UNEXPECTED ATTRACTION

"Listen to me one moment longer, *Miss Timberlake*. I would bet everything I hope to gain in my life that this ranch will be managed for a time by a man. Not you."

She scoffed at him, eyes disdainful. "If my father said it once, he said it a million times. Timberoaks would be mine when he was gone. My father never went back on his word in life, Walker. I do not expect him to do so in death."

Without warning, Walker drew her against him. She felt his heat, and her breasts pillowed against his hard chest. Protest failed her. One hand still held her in place; his free arm circled her body. His thighs felt like tree trunks pressed against hers. An answering heat sluiced through her entire length.

"Miss Timberlake, I will be gone for a few days, but I *will* be back. That is a promise. I suggest you heed my words and guard your tongue."

WALKS IN SHADOW

JOYCE HENDERSON

LEISURE BOOKS NEW YORK CITY

A LEISURE BOOK®

February 2005

Published by

Dorchester Publishing Co., Inc.
200 Madison Avenue
New York, NY 10016

ISBN 0-8439-5508-2

Printed in the United States of America.

Visit us on the web at www.dorchesterpub.com.

ACKNOWLEDGMENT

My eternal thanks to Lynette Hallberg and Diane O'Key, critique partners extraordinaire. You were with me every step, every word. I couldn't have done it without your insightful comments. Tough sometimes, but unfailingly delivered with a large helping of love.

And to Bob...our journey through life has been, still is, an adventure. You never lost faith.

WALKS IN SHADOW

Prologue

Central Texas, 1855

Walks in Shadow stood amid the oaks, shrouded in the inky darkness for which he'd been named. Overhead, tree limbs bent and groaned. Their leaves rattled in the slicing rain of a blue norther. Dawn, dreary and icy, would creep over the land before long.

Focused on the squares of light in the ranch house windows fifty yards away, he didn't bother to brush away the strands of shoulder-length hair whipping against his lips and bronze-skinned cheeks. Water cascaded from the brim of the white man's Stetson he wore. He looked down at the oilskin-wrapped boy-child in his arms.

Little Spring slept peacefully. His small body and breath warmed Walks in Shadow's buckskin-clad chest. In, out—relaxed, trusting. The fifteen-month-old boy had been played with, protected and loved by the man who held him. Trust for his adopted uncle was all the little Comanche had ever known.

That was about to change.

Walks in Shadow clenched his jaw and shook his head. Water droplets sailed from the hat's brim.

I do not want to do this. I cannot.

I must. A promise is a promise.

He glanced up when a distant, indistinct sound carried above the wind's wail. A figure stepped out on the porch and spoke to another inside the house. Thunder cracked, drowning out the voice as he closed the door and turned toward a shed. A bucket swung in his hand as he dashed through the downpour, head angled against the buffeting rain.

The figure was garbed in trousers, a hip-length coat and a wide-brimmed hat. Bubbling Water had not mentioned a boy. Only a woman, a kind man, and a girl.

Walks in Shadow's eyes dimmed as he remembered how enraged he had been when his adopted sister disappeared. A tested warrior, having seen twenty-three winters himself at the time, he had joined three others to scour the countryside for her. That had been over two years before, but he could still feel the rage, the gut-wrenching fear when she had not been found.

Twelve suns later, Bubbling Water walked into camp wearing white women's clothes. The tale she told still made his stomach clench. While gathering herbs, she had been abducted by a white man, raped and left to die. The man who owned this ranch where Walks in Shadow now stood had found her and cared for her until she recovered.

The names of its inhabitants were imprinted on Walks in Shadow's heart. Hiram Timberlake, his daughter, Samantha, and the older woman, Mattie Crawford. Another name circled in his mind, too.

Clarence.

The man had uttered his own name to Bubbling Water when she scratched him in a vain attempt to escape.

"Ya goddamn bitch! What Clarence wants, he takes!"

He had.

Now holding the results of that rape in his arms, Walks

in Shadow trembled with the same rage he had felt when Bubbling Water haltingly told of the evil committed against her. Clarence would die, Walks in Shadow vowed. One day he would find the man.

Only fourteen at the time, Bubbling Water had given birth, then within a few months she was taken to the Spirit world, defenseless against the white man's measles. Walks in Shadow shifted the sleeping child in his arms and watched the youth disappear into the shed.

"You are white, my brother." Bubbling Water's voice rose from the past to carry on the wind. "Disease and starvation are all that remain for the Comanche. Promise you will take Little Spring and return to the white world."

"I am Comanche by everything but birth!" Walks in Shadow had argued. A name from the past was all he remembered of the world whence he had been taken many years past. Holden. His life as a white child before age three was only fleeting images.

Conditioned to think like an Indian, he felt hate burning in his breast when he thought of the white scourge overrunning the Comanche. On the other hand, Bubbling Water had said Hiram Timberlake was kind, his family gentle and caring.

A thunderclap boomed and rumbled across the sky, jolting him from his musings. He looked down at the dark head peeking from beneath the oilskin, then slid his gaze to the windows and the shed.

Now or never.

His night vision keen, he circled behind the shed and angled toward the house. He lightly stepped onto the porch and laid his sleeping burden next to the wall. The porch roof shielded Little Spring from direct rain. For an instant he longed to pick up the child and run.

He could not.

He must leave Little Spring with these white people until he was sure he could live among white men himself. Only then could he protect the child. Only then could he secretly teach Little Spring about his Comanche heritage. His shoulders tensed with resolve.

Pulling aside the oilskin wrapping, he looked into Little Spring's sleeping face. His heart like a stone in his chest, Walks in Shadow caressed the babe's cheek one last time. "I will be back one day, little man." He re-covered the child's face and stole away as soundlessly as he had come.

Walks in Shadow had just regained the safety of the gloom beneath the oaks when the door opened and a man's silhouette filled the space.

He could not watch anymore. Tears stung his eyes as he vanished into the trees.

One day I will be back, Little Spring. That is a promise.

Chapter One

Timberoaks Ranch, Central Texas, 1860

Samantha Timberlake wanted him from the first time she saw him. The yearning was so intense, so primal, it took her breath. She was twenty-five years old, and though she loved her father, Aunt Mattie and little Guy fiercely, she'd never experienced a desire so strong—until that moment.

He'd stood on a hill, wild, proud, fierce, as beautiful as Texas was brutal. Then he disappeared from view. The search lasted three weeks before she and a couple of ranch hands had found and captured him. She'd wanted him and now she had him. But at what price?

Dust flew as he twisted and fought against Oscar's rope. Oscar Dupree was strong, even if he stood only five-five, shorter than Samantha by two full inches. His compact, wiry frame attested to a life of hard work. For once, he'd donned gloves over hands that appeared old beyond his forty years. Crookedly healed broken fingers, wire cuts, and old flesh-eating rope burns marred the skin. A ten-year veteran on Timberoaks, Oscar was the best broncobuster around, but he might lose the battle with this wild, beautiful black stallion.

The stallion's breath rasped. Deceptively spindly looking forelegs shot skyward as the animal leaped up, then came down stiff-legged, humpbacked, his head diving toward the ground. He bucked across the enclosure, dragging Oscar as if he weighed no more than a barnyard cat.

"Whoa!" Oscar yelled to no avail.

Guy, the six-year-old boy who was like a brother, whooped and laughed. He straddled the top of the corral fence an arm's length from where Samantha stood. "Ain't gonna win, Oscar!"

"You aren't going to," she automatically corrected, though her chocolate-brown eyes remained fixed on the writhing stallion.

"Yeah," Guy agreed.

From the corner of her eye, Guy's snaggle-toothed grin told her he hadn't listened to a word she'd said. For that matter, he didn't care about proper grammar, and probably never would. Like hers, his world centered on horses, and he was caught up in the war raging between tenacious man and obstinate horse.

Several ranch hands stood on the far side of the corral, arms crossed atop the fence, as enthralled by the tableau as Samantha and Guy were. This was simply the way a horse was broken to saddle. But the stallion might break a leg in the process. More than one leg if he continued the violent pitching. She scowled. Worse, if Oscar ultimately won the battle, the stallion's spirit might be crushed.

Samantha didn't want that. Part of the horse's allure was the untamed spirit she sensed in the animal. She wanted him gentled, not broken. There had to be a better way.

"Oscar, stop!" She scraped her booted foot off the bottom rung of the fence and strode toward the gate. "Oscar!" she called again. The buster couldn't hear her above the men's shouts of encouragement and the horse's frantic snorts and grunts.

Samantha opened the gate and stepped inside. The stallion bolted directly toward her. His surprise move jerked the rope from Oscar's hand.

"Samma!" Guy cried.

She raised a reassuring hand in his direction. "It's all right." That was debatable, but she'd left herself no room to maneuver. She stood her ground, back against the gate. "Stop," she whispered from a suddenly dry mouth as the stallion bore down on her. Even if the horse were inclined to obey—which he undoubtedly wasn't—her faint command was lost amid concerned male shouts.

She stood mesmerized, watching the stallion plunge toward her. Then, as if he'd been grabbed from behind by the scruff of his sleek neck, he arched that neck, stiffened his forelegs, and slid to a halt not three feet in front of her.

Dust billowed up, coating her trousers and white shirt, surrounding her, choking her, but she could see the stallion's dark, challenging eyes. Head held high, sides heaving with each breath, the magnificent animal stared with disdain—and fear—down the length of his nose. The stallion probably tipped the scales at eleven hundred pounds, but the fence and the people scared him to death.

"Come out of there right now!"

Samantha recognized that authoritative voice. Her father's. Hiram Timberlake might be ill, but his spirit was still intact, strong as a bull's.

She licked dry lips. "Maybe I should—"

"Out!" her father snapped.

Samantha continued to face the horse as she opened the gate and stepped back through, pulling it closed. Her shoulders slumped with relief when the latch clicked. The stallion threw his head up at the tiny sound, whirled, and galloped back to the center of the corral.

Her father dragged her around to face him. His green

eyes pierced hers, and she heard the concern in his gruff voice that others might not.

"Whatever possessed you to go into that corral, daughter?"

Shaking, she took a breath. "Oscar didn't hear me when I told him to stop. Pa, I don't want the stallion if it means he'll be—"

"Don't you go near that horse again until he's gentled. You got that?" He stood with his elbow cocked, thumb hooked on the gun belt he wore.

She reached out and touched his upper arm. "That's my point, Pa. I want him gentled, not broken." She shook her head when her father's eyes narrowed. "You don't understand—"

"What you want may not be possible. What you get may be a disappointment."

"I'd rather let him go."

"Yer kiddin'."

Guy's drawl snapped her head around.

"No, I'm not kidding."

"Holy moly, Samma—"

"Watch your mouth," her father growled.

Guy paid no mind. He had a head of steam already primed and chugging away. "You look-ted and look-ted. Now you wanna let 'im go? Geez—"

Still able to muster enough strength for his purpose, Hiram grasped a fistful of Guy's shirtfront and yanked him off the fence. "You, young man, can hie yourself off to the house. Your mouth is about to run away with you and take the Lord's name in vain. I'll not have it." Hiram pointed in the direction he wanted Guy to go.

"Pa, I di'n't—"

"Not yet. But your smart mouth is going to get you a strop mark or two on your backside. I'd be mighty sorry to have to administer those marks, boy. Mattie has fresh bread cooling. Go ask her for a big slice slathered with her peach jam."

Guy's pale blue eyes lit, and Samantha suppressed a grin. Aunt Mattie's jams and jellies could bring men to blows if one hogged up the last of a jar without offering to share.

Guy took off at a run toward the house. His too-long black hair swung below his collar.

Her father's lips lifted in a half smile as he turned back to face her. The chance of his taking his razor strop to her sturdy brother's backside was so remote that she wanted to laugh.

"Oscar, take that rope off the stallion."

"Whatever you say, Hiram."

"Samantha," her father said, "I don't know of another way or a better man to tame that stallion than Oscar. You know how he works. You know how horses are broken."

She gazed into his gaunt face. Her heart constricted at the thought that he might not live much longer. How could she let him go?

How could she be so arrogant as to think she had a choice in the matter?

"In His good time and by His grace, I live," her father had admonished. "I'll die when He says it's my time, Samantha."

When the time came, she'd have to be strong like her father. She willed away the worrisome thoughts.

Holden Walker glanced up. Between the leaves and far, far away, the evening star glittered in the vast purpling sky. Before long, total darkness would be upon the land. Countless stars would splash across the heavens, joining the one that heralded the night. He tethered his dapple-gray cow pony to a spindly bush among the shadowy stand of oaks. He knelt to remove his spurs, then stood and stuffed them into his saddlebag.

A whippoorwill's call carried on the wind. Another answered, hidden in the spreading limbs directly over his head. Brush rustled in the breeze. A squirrel scolded.

Holden smiled, listening to the familiar sounds of approaching night as he adjusted the gun belt circling his narrow hips, then wove his way among the oaks. Though he wore white man's boots, he moved as quietly as a wolf, always had. His affinity for the night and ability to roam undetected had prompted the People to name him Walks in Shadow. Now, other than an occasional visit with Two Horns and Swift Arrow, that life was behind him—by five long years.

A clearing stretched before him as he reached the edge of the trees' canopy. He paused and leaned a muscled shoulder against an oak's gnarled trunk. Not much had changed since he had stood in this spot once before. The house and barn had since been whitewashed, perhaps.

No. Another structure now stood north of the barn. Maybe a bunkhouse. Square windows flanked either side of the door in the plank walls. Lantern light shone from the windows in the new building and those downstairs in the ranch house.

He searched the area. His piercing gaze missed nothing. Other than a hound that lay on the porch scratching fleas, not a soul stirred. Supper time, perhaps.

While learning to live in the white man's world, he had worked on several ranges such as this, but often escaped to the prairie. Sometimes he went off during the night when a Comanche moon lit the sky. On those occasions he spread a blanket and communed with the Spirits. Though he should have cut all ties, twice a year he rode out to find his former band. Speaking with the People he still thought of as his own gave him the strength to live in the white man's world, to learn their ways.

His longest stay in a town had been in Waco, where he met Lillibeth. She had not only appeased his sexual needs, but she had also taught him to read and write. Now he was back, his promise kept.

Seeing Little Spring would have to wait until tomorrow. The boy was probably headed for bed before long. Holden sent up a prayer to the Great Spirit that Bubbling Water had not misjudged this family, that Hiram Timberlake had reared the boy.

Retreating through the trees to his tethered horse, he pulled a bedroll from behind his saddle and prepared to settle down for the night, with the sky as roof and the ground his bed. It was summertime in Texas, and with the coming of night, the searing heat had diminished.

With just a pinch of luck, maybe Timberlake would give him a job. Timberoaks was a horse ranch, and Holden was a master at handling horses. Gentling mustangs, herding and tending the remuda had been his job on cattle drives. While working in Waco, he had trained more than one horse so a greenhorn could ride without breaking his fool neck. That was how Walks in Shadow had become Holden Walker, horse trainer.

Until he was sure he could again live in the white world, Holden had resisted the temptation to check on Little Spring. Consequently, the boy would not remember his adopted uncle. Besides, Walks in Shadow had left Little Spring here under Timberlake's care. The man would not take kindly to a stranger who claimed to be kin carting off the child.

What could he say, anyway? *You have harbored a half-Comanche for five years, Mr. Timberlake. Now I want him back.* Holden grimaced. Oh, yes, that would sit well with a Texan! Perhaps he would never be able to reveal his former relationship with Little Spring. If that were the case, could he move on and leave the boy again? Doubtful.

Holden removed his black hat and gun belt and laid the weapon within easy reach. Settling his long frame on the blanket, he stared up through foliage with unseeing eyes, unsure if the boy was still on this ranch. Tomorrow he would know, and then he would take whatever came one day at a time.

* * *

That evening Samantha's thoughts were on her empty stomach. Her mouth watered at the scrumptious smell wafting through the kitchen. Surreptitiously, she lifted the corner of a flour-sack cloth. Before she could filch a slice of the warm bread, a wooden spoon whapped her knuckles.

"Ow!" She snatched her hand back and stuck stinging fingers in her mouth.

"Keep your grubby hands off the food, young lady," Matilda Crawford ordered.

"But it smells so good, Aunt Mattie. And I'm hungry."

"Then get washed up for supper. It'll be ready in a jiffy. While you're at it, change your clothes."

Samantha turned so Mattie couldn't see her face and mouthed verbatim her aunt's next words. "You may wish you had been born a boy, but you're a girl. A girl comes to my table looking like one. Put on a clean shirtwaist and skirt."

Samantha rolled her eyes at the last order. It was her aunt's fondest hope that she would settle down and marry. Sooner rather than later. Though her father hadn't pressured her, he felt the same way.

Shoot, had she been born a boy, they wouldn't think twice about when she married. And, most importantly, there would be no question in her father's mind that she could run the ranch as well as he.

Since she was a girl, Aunt Mattie and every man on the place protected her from the heavier work: shoeing, occasional branding, and night riding or fence mending. She grimaced, then consoled herself with the thought that at least she had learned from her pa how to get the best price for Timberoaks's stock.

One day—she prayed that day would be far in the future—Timberoaks would come to her. When it did, she needed to know all there was to know about the horse business. As a woman, she'd have to work doubly hard to earn respect from men who considered females weak in the head about such matters.

Samantha climbed the stairs and walked down the short hallway to her bedroom at the back of the house. She went directly to the mirrored armoire and pulled open one door. She eyed the few feminine garments she owned.

Glancing sideways, she peered at her image in the looking glass mounted on the inside of the door panel. Dirt smudged her cheek. Beneath the brown Stetson, her hair was dust-laden, windblown and tangled. She crinkled her nose; the smattering of freckles all but disappeared.

"You *are* filthy," she muttered.

Pulling off her hat, she gave it a toss. The headgear sailed unerringly and plunked against the wall, squarely hooked by half of an old horseshoe.

After shucking her dirty outer garments, she made quick work of a spit bath, then donned a shirtwaist. Reluctantly, she fastened the buttons clear to the base of her throat. That was another thing that galled her about her aunt's insistence that she look and act like a girl. Comporting herself properly when necessary was not a problem, but women's clothing, fashioned for total cover-up, was so blessed hot.

She smoothed the long skirt over generous hips and took a modicum of satisfaction that she'd won a crucial concession from Aunt Mattie. Samantha had vowed never to wear a corset. That contraption harkened back to medieval torture and ranked right up there with chastity belts.

Grinning as she pulled a brush through her thick hair, she spoke to her reflection. "Aunt Mattie would be shocked if she knew you even thought of such a thing."

She arrived back in the kitchen in the midst of a conversation. Her heart sank at Aunt Mattie's stern words to Guy. "Yes, you will, young man. Reverend Fuller only gets around this way a couple of times a year. Listening to his sermon and taking his words to heart won't hurt you one bit."

Samantha might have argued that point. Reverend

Fuller preached "fire and brimstone." She doubted even one person had ever been brought to salvation through the grim preacher's harsh words.

"He's coming here?" she asked as she took a seat. The smell of fried chicken added to the lingering aroma of warm bread made her mouth water again.

"Not here," Aunt Mattie replied. "He's staying at the Butchers'."

Holy moly, far worse! Not only would she be forced to sit through a two-hour sermon but she'd have to do so in proximity to the two most odious men alive. Uriah Butcher was a tyrant, and his son, Clarence James, made her skin crawl. Older than her by ten years, C. J. believed her destined to be his wife.

Not if she had anything to say about it!

"Rev'end Fuller's a mean old man," Guy groused.

"He preaches the gospel, boy," Hiram interjected, then coughed.

Samantha's heart lurched when her father clapped a napkin against his mouth. His shoulders heaved as he rose and left the table, spasms racking his body. Aunt Mattie watched her brother-in-law, five years her junior, with troubled chocolate-brown eyes that matched Samantha's.

Samantha eyed his plate. He'd taken one bite of chicken and perhaps two of mashed potatoes and gravy. Six months before, Dr. Bennett, in Waco, had diagnosed her father's illness as consumption, but she wondered if starvation wouldn't take him first.

Samantha's gaze met her aunt's. Without uttering a sound, Mattie's compassionate expression spoke clearly. *Not long, not long for this world.*

"Is Pa gonna die?"

Guy's timid question slammed into Samantha's heart so hard that he might as well have hit her with a hammer. She sometimes forgot he was still a little boy. Rambunctious, for sure, but scared right now. Before she could respond, Aunt Mattie closed her hand over his.

Mattie never lied. She had never glossed over the truth for the sake of misplaced kindness. But thank God, this time she equivocated. "We all will die one day. We just don't know when the Lord will take us home."

"Pa *is* home!"

Mattie nodded. Her eyes glittered with unshed tears. "His earthly home, yes, Guy. But we all have a better place awaiting us on the other side of eternity."

Tears silvered his pale blue eyes, turning them gray. "I don't want him to die."

I don't either! Samantha wailed inwardly.

"Come, child." Aunt Mattie rose and drew him to his feet. "It's time to call it a day. Your pa will be with us a while yet."

Samantha stared at the uneaten supper on the plates and in the serving dishes. It had been over a week since her father had had such a coughing fit, and she'd hoped . . . She looked up at the ceiling, still able to hear him, though she knew he tried to suppress the sounds.

Rising, she began to clear the table. The hunger she'd felt moments ago had drowned in a heart awash with tears.

The next dawn, a faint tinge of orange lightened the gun-metal gray sky on the eastern horizon. Anxious to check the black, Samantha hurried through her morning ablutions.

As she descended the stairs, lantern light glimmered across the floor from her father's small office off the parlor. She stepped to the door. Undetected, she gazed at him bent over a ledger lying on the oak desk. The gray salted through his midnight hair gleamed silver in the lantern's light.

A faint hiss from the lamp mixed with the sound of his quill scratching on paper. Although she hadn't made a noise, he must have felt her gaze on him, for he glanced up. His smile reached his green eyes. Dear God, how would she live without a daily dose of that cheerful expression?

"Morning," he said. "You're up early."

"Um, I wanted to check on the stallion."

"He's still out there." His grin widened. "Full of spit and fire, and not the least bit pleased at being penned."

He'd already taken a turn outside to see that everything was okay. One day that would be her job. A faint noise from the back of the house told her Aunt Mattie was also up, fixing breakfast.

Suddenly her father sobered. "I've been meaning to talk to you, Samantha." He motioned to the overstuffed wing back chair angled at the corner of the battered desk. "Come sit down for a few minutes. That stallion will hold for a bit."

Vaguely alarmed, Samantha didn't like the serious look in his eyes. Her boots thudded hollowly on the wooden floor until she stepped onto the circular rag rug her mother had made some thirty years before, when her parents had first come to Texas.

"Samantha, I have the feeling that before long I'm going to be treading ground in the 'Promised Land' we've heard so much about."

"Oh, Pa!" She sank onto the brown cushion and flung up a defensive hand, a futile gesture to ward off his pragmatism. His attempt at casualness failed—miserably.

"It's got to be faced," he went on relentlessly. "When I'm gone, this ranch will go to you, eventually."

Eventually? Her brow creased. "Is that supposed to make me feel better?" She couldn't help the sarcastic retort. "I don't want to listen to this." She didn't want to cry, either, but tears threatened.

"Sass won't change a thing, Samantha." He smiled lamely. "After I'm gone—"

"Must you harp on that?" She stood and took a backward step. "Please, Pa, not now."

She left her fears unsaid. If he'd stop talking about his death, maybe it wouldn't be so hard to listen to him. She'd learned some things about ranch operation, but there was far more her father needed to teach her if she was to run Timberoaks at a profit. Her gaze flicked to the ledger on the desk, which she knew nothing about.

He emitted a resigned sigh. "All right. But we must talk soon. You may not wish to face it, but time is short." Before he could continue, a fit of coughing shook him.

He drew out a handkerchief and covered his mouth until he breathed more easily. A telltale splotch of blood appeared on the cloth. He wiped his lips, crumpled the linen in his fist, then lowered his hand to his lap.

"Pa." Her voice quavered.

"I'm all right."

"But you're spitting—"

"It goes with this blasted ailment, Samantha. There's nothing to be done about it."

That was true. No one seemed to know how to stop the insidious march of consumption. Still . . . Heartsick with what she had seen, she wondered if her aunt knew his lungs now bled.

"Anyway," he said, as if there had been no interruption, "I need to explain some things so you don't think unkindly of me."

"What?" She shook her head, struggling to concentrate on his words. *Think . . . unkindly . . .* "Pa . . ."

He waved his hand in dismissal. "You'll understand soon enough. Now, if we aren't going to discuss ranch matters, you need to figure out what you want to do about that stallion. Oscar can break him, but that's what he'll do. Break him. It's the only way."

"You expect me to forget . . . You think I can—"

From one breath to the next, his mouth hardened. "You can and you will! Life goes on. Yours certainly will, Samantha. You can't avoid responsibility because you're upset or something strikes you as unfair. You were determined to have that horse, and now you've got him. Tell Oscar if you want him broke. If you've changed your mind, let him go."

* * *

Once again Holden stood half-hidden under the oaks, his dark clothes an effective camouflage. He scanned the clearing as daylight strengthened. A short-statured cowboy ambled out of what he assumed was the bunkhouse, a toothpick stuck in his mouth. At the same time, the front door of the main house opened.

As the figure stepped to the edge of the porch, the sun burst over the horizon and bathed the front of the house in golden light. A tall, willowy woman stood looking toward the corral. Holden's breath stalled.

She was the most striking woman he had ever seen. Hat in hand, she wore men's clothes—a surprise in itself. But it was her hair, lots of it, that claimed his admiration. Lit by the sun, gleaming tresses cascaded to the center of her back, golden around her shoulders. His gaze slowly tracked her length.

Ample breasts rounded beneath the white shirt, taunting a man to cup them, caress them. Below a tiny waist circled by a wide belt, denim hugged generous hips. And long legs. Lord of the white man, she had the shapeliest legs.

She stuck the hat between her knees and clamped them together. Heat boiled through Holden and settled heavily in his groin. He could actually feel silken thighs wrapped around his waist.

When she raised her arms, the shirt snugged across her breasts, outlining them so effectively she might as well have been naked. He shifted and licked his lips. With both hands, she gathered that gorgeous hair at her nape, twisted it several times, and flipped it atop her head. She retrieved the hat and hid the glorious tresses inside the crown.

He felt oddly deprived, but only for a moment. When she stepped off the porch, her hips swayed provocatively. He wanted to rush forward, throw her down, and mount her like some green boy.

He forced himself to take slow breaths, coming out of a trancelike state. In the name of the lightning spirit, what was wrong with him? A woman was a woman was a woman. He had proven that to himself time and again. Not a one was worth getting hot in the trousers. Other than Lillibeth, most women he had ever come in contact with could be had with a look, a smile. Since his return to the white world, even a half-pleasant expression usually brought a woman to his bed.

He watched her easy stride as she approached the man who now stood next to the corral fence. When she halted beside him, Holden noticed she was taller than the wrangler. She hooked a boot heel on the bottom rung and rested crossed arms atop the fence. The movements stretched the shirt across her narrow back and cupped the denim around her derriere.

He envied the material caressing her bottom—which was lunacy. Still, he wanted to cup that derriere. He wanted to twirl her around, unbutton her shirt, and feast his eyes on her generous breasts. Damnation, the way he felt right now, he would rip off the shirt, not take the time to release the buttons!

"Samma, you gonna ride 'im?" a child's voice called.

A boy banged out the door and crossed the porch. He leaped to the ground and ran pell-mell toward the corral.

Little Spring? Holden's breath slowed. He eyed the boy with speculation. Black-as-night hair straggled below his ears. He clambered up the fence on sturdy legs, agile as a bear climbing a tree.

Holden's gaze wrenched to the woman, who looked over her shoulder and said something. He failed to catch her words; only a husky timbre registered. *Samma,* the boy had called her. Perhaps this was Bubbling Water's Samantha.

Could be, he thought, counting backward. Twenty-four, maybe twenty-five by now. More than old enough . . .

He shook his head. No. Samantha Timberlake had nursed Bubbling Water. She deserved his gratitude, not his lust.

"I don't know that I'll ever ride him," the woman said.

"Geez, Samma—"

"Guy," she interrupted, her voice stern. "You know what Pa said about your mouth."

"I know't. But 'geez' ain't 'Jesus.' "

Holden smiled at the boy's feisty retort.

"Isn't," she corrected, and argued further. "Pa draws a fine line."

A whinny shifted Holden's gaze to the handsome black that stood on the far side of the corral, distancing himself from the humans by the fence. Ears alert, the stallion eyed them, the boy in particular. The animal lowered his head, snorted and pawed the dirt. Dust billowed up to coat his fine head.

"Ain't he sum'pin," Guy said, clearly disregarding Miss Timberlake's admonishment.

The boy laughed and clapped his hands when, for no apparent reason, the stallion reared and pawed the air. He dropped to the ground, pranced one way, whirled and trotted in the other direction, prowling the fence, looking for a way out.

Holden's interest snapped back to the conversation when he caught the man's words.

"I been breakin' horses a lotta years, Samantha. There's only one way a cantankerous stallion is gonna accept a saddle. Blindfolded, hogtied, and thrown."

Samantha listened to Oscar's arguments and grew frustrated. "You could break his legs!"

"Them's the chances you take ever' time you break a horse. You knew that goin' in."

"If we can't do better by him, then let him go."

Oscar snorted. "That's all-fired loony, Samantha. We winded three good horses catchin' that critter. Now you're turnin' lily-livered over breakin' 'im?"

"Not lily-livered . . . exactly."

"Don't know what else to call it," Oscar snapped.

Sighing, she stared morosely at the best-looking horse

she'd ever seen. Blessed heaven, how she had wanted him. How she *still* wanted him. "There must be a better way," she murmured. "There has to be."

"There is," a voice said behind her.

At her side, Oscar turned and Guy looked over his shoulder.

"Says who?" Oscar challenged.

"Walker. Holden Walker."

His deep voice vibrated along Samantha's nerves like a cat's purr. She was glued to the spot as if a tub of thick, sticky honey had been poured over her head. For some insane reason, she wondered if she dared look at the man with the extraordinary voice. Deep inside, heat coiled in her belly, flashed through her veins. At the same time, inside, she was on fire, and gooseflesh erupted on her skin. She shuddered.

Holy moly, what's wrong with me? This Holden Walker was only a man, for heaven's sake. Not . . . Well, she didn't know what. Taking a deep breath, she steadied her shaking limbs.

"You got a lotta experience, I suppose," Oscar further challenged, sounding as though he thought the man had taken leave of his senses.

"Enough."

She was being ridiculous and rude. *Turn around, you ninny!*

Squaring her shoulders, she turned ever so slowly. A buckskin-clad chest met her gaze. Delaying the inevitable, she glanced down and inspected the man from the ground up. He wore black boots and black trousers that hugged muscled thighs. Two belts circled his narrow waist. One was black; the other, his gun belt, was brown, tooled leather. A six-gun's long barrel rode his lean thigh, a rawhide thong anchoring the tip of the holster to his leg. Like a shootist usually wore a gun. Samantha was certain he could use the weapon—with deadly accuracy.

Even at her height, she was uneasily aware that this man

towered over her. His buckskin shirt looked surprisingly clean. Ax-handle-wide shoulders filled the soft leather. Lines bracketed wide, well-defined lips curved in a slight smile. His face was burnished and clean-shaven. Backlit by the morning sun, gleaming sable-brown hair dusted his shoulders below a black hat whose low brim left his eyes in deep shadow. Until he nudged up his hat brim with a thumb.

God in heaven! Gold-centered, circled by greenish gray, his eyes seemed to glitter with inner light. She swallowed. *Cat . . . No.* Only once before had she seen eyes like his. And they weren't human. Wolf's eyes. Dangerous. Compelling.

Befuddled, Samantha could say nothing. Caught by his gaze, she was unable to look away.

He was so still that he appeared not to breathe, while his rude, intent gaze roamed over her as hers had over him. Her lips tingled with a burning sensation when his perusal lingered on them for what seemed like forever. Then he refocused on her eyes.

Her breath was labored, but she forced herself to speak. "I don't believe we've met. I'm Samantha Timberlake."

"It is my pleasure."

While the greeting sounded ridiculously formal coming from a Texan's mouth, his brilliant eyes promised . . . what?

Tremulous with disquiet and wonder, she felt her heart thump with undeniable excitement.

Chapter Two

"Do I know you?"

The boy's question yanked Holden's attention from the woman. Still perched atop the fence, the child narrowed pale blue eyes on him, speculative and a tad bewildered.

Holden's heart beat like a ceremonial drum. Not only were his eyes those of the child Walks in Shadow had left here, but his round cheeks and gently curved mouth were exactly as Bubbling Water's had been.

He smiled. *Yes, you do, Little Spring. Or you did.*

But he could not say so. Not yet. Boots crunched on the rocky soil, drawing his gaze to a man walking toward them from the house, saving him from the need to answer Little Spring's question. Five years ago it had been dark and stormy when he last saw him silhouetted by lantern light, but Walks in Shadow knew he was the same man.

"Hello, young fella," the older man said affably, his expression welcoming and curious. "I'm Hiram Timberlake, chief honcho here on Timberoaks. And you are?" He extended a callused hand.

Holden shook it and grinned inwardly when the woman stepped to her father's side and tucked her hand inside his arm. She appeared anxious about something. About meeting him, perhaps. He was not surprised. Moon madness must have claimed him when he appraised her as brazenly as he would a whore.

"Mr. Walker, Pa."

"Holden Walker, sir."

"Don't believe I've heard that name before. You new in these parts?"

"Yes, more or less. I've just come from over Waco way. Looking for work."

Interest sparked in the older man's green eyes. "You know horses?"

Holden nodded. "You might say that. I gentle them."

"Gentle?" Samantha Timberlake's fathomless dark eyes rounded, then narrowed with speculation. "What do you mean?"

Holden wanted to laugh at her sudden interest. He could read her as easily as the books he had devoured in Waco. He had heard part of her conversation with the shorter man, who looked at him expectantly. Oscar, she had called him.

"I can gentle that stallion for you." He tipped his head toward the black, which had moved as far from the humans as the corral would allow. "Without breaking his spirit."

"Yeah, right," the short man countered, his tone just shy of a sneer.

"My foreman, Oscar Dupree," Timberlake said.

Holden touched his hat brim in a half-assed salute. "I just came off a cattle drive where I handled the remuda. If you question my ability, talk with Simon Donlevy. I worked for him."

"Don't know that we have to do that," Timberlake interjected. "Maybe you could show us what you can do."

"You looking for hands, Mr. Timberlake?"

His smile appeared genuine. "Call me Hiram." He glanced at his foreman, then back at Holden. "We can always use a good hand, Walker."

Timberlake was gaunt. That was the only word that came to mind to describe the older man's lined face. He stood straight, his shoulders thrust back, but had the look of a man one step away from walking with the Spirits.

"All right, Hiram it is." He turned to the short man. "Do you mind?" He did not want to antagonize him. If Oscar was the foreman and Timberlake hired him, he would work for Dupree.

Oscar's grin split his homely face. "Nah. I been scrapin' whippersnappers off the ground for a long while. Just don't go and break somethin'. Miss Mattie gets a might twisted when the boys comes in banged up."

Across the corral, a man of about forty exited the building that Holden figured to be the bunkhouse. Hats clamped on their heads and carrying lariats, two followed, one of them a black man.

"Hey, Grogan, we got a show about to start here," Oscar yelled.

The lead man paused, his gaze trained on the clutch of people. "Show?" Grogan repeated. The three men headed for the fence on the far side of the corral.

Oscar jabbed his thumb toward Holden. "This here young feller is gonna *gentle* that black devil for Samantha."

Holden glanced at Samantha. The name fit her better than "Samma." Tall, regal in bearing, she was all woman. Samma sounded more like a boy's name. His body never heated when he looked at a boy, but a mere glance at Samantha Timberlake set him afire.

First things first, Walks in Shadow. He would forever think of himself by his Indian name. *You need a job on this ranch to be near Little Spring. Get on with it.*

"I would ask that no one speak after I enter the corral."

"Why?" the boy challenged.

"The stallion is already spooked. He does not like to be penned."

"How do you know?"

He smiled at the youngster's belligerent tone and winked. "He told me."

Little Spring hooted with laughter. Holden's heart constricted. Oh, how he had missed this boy.

"Guy, don't be rude," Timberlake said. "If Mr. Walker wants quiet, we'll give it to him. Understand?"

Most of all, Holden hoped someday to see the dawning of respect for *him* that the boy now showed the man who had reprimanded him.

"Little Sp . . . man, I would also have you off the fence."

"But I can't—"

"Look through the slats. You will be able to see just fine."

Little Spring reluctantly climbed down and stuck his hands in his pants pockets, the pugnacious expression back again. Holden steeled himself to look at Samantha without betraying his lustful feelings.

"I would have your saddle, bridle, and blanket to use."

"What about a rope?" Oscar asked.

"I will use my own." He raised his arm, then dropped it downward. Instantly, his gray trotted from beneath the oaks where he had been standing for the past half hour, unattended.

"Gol . . . ly!" The boy's eyes rounded with wonder. "He wudn't tied er nothin'."

Samantha frowned while getting her tack. The way the man's horse responded didn't prove a thing. Men used *gentle* interchangeably with *break* when training a horse to accept a saddle and rider. It remained to be seen what Holden Walker meant.

"Thank you."

He again spoke in an oddly formal manner, without a trace of Texas drawl, as he lifted the saddle and blanket . . . with one hand. He must be as strong as he looked. She shivered when his fingers brushed her hand as she let go of the bridle.

Without glancing at the horse, Walker dropped the tack in the center of the corral. He uncoiled his lariat and fed several feet to the ground, then slapped the tail end down, but not directly at the horse.

The stallion bolted around the perimeter of the corral, his dark eyes wild, his ears scissoring between the man in the center with the rope and the people clustered outside the fence. He slowed a bit when Walker made no move toward him. Again Walker flicked the rope, striking the ground, then pivoted slowly. His extraordinary eyes never left the stallion.

When the black started to turn on his own, Walker said nothing, only jiggled the rope, and the horse kept on in the same direction. After several rounds, he turned the horse by flipping the rope ahead of the nervous animal.

"How'd he do that?" Guy asked.

Before Samantha could reply, Walker spoke from the center of the corral. "I asked you not to speak, little man."

She put her arm around Guy's shoulders when he ducked his head. Though Walker had spoken quietly, authority rang in his voice, and Guy was duly chastised. At times she wanted to wring Guy's neck. Still . . . She resented this man's ordering her brother around. Glancing at her father and Oscar, she realized they hadn't noticed, their attention trained on the tableau in the corral.

Her eyes widened when she saw that Walker had turned his shoulder to the horse. Holy moly! If the stallion took it into his head to run him down, the big man was paying no attention.

The black stood for another second, then he lowered his

head and walked—*walked!* she thought with wonder—
toward the motionless figure. Still facing away from the
stud, Walker smiled.

"So, you want to be my friend."

It took a moment for her to realize he was speaking to
the horse as if it were a person. Was the man chewing
locoweed? She looked at her father, then at Oscar. Her
gaze skipped to Guy and to the men across the corral. All
stood stone-still.

"That can be arranged."

He spoke as if carrying on a conversation, turned, and
scratched the stallion on the muzzle. His big hand moved
slowly up the horse's long face, paused and massaged
between his pricked ears, then skirted down to rub the animal's jowl.

Out of the blue, Samantha wondered how it would feel
if his strong hands stroked her body. Her nipples beaded in
response. She shivered.

Walker continued stroking the sleek neck, the withers
and shoulder, stepped back and rubbed from the horse's
flank to his rump. Then he returned to the horse's head.

The animal stood, docile. The only thing that moved
was an ear. It swiveled, tracking the man when he moved
back, then forward.

Samantha shook her head in disbelief. From the corner
of her eye, she saw Oscar's mouth drop open. After a second of pure wonder, he snapped it closed, but never took
his gaze off Walker.

The stranger repeated the rubbing with the blanket
before he laid it on the stud's back. He allowed the horse
to snuffle the saddle, then settled it on the withers and
slowly pulled it into place. He threaded and tightened the
cinch, but not snug enough for a rider to mount. The stallion's only response was a snort and sidling sideways a
step or two.

Walker put the horse back to circling the ring, merely
flicking the rope in the direction he wanted the stallion to

go. After several revolutions in each direction, he drew the horse in again by turning his back, then cinched the saddle tight. He examined Samantha's bridle, the bit in particular. She wondered why, but said nothing. No one made a sound as Walker worked the animal for some time.

Though he didn't bolt, the horse took a backward step when Walker nudged the bit against his lips. The wrangler made a soothing sound in his throat, and the stallion opened his mouth. Before he could close it, the bit was in place.

"Do you know how to ride, little man?"

When Guy didn't answer, Walker glanced over his shoulder and smiled. Which sent Samantha's pulse skittering.

"You may speak when I ask you a question."

Guy didn't. Instead, he nodded.

"Would you like to ride this horse?"

No! Holy moly, the man *was* loco. Just because the stallion had cantered around in the corral at Walker's bidding, just because he'd allowed the saddle on his back, didn't mean a small boy could ride him. But Samantha's tongue felt pasted to the roof of her mouth. She couldn't say a word in protest. Apparently, her father and Oscar were as speechless as she.

"Come," Walker said. "But move slowly, little man. This fine fellow is not too sure about all this just yet."

She put out a restraining hand when Guy started through the slats. "No," she whispered.

"But he said—"

"The boy will be fine, Miss Timberlake."

Her gaze snapped to the honey-tongued man. Guy could be killed! Apparently her mute worry was telegraphed to Walker in some way. A smile that went all the way to his extraordinary eyes set her heart pounding.

"I promise you, he will be fine." He extended a hand. "Come, little man."

Guy went, slowly as the big man had cautioned. First Walker attached the lariat to the headstall, adjusted the cinch, then laid her brother stomach down over the saddle and put the horse to a slow walk. Guy made no protest, but he looked like a sack of grain. Then the man told Guy to pull himself up and sit astride. After two or three circles, Walker handed the reins to him. Backing up, the big man allowed the lead rope to slip through his fingers until he was fifteen feet away from the animal.

"Show me how well you walk and trot a horse."

He instructed Guy to ease up on the reins a couple of times, but otherwise he maintained a firm grip on the lead, slowly pivoted, and remained silent. After several minutes, her brother pulled up the stallion. His grin was as wide as the sky when he looked at her father and Oscar, then at her.

"You may dismount now." Walker took the reins from Guy, who scooted out of the corral.

Samantha was so relieved that her brother had come away unscathed that it was a moment before she realized Walker had spoken again . . . to her. He had removed the long lead and coiled it in one hand. The other was extended toward her, the reins looped over his fingers.

"He is all yours," he said, offering the horse for her to ride.

"Just a gol-durn minute." Though Oscar had been tongue-tied moments ago, he wasn't now.

"Perhaps you should ride him, Walker," her father said.

Now Oscar and her father questioned him? A six-year-old boy could ride, but they protested when it was her turn?

"The stallion is Miss Timberlake's, is he not?" the stranger asked in a reasonable tone. "It would be best if he is handled by the person who intends to ride him."

"Maybe so, but he could buck her to the other side of hell before we blink," Oscar argued.

Heat coiled in her stomach and warmed her body all the way to her cheeks when Holden Walker refocused his remarkable eyes on her. "Are you afraid?"

"Fear has nothin'—"

"No," she interrupted Oscar. Wasn't that just like a

man! She'd been riding since she was three years old, as had Guy. But because she was a woman, every man on the ranch jumped to protect her, as if she didn't have the sense God gave a goose.

Dang it! I'm as capable as any man on the ranch.

Before more objections could ensue, she slipped into the corral and reached to take the reins from his hand. When her fingers curled against his bare, callused palm, a shiver quaked inside her. Again, her gaze darted to his.

Smoldering. That was the only way she could describe his eyes. She gulped air and looked away.

"Good," he said, a smile in his tone.

Had he read her mind?

"Move slowly, but without hesitation. This horse will go the way he is started. If you let him get the upper hand, you will never gain his respect."

"Respect? He's a horse, for God's sake!" Oscar said.

"That will be quite enough."

Oscar flicked a glance at her father, then stared at the stranger. "Sorry, Hiram, but I never heard the like in my life." He hooted with amiable laughter.

A smile lit her father's features. "That's a fact, but we've come this far. Let's play it out."

Samantha gained control over her racing pulse. What in heaven's name was wrong with her? Holden Walker was a drifter. A ranch hand. Nothing more. Okay, so he could gentle a horse. She was glad of that, wasn't she? Why get herself in a twist over his penetrating gaze, his . . .

Warmth would be an understatement.

She could feel the heat, not just of his hand but his entire body, for he stood close. Too close.

Concentrate on the horse!

As she stepped up to the animal and gathered the reins in one hand, Walker said, "Talk to him. The stallion is smart, but he is green. Stroke him."

As I would your body?

She blinked. Dear heaven. Where had that thought come

from? She'd never touched a man that way. Didn't know how, in fact.

"Let him know you are no threat," Walker added.

Thank God he was behind her and couldn't see her face. Surely her cheeks had blossomed to a rosy hue from the sudden heat coursing through her. She started to lift her foot, but Walker stopped her.

"Wait. I will give you a leg up so you will not be off center in one stirrup. The stallion will notice your weight more than the boy's."

Undoubtedly, he would. Guy weighed about seventy pounds. Her weight was 125. She glanced over her shoulder. The stranger had laced his fingers together, making a basket.

"Your knee," he said when she moved to place her boot in his hands.

He pitched her up with no effort at all. Samantha glanced down at him and wished she hadn't. Again, light spangled in his eyes, but he spoke as if passing the time of day.

"Walk until I tell you differently."

She gathered the reins loosely and nudged the horse's flanks. She'd failed to wear spurs this morning, not realizing she'd be riding, but it made no difference. The stallion moved out smoothly. After several revolutions, Walker told her to trot, then lope. Amazing! The stud responded like a seasoned saddle horse.

What a joy to ride. She'd known he would be. All his gaits were smooth. His hooves struck the hard ground like dance steps. A smile curved her mouth when she caught the expressions of wonder on the men's faces as she passed time and again. She reined in the horse, even backed him a few steps.

"You're wonderful," she murmured, and reached to caress his withers. His thick mane was matted, his coat hot. She chuckled when he nodded his head as if in agreement. The bridle chinked in the stillness.

Oscar spoke. "Bet you can't do that again."

She glanced around and found the foreman grinning at the stranger. Though Oscar was secure in his position with her father, he obviously felt challenged by the newcomer.

Holden Walker lifted a corner of his generous lips in a faint smile and shrugged. "I can and I will if you have other horses that need gentling."

Samantha believed him, and knew she would never forget the extraordinary performance she had watched unfold this morning.

The stranger looked at her father. "If I am hired, that is."

"I believe that goes without saying, young man. That was quite a demonstration. Like Oscar, I'd like to see you repeat it. We have a dozen horses that need work."

"I want to ride him outside the corral," Samantha said.

Walker looked up at her and shook his head. "Tomorrow. He is nervous."

Right on cue, the horse blew and mouthed the bit.

Well, shoot. Walker was right. But she wanted to put the stallion into a flat-out run. She wanted to feel the wind in her face. She wanted . . .

"He has worked enough his first time under saddle," Walker said.

Of course. Why hadn't she realized that? The man's voice bore a chiding quality, as if he were speaking to a young child. Her back stiffened.

"Can I ride him again, Samma?"

Before she could answer, Walker looked at her brother with a smile that made her mouth go dry. Lord in heaven, he was too handsome by half. Her thoughts were as scattered as leaves falling in autumn. One minute her pulse raced and she burned inside, the next her teeth were on edge because of his arrogant manner. Well, not arrogant, exactly . . .

"Perhaps you would like to have your own mount, little man."

Guy's eyes rounded. "Can I, Pa? Can I have my own horse?"

"May I," Aunt Mattie corrected. Undetected, she had walked up behind Samantha's father with old Bengy, the hound that would follow her into fire, on her heels.

As the men turned to her aunt, Samantha carefully dismounted. She remembered Holden Walker's instruction to move slowly.

"Who have we here?" Mattie took the stranger's measure from her diminutive height, her expression sober. Hiram made the introductions.

"Ma'am," Walker said, and removed his hat with that grave politeness that seemed so at odds with his dangerous-looking exterior.

His speech reminded her of the Eastern nabobs she'd met the past summer in Waco. Each word so precise. Odd, too, how he called Guy "little man." Every time he did, her brother's chest puffed out.

Walker's dark hair feathered across his lips in the morning breeze. A breeze Samantha hadn't noticed until now. Her fingers itched to brush the silken-looking strands from his chiseled face. He did so himself, the hair resisting the attempt, caught in the dark stubble shadowing his firm jaw.

"You're a big one." The top of Mattie's salt-and-pepper head came to the middle of the tall man's chest. "Walker," she said thoughtfully, and didn't crack a smile. "Don't know the name."

"No, ma'am," he agreed and offered no more.

"Aunt Mattie, you shoulda seen him workin' Samma's horse!"

Her brother's exuberance seemed to bring Mattie out of a trance. She blinked and looked at Guy.

"I should *have* seen," she said.

"Yeah! He done—"

"Breakfast is on the table getting cold," she interrupted. Glancing around, she spoke louder. "There's work aplenty for you men. The day isn't getting any younger. Sounds to me like Hiram hired this here fella." Mattie cocked a thumb in the stranger's general direction, but she was looking at Oscar. "Maybe you can put him to earning his keep."

Why in heaven's name was Aunt Mattie . . . She sounded plain rude. Casting a glance at the man from beneath her lashes, Samantha saw him smile faintly and turn to walk with Oscar.

Like the other ranch hands, Oscar hopped when Mattie Crawford spoke. So did her father. It never ceased to amaze Samantha how her tiny aunt commanded so much respect from the strapping men. They never, ever, gainsaid her. Someday, when she was top dog here, Samantha was determined to have them do her bidding as readily.

Walker's horse followed him like an obedient dog. She gazed after the stranger, who was far too intriguing, and dangerous in more ways than one, she thought. Who was he, really? Where did he come from? Why was he here? She didn't believe he was a mere drifter. Why, she couldn't say. But he didn't look like any saddle tramp she'd ever seen. He didn't sound like one either. She wondered if anyone else had noticed his odd way of speaking.

For her own peace of mind, she'd have to guard against her building curiosity.

"Are you coming?"

She whipped around as if her aunt had caught her committing an unpardonable sin. A crazy thought, but her cheeks warmed anyway.

"Yes. Of course."

She trotted toward the smaller woman, who gazed at her with narrowed eyes.

"Samantha, he's far more dangerous than he appears. Keep your distance."

She blinked, astonished that her aunt had come up with the same conclusions as her own.

She frowned. "You needn't worry about me, Aunt Mattie. I can take care of myself."

"Can you really?" Mattie said dryly.

*   *   *

Oscar put Holden to work, but not gentling horses. Not that day. Instead, he sent him out with Lemuel Baker, the black man. Only a couple of inches shy of Holden's six-three, Baker was formidable looking as hell, with wide, beefy shoulders.

Holden could handle horses with his eyes closed. He suspected Baker could, too. Although Holden was surprised that Baker had been given the chance. Few Texans hired colored men.

Between them they rounded up two dozen head and hazed them into a holding pen about a mile from the ranch house. The horses were unbranded, but already green-broke.

Walker closed the makeshift gate and paused to wet his mouth with a slug of warm water from his canteen. He squirted a tiny bit on his sleeve, laid the damp buckskin against his hot forehead and looked over at Baker, who was checking his cinch.

"Problem?"

Baker glanced up, his fathomless black eyes surrounded by light chocolate skin. The man did not look much different from many Indians Walker had known, except for his hair. Baker's hair was thick, haphazardly whacked just above his collar, and nearly untamable. He had pulled his hat down almost to his ears so it would not fly off.

"Frayin'," he finally answered. "But it'll hold till nightfall."

"Why have we corralled these horses?"

"They's been sold to some fella down San Antone way," he drawled and remounted, sending his fidgety gelding into a tight circle until he drew him up.

Walker's gray sidestepped away and eyed the bay rather than nipping his butt. Walker patted his mount as if commiserating with him. Leaning slightly back to settle his canteen into his saddlebag, he squeezed the gelding with his knees. The animal ambled forward at a walk. It was a moment before he took up the reins that draped loosely over the saddle seat.

"Y'all train that horse yerself?"

Walker nodded. "About six years ago."

"Can he run?"

Walker's mouth lifted in a half smile. "You are interested in racing? That is what you are asking?"

"Yeah. I like ta wager, but I'm too heavy to ride a race. Oscar, he can ride rings 'round most fellas in these here parts. I won a heap o' eagles on him an' the li'l mustang he rides."

This was the most conversation Baker had offered all day. Which bothered Walker not at all, since he was quiet himself. But the black man's eyes sparkled when he talked about racing, which amused Holden. He said just enough to draw out Baker.

"Fast, is he?"

"Ya betcha. They's not a horse 'round these parts that ain't seen that li'l mustang's rump drawin' away. The Butcher boy tries ever' chance he gets to beat 'im, but Oscar just gives that horse his head an' off they goes."

"Butcher boy?"

"C. J. Uriah Butcher's young'n." Baker frowned fleetingly. "Them's the folks owns the neighborin' ranch north o' here. Between you an' me an' the fence post, C. J. is sweet on Samma."

Walker went utterly still. He hadn't even considered that Samantha Timberlake might have a suitor. What did it matter, anyway? He might be attracted to her, but he would not act on it.

"Between you an' me an' another o' them fence posts," Baker rambled on, "Samma don't think much o' him a'tall."

Walker shook himself from his musings about the woman. "Why do you say that?"

Baker flashed a humorless smile. "When ya meet up

with 'im, y'all'll see right off. He's a banty rooster what likes to dig in his spurs, if'n you know what I mean."

Mean-spirited son of a bitch, Walker surmised. Well, he would not be the first one Holden Walker had encountered since returning to the white eyes' world. And likely not the last. Besides, he had nothing to say about who courted Samantha.

Three days later, Samantha bounced on the buggy seat next to Mattie. Guy sat hunched next to her father, who still insisted he commanded enough strength to drive the rig. Not only were they headed toward the Butcher place, but she was forced to ride in the blasted buggy—like a lady—at Aunt Mattie's insistence. Her bottom already numb, she had yet to sit for a couple of hours on a hard bench while Reverend Fuller ranted.

At moments like this, she wished she *had* been born a man.

Not one of the ranch hands on Timberoaks had ridden along. The only time any of them heard Reverend Fuller preach was when her father's porch was the pulpit and the booming voice couldn't be avoided.

The image of the new man lingered in her mind for a moment. She'd not hesitate to wager that Walker wouldn't be caught dead in church. The gun he wore bespoke violence in direct conflict with God's commandment: *Thou shalt not kill.*

"The Lord served up a beautiful day, didn't He?" Aunt Mattie asked.

Samantha reluctantly let go her thoughts about Walker and looked around. Her eyes crinkled despite her bonnet. She lifted her hand to shade them. The sky appeared white-hot in the glare. Heat shimmered off the prairie in the distance. Not even noon, and already the air sweltered.

"Yes, He did," she answered halfheartedly. Lordy, it was going to be a very long day.

Her attention narrowed on her father's straight back in front of her. If Reverend Fuller hadn't been here, she knew her pa would not have ventured off the ranch for the whole day. His uncontrollable coughing fits embarrassed him.

"Almost there," he said.

She leaned and gazed beyond the horses' bobbing heads. The huge, pretentious portal Uriah Butcher had erected to announce passage onto Singletree Ranch loomed ahead. In seconds, they passed beneath the crossbeam where a singletree was attached to one of the uprights that bore the heavy timber's weight.

Ahead lay Butcher's sprawling ranch. Though his house was sod, the rest of the buildings were impressive in size. Set a quarter mile from the house, the barn's pitched roof reached for the sky and dwarfed the dwelling. The hands occupied a bunkhouse half again the size of Timberoaks's quarters for its men.

C. J. had built a place of his own. It stood isolated from the main house and buildings by a line of cedars and hackberry trees. Though she didn't like C. J., she could understand his need for peace away from his father. Uriah was forever on him about something. Like right now.

Uriah bellowed from where he stood on the porch watching their approach. "Clarence, git yerself out here and help the ladies down!"

Even though C. J. hated it, his father always called him Clarence. Years before, Samantha had seen C. J. sock boys, and now that he was grown, he glared at ranch hands who dared call him that, even though it was a family name.

He came forward, a smile on his thin lips, but as usual, it didn't light his cold eyes. "Mornin', Miss Mattie." The barrel-chested, bow-legged man swept his hat off respectfully as he approached her aunt.

"Hello, C. J. Nice day for the sermon." She extended her hand and accepted his assistance out of the buggy.

"Yes, ma'am."

He resettled his hat on mouse-brown hair and started around the back of the buggy toward Samantha. She leaped down before he got there, unable to abide his touch.

C. J. turned and spoke under his breath so only she could hear. "How's my girl?"

"I have no idea how *your* girl is," Samantha sneered, "but I'm fine. Or I was until just a moment ago."

"I'm really lookin' forward to the day all that fire is spent for another purpose, honey." A leer stretched his lips. "I'm gonna enjoy the hell out of tamin' you."

"The day you shoulder your horse's weight on your back is the day you'll be man enough to tame me, C. J."

"Everything all right?" Mattie asked.

"Why, yes, ma'am!" C. J. grinned down at her aunt.

He wore boots with two-inch heels for added height. Otherwise, he'd have looked Samantha straight in the eyes.

She moved, anxious to get away while he was occupied with her aunt. Ahead of her, Uriah, Reverend Fuller, the Tuckers and the Sylvesters stood near the doorway or sat in chairs arranged in front of the house.

Following her father, she glanced at her brother as he ran off toward a cluster of youngsters beneath the trees. Children on the range seldom had the chance to play together. By tonight, when they headed home, Guy would be exhausted and dead to the world five minutes into the ride.

"Well, now," Uriah said, and walked toward them. "Here's the little lady I'm pinin' to call daughter before long."

Samantha bit back a hot retort. She'd heard it before from the burly man, a bully if there ever was one. Like father, like son. She didn't trust either any farther than she could throw them.

She endured a smooch on her cheek, and smiled as if she were glad to see him. At least he hadn't put his arm around her shoulders the way C. J. would try to do at every opportunity.

"Morning, Mr. Butcher. Nice day for a sermon and picnic."

"Um," he said, and extended a welcome to her father and aunt. "Miss Mattie, you're a purty sight for these old eyes!"

"If I am, you haven't looked beyond your nose."

He laughed and clasped her elbow. "Full o' sass as usual. That's what I like about you." He started toward the crowd of guests. "It's a puzzle why we ain't married up."

"Because I wouldn't have you on a silver platter."

Striding forward, Samantha clasped her father's arm before C. J. could lay claim to her.

Chapter Three

"Damnation and hell await you who walk the path of sin!" Reverend Fuller roared.

Sanctimonious rot.

Samantha hid her thoughts behind a bland expression. *You* who walk the path? Obviously the reverend didn't believe *he* was a sinner.

"The Good Book says the Lord is a God of wrath. You must ask His forgiveness for your sins every day!" Reverend Fuller's eyes burned into each of the young people listening to his sermon, the females in particular. "Idle thoughts lead to lustful thoughts!" He *amen*ed, waved his arms, and pointed toward the sky. "Cleave unto God's word, and await the man or woman He's chosen for you!"

His stern gaze slid to C.J., then to Paul Sylvester. Samantha could understand the remarks aimed at C.J., a man in his thirties, but Paul was barely fourteen. She shook her head, harboring more than a few suspicions that the reverend was as easily led astray as the next man.

She sat behind her father, aunt, and the Sylvesters, hemmed in—thank you, God—by the twins, Mary and Minnie Tucker. Mary turned to her and crossed her sky blue eyes, then rolled them heavenward. Samantha bit back a laugh and ducked her head.

At the same time, Minnie grumbled, "And just where are these chosen men?"

Samantha seldom had the opportunity to see Mary and Minnie. Not quite twenty, the twins were fun-loving, and she enjoyed their company. But a trip to Uriah's ranch always put her on edge and left a foul taste in her mouth, so the visit with the twins wasn't as pleasant as it might have been.

Again, she glanced at C. J. and found him ogling her. He wiggled his brows. Did he believe his suggestive manner-isms made her heart beat faster? *Think again, C. J.* She wanted to shout at him to aim his lecherous thoughts else-where. Not that it would do any good. Samantha had long ago surmised that C. J. thought women panted after him like bitches in heat.

"Prayer is my personal link to God! Perhaps He will lis-ten to you if you come before me now on your knees so I may pray for your souls!" the reverend thundered, recall-ing Samantha's attention.

What he'd said in the interim, she didn't know and didn't care. Her thoughts wandered; she stared directly at the minister, not seeing him. Instead, eyes the color of a wolf's leaped to mind. Eyes that had traveled her length with bold regard.

Even his hands were intriguing. Hers would undoubt-edly disappear from view if cocooned by his wide palms and long, tapered fingers. She blinked several times when she found herself wondering what it would be like if he . . . touched her. A shiver rippled through her.

His manner fairly screamed self-assurance, and that thought brought her up short. He'd probably make an overbearing husband. And the gun he wore scared her a little. Had he ever shot, maybe killed a man?

Her father's cough captured her attention. She was on her feet by the time he'd fished a handkerchief from his back pocket. He walked around the side of the house, out of sight. She started to follow.

Reverend Fuller sputtered to a halt, glanced toward the corner of the house, then back as Mattie joined Samantha.

"Ladies?"

"I'm sorry, Reverend. I fear we must take our leave," Mattie said.

"I was about to offer the last prayer." His voice rang with indignation.

"I'm sorry, but we must head home." Her aunt didn't stop walking.

Neither did Samantha. Too bad if the minister was upset that they were more concerned about her father than his self-important ranting. She scooted around the building. Her father slumped against the side of the buggy. Before she reached him, he pulled himself into the seat—the back seat. She would drive home.

Mattie scrambled in next to her brother-in-law while Samantha lifted her skirt to climb into the front. Suddenly, C. J. appeared, clasped her elbow and gave her a boost up.

"Move over, Samma. I'll drive ya home."

"No." She and Aunt Mattie spoke at the same time.

"That won't be necessary," Mattie continued. "But you can . . ."

Before she finished her directive to find Guy, he bounded into view.

"Pa!" He sprinted forward, took one leap and landed in the seat next to Samantha. He half turned and stared back. "Pa," he said more softly. "You . . . okay?"

Of course he wasn't okay, but as Samantha took up the reins, out of the corner of her eye she saw her father squeeze Guy's hand, a reassuring gesture.

"Samma," C. J. said.

She signaled the horses into motion. "Get out of the way."

He jumped back. "I'll come by tomorrow to see how he's doin'," C. J. called as the buggy picked up speed.

Her father was gone!

Hiram Timberlake had taken to his bed upon their return from the Butchers' and not risen again. His last labored breath came a short two weeks after that awful ride home. Convinced her father's strength had been depleted by the twenty-mile round-trip buggy ride and the long day, she blamed Reverend Fuller and his stupid, endless sermon. And God.

Her father's strength had drained away before her eyes. No matter how hard Aunt Mattie worked to relieve his cough, he quickly weakened.

Another six days had passed since the funeral. Samantha sat next to her father's grave, her eyes full with heavy tears that wouldn't fall. She stared at the mound of rocky soil that would gradually sink and leave little evidence of the dear man's last resting place. But of a certainty she'd remember her vital, loving father.

Glaring up at the impossibly blue sky, she wondered how the day could be so lovely. How could the sun shine and warm the earth, heat her back, while her heart rained tears?

"Why did You take my father?" she berated God for the umpteenth time.

Fifty-five was not old.

Samantha leaned forward and placed her hand on the warm earth, then sifted dry dirt through her fingers. "What will I do without you, Pa? How am I going to manage Timberoaks without your steady hand? Your . . ."

Boots stepped into her side vision. Unheard, someone had walked up next to her. She grimaced. She'd had a belly full of C. J.'s presence. He'd made a nuisance of himself, especially this past week. Samantha looked up . . . up.

Wolf eyes returned her gaze.

Holden Walker carried his black hat in his hand. The incessant wind lifted his long sable hair as his gaze shifted to the grave. Oscar had told her just this morning that Walker was working out fine. He'd exercised the black every day while Samantha cared for her father. No matter how long his day, the wrangler had walked or lunged the stallion after everyone else had slipped into the bunkhouse for evening chuck.

"Your father was a fine man," he said in his silky, quiet voice.

She glared at him. "How would you know?"

For several seconds he remained silent, his gaze upon the grave, then he settled the hat on his head and turned his attention to her. He probed her eyes so intently that she felt like an insect trapped on flypaper.

"You are angry with your god."

Put so baldly, it sounded presumptuous of her. And what an odd way to say it. *Her* god? "What I feel, what I think, is none of your affair, Walker."

"That is true, Miss Timberlake. Nonetheless, I am sorry for your loss."

His deep voice unsettled her. Much more and she'd succumb to tears. Irrationally, at that moment she wanted to fling herself into this man's strong arms and cry her heart out. Yet she barely knew him. Her wits must be addled.

With a resigned sigh, she asked, "Did you want something?"

Her attention shifted at the sound of pounding hoofbeats. Walker looked across her father's grave, and she glanced over her shoulder. In seconds, Willis Nabors drew close and slowed his buckskin.

"Howdy, Samantha." He halted in a cloud of dust, dismounted, then swept off his hat.

"Hello, Willis. What brings you this way?"

"On my way home from Waco." He walked toward her, fishing in a shirt pocket beneath his black vest.

"How's Emma?"

His smile revealed one gold tooth slightly off center in his wide mouth. "Fit as a fiddle. The little mite's due next month."

Married just over a year, Willis and Emma expected their first child, and Willis's buttons nearly bursted with pride.

He extended his hand, a battered envelope clutched in his fist. "I brung this for ya, Samantha."

Her eyes widened with surprise. Mail was so rare. She read her name in bold writing she didn't recognize.

"I was at the courthouse, and a feller handed it to me when he found out I lived near ya. Crocker, I think he said his name was."

Remembering her manners, she said, "It's so hot, Willis. I suspect Aunt Mattie has a pitcher of lemonade in the icebox. Go to the house and rest yourself for a spell."

He shook his head and took a backward step. "My thanks, but I best be headin' on. Heard Injuns is roamin' the area."

"Indians? Where?"

Samantha jumped at Walker's questions.

"Just north o' Gatesville. Stole a couple horses from a farmer, then splashed into the Leon so's nobody could follow their trail."

"Anyone hurt?" she asked, even though she feared the answer.

He shook his head. "The sneaky bastards just took horses."

Out of the corner of her eye, she saw Walker's jaw set. The big man's fingers curled into fists.

Willis looked at the grave, his expression sober. "Shore was sorry to hear about yer paw, Samantha, but I ain't anxious to hang around too long. Emma and Maw is alone."

She understood. It had been four or five years since they'd had trouble with marauding Indians, but that didn't mean there was no danger.

Willis left and Samantha ripped open the envelope, ignoring Walker. As she read, her heart constricted.

Dear Miss Timberlake:

My condolences on the death of your father. Last year, according to his wishes, and the law by which I am governed, I drew up Hiram's will.

"A will?" she murmured and returned to reading.

As executor of the estate, one of my duties is to read that will in the presence of his heirs. To that end, I shall arrive at Timberoaks Tuesday next, 6 July 1860, at 10 o'clock. Please be advised that Miss Matilda Crawford and Guy Timberlake should be in attendance.

> *I am at your service,*
> *Judge Hazlett Crocker*

Samantha brushed her hand over her brow. Her unfocused gaze wandered to her father's grave. "You thought it necessary to appoint an executor over me, Pa?"

She squeezed her eyes shut, dropped her hand to her side and crumpled the letter. What had her father said? *"When I'm gone, this ranch will go to you, eventually."*

Eventually. The word screamed in her head.

Why hadn't she listened to him? Asked him what he meant? If she had, maybe she could have changed his mind.

"Miss Timberlake."

Samantha opened her eyes and whirled to face Walker. Heartsick and angered by this turn of events, she'd forgotten he was standing there, hearing everything Willis said, and every word she uttered.

"What?" she snapped, transferring her anger to him.

"I am leaving Timberoaks for a few days."

Her pulse raced. She didn't want him to leave. An absurd thought, but she couldn't deny it. "Just because my father died—"

"I have . . . business to attend to."

"Will you be back?" Blast it, she shouldn't have asked. It made her appear weak.

He nodded. "I will take the black with me."

"What?" Her eyes rounded in astonishment. "You think I'd allow you to take my horse? Are you crazy?"

A half smile lifted the corner of his generous mouth. "I think you should, answers your first question. And no to the second."

"What?" She sounded like a magpie, but his reply confused her.

"Miss Timberlake, you would be wise to let me take the stallion away from the ranch."

"Why?"

"Your father's will is to be read soon."

"What does that have to do with my horse?"

He shrugged one massive shoulder. "Maybe nothing, but I would advise you not to claim that stallion as yours for a while."

Mystified, Samantha planted her hands on her hips. "You're advising me? I'm your new boss."

"Miss Timberlake—"

"For God's sake, stop calling me that!"

She glanced at her father's grave. *Sorry, Pa.*

"That is your name, is it not?" Walker asked in his maddeningly reasonable tone.

"Of course it is." She shut her eyes in an attempt to rein in her anger. Drawing a deep breath, she opened them and willed herself to control her temper. *Just listen to what he has to say. Maybe he'll make sense eventually. That word again.* "Why would I let you take my horse?"

"It might be wise if people believe you have sold the stallion to me."

She glanced around, hoping someone would appear to explain this crazy man's babble. After another deep breath, she said, "The black is not for sale. Why would I tell people—"

"I have a hunch you may lose him to another if you do not take my advice."

"You *are* crazy! Do you fancy yourself some sort of . . . of a seer?"

Walker said nothing, his expression enigmatic.

"Who would take him?" she demanded when he failed to respond to her taunt.

"Do you not think it strange that your neighbor has been here every day since your father's death?"

Baffled by his question, she asked, "C. J.? He's a pest, but he—"

"Intends you for his wife."

She blinked. *Dear God, who other than C. J. and his father thought . . .* Hearing someone else, a near stranger, speak her fears stole the breath she'd struggled to get into her lungs. "Where did you hear that?"

"It matters not. When you marry, he will claim the black for his own."

"That's ridiculous. In the first place, I'm not marrying anyone. Least of all C. J. You warn he'll take the stallion, but you want me to sell him to you? Same thing, Walker."

His eyes gleamed, lit by internal flames. She stepped back. He gave her a tight smile.

"You are not listening, Miss . . . Samantha."

Her name rolled off his tongue as if he tasted it, savored it. The sensual sound ignited sparks in her stomach. Her knees weakened as heat warmed her entire body. Handsome, virile, mysterious . . .

Stop it, Samantha!

She stood by her father's grave fantasizing, if that was the right word, about a ranch hand. A man who had announced he was leaving. A drifter who tried to trick her into giving up the best-looking horse she'd ever seen.

"Maybe you think I'm not listening, Walker. But I hear you loud and clear. Now you hear me. I will *not* sell Black Magic to you." She paused, surprised as the perfect name for the magnificent stallion slipped past her lips.

"You are correct. You will only let people believe you have sold him to me."

"So you can run off with him? Steal him from me?"

Walker dug in his pants pocket, then extended his hand. When he opened his fingers, Samantha gasped. Two gold nuggets as big as pigeon eggs nestled in his palm.

"Something to hold," he said. "If I fail to return your horse, they are yours to keep."

Her startled gaze shot to his eyes. "Where did you get—"

"It matters not. I will leave the gold in your care while you place the stallion in mine. Later, we will trade back."

"And I'm a monkey's uncle."

"I beg your pardon?"

Walker looked so perplexed, she wanted to laugh. A grown man, and he'd never heard the expression before?

"It means . . . Never mind."

She glanced toward the house. It wouldn't be long until supper. Though she found it next to impossible to eat, she needed to freshen up and sit at the table, for Guy's sake if nothing else.

"I must go, Walker. My father's will—"

"In a few days, you will lose Black Magic," he interrupted.

Vexed by his insistence, she started past him. Walker's hand shot out, and those long fingers she'd imagined caressing her clamped around her upper arm. She couldn't move another step.

"Listen to me one moment longer, Miss Timberlake. I would bet everything I hope to gain in my life that this ranch will be managed for a time by a man. Not you."

She scoffed at him, eyes disdainful. "If my father said it once, he said it a million times. Timberoaks would be mine when he was gone. My father never went back on his word in life, Walker. I do not expect him to do so in death."

The words had barely left her mouth when she mocked her own bravado. *Eventually. Executor* haunted her. Dismissing uncertainty, she squared her shoulders. It made no difference. Not now.

Without warning, Walker drew her against him. She felt his heat, and her breasts pillowed against his hard chest. Protest failed her. One hand still held her in place; his free arm circled her body. His thighs felt like tree trunks pressed against hers. An answering heat sluiced through her entire length.

"Miss Timberlake, I will be gone for a few days, but I will be back. That is a promise. I suggest you heed my words and guard your tongue."

The nerve of the man! She looked up into his enigmatic eyes. Before she could give him the tongue-lashing he deserved, he lowered his head. His mouth covered hers.

Thought fled. Nothing remained except the warmth of his lips, claiming, coaxing, nibbling. He sucked her lower lip between his, then nipped with his teeth. She gasped. His tongue darted to meet hers. She was lost.

My God, my God, my God. The litany played through her otherwise paralyzed brain. In the next instant, *don't stop, don't stop, don't stop* echoed in her head.

But he did.

Floating, as if in a fog, ever so slowly she realized he was no longer kissing her, though her pliant body was still crushed against his hard frame. His lips were . . . speaking.

"I must travel from here for a time. Remember, guard what you say, and do not be upset by what I do. It is for your own good."

She lingered on the threshold between exquisite feeling and rational thought, unable to wrap her mind around a word he said. He could have kissed her forever if he'd wanted to.

When her eyes focused at last, she stood alone next to her father's grave. She shook her head and glanced around. Walker was gone as though he had never . . . kissed her witless. Yet she felt as if she still stood in his shadow, crushed against his unyielding frame. It made no sense, but she felt his heat, his . . . She reached up and touched tender lips with trembling fingers.

His last words echoed in her mind.

"Do not be upset by what I do. It is for your own good."

Her father had said something similar.

Samantha circled around the barn before returning to the house. She didn't know what Walker had meant about not being upset, but she was reassured to see that Black Magic paced the perimeter of the corral. She paused, recalling the wrangler's other ridiculous prophecy.

". . . this ranch will be managed for a time by a man."

Absurd. The comment of an arrogant man, nothing more. Executor, Judge Crocker might be, but by glory, she would manage this ranch on her own. With a shake of her head, she strode on. She needed to tell Aunt Mattie the astonishing news about the will.

Approaching the house, she saw Guy seated on the porch, petting Bengy. The old hound was more or less asleep, his usual pastime. Guy's little face looked as sad as the hound's. Since her father's death, her brother was no longer the into-everything, ask-a-question-a-minute child. He'd grown quiet, in fact. Too quiet.

She sat on the step and fingered Bengy's soft ear. The brindle-colored hound stretched his legs and moaned.

"Guy, it's time to get cleaned up for supper."

"I ain't hungry."

His belligerence irritated her, but she bit back a harsh response. Besides, a six-year-old boy was always hungry. "Aunt Mattie has cooked, so we'll eat."

When he didn't respond, Samantha brushed the top of his head. "Guy . . ."

He shied away and muttered, "Why'd Pa die? It ain't fair."

Samantha felt the same, except she was glad her father was no longer suffering, as he had at the last.

Why was it that no-account rustlers, horse thieves, savage Indians, and the dregs of society lived long lives, while the good died young? Guy was right. It wasn't fair.

She stood, reminding herself that he was a child. He needed time, time to think about death, its suddenness, its finality. Aunt Mattie would know what to say, how to help him. Heaven knew Samantha didn't have the right words, so she ignored his question.

"Come in soon. You don't want to upset Aunt Mattie."

A few minutes later Samantha lit the lamp in her room to augment the waning daylight. Absently, she released the waistband button as she walked toward the armoire to find fresh clothing. The skirt slid over her hips and hit the floor with a faint *clunk*.

Scowling, she leaned and picked it up. Spreading the cotton in front of her, she stuck her hand into the pocket. Her eyes widened as she pulled out two gold nuggets.

"What in the world . . . ?"

And then she knew. Holden Walker had slipped them into her pocket when he kissed her. Lost in the magic of his warm lips, she had felt nothing.

"The nerve of the man."

Despite her half-dressed state, she ran out to the hallway and into her father's room at the front of the house. She swept aside the lace curtain and peered out. Though shadowed by approaching darkness, she could see a quarter of the corral where Black Magic should have been penned. Unless the stud was hidden by the barn . . . Wishful thinking, she knew.

"Do not be upset by what I do."

Damn Walker to perdition! Now she understood his words. The no-good sidewinder had waited until she had come in the house, then taken her horse. After she'd told him . . .

She yanked the curtain back in place so hard that it was

a miracle the lace didn't rip. He'd understand exactly what upset meant when he came back. If he came back.

"Wait till I get my hands on you, you low-down cur!"

Just past ten o'clock the next morning, Samantha sat on a settee in the study. Guy perched next to her, and Aunt Mattie occupied the worn wingback chair. Judge Hazlett Crocker sat at her father's desk, dwarfed by the big leather chair. For ten minutes his voice had droned, spouting the legal jargon of her father's will.

Judge Crocker was doubtless the one who had reduced Hiram Timberlake's vital, loving life to all this legal mumbo-jumbo. The man she had called Pa, the man she had loved—still loved—would not speak the way the legal document read.

Closing her mind to his voice, she studied the judge. He was not what she had expected an important attorney to look like. This rotund individual appeared to have been stuffed into too-tight clothes.

His almost perfectly round, balding head sat atop an equally round body, choked in at the neck by a stiff collar. Starched collar tips jabbed into his jowls, the apparent cause of his unnaturally rosy cheeks.

"To my sister-in-law, Matilda Kathryn Crawford, I leave the sum of five thousand dollars, and a home at Timberoaks." Judge Hazlett gave her aunt a cryptic smile.

Samantha seethed at his tight expression. Did the barrister mean to suggest that Aunt Mattie had lived here these many years in the hopes of monetary gain? *Think again, Judge.*

"To the boy bearing the name Guy Timberlake, I leave . . ."

No. Guy was her brother! Her father would have called him his son. "Judge Crocker."

He glanced up as if startled that anyone would interrupt him. She smiled as tightly as he had moments ago.

"What is it, little lady? If you'll be patient, I'm coming to the portion of the will pertaining to you."

"I'm having trouble with some of the wording of this will, Judge."

He frowned, casting a quick glance at Mattie, then back at her. "I beg your pardon?"

"Guy is my brother. I don't believe my father would have referred to him as 'the boy bearing the name Guy Timberlake.' Guy was and still is his son, in every way but blood."

"That may be true, little lady, but legally he's an orphan your father took in."

Samantha curled her hands into fists that bunched the fabric of her skirt. *Little lady?* Twice now he'd called her that. She hated his condescending tone. "There's no *may be* about it, sir. Pa always referred to him as his son."

"Samantha."

She glanced around. Brow furrowed, Mattie nodded ever so slightly toward Guy. Samantha looked at her brother. He made not a sound, but his chest heaved and tears rolled down his cheeks. Like hers moments ago, his hands were fisted in his lap, white-knuckled and shaking.

"Oh, Guy. I'm so sorry." She slid off the seat to her knees, but he was faster. Before she could put her arms around his trembling shoulders, he shot from the chair and ran from the room.

She jumped to her feet to go after him, but Mattie snagged her skirt from behind. "Sit down, Samantha. Leave him be for a little while. Hear the rest of the will; then we'll deal with Guy." Mattie turned to the judge and said pointedly, "Hiram's son."

Judge Crawford cleared his throat, obviously discomfited. Then he squared his shoulders and spoke as if presiding on the bench. "Miss Crawford, Miss Timberlake, a will is written to the letter of the law. At no time did Hiram formally adopt the boy. Thus, he's legally an orphan. My hands are tied—"

"Never mind. Get it over with, Judge Crocker," Mattie said.

Wearily, Samantha regained her seat and kicked herself for bringing the matter up in Guy's presence. She should have waited or let it pass.

". . . and to my daughter, Samantha Rose Timberlake, I leave the twenty thousand acres known as Timberoaks, all its buildings and stock, and the sum of fifteen thousand dollars plus interest accrued, on deposit at Wells Fargo Bank in Waco, Texas."

Her father had settled five thousand on Aunt Mattie, the same amount on Guy, and now he'd left another huge sum to her. Hiram Timberlake had been a rich man by any standards. Why hadn't she known? With that kind of money, he wouldn't have had to lift a hand.

"Management of Timberoaks shall rest in the hands of Judge Hazlett Crocker, or his designee, until such time as my daughter, Samantha Rose, marries or reaches the age of thirty, whichever comes first."

"What?" She half rose off the chair, then crashed down against the back as if her legs had been kicked from beneath her. Her throat seemed to close. She couldn't breathe.

Crocker looked up, his expression indignant. "Aren't you listening, little lady? This document is important. Your father made every effort to protect you in a legal manner. The least you can do is pay attention."

Samantha scooted to the edge of the chair. After several seconds of gulping air, she narrowed her dark eyes on the judge. Anger laced her terse words. "Judge Crocker, if you call me 'little lady' one more time, I won't be responsible for my actions."

She ignored him when he reared back as if struck. "My father left Timberoaks to me. That is no surprise. What is a surprise is the last stipulation. Indulge me," she snapped. "I want to make sure I understand Pa's instructions."

As he reread, all Samantha could see was crimson surrounded by impenetrable black. She couldn't suck air into her starved lungs. Marriage or five long years stood in the way of claiming her birthright? How could he have done this to her? Unable to sit still, she leaped up and stalked to the window.

"Samantha." Mattie's voice shattered the stark silence.

She whirled around and cast venomous eyes on her aunt. "You've wanted me to marry. Was this your doing?"

Mattie stiffened. "I told you the will was a surprise to me."

Though scarlet still colored her vision, Samantha realized she'd gone too far. Of course Aunt Mattie wouldn't have had a hand in it.

She glanced at the judge, his eyes round as biscuits. His gaze shifted from her to Aunt Mattie.

She returned to the settee. "I'm sorry, Aunt Mattie. It's just that—"

"Are we finished, Judge Crocker?" Mattie rose stiffly and turned her back on Samantha. "I must go to the boy."

"Yes." He cleared his throat and gathered the sheets of parchment into a neat pile. "There are only a few things I must settle with your niece."

"I'll serve midday meal in an hour or so. If you wish to stay, you're welcome, sir."

He cleared his throat again and scowled at Samantha. "I . . . Perhaps. I'll let you know, ma'am."

Without another word, Mattie swept from the room, never once glancing Samantha's way. She deserved her aunt's ire. The woman had loved her all these years, and how had she repaid her? She cringed. The hateful words of moments ago rang in her head. Would Aunt Mattie accept her apology? She must, for Samantha loved her like a mother.

"Miss Timberlake."

She blinked and focused on the judge.

"About the matter of managing this ranch. We must discuss—"

"What do you know about raising horses, Judge Crocker?" She neatly transferred her anger to him. The man she wanted to shout at, the man she was really angry with, was dead. Angry with herself, too, she again wished she had pursued the matter that morning with her father.

"That is the point, Miss Timberlake. Your father's wishes were that management of Timberoaks be placed under the court's jurisdiction for a time. And to answer your question, I know nothing about ranching."

He cleared his throat again, which set her teeth further on edge. She didn't know if it was a nervous habit or a self-important tick. But she'd had enough of him, enough of this whole affair.

"So where does that leave me?"

"If you'll recall, your father's will states that I may designate a manager for your ranch until you marry or—"

How in heaven's name did Walker know?

"Which means another man will take over Timberoaks," she sneered. "My father didn't think I could handle the responsibility." Voicing the thought hurt like the dickens, but that was the only conclusion she could draw.

A sad smile curved Judge Crocker's lips. He actually looked as though he commiserated with her on this point. Perhaps he had dealt with many women who found themselves dictated to by men who wielded power, even from the grave.

"I don't presume to know what your father thought," he said diplomatically. "But I'm in the uncomfortable position of installing a manager over your affairs for the foreseeable future." He sent her a hopeful look. "Are you contemplating marriage anytime soon, Miss Timberlake?"

She grunted with disgust and glanced out the window. Her life had turned to ashes, but sunshine splashed over the ranch.

Unbidden, the drifter's incredible eyes swam into her inner vision. She shook her head. Her lips thinned to a straight line. That one would feel the imprint of her hand on his square jaw if he ever dared show his face again.

"No," she finally responded. "It's doubtful I shall ever marry, Judge Crocker."

Though his eyes clouded with skepticism, he didn't argue. Instead, he irritated her again by clearing his throat.

"Well, then, I've already spoken with a fine, upstanding man who does know about ranching. In fact, he's anxious to take over for you until . . . How old are you, by the way?"

"Twenty-four." Six long years to endure . . . Actually, not six. Her twenty-fifth birthday was only two months away, in September.

Crocker's countenance brightened. "Well, at least you know the manager I have chosen. That should ease the way considerably."

Unease prickled. The hair on her nape rose. *Know the manager?*

"I stopped by his place last evening and spoke with him about the matter. He graciously put me up for the night." The judge reached into his vest pocket and withdrew a large pocketwatch. Flipping open the case, he peered at the face. "He'll be here before long, in fact."

Judge Crocker had arrived at quarter to ten. He'd stayed somewhere within a two- to three-hour buggy ride. And that could only mean . . . She tensed, her throat closed. *Oh, God, no!*

"He is a longtime acquaintance of mine, Miss Timberlake. You'll not find a better man to manage Timberoaks for you than Uriah Butcher."

Chapter Four

Unfair, unfair, unfair!

Samantha frowned at Uriah Butcher, who was seated on her father's comfortable chair in the parlor as if he owned Timberoaks. C. J. had appropriated Aunt Mattie's gingham-covered rocking chair on the opposite side of the fireplace. His pale eyes assessed Samantha's length as if mentally undressing her. Her skin crawled.

Aunt Mattie was nowhere in sight, probably consoling Guy. Though Samantha didn't begrudge her brother the needed attention, she wished her aunt were present. Filled with anger at the turn of events, she refused the chair Judge Crocker offered before taking it himself. Instead, she stood with her clenched hands hidden in the folds of her skirt.

"I've explained our arrangement to Miss Timberlake, Uriah," Judge Crocker said. "I realize running two large ranches will present quite a burden for you, but . . ." He shook his head. "I certainly can't stay here for the task, even if I knew how."

I know how. I can run this ranch as well as Uriah Butcher. Better!

Samantha wanted to scream those thoughts aloud, but knew they wouldn't change a thing. Her father had doomed her to live under a man's thumb for the next five years. Her shoulders slumped. Despair sat heavily in her breast.

"It won't be no burden, Hazlett. I'm puttin' C. J. in charge."

No! She shook with the horror she felt at those words. C. J. was a yes-man to his father's wishes. He'd never make one decision without Uriah's guidance. The older man made sure his son was dependent on him, too.

"Oh. Well." The judge smiled. "It's wonderful you have a son to handle this place. When he moves onto Timberoaks—"

"No!" Samantha blurted the single word just as her aunt came into the parlor and echoed the same sentiment. Relief flooded her when Mattie calmly continued.

"The bunkhouse is full, Judge Crocker. There's no room for C. J. or anyone else to live here."

Crocker's brow creased in a perplexed frown. He rose and offered Mattie his chair, but she remained standing, her posture ramrod-straight.

Disgust for Uriah and C. J. ripped through Samantha when neither man moved. The simple courtesy the judge had shown apparently never entered their minds.

"Surely you jest, Miss Crawford. Since Hiram's death—"

"You aren't suggesting Hiram's room be turned over to . . ." Mattie shook her head emphatically. Her next words sliced the air like shards of glass. "If Uriah intends for C. J. to manage Timberoaks, he will ride here each morning and home each night, Judge. I will not allow another man to live in this house until Samantha marries. It's unseemly for you to even mention it."

"Now, Mattie . . ." Uriah sounded as though he were soothing a demented person.

She glared at him, her head held high. "Don't 'now Mattie' me, Uriah Butcher. Hiram's will says this is my home for as long as I live or want to stay. A single man will not dwell under this roof while I draw breath. Do I make myself clear?"

If she dared, Samantha would have applauded her aunt. As it was, relief danced along her nerves and wobbly legs.

"Miss Mattie, it ain't as if'n I was a stranger," C. J. said. "It's a mighty long ride over here, ya know."

"That's not my problem," she snapped.

He scratched his whiskered jaw. Samantha wondered if mites lurked in the dark, unkempt beard, then castigated herself for the childish thought. She disliked everything about C. J. Butcher, but she really didn't believe he or his father were unclean.

"Precisely because you aren't a stranger is why I won't allow such familiarity," Mattie said.

"Well, then, maybe I'll let one o' the hands go so there's a bunk for me."

Uriah put a stop to C. J.'s flapping tongue. "No, you won't, boy. Good hands ain't easy to find. Hiram's got some of the best around, and they'll be mighty helpful as the days and weeks go by. You'll have to abide by Miss Mattie's wishes." He grinned at Samantha. His bright blue eyes flashed. "Besides, ain't I been sayin' this here little gal will make me a fine daughter-in-law one day?"

Cheeks flushed, Samantha turned on her heel, walked past her dear aunt, and left the room. She might die a spinster, might not bear the children that in her heart of hearts she wanted, but she would never agree to marry C. J. *Not in this life, Uriah Butcher.*

Seconds later she closed the screened door and met Oscar on the porch, his brow creased in a frown.

"Samantha, I've looked ever'where and I can't find the stallion."

She wasn't about to tell Oscar that Holden Walker had taken her wits with a simple kiss. She'd deal with the man in her own way when he returned. If he returned.

"I let him go," she lied.

She might as well have struck Oscar. He reared back and stared at her in disbelief.

"You done what? You done lost your senses, girl? Christ almighty! Sorry, Hiram," he said as if her father were standing there. "That horse was ready to ride. What got into you?"

She shrugged. "I don't know. I watched him circling the corral and decided he should be free."

Oscar shook his head, then swept off his hat and scratched above his ear. "Well, I never." His expression dazed, he plunked the hat back on his head. Muttering under his breath, he started to turn away, then swung back. "That Walker feller is gone. For a few days, he said." He scratched his stubbled chin this time. "Wasn't nothin' I could do. But I sure hated to lose him. He's a good wrangler. One of the best I ever did see, Samantha. Hope he weren't joshin' me about comin' back."

"He said the same thing to me yesterday afternoon." She recalled her brief encounter with the tall man, and anger seethed anew. "If he comes back, he does. If he doesn't . . ." She shrugged as if it didn't matter. "Well, we'll just wait and see."

He started away again.

"Oscar, Judge Crocker read my father's will this morning."

A pained expression lit the man's homely face at the reminder of his boss's death. "Yeah. I heard 'bout him comin' today."

"Because of Pa's will, we have a . . . situation you may not like."

"Yeah? What?"

She hesitated, loath to tell him. Between herself and Oscar, they could have managed Timberoaks just fine. Now . . . "Pa left the ranch in the hands of a manager until I marry or turn thirty."

"Huh? What you talkin' 'bout, girl? You plannin' to marry?"

"No. That's the point. We'll be answering to Uriah Butcher for a long time."

Oscar's face changed so quickly that she blinked. Anger painted his features.

"I ain't takin' no orders from him, Samantha. You best understand that right now."

She put out a hand and touched his arm in a placating manner. "Please. Don't say that. Actually, it's worse than you can imagine."

"What could be worse?" He bit off each word with disgust.

"C. J. will be coming here every day, Oscar. Uriah says he'll manage the ranch. He'll be calling the shots."

"Over my stinkin' carcass! That boy ain't got no sense a'tall. Why, I wouldn't let him handle ma dog."

Her sentiments exactly, but what could she do? One thing she had to do was convince Oscar to help her. Somehow she would get through the bad times ahead. But not without Oscar. He couldn't leave Timberoaks. He'd been here for so long; he was a fixture, an important fixture.

"Oscar, I need your help. If C. J. makes bad decisions, we must somehow get around him."

"Maybe you must, Samantha, but I don't have to take nothin' from that idgit. And I ain't gonna. I worked for your pa, but I ain't workin' for no Butcher. No, sirree."

"You won't work for me?" Panic squeezed inside her chest. How could she get along without Oscar?

"Course I'd work for you, girl. But you just said—"

"What I said was that Uriah has put C. J. in charge of Timberoaks. But that doesn't mean he'll *be* in charge. We

can go on just like we always have. All we have to do is
fool him into thinking he's the one making the decisions."

"I ain't no dip-lee-mat, Samantha."

She clung to his arm, panic shaking her right down to
her toes. "What you are, Oscar, is the best foreman
around. And I need you. Please. Please don't leave me to
face C. J. and Uriah alone. I don't think I . . ." Tears
pricked her eyes. She hated to beg. She hated this feeling of
helplessness.

Clearly, Oscar was torn between walking away and
helping her, and her pleading made him uncomfortable.
But she'd crawl on her knees if she had to. Though Mattie
Crawford was a formidable woman, she was a woman.
Her power extended only so far, and she knew next to
nothing about ranch management. That left Samantha to
deal with C. J. every day.

Again, panic clawed at her. To admit it even to herself
was hard, but something about C. J. scared her a little. She
never wanted to be alone in his company. Uriah, too.
Sometimes his glance seemed more lecherous than C. J.'s.

Gazing into the foreman's swarthy face, she pleaded
despite tears that clogged her throat. "Please, Oscar, don't
leave me alone to deal with C. J."

Seemingly endless moments ticked by while Oscar
searched her eyes. A muscle twitched in his clenched jaw,
but ever so slowly his features softened and his stormy eyes
calmed. Then his gnarled hand closed over her fingers
clutched on his shirtsleeve. He gave a reassuring squeeze.

"All right, Samantha. I'll stick around for a spell. But I
can't make no more promises than that."

Her eyelids shut, unshed tears wetting her lashes. Air
whooshed from her lungs. She clamped her teeth together
to still quivering lips. Embarrassed by her weakness, she
managed a tremulous smile. "Thanks. You'll never know
how . . . relieved I am."

His mouth kicked up at one corner as he turned his head

and spat a stream of tobacco juice into the dirt. He looked pointedly at her fingers still clamped on his shirt, the material bunched in her fist.

"Think I do, girl. Now, I best git back to work."

She snatched her hand away. As he turned to leave, she clasped her hands together and hugged them to her chest, offering a quick prayer of thanks. Heaven's angels must surely have smiled on her these past few minutes. She took a deep breath. The pungent smell of sage entered her nostrils, battling with the sweet fragrance from Aunt Mattie's rosebushes in full bloom at the corner of the house.

Thank you, God.

She heard a step on the porch behind her, followed by a drawling voice that made her want to clamp her hands over her ears. She knew she would come to hate that sound even more than she already did.

"Well, well. Here we are, Samma. Just you an' me. Now I can get down to serious sparkin'."

Though a tremor quaked down her spine, she stiffened her back. But as she slowly turned to face C. J., his oddly lifeless hazel eyes focused over her shoulder.

"Oscar!" he called. "Hold up there. I gotta talk at ya."

The crunch of the foreman's boots on the hard ground ceased. Then she heard him draw close again. She didn't need to look to know Oscar had stopped after a few steps, leaving quite a distance for C. J. to go to him.

Don't antagonize him, Oscar. She bit her tongue rather than voice the thought. Oscar was no fool, but he wouldn't take a thing from C. J. One way or another, he'd gain the upper hand with the manager forced upon them.

As C. J. approached, he gave her a sneering grin. His teeth were yellowed from the Bull Durham cigarettes he smoked, and his clothes reeked of stale tobacco. She refrained from pinching her nostrils against the foul odor.

"We'll talk later, Samma me girl," he whispered.

Until her unwanted encounters with C. J., and the latest

one with that . . . that *drifter,* Samantha had never considered herself a violent person. But C. J.'s suggestive grin made her want to slug him.

She fisted her hands at her sides. "You'll need some instruction regarding Timberoaks." Exasperated by his stupidity, she snapped, "I'm not your girl. Get it through your thick head, C. J."

He laughed. "Now, honey, is that any way to talk to yer intended?"

Fuming, she rolled her eyes skyward as C. J. stepped off the porch.

Are You there? Can You hear me, God? Deliver me from overbearing men!

Many hours' ride north of Timberoaks, in the area where Willis Nabors said Indians had been spotted, Walks in Shadow sat before a campfire wearing nothing but a loincloth and moccasins. Though it would not last, it felt good to return to the freedom of his former life, the simple apparel that afforded quick, easy movement.

He had set his course on the white man's path. For Little Spring's sake, he would again don trousers and boots and return to where the boy now lived. A faint, self-mocking smile curved his lips.

He fancied he heard the Spirits' chuckles in the wind soughing through the trees. They knew how strongly Samantha Timberlake lingered in his thoughts, too. In truth, his body's reaction went far beyond mere thought. He wanted that woman like no other.

He glanced sidelong into darkness when the horses stamped and snuffled. Black Magic, she had called the stallion. A good name for him. Dominant by nature, he had trailed with reluctance, tethered behind the gray. Walks in Shadow meant what he had said. The horse belonged to Samantha Timberlake. If he was to be her mount, no other should ride him before she set her stamp on the horse. That included him.

Night sounds intruded on his thoughts. A wild turkey's gobble, followed by another, chattered on the faint breeze. Then an owl's hoot. He tilted his head when an answering hoot sounded from a different direction. He smiled. *Very good, but not perfect.*

His bare shoulders lit by the fire's glow, Walks in Shadow sat perfectly still, waiting. It was more a feeling than sound that told him one or more warriors stalked directly behind him. They were now silent as a rattler before it strikes.

"May you be at peace this night," he said quietly in Comanche.

"Ha," a voice said.

The short affirmative did not allow him to recognize the voice. After a moment a twig snapped, then moccasins appeared in his peripheral vision. He picked up a stick and stirred the flame-licked wood.

"You are welcome at my fire, but I seek Two Horns, his brother Swift Arrow and their band."

The moccasins next to him crossed at the ankles, and the warrior gracefully sank to the ground. Not until the brave leaned forward and rested his elbows on his knees did Walks in Shadow see the silver bracelet circling his upper arm. At the same moment that he recognized the familiar ornament, the Indian spoke.

"You court death, my brother. Your fire signals in the darkness to foe as well as to friend."

He looked into Swift Arrow's eyes, the brave who had become his blood brother following his adoption by the Comanche. Each still carried the scar on his wrist from cuts made much too deep. So much blood flowed that Blanket Over Her Head had feared for the four-year-old boys' lives.

Walks in Shadow glanced around and nodded as four other braves stepped into the dim light cast by his fire. He was exceedingly glad to see Swift Arrow, but he searched the other men's faces in vain for Two Horns.

Swift Arrow's long hair dusted his crossed knees as he picked up a stick and absently stirred the fire. Walks in Shadow noted the men were painted for war.

"You have been raiding, my brother?"

"Your fine mounts are what brought us to your fire." Swift Arrow grinned. "But you may keep your mount and packhorse." He cast a glance into the darkness as Walks in Shadow had done only moments ago. "The stallion is a fine-looking animal."

"The gray is my mount, Swift Arrow. I search for the band because of the stallion. I would ask Two Horns to care for him for a while."

Swift Arrow shook his head. "Two Horns is four, maybe five suns' ride into the *Llano Estacado*. The band moves toward the far mountains. Buffalo were sighted before I left to claim horses."

Disappointment cloaked Walks in Shadow. He revered the chief like a father, though Two Horns was only twelve summers older than he. Another plan for the horse's care must be devised.

The brave seated closest to Walks in Shadow's left laid his bow next to his knee and pulled a pipe from the band circling his waist. From a pouch he scooped out tobacco to fill the small bowl, picked up a burning twig and lit the pipe. After several puffs, he saluted the four winds, then handed the pipe to Walks in Shadow.

"I, Tail of the Buffalo, would be honored to share my pipe with you. Many talks have I heard about you around our campfires, Walks in Shadow. You stalk the night like the wolf. You run like a swift eagle crossing the sky. You loose arrows straight and true."

As he accepted the extended pipe, Walks in Shadow smiled at the description of his exploits. Exaggerated, perhaps, but nevertheless his chest expanded with pride that his people remembered him in such glowing terms.

He dipped his head in recognition of the praise. Then he, too, lifted the pipe to the four corners of the earth in the Comanches' age-old reverent fashion. Stars danced before his eyes when he sucked on the pipe. It had been months since he had last tasted Indian tobacco. "I am honored to share this smoke with you, Tail of the Buffalo."

He passed on the pipe.

"How fares your quest?" Swift Arrow asked.

"Little Spring is well. He dwells where I left him. The white man, Timberlake, gifted him the name Guy."

"You would take him to his people?"

Walks in Shadow shook his head. The remembrance of Samantha correcting Little Spring's speech was fresh in his mind. Though she sounded stern, he knew she loved the boy. Her protective embrace spoke more than words could. Taking the child from the Timberlakes would not be easy.

"Little Spring remembers naught of Bubbling Water or me." Spirit of the Sun, how it hurt to say that.

"His blood is that of the Comanche, my brother."

True, but the boy was now white in manner and beliefs.

Swift Arrow searched his eyes for a moment, then let the subject drop. "It pleases me to see you in the old way. How fare you among white men?"

"Fair to middling, as the white man says. My heart still dwells with my Comanche people, but I have found . . ." Perhaps it was not wise to reveal his foolish desire for Samantha Timberlake.

"A woman who pleases you," Swift Arrow finished. He grinned, teeth flashing in the dim light, dark eyes glinting with mischief Walks in Shadow remembered so well.

He returned his friend's smile. "The woman, Samantha Timberlake, is one I would take to my blankets."

"You have not?" Swift Arrow's dark eyes rounded in mock astonishment. "My brother's medicine is soft and will not rise?"

Walks in Shadow chuckled. "My medicine is as strong as ever, brother." He looked down, then glanced back up. "It fills my breechclout at the mere thought of the woman."

"Speak, so I may see this woman."

Walks in Shadow's gaze wandered to the other warriors seated comfortably around the small fire. Maybe if he described Samantha Timberlake to his brother, it would ease her from his mind, cool his blood.

"Her eyes are the color of a fawn's. Brown, in the white man's tongue."

"Brow . . . un," Swift Arrow repeated, and curled his mouth in distaste. "This word does not please my ears."

"The word may not please you, but her eyes would. Fire leaps in them when she is angry."

"You have seen her angry, my brother? Sa . . . man . . . ta is not biddable?"

"I have, and I will see more upon my return." He shook his head. "Biddable she is not."

The warriors stirred, whispered to each other, obviously bewildered by his words. He could see the question in the eyes of more than one man.

"Sings Like a Bird is not biddable." Tail of the Buffalo smiled slyly. "But she warms my blood when I take her between the blankets."

Walks in Shadow knew with certainty that Samantha would do the same for him. He burned just thinking about her. "It was her hair that took my fancy when first I saw her."

"Ah. A trophy for your lance?" Swift Arrow teased.

He laughed. "Her hair will stay on her head, brother. It is washed with gold. It pleases my eyes." He raised a hand level with his chin. "She stands here. Tall, white men say, and supple like the willow."

"I would see this woman one day," Swift Arrow said. "You would bring her to our village?"

He shook his head. The Spirits knew he wanted her, but Walks in Shadow thought it unwise to take her. One day he would move on. If all went well, Little Spring would go with him. Samantha Timberlake was wedded to her ranch. Walks in Shadow could not really understand that. He did not believe he could "put down roots," as white men described their feelings about their homes.

"The vile man you seek, you have found him not?"

Walks in Shadow was caught off guard by Swift Arrow's quick change from lighthearted banter to grim contemplation. The question sent rage sizzling through him. He knew he was in the vicinity where Bubbling Water had been violated, but not once had he heard the man's name. It was possible her attacker had been a drifter passing through. If that were the case . . .

"In vain I have searched."

"That is his name?"

Walks in Shadow glanced down. Without even realizing it, he had drawn crude letters in the dirt. *Clarence.*

Swift Arrow's gaze lingered, studying the name. His expression hardened as he traced over the letters with a finger, then he nodded once as if he had memorized the letters or come to some conclusion.

The next morning, Walks in Shadow clasped Swift Arrow's forearm in farewell. The gesture pressed the scars on their wrists together, a strong reminder of their nearly lifelong regard. Feeling a strong urge to return to his Comanche life, Walks in Shadow snatched his arm back and stuck his hands in his pants pockets. He was again Holden Walker as he watched the warriors out of sight.

Although he had honored Bubbling Water's dying wish, he had denied Little Spring the care and rich teachings of his Indian people. The boy knew not what he had missed. Palefaces looked upon the Indians' way of life with disdain, but Holden knew how soul-satisfying it was. Wherever life might take him, his spirit would forever be one with the Comanche.

Troubling thoughts about Little Spring lingered. Even if he reclaimed his nephew, it was doubtful they would return to the Indians' way of life. Bubbling Water had been right; starvation and death stalked the Comanche. As he had ever since returning to the white man's world, he must trust the Spirits would guide him.

Now, Black Magic must be stabled . . . somewhere. He paused with the lead rope loosely held in his strong hand. Looking into the stallion's dark eyes, he saw those of another. Wide, lovely, soft doe eyes. The memory of Samantha Timberlake's lithe body pressed to his length thrummed through him. His pulse quickened.

Fool that he was, he wanted to see her again. Needed to see her. The time was near when she would need him, too. Samantha Timberlake did not realize how close she had come to his visionary abilities when she'd asked if he was a seer. He knew deep in his gut that returning to Timberoaks was imperative. He sensed that danger stalked her.

Holden leaped high and clamped his hands on the corner of the bordello's balcony. Muscles bunched in his arms and back, he chinned himself up and grabbed the rail. He pulled himself upward until he sat on the top rail, then swung long legs over and to the floor. He backed against the wall and looked around. At two A.M. the street was deserted, though he could hear the tinny clink of pianos from several establishments that lined the street. Voices droned and occasional laughter drifted in the dark. Waco's saloons did a roaring business all night long.

Lillibeth carried on her business in the corner room of the Palace Sporting House. Sliding sideways toward the window to his right, he knelt and peered inside the first of four upstairs quarters fronting the building, usually full this time of night. The room he hoped was still Lillibeth's was empty.

Wick lowered, a single lamp glowed atop the spindly table next to the bed. He tested the window. It squeaked open. He raised the sash and stuck a leg over the sill, then followed it with the rest of his body, swiping the lace curtain out of his way. He pushed the window down, then stepped aside so he was not silhouetted against the lantern's dim light.

He looked around and breathed with relief. The furnishings were as he remembered. Other than the garish red wallpaper, the room was tastefully decorated, a testament to the kind of woman Lillibeth was despite the circumstances that had forced her into a life of . . . Well, he disliked thinking of her as a whore, but that was what she was.

Holden doffed his hat and laid it on the side table as he settled on the divan. The furnishings were simple pine, and Lillibeth kept them polished to a shine. He suspected she had made the colorful counterpane herself. White, lace-covered pillows lay against the headboard. The bed was unmussed, which could bode ill for him if she had yet to bring a cowboy up tonight. He certainly did not want to embarrass her. He needed her help—again.

A step sounded outside the door, a key turned in the lock, and the door swung open. Lillibeth did not see him seated on the far side of the bed as she entered.

Her red-and-white candy-striped skirt swirled as she turned, shut the door, relocked it, and pressed her forehead against the panel. She sighed.

Utter exhaustion radiated from her, and maybe despair. A half second later, she raised her head and squared her bare shoulders. Lillibeth walked away from him toward the armoire on the far wall, stripping off lacy gloves as she went.

She opened one door and stored the gloves in a narrow drawer. Then she reached back and fumbled with the hook on the low-cut gown. As one strap slid off her shoulder, she opened the left door of the armoire. Holden's image flashed into view, framed in the oblong mirror.

Emitting an inarticulate squeak, she slammed her hands against her breasts to halt the slide of the gown, and whirled to face him. Eyes as round as gold pieces, she stared at him, mouth trembling.

His lips kicked up at one corner in a half smile. "Hello, Lillibeth. It has been a while."

Chest heaving, she sucked in a breath and glared at him. "Holden Walker, you frightened the liver out of me! Why don't you use the door downstairs like everyone else?"

Grinning broadly, he rose and strode toward her. "I never have. Why would I do so now?"

"Why, indeed?" Her voice shook.

Holden's arms encircled her. He leaned down and bussed her on the cheek. The top of her head only came to the middle of his chest. He felt her tremble. Her hands still clutched the top of the satin dress, her arms imprisoned against his frame. His nose twitched with delight. Unlike other women of the night, who doused themselves with cheap perfume in an effort to mask unwashed bodies, Lillibeth's delicate lilac fragrance mingled with her own clean womanly scent.

"I did not mean to frighten you, little one. But I was enjoying the show. You look beautiful, as always."

Lillibeth made up her face as artfully as she could and used less paint than other lightskirts he had bedded. Inside, where it counted, she was a good woman. Though he had sampled her charms many times, he respected her. Had she not taught him to read and write, and refused payment for those many nights he pored over books in this room, which kept out paying men?

She had even tried to stop him from paying for the pleasant evenings spent in her bed. But it was her livelihood, and there he had drawn the line. He left gold in the armoire rather than embarrass her by placing greenbacks in her small hand.

"What are you doing here? I thought you were . . ." She shook her head as he released her. "Well, I don't know what I thought. But now that my heart has restarted, it's good to see you."

Holden returned to the divan. Once settled, he extended

his arms along the back, stretched out his legs and crossed them at the ankles.

Lillibeth walked back to the armoire, still clutching the dress's bodice. She reached into the depths of the tall chest and brought out a wrapper. Rather than change before him, she stepped behind a screen angled across the corner of the room.

He had seen her lush body in all its glory, but she still retained an endearing modesty about her. Perhaps that was why most men she entertained treated her well, even while lusting after her.

"What are you doing here?" she asked again.

He did not answer. Instead, Samantha Timberlake's image flashed in his mind's eye, her dark eyes spitting fire as they had the last time he had seen them. His body tightened. Here he was in the room of a woman he could bed if he so desired, a woman from whom he needed a favor, but his body ached for another.

"Holden?" Lillibeth came toward him, cinching the wrapper's belt around her tiny waist. "What's wrong?" She eased down next to him, her back as straight as the schoolmarm's she had wanted to be.

"There is nothing wrong. I just . . ." He frowned, unsure how to ask yet another boon of this woman.

Holden had given the liveryman, Rudy Sanders, a chunk of gold to stable the stallion while he returned to Samantha Timberlake's ranch. The man was honest, but Holden was unsure if Sanders would have the time to care for the horse as it deserved. He intended to ask Lillibeth to check on the stallion every day. But if he told her the horse belonged to another woman, he feared it might hurt her feelings.

Lillibeth sighed when he remained silent so long. She rose and headed toward the bureau, where a brandy decanter sat atop a silver tray, flanked by two crystal glasses.

"May I get you something to drink?"

Two Horns had frowned upon drunkenness. Few in the band had ever tasted liquor, though Holden had indulged occasionally since leaving the Indians. Maybe a sip or two was what he needed to untie his tongue.

"Thank you."

As she splashed amber liquid into the glasses, he heard heavy footsteps pause in the hallway. The door rattled as a fist pounded. Holden tensed, aware the Palace's owner, Sid Henshaw, did not know he was in her room.

"Lillibeth, Buster Monroe is askin' for you," a voice boomed.

Holden glanced up at her. She lowered the decanter, closed her eyes and sighed.

"I'm busy, Sid. Mr. Monroe will have to come back another night."

"Whataya mean? I didn't see no payin' customer come up the stairs with you."

"One did," Holden snapped, irritated that Henshaw would badger her so late. It had to be nearing three o'clock.

"Oh. Sorry," Henshaw said. "Didn't mean to interrupt your sportin'."

Holden could hear the curiosity in Henshaw's voice. And greed. Whatever the girls at the Palace earned, Henshaw took a chunk right off the top.

"Y'all spendin' the whole night?" Henshaw persisted.

"What is left of it," Holden said.

He looked up at Lillibeth standing next to the bureau, her expression one of resignation. Lumbering steps receded down the hallway.

"I am sorry," he said quietly. She appeared so achingly tired.

"For what?" Lillibeth picked up the two glasses and came toward him, a smile plastered on her face. She sat and extended one of the small goblets.

"For him. For me. For what you must—"

"Come now, Holden. This is my life. I make the best of it."

"I guess you do."

He gazed at her thoughtfully, and wished this good woman's life had played out differently. If she could have been the schoolteacher she wanted to be, she would not have to endure men pawing her night after night. Men had been the culprits who deterred her from being a teacher. If teaching positions were to be found, more often than not, men took those posts ahead of women here in the West.

Lillibeth raised her glass in a toast, then took a sip. Her golden eyes focused on him. "Now, will you please tell me what has brought you here? I'm pleased to see you, Holden. But I thought you dusted Waco off your boots for the last time long ago."

He shrugged. "So did I, but I need . . ."

When he paused again, exasperation lit her eyes. "Spit it out, will you? What do you need? My help? You know you have it without asking. You're as reluctant as a mule. Just like you were before you finally asked me to teach you to read."

"I have a stallion stabled with Sanders. I wondered if you could check on him now and then." *There. That was not so bad.* And he had not told her to whom the horse belonged.

"I take it you're only passing through Waco on your way to . . . wherever."

"Umm."

She hesitated, fiddling with a fold in the wrapper that covered her knee. "I will be happy to do that, Holden. But . . ."

"What?"

"Rudy Sanders is one of the few citizens in this town who treats me as if I were a lady. Many townspeople turn away when my . . . kind enter his establishment."

"Your kind," he repeated, anger swirling through him like a tornado.

She touched his sleeve. "I don't want any trouble, Holden."

"There will not be any. No one has the right to say who enters his livery except Rudy. Sanders strikes me as his own man." Which was more than Holden could say for many white men he had met.

"You're right. But if I frequent his place, others may not offer him their business. He has four little ones who depend on him, you know."

He reached for her fidgeting hand and squeezed her fingers ever so gently. "I am sorry I asked. I will—"

"I'll do it," she said quickly. "It's . . . well, I'll work it out with Mr. Sanders."

Holden eyed her a moment, grateful he had met her long ago. Basking in her gentleness, her unselfish desire to teach, had eased some of the bitterness he had harbored in his heart for all white men five years before. He wished it was in his power to take Lillibeth to another place, a place where she could find respectability as a schoolmarm.

Chapter Five

C. J. gazed at the buildings that made up Timberoaks's main compound. Afore long the place would be his. Its twenty thousand acres added to Singletree's thirty thousand would make a substantial holding no matter which way the steer leaped. He'd be king of the prairie!

Once he bedded Samma, she'd have to marry up with him. It would be easy as shootin' a can off a log to corner her in the barn or someplace. He grinned, recalling all that spit and fire she aimed at him ever' time he talked to her. Hot damn, beddin' her was gonna be rousin' good sport. As sassy and smart as she was, wouldn't take long a'tall to teach her how to please him in bed.

His groin tightened just thinkin' 'bout her pert tits hidin' behind them shirtwaists. Lightheadedness claimed him as he envisioned her round ass fillin' his hands, his member poundin' into the softness between her legs.

He stilled. Was the hair inside them pants the same color as the golden flame on her head? Woo-wee, he hoped so. His pecker rose, hard as a rock.

"Clarence, a word with ya afore I leave."

C. J. cringed. His member instantly shriveled inside his trousers. *The old he-goat!* Insistin' he needed to get things straight with Oscar afore he turned over the reins to C. J., Paw'd moseyed over each mornin' with him. One day C. J. was gonna own the whole shebang, and when he did, he'd give the old man the boot all the way to Waco.

"Yeah, Paw." He schooled his features, turned and casually leaned against the corral fence.

His father came to a halt, his burly shoulders thrust back, chest puffed out like a rooster's. "I want ya to behave yerself here, boy. Don't give me no call to whap ya upside the head."

"Aw, Paw, why do you talk thataway? I'm a grown man. I know how to run this place." *Goddammit. Why does Paw always treat me like a snivelin' kid?*

"Ya don't know spit, Clarence. Yer mind ain't on the business at hand. I seen the way ya been eyein' Samantha. Keep yer pants buttoned. Ya hear? Court that girl proper-like, how I told ya, and this place will be signed over on a marriage certificate, purty as ya please. But it ain't gonna happen if'n ya treat Samantha wrong or Miss Mattie gets wind o' trouble."

"They's only women, Paw. You can have a little talk with Judge Crocker next time ya see 'im. He can fix them papers—"

Uriah grabbed C. J.'s shirtfront, bunching the material in his fists, and hauled him up on his toes. He stuck his nose close. "You listen to me real good. Hazlett is honest as God. That's why Hiram trusted 'im. This place belongs to Samantha. There ain't nothin' I can do to change that less'n ya do as I tell ya."

"But I'm runnin' Timberoaks!" C. J. brushed his father's hands away and stepped back. Straightening his shirt, he seethed inwardly and looked around. Thank God there weren't nobody to see what just happened.

"No, ya ain't. *I'm* runnin' Timberoaks, Clarence. You'll

do as I say, or by cracky I'll haul yer ass home and make ya stay there. Now, listen to Oscar Dupree. He knows this place as well as Hiram did. Learn from him, boy. You ain't never gonna amount to a hill o' beans if'n ya don't learn to listen to yer elders."

"Oscar ain't more'n forty."

"That's a fact, but he's got eighty years of experience when it comes to handlin' horseflesh. You ain't got spit. Neither do I, not like I got with cattle. I'm dependin' on ya to learn how to run Timberoaks proper-like. When Single-tree and Timberoaks is combined, we'll have the best durned spread east o' the Brazos, seein' as how we'll run critters *and* horses. Don't know of another ranch can boast that 'cept King's down south."

"I was just thinkin' that myself, Paw. Honest. I'll do a right smart job here."

C. J. maintained a straight face under his father's penetrating stare. After long moments, he let out a breath when the old goat turned away.

"Well, see that ya do," Uriah mumbled. "Git yerself home tonight afore too late."

"Yes, Paw."

What the hell was "too late"? He'd hauled his ass out o' the bunk afore sunup to get over here by eight ever' mornin' for several days. And once't that was too late. Dupree roused with the chickens like everyone on Single-tree. A body had to work from sunup to sundown on a ranch. No way around it. Well, that weren't exactly the way of it. He didn't work that long, but he made sure the men did. Paw expected it.

It was unusually quiet, he realized. Not a horse or man in sight other than Paw headin' home. He hoped to God this was the last day the old man came along to check up on him. C. J. fished a watch out of his shirt pocket. Half past noon. Maybe he'd find the men in the bunkhouse and get some vittles down his gullet.

He spied that little pissant, Guy, sittin' still as death

under a tree some fifty yards away. He frowned. That kid slipped around undetected like none he'd ever seen. Weren't natural. Boys ran and hollered most of the time. Shouldn't he be inside eatin'? After he married Samma, by God, he'd take the little brat in hand.

Sure as shootin' the Timberlakes spoiled Guy like a girl. Oh, sure, he'd seen the kid ride. Guy could even rope, but he weren't near as accurate as C. J. had been when he was Guy's age. Hell, Paw woulda stripped a layer off his hide if'n he hadn't done good, even back then.

He approached the bunkhouse and slowed. Better put on a good face this first time he approached the men without Paw hangin' around. Timberoaks's hands weren't no different from other reg'lar hires. They were territorial about their home spread, and it didn't make a lick of difference that C. J. was manager; he'd have to prove himself to these rough men.

"Hup, hup."

Samantha slapped the lariat against her thigh as she hazed three horses into the holding corral built a mile from the main compound. The pen was backed up against a sharp embankment, where piled brush, too thick and high for the horses to jump, made up a second side. Poles and timber had been nailed together to finish the enclosure. They had plenty of water in two troughs lined up side by side against the abutment.

Old Henry Sullivan and Buddy Grogan had left the half-wild animals in her care a half hour ago while they rode off to look for more mustangs. The horses rounded up today would be trailed to the new owner tomorrow.

Dust clouded the sky as the skittish animals milled about, ears back, snorting and nipping at each other. She nudged her gelding forward and dropped the rope around the pole to secure the gate.

The wind shifted, sending the dust away from her, but

not before grit covered her. She snagged the corner of the bandanna over her mouth and nose and pulled it down.

She counted fifteen head. Oscar had sold twenty mustangs to a rancher gathering a herd to trail north this fall. He needed these horses to fill out his remuda. She'd never been on a cattle drive. Though doubtless it was a grueling job, Samantha would go along in a minute if allowed.

But joining a cattle drive was an extremely remote possibility. Unless a woman owned the herd, few engaged in the risky venture of heat, dust, long days, and longer nights in the saddle. Pa had told her that more times than she could count when she badgered him on the subject.

Besides, cowboys were a rough lot, some rumored to be murderers or thieves hiding from the law. Maybe so. But in Samantha's experience, no matter how rough the man, he usually treated a good woman with respect—even awe.

Except for C. J. She grimaced. Ten days since the blasted will had been read. She had been forced to speak with Uriah, but since he'd stopped coming over every day, she'd managed to avoid C. J. Oscar dealt with him. Thank God.

She pointed the gelding toward home. Might as well call it a day. Grogan and old Henry wouldn't return for hours. She glanced back at the stock one last time, confident these horses weren't going anywhere.

She hadn't ridden a quarter mile before she spied a rider heading her way. Lifting her hand, she clasped her hat's brim and angled it farther down to shade her eyes against the glare.

"Oh, blast it." Had she conjured him from her thoughts?

Nudging her horse to a lope, she hoped to pass C. J. without more than a wave of recognition. But as they neared each other, he angled his mount so she would have to stop or ride around him. Well, he wasn't going to intimidate her. She drew rein and glared at him.

He spoke before she could. "Where ya headed in such a all-fired hurry?"

With a long-suffering sigh, she pointed the way he had come. "It doesn't take a genius to know what lies in that direction."

He grinned; the corners of his eyes crinkled. On most people, she found hazel eyes pleasing, but C. J.'s merely looked lifeless and cold, even when he appeared amiable.

"How many horses y'all round up today?"

He reined about and fell in beside her as she nudged her horse forward. Conversation with him could not be avoided today. She would have to bear it.

"Fifteen, so far. The men are off again looking for more."

"That's all? Dang it, Samma, we need twenty head for that sale comin' up."

We? C. J. spoke as if he'd had something to do with the sale set up by Oscar before her father's burial.

She gritted her teeth and spoke without temper. "They'll find the rest. You needn't fret." And why was he? He promptly answered her thought.

"Paw expects that sale to go without a hitch. So do I. It's the first since I took over, and I ain't gonna tol'rate no foul-ups."

"There won't be any." She stared straight ahead.

Precisely because she avoided looking at him, squelching the urge to spit in his pompous face—a childish thought, she knew—she didn't see it coming until it was too late. C. J. snagged her horse's nearest rein.

"What the devil do you think you're doing?" she sputtered as he led her beneath an oak.

"I been wantin' to talk at ya for days, Samma. Ain't seen hide nor hair of ya. Guess now's a good time." He dismounted and dropped his own reins, ground-tying his gelding. "Get down."

Surprise and anger roiling inside, she glanced from his face to his hand. He held the rein with a death grip. She could wrench away, perhaps, but the bit would saw cruelly in her mount's mouth if she did. She wouldn't do that to one of Oscar's well-trained horses.

"Ya deaf, Samma? I said, get down."

"All right."

Reluctantly, she slid to the ground and looked around. Not a soul in sight. Trees and rolling terrain hid the ranch buildings from view, though she knew they weren't far. Birds twittered in the trees, intent on their own pursuits. *It's broad daylight,* she scolded herself. *Don't be chickenhearted.*

C. J. flipped her horse's reins over a tree limb and tied him. Then he sat against the tree and patted the ground next to him.

"Set yerself down, Samma."

"I'll stand, thank you." She looped her arm over a low-hanging branch. No way would she go near this man.

"We've knowed each other our whole lives, Samma. Why do ya act thataway? Ya don't like me or somethin'? It ain't as if'n I ever done anythin' to ya."

True. But what she saw in his hazel eyes troubled her. She didn't believe for one minute C. J.'s intentions toward her were honorable. And, as she suspected of Uriah, C. J. appeared downright mean sometimes. One could tell a lot about a man by the way he handled the men who worked for him and how he handled his stock.

When she didn't answer, he cocked his head questioningly.

"See? That's what I mean. Ya act like I ain't even alive. Christ almighty, Samma—"

"I'd appreciate it if you wouldn't take the Lord's name in vain."

" 'Cause yer paw didn't? Jesus, Samma, that's the way men talk. Don't mean nothin' by it."

"Some men," she snapped.

He spread his arms wide. "Okay. Some men. If'n it riles ya, I'll watch my mouth."

"What did you want to talk about?" She plucked a leaf from the tree and rubbed it between her fingers. "I've got chores waiting at the house." Dropping the leaf, she crossed her fingers at the lie. The house was Aunt Mattie's domain. Sure, when heavy cleaning was afoot, Samantha pitched in to help. Her aunt performed the day-to-day housework, though, and when it came to cooking, Samantha was a dead bust.

"Well, there's a couple o' things." C. J. picked up a fallen stick and scoured the dirt as he looked up at her. "Where's the black stallion I heard ya captured a while ago?"

Surprise took her wits for a moment. "Who told you that?"

"Don't make no never mind; I heard." His expression hardened. "Ain't proper for a girl to ride a stud, Samma."

She couldn't help it; she laughed. "What in the world are you talking about? If I owned a stallion, I'd certainly ride him. I ride as well as any man."

"Yeah, ya do, and ya ride astride. It ain't proper for a girl to wrap her legs 'round a stud." He leered. "Less'n it's a man."

She should have expected it. C. J. seemed to have two things on his mind all the time. Women and bedding them. Tsking with disgust, she clutched her fingers into the tree bark and counted to five. It didn't help.

"You said I act as if I don't like you, C. J. It's your dirty mind I dislike."

All innocence, his eyes widened. "Me? Jesus, Samma, where'd ya get that notion? Maybe it's you what's got the dirty mind if'n ya think—"

"Please, don't take me for a fool just because I'm a woman."

"I ain't. Hell, I think right highly of the woman I intend to marry up with."

She stiffened. Would he never get it through his thick head? "C. J., I will never marry you." She enunciated each word.

"Aw, now, Samma. That's no way to talk. Who else ya gonna wed? There ain't 'nother man my age for a hundred miles 'round."

A tall drifter sprang to mind, but she slammed the door shut on that thought as quickly as it surfaced. The man who now scrambled to his feet made her skin crawl, and the other one, who commanded her thoughts whether she willed it or not, was sneaky as the dickens. Some choice she had, if she were inclined to pick either one.

"I'm not marrying anyone."

"Aw, Samma," he said again and stepped toward her, arm raised.

She backed away. "I have to get back to the ranch."

He stopped and lowered his hand, his eyes glinting. Try as he might to hide it, she saw his anger. She glanced around again, wishing someone—anyone—would come along.

"Well," he said, visibly reining in his ire, "we'll talk about this some other time. I want ya to tell me where that horse is. I'm gonna take him in hand. Make sure he's docile enough for a woman. If'n ya want to ride him, I'll see him gelded proper."

"No," she snapped. "He's gone."

"Huh?"

"I let him go, C. J."

"Ya what?" He took another step toward her; his mouth worked like a fish's until words exploded from him. "Ya had no right to do that, woman! The stock on this ranch is my responsibility. I say what animal goes or stays. I say who rides what."

"In a few days, you will lose Black Magic."

Walker's prediction echoed in her head so strongly that she blinked. He'd also said she would be under the thumb of a man who would run Timberoaks. He'd been right about that, too. Blast his hide. Maybe Walker had spirited the stallion from under her nose, but at least C. J. wouldn't take him. She gleaned a modicum of satisfaction from that thought and glared right back at him.

"You may be managing Timberoaks, through your father"—she stressed the last three words—"but you aren't managing me. I let the stallion go because he was mine to do with as I pleased. Mine."

Ruled by her own anger, she was taken off guard when he lunged and clamped his hands around her upper arms. His fingers bit into her flesh. Startled, she flinched and yelped in sudden pain when he squeezed hard, holding her in place.

"Goddamn you! Yer gonna learn who's boss 'round here if'n I have to beat it into yer hide, Samma!"

"Let her go."

Though soft, the low words rifled through the air, stilling them both as if a rope had drawn tightly around them. She glanced over her shoulder, unsure from which direction the man had spoken. She saw no one. C. J. looked the other way, as confused as she, but still held her arms with bruising hands.

"Let her go." The order came again.

Then she spied Holden Walker on the other side of the tree. He sat his horse with unconscious grace, though his big body looked tense, ready to spring. His remarkable eyes pinned C. J. where he stood. The fingers of Walker's left hand curled over his belt just above the butt of the six-shooter riding his thigh.

"I will not tell you again."

Not once had he raised his voice. His few words, spoken with such deadly intent, caused Samantha to gulp, afraid of what this man might be capable of. She didn't want to find out, either. Apparently C. J. thought the same. He released her and stepped back sharply.

She rubbed her hands over numb upper arms, eyeing Walker. It was spooky the way the man seemed to appear out of thin air. He moved about like a . . . a shadow. Her gaze shifted to C. J.

From one breath to the next, he regained his bluster and confronted the wrangler. The tree between them offered a measure of protection. C. J. bullied when he thought he could get away with it, but she was sure he flew in the face of disaster if he challenged Holden Walker.

"This here's Timberoaks land, mister. I manage this place, and yer trespassin'. Who the hell are ya?"

"I work here." Walker offered nothing more.

He looked her way, eyes narrowed as they traveled her length from toe to head. Staring into his unwavering gaze, she was claimed by the same heat she'd experienced while in his embrace.

It was uncanny the way his body seemed to relax all over, all at once. What had he seen in her that made him relax? And why should he be so tense, anyway? He wasn't her . . . keeper.

"The hell ya say." C. J.'s voice brought her back to the present. He scowled, his fists planted at his waist. "I ain't never laid eyes on ya."

"I was delivering a horse," Walker said.

That reminded Samantha that she was as riled as a pitching mare at Walker, but she held her tongue. She'd have her say with this no-account, sneaky skunk later.

As if he'd read her mind, a faint smile tilted Walker's lips. "That true, Samma?"

Easing the frown from her brow, she looked C. J. in the eye. "It's true." *As far as it went,* she added silently. Her father had hired him, but taking her horse bordered on theft. Though he'd been right, blast his hide.

C. J. swung his attention back to Walker. "Ya ain't answered my question. What's yer name?"

"Holden Walker."

"Ya got money for Timberoaks?"

"Payment changed hands before I delivered the horse."

Before you stole him, you mean. What a lying, silver-tongued devil.

C. J. grinned. "I ain't surprised. I wouldn't trust no ranch hand with my money, and Hiram musta not neither."

Silence stretched between them while Walker stared at the smaller man, his expression giving nothing away. The only sound was the skitter of a small animal high in the tree's branches.

"Well," C. J. muttered, shifted his feet and looked uncomfortable. "Ya best head on to the ranch. Won't be long till chuck is dished up."

Walker nodded but moved nothing except his eyes, which again pierced Samantha.

After several seconds, C. J. sneered, "What ya waitin' for?"

"Miss Timberlake."

"Samma an' me is discussin' business." He flapped his hand. "Go on. She'll be along d'rectly."

Walker remained still and silent. At last he asked, "Is your *discussion* finished, Miss Timberlake?"

She grasped the opportunity with the same dispatch C. J. had when he stepped away from her moments ago. Pulling the half-hitch in the rein, she swung atop the gelding before C. J. could do a thing.

"Samma! Come back here."

A string of curse words erupted from him as she pounded away. She didn't look back. Seconds later, Holden Walker's horse loped into her peripheral vision.

Taking a deep breath, she glanced sidelong at the tall man who rode with the grace of a born horseman. He looked straight ahead, his chiseled profile accentuated by a firm jaw. A hard-set jaw. She was intrigued by him, angry too, but above all she was ever so grateful he had come along when he did.

"Thank you," she said.

Walker pinned her with eyes that made her shiver every time he looked at her. Saying nothing, he merely touched his hat brim in a salute, then turned his face forward again.

Disturbed by what had taken place between her and C. J., she felt her stomach churn. She had always believed she could take care of herself, though in the back of her mind she knew her father and the men on the ranch had always been ranged behind her like an invisible shield. Now her father was gone. But the men were still there; Walker had just proved it.

She glanced down at her still-throbbing arms. C. J. was far stronger than he looked. She had the uneasy feeling she wouldn't have escaped him without help.

Rage such as Holden had never felt before pounded in his head in cadence with the gray's hoofbeats on the hard ground. It did no good to tell himself Samantha was unhurt. That he had interfered in time. He knew that, yet his gut clenched at the thought of the vermin's hands on her.

C. J. Butcher.

He had not been introduced by name, but Walker knew he'd just met the "banty rooster" Baker had mentioned. Though not surprised her father had put a man in charge of Timberoaks, he was livid to learn it was this man. And to have met the son of a bitch in these circumstances!

His eyes narrowed. It made no sense, this all-consuming rage. Samantha Timberlake did not belong to him, even though the taste of her, the smell of her, the feel of her in his arms a couple of weeks ago still stalked his dreams. Damnation, not just his dreams. Awake and asleep, he wanted her.

He glanced at her riding next to him, silent and introspective, and battled the thought of what might have happened if he had not come along. She had been struggling to break Butcher's hold. Without success. And that brought to mind Bubbling Water's long-ago horror when he had not been there to save her.

Suddenly, Samantha veered toward a stand of trees, bypassing the main compound of the ranch. She headed toward the spot where his camp lay hidden in the grove of oaks. Holden spurred his mount. He caught up with her as she entered the shade of spreading limbs.

"Miss Timberlake!"

She ignored him, weaving between the trees a few yards before she hauled in her horse. Holden brought the gray to a plunging halt next to her.

"Where do you think you are going?"

"None of your business. Go away."

"I will when you go home where you belong."

She glared at him. "I am home!"

"That is true. But better you put yourself in the midst of people who care about you than to wander off alone."

"I can take care of myself, Walker."

"Like you did back there?"

Fire sparked in her dark eyes. He fancied he could see smoke curling from the top of her head.

"What have you done with my horse?"

Her vault to that particular subject came as no surprise. He had expected her anger. "He is well cared for, Miss Timberlake."

"Well cared . . ." she sputtered. "I want him back! You stole my horse."

"You have the gold, do you not?"

He knew she did, remembering how he had slipped the nuggets into her skirt. He had been so heated by her responsive kiss that he had almost missed the opportunity. His gaze lingered on the sweet curve of her lips. Kissing her again consumed his thoughts. The gray sidestepped nervously when he gripped the reins in response to the hardening in his groin.

"I'll return your gold as soon as you bring him back. I told you, Black Magic is not for sale."

"Would you rather that man owned your horse?"

Her eyes widened. "How did you know . . . ?" She clamped her mouth shut.

"I know how men think."

"And gloat!"

"Gloat?" He did not know the word.

"Why don't you say it, Walker? 'I told you so.' I know you're itching to."

He grinned. He could not help it. She reminded him of a scrappy young cougar. He sobered when she glanced away, not quite quick enough to hide her eyes sheened by tears. Understandable, he supposed. She had lost her father. Fast on the heels of that calamity, her ranch had been taken from her. And the stallion . . .

"I am sorry, Miss Timberlake, but I believe it best your horse remains where he is."

"And where is that?"

He hesitated. If he told her he had stabled the horse in Waco, she would probably go after him.

"Answer me, you low-down . . . ranch hand!"

"Ranch hand? That is what I am, Miss Timberlake."

She doubtless wanted to call him worse. It mattered not that he could be a chief or a shaman to his people. She would be horror-struck if she knew he was more Indian than white.

Without warning she reined close. Her free hand lashed out, but he clasped her wrist and blocked the intended blow. Though he would never intentionally hurt her, delicate bones ground together beneath his firm grip.

His quick action overbalanced her. She tilted toward him. His other arm circled her waist, pinning her upper body to his chest. Her hat slipped awry, then tumbled to the ground. If he had not pulled her to him, she, too, would have fallen between the horses.

Breath whooshed from her, feathered over his jaw. Mind-numbing need galloped through him like a runaway team. He lost the battle with himself, swooped down to possess her parted lips, even as he reminded himself to go easy, the episode with Butcher fresh in his mind.

She stilled, her sweet breasts pillowed against his chest. Her nipples hardened, teasing his already heated body. He released her other hand and circled her back, anchoring her more firmly with both arms.

She moaned. Her hands slid up and over his shoulders; her fingers tunneled into his hair. His hat toppled to the ground, but he paid no attention. She gasped when his tongue slipped between her teeth.

Savoring her moist, soft mouth, Holden blindly slapped at her horse's rump to send it away. He lifted his leg over the gray and slid to the ground, carrying her with him. His cow pony never moved. Holden stood pressed against the horse's shoulder, his back warmed by that contact. But his chest and then his loins were licked by flames as Samantha's lithe body pressed to his. Spirits of the People, he was lost.

He leaned slightly, cradled her bottom in his broad hand, then lifted her up and forward to press his burgeoning sex at the juncture of her thighs. She trembled. Instinct told him she had never been with a man, but he could not conquer his raging need.

This is moon madness! Stop!

At that moment something banged against his hip, and a voice wailed, "Leave Samma alone!"

He jerked up his head. Her eyes glazed, Samantha appeared to be in a trance. Then he realized who had yelled, who was pummeling his leg.

Little Spring. Guy.

"Don't hurt my sister!"

Samantha came to her senses at that moment. Her eyes enormous with wonder, then confusion, she clamped a hand over her mouth and struggled for release. He let go, but gripped her again when she nearly toppled backward.

"Easy." His voice rasped hoarsely. Need still raged within.

"Leave my sister alone!" Guy punctuated each word with his fists, slamming Holden's thigh.

He looked down at the boy. Samantha whirled away, snagged up her horse's rein, leaped into the saddle, and galloped off.

He watched her go, knowing it was for the best, though his body did not appreciate the thought. *Bewitched.*

Crazed. He must be, to have kissed her like that. To have lost control. That was all it was. Loss of control.

You lie.

The boy hit him again. He blocked Guy's other hand before it also connected with his hip. "Easy, little man."

"You hurt Samma!"

"I would never hurt your sister, Guy."

He took a deep breath to ease his desire, released the boy's clenched fist, and stepped back. No. If anyone hurt, it was he. He burned, could still feel her nipples against his chest. Holden liked . . . loved . . . large nipples on a woman. Samantha's were large, the better to taste.

"I saw ya!" The boy was not giving up. "You was bitin' her."

"Biting . . . ?"

It took a moment for Holden to understand. The boy had never seen a man kiss a woman? He stared at Guy's angry face. Perhaps passion shown in that way—any way, in fact—was unknown to the boy.

"I did not bite her."

He squelched a grin when Little Spring's mouth pouted. Clearly, he believed Holden was lying. To give himself a moment to gather his thoughts, Holden turned to his horse. He lifted his canteen from the saddle horn, uncorked it, and took a long swallow. He extended it, offering to share, but the boy shook his head.

Looping the strap over the saddle horn, Holden thanked the Spirits his desire had subsided. His gaze swept the open ground toward the ranch buildings. Samantha was long gone. The thought that he was possessed by madness, which had challenged him while he kissed her, now came back with a vengeance. Somehow he must master this unbridled lust that overtook him every time he saw her.

But right now, he must deal with Little Spring. "Come. We will talk."

Perhaps if he were on Guy's level, the boy would not be

so wary. Holden sank down beside the nearest tree and braced his back against the trunk. Guy had not moved other than to jam his hands in his back pockets.

"I did not bite your sister. Sometimes men and women kiss. That is what we were doing."

"Why?" Guy's eyes narrowed further in disbelief.

Why, indeed? "Because it is . . . pleasant. Men and women like it."

"You was squeezin' the life outta her. Bitin' hurts. Daniel Sylvester bited me once't when we was fightin'." He pulled a hand from one pocket and crooked a finger. "See?"

Holden saw nothing. But clearly Guy remembered an unpleasant scuffle with another boy.

"Did you win?"

"Huh?"

"Did you win the fight with Daniel?"

Guy ducked his head, stuck his hand back in the pocket, and swirled a boot toe in the dirt.

"Yeah. But Pa . . ." His eyes teared.

The only father he had known was dead. Holden understood the heartache of loss.

Guy took a shaky breath. "Pa walloped me good fer fightin'. Made me 'pol'gize and shake hands."

His expression was so woebegone, and he seemed so alone that Holden wanted to comfort him.

"Did Daniel apologize too?"

"Sorta. We's friends. Don't see him much."

Arm extended, Holden beckoned. "Come."

He might as well have asked Guy to jump off a cliff. His head snapped up, his expression again wary.

Pain lanced Holden's chest as he curled his fingers on thin air and dropped his arm to his side. Had he not left him here, had he raised the child himself, Little Spring would not be cautious. It had been so long since he had carried the little man cradled in his arms, ruffled his hair. Tickled his round belly until he squealed with laughter.

The boy had liked nothing better than for Walks in

Shadow to take him up on his horse and carry him across the prairie. Baby though he had been, Little Spring showed no fear. Holden still carried the small bow and arrows he had made for him. The weapon he would have taught the child to use by the time he saw three summers.

Holden wanted so badly to touch him, but knew Guy would not allow it. He envisioned Samantha hugging the boy that day in the corral. No longer Little Spring, he was now Guy, and belonged heart and soul to the Timberlakes.

Frozen where he sat, Holden watched Guy turn away and head toward the house. The plan to reclaim him had seemed so simple when he left Little Spring here. Now he wondered.

Would he ever be able to reveal himself as Guy's adopted uncle?

Samantha stormed into the house. Behind her, the screen crashed against the doorjamb. She headed straight up to her room. For the first time in her life, she had ridden her mount into the barn and walked away, leaving the animal's tending to someone else.

She didn't give a good grunt who brushed the horse, who watered and fed him. "Some *man* will do it. Some *man* will take charge."

Silence met her burst of sarcasm.

She stomped toward the bed and plopped down on the mattress, hard. Aunt Mattie would doubtless have fit number ten if she'd seen her, but Samantha didn't care. If the abuse broke down the mattress, so be it.

Hands fisted, she pounded her thighs—and cursed for the first time in her life. "Dammit!"

Her father probably turned over in his grave, but she didn't care about that either. Everything was his fault.

Glaring defiance at the ceiling, she exclaimed, "That felt good, Pa!"

If he hadn't tied her hands with that damned stipulation in his will . . . There. She thought it, even if she didn't say it a second time. If he hadn't . . . No. If he had trusted her with the ranch, C. J. wouldn't be here strutting like a rooster with a pen full of chickens.

Well, she was no chicken. She would not cluck to his crow.

Samantha pushed herself up and stalked to the armoire. She yanked open one door. Her mirror image flashed before her. Eyes the color of umber burned bright and glowered in the glass. "It isn't fair, Pa. Timberoaks is mine. You had no right to give it away."

Her dim-witted speech to Oscar about bypassing C. J. in making important decisions was just that—dim-witted. The odious man appeared every single day, and would for the foreseeable future. If she couldn't control her own temper, she'd never be able to control anything else. Least of all C. J., who had proved stronger than she'd realized.

Samantha gripped her upper arms and rubbed her shirt-sleeves against still-smarting flesh. If Walker hadn't . . .

Her eyes clouded. Anger seeped away. Frustration and disquiet took its place. Frustration that he had taken her horse against her wishes, disquiet at the inexplicable heat that sparked inside her at the mere thought of him.

Long ago, she had figured out that all the begatting spoken of in the Bible had something to do with making love. Not something. Everything. There had to be more to it than simply populating the earth. Love, emotion, touch . . .

Focused on her mouth reflected in the glass, Samantha raised her fingers and caressed tender, slightly swollen lips. She stared at them, wondering how she could still feel his warm ones. Ever so slowly, she slipped the tip of her finger into her mouth and sucked. Walker had done that . . . to her tongue. She shivered.

Heat flared once again, delicious heat that slithered through her entire body, then settled in her breasts and between her thighs. Her nipples beaded against her shirt. She had experienced the same burning-inside, freezing-outside sensations both times he'd kissed her. Her breathing mere shallow pants, she closed her eyes.

Dear God, his kisses haunted her. She wanted the sensations to continue . . . in his arms. To see . . . no . . . feel where they led. Adrift, helpless to rein in her imagination, she relived those moments when Holden Walker wrapped his arms around her, pressed her close to his hard body. Overpowering he was but, oh, so gentle, too. So warm. So strong.

Stronger than C. J., I'd wager.

Her eyes popped open at the thought. She gasped with shock.

The warmth fled her body as quickly as it had come.

"Are you mad?" she asked her image.

Here she stood, dreaming about a man she intended to give a tongue-lashing the next time they met. A man from whom she intended to pry the whereabouts of her horse. Not . . . not . . .

She whirled about and came face-to-face with Aunt Mattie.

"We need to talk about what's got your drawers in a twist, Samantha."

Chapter Six

"Wh-what?" Samantha stuttered.

Aunt Mattie's dark eyes snapped fire. She looked ready to spit nails, and pointed to the single chair angled in the corner of the room.

"Sit."

When Samantha hesitated, Mattie planted her hands on her hips. "You're not too big for me to turn over my knee. I swear by the Almighty, I'm vexed enough to do it. Now sit!"

She did. Samantha had learned long ago that when Matilda Crawford had her back up, she'd better do as told, without argument.

Mattie eased onto the end of the bed and rested one arm on the iron foot rail. "Now, you're going to tell me what you're so riled about."

"I . . . I'm not, Aunt Mattie. It's—"

"Samantha Rose, I'm not blind, and I'm blessed with two good ears. For the past ten days, you've slammed doors fit to fly off their hinges. The way you just stomped up the stairs sounded like a horse galloped through the house."

"I'm sorry." She was, for that and more. She still hadn't apologized properly for her attack the day Judge Crocker read the will. "I—"

"You've snapped at Guy so many times, the boy ducks like a turtle pulling its head into its shell."

Was that true? Maybe so, but she hadn't meant to. "I'm sorry," she repeated. "I didn't mean to hurt Guy. None of it is his fault. . . ." She paused, unsure whether or not to tell Aunt Mattie about her encounter with C. J.

"No, it isn't. Whatever it is. You're going to tell me, and have it over and done with. Then maybe I won't feel the need to take a switch to your backside every time you enter the house."

Mattie's feet dangled a couple of inches above the floor. But it didn't detract from her ramrod-straight posture or her unwavering gaze leveled on Samantha.

"So, tell me, and do it now while I still have the patience to listen."

Samantha looked down at her white-knuckled fingers laced together. Pa, the will, C. J., her stallion, and . . . Walker. Everything jumbled in her mind. Where to begin? She shook her head.

"What good will talking do, Aunt Mattie? Pa . . . the will . . ." She looked up, mortified to feel tears burn her eyes. She would not cry! Somehow she would deal with her father's . . .

"The will," Mattie said. "Yes. I can certainly understand your consternation." Her brow furrowed. "You know, several years ago your father and I talked about your finding a husband. It isn't as if we live in Austin or Waco where there would be eligible young men aplenty to choose from."

"So you push me to marry C. J."

Mattie's expression sharpened. "I beg your pardon?"

Then she softened. "Samantha, when have I ever pushed you about marriage to C. J.?"

Her aunt's reaction raised second thoughts. Samantha knew she sounded like a mewling cat, but she couldn't seem to help herself. "Well, that's how it seems. You insist I behave like a lady every time we see the Butchers. And Pa put that stipulation in his will."

Mattie shook her head and sighed. "I'll not apologize for teaching you to act like a lady. As far as your father's thoughts, I can't say. But I don't think he envisioned you marrying C. J."

"Then why did he—"

"I just said I don't know. Besides, it's doubtful Hiram could have foretold that Judge Crocker would appoint Uriah Butcher to manage the ranch. He failed to stipulate it in his will, but he probably thought Oscar would work with the judge. One thing I do know, though. Hiram wanted you to marry for love."

Without warning, she felt Holden Walker's overpowering presence, the heat of his body pressed to hers. Yes, she was attracted to him, but love? She quickly ducked her head, her cheeks warm, doubtless blooming to a rosy hue. Her aunt's next words told her she hadn't been quick enough.

"Glory be, Samantha, are you in love with—"

"No!" She jerked up her head and found confusion on her aunt's face. Mattie had seen how she avoided the Butchers whenever possible. Her feelings in that regard were plain and simple. And, thank God, Mattie didn't know about Walker. "I can't stand C. J. He scares me sometimes. He . . ."

No, she wouldn't tell her aunt about the encounter today. If she did, it might lead to revealing what had occurred between her and Walker.

"Every time I turn around, C. J.'s here. He never misses the opportunity to talk about marriage. Uriah is no different."

Mattie's lip curled as if she'd tasted something sour. "The Butchers are tiresome, but you needn't ever say yes to C.J."

"He's here every day. He annoys me. And he's getting in the way of ranch business."

"What have you done in the past ten days to prove you can manage Timberoaks?"

The question took her by surprise. "What?" She frowned. "Well, Oscar—"

"Oscar is an excellent foreman, but he doesn't own the ranch. You do. Not once have you looked at the books your father kept so religiously. Not once have you planned the next sale. The ranch prospers or dies on horse trading. What have you done to learn?"

"Aunt Mattie!" Guy's voice floated up from belowstairs.

Mattie heaved her small body off the bed and walked to the door. "Up here," she called.

Samantha heard his boots pound up the stairs, then slow in the hallway. "You shoulda seed 'em, Aunt Mattie. They was kissin'."

If she could have dropped through the floor, Samantha would have. She had forgotten that Guy had seen her with Walker.

"Who?" Mattie questioned.

"Samma and that Walker feller."

Mattie turned, her questioning eyes on Samantha. An excited Guy plunged into the bedroom. He drew up short when he spied his sister.

"Shut up, Guy," she snapped.

He ducked his head, but stood his ground. "Well, you wuz," he mumbled. "Walker said grown-ups like—"

"Guy!" Would he ever close his trap?

"Guy," Mattie parroted in a much quieter tone. "You look like you've brought in half the dirt from outside. Go wash up, please."

"Don't need no bath."

"You do. But for now a good wash of your face and hands will help." She clasped his shoulder and turned him around. "Now, young man. We'll talk at supper."

Casting a belligerent frown at Samantha, he scuffed his boots on the hardwood floor as he reluctantly left to do his aunt's bidding.

Silence reigned for endless seconds as Samantha looked down at her hands, hoping to avoid a confrontation with her aunt. It didn't work.

"You didn't tell me Holden Walker was back."

"It didn't seem . . . important."

"Samantha, a few minutes ago I reminded you I see quite well, and my ears work just fine, too. Do you think maybe my wits have deserted me?"

"No."

She wanted to scream. *Please, I don't want to talk about Holden Walker. I don't know how I feel about his kisses myself.* But she didn't say a thing. Instead, she waited, sure Aunt Mattie would have plenty to say.

She was mistaken.

After another endless moment, her aunt broke the silence. "There's far more to Holden Walker than we know, Samantha. I would advise you to make a wide path around him. He reminds me of a man I once knew."

Certain she had heard pain in Aunt Mattie's voice, Samantha glanced up. The doorway was empty.

As darkness descended, Holden put away the tin utensils he had used to prepare his supper. Would that he could rein in his wayward thoughts as easily as he cleaned up the camp.

He listened to night sounds. Overhead, leaves whispered in a gentle breeze. One moment he felt the draft on his face, the next on his nape. The wind was as ambivalent about which way to blow as he was. Never before had his thoughts, his desires, shifted so.

No surprise that C. J. Butcher had announced himself manager of the ranch. White men were predictable. One way or another, they would have this land. If it meant taking it from the Indians or bending a woman to his will, Butcher would do it.

Not if I have anything to say about it.

Samantha Timberlake's dark eyes haunted him. They had held fear today. Rightly so. If he had not returned . . . Holden shrugged his shoulders, a futile effort to throw off the image of what Butcher had planned for her.

Thank you.

Those words had not come easily. He wanted to stay and protect her, but he should go. If she knew who he was, her eyes would hold fear, but of him rather than Butcher.

He looked down at himself. Seconds later, he pulled the buckskin shirt from the waist of his trousers and threw it off. Releasing his gun belt, he used more caution laying it next to his saddlebags. In moments he stood naked, then donned a breechclout and moccasins, crossed his ankles and sank onto his blanket.

"*This* is who you are," he said grimly.

Convincing himself of that seemed hopeless. Each encounter with Samantha and Guy increased his doubt that he was the nomadic warrior he had once been. Did he really want to be Walks in Shadow anymore? Perhaps he should settle himself into the skin of the white man he pretended to be and accept that way of life. All of it.

He tipped his head back and gazed up through foliage at stars winking in the black velvet sky. Even if he lived in a house with a roof over his head, at times he would camp like this. He needed the freedom open space afforded.

He rested his palms on the earth. His bed would be a mattress in a house, not this soil still warm from the day's sun. And lying beside him, beneath him . . . He tensed and closed his eyes.

Think of something else. Think of Little Spring.

Rising, he moved to the rolled tent and extra blanket stashed near the tethered gray. He returned to sit by the fire and unwrapped the bow and arrows he had carried these many seasons, hoping to gift them to the boy one day.

He lifted the small weapon and brushed his hand along the smooth wood. Eyes bleak, he allowed the thought to come. *Guy is no longer Little Spring. He is white.* A few years—even a few weeks—ago, Walks in Shadow could have stolen him from the Timberlakes with no compunction. But now, when he considered it, Samantha's face came to mind.

Walks in Shadow had seen the pain of loss in Bubbling Water's eyes before she died. Holden Walker did not want to see that same pain in Samantha's, only passion. The aftermath of pleasure he had given her. He wanted . . . more.

"Fool," he muttered. His thoughts invariably circled back to her.

He laid the bow aside, then pulled his saddlebags toward him. Fishing to the bottom, he drew out his flute, given to him when he was fifteen summers by Flies With The Eagle. Holden blew gently, testing the finger holes.

If he put his mind to it, he could make the sounds of many birds with the wooden gift. He had even composed a melancholy-sounding tune, full of anguish only a youth of seventeen summers could imagine, when a maiden he desired had gone to the blankets of another warrior.

It had been weeks since he played the crude instrument. Usually it soothed him. Maybe it would tonight.

Restless, too warm, Samantha threw back the sheet. Intermittently, the lace panel billowed at the window, but the breeze didn't make it into the room. She didn't know what time it was; the house had been quiet for maybe an hour.

Sleep would not come. She rose, pulled on her trousers and a shirt she didn't bother to tuck in. She found her boots in the dark and carried them, tiptoeing down the hall and stairs. Ever so carefully, she pushed open the screened door, then eased it back against the door frame without making a sound.

She shoved her feet into the boots, leaned back in the old rocker and sighed. It wasn't much cooler out here, but occasionally a breeze ruffled her tousled hair. She combed her fingers through it to achieve a semblance of order.

Without thought, she put the rocker in motion. One squeak and she stilled the chair. Wouldn't do to wake Aunt Mattie or Guy. Not after sitting through an unnaturally quiet supper. Not after Guy had shied away from her good-night hug.

She'd never intended to hurt Guy. Her life was such a jumble these days. Somehow she'd have to mend the breach. Maybe she'd ask him to ride along with her tomorrow. Problem was, he might not want to. Aunt Mattie was right; she'd been a shrew.

A distant sound caught her attention, then was gone. She cocked her head, listening. It came again, but was like no bird call she'd ever heard.

Rising, she stepped off the porch and walked to the center of the clearing. A moment later she heard the plaintive notes again, wafting from the direction of the oaks on the east side of the ranch. She strolled toward the trees, then paused and peered into the dark, dense foliage.

The sweet sound tickled her ears again, and this time it sounded like a tune. Some sort of instrument.

Curiosity won over her better judgment. She started into the forest, careful as near-impenetrable darkness cloaked her eyes. She paused, and finally recognized the sound. A flute. Who owned one, let alone played?

With that thought, she walked smack into a tree. "Ow!" She rubbed her forehead. Only a pace away, she could barely see the tree. "Not the smartest thing you've ever done, Samantha," she muttered.

Prowling in this small forest in daylight was unwise; in

the middle of the night, she courted all kinds of danger. That tree could have easily been a bear. But surely she would have smelled a bear.

She listened again. "Well, shoot." Now all she heard were leaves rustling. Taking one cautious step sideways, she peered around the trunk. Faint light flickered in the distance. A fire, or perhaps a lantern. She wasn't sure, but it gave her the heart to go on.

Moments later, Samantha came upon a camp. The fire in the center of the clearing was so small, it was a wonder she had seen it at all. A coffeepot rested on one of the rocks circling the flames. One cup sat on a nearby blanket, and the flute lay there as well. A piece of soft leather lay in a heap.

Moving cautiously, she walked the few paces to the blanket and stared down at a saddle. She knelt and brushed her fingers on the cantle. Recognition dawned. *Holden Walker's gear.*

Her eyes widened when she spied an Indian bow. She picked it up and wondered why it was so small. Surely a warrior carried a larger weapon. Odd that Walker would have it.

Unease prickled her nape. She rose and looked around, but the meager firelight didn't extend past the surrounding trees.

"Walker?"

Silence.

Her brow furrowed. "Are you here?"

Samantha pivoted ever so slowly, searching the darkness. Then she saw him. Or what she thought—hoped—was him. "Walker?"

Obviously reluctant, the wrangler ambled into the clearing, but he stopped a distance from her, propped a shoulder against a tree and crossed his arms. Her breath whooshed from her lungs when she got a good look at him. He wore only trousers and moccasins, though his gun belt rode his lean hips. Faint firelight danced on his bronzed skin from the waist up.

Some years ago, Samantha had seen her father's bare back when she'd walked in on him while he shaved. But she had never seen a man's bare chest. She was sure Walker's must be a rare sight. Sculpted by hard muscles, his upper arms bulged and sinew ribboned his forearms, but it was the rippling muscles across chest and stomach that stole her breath. The same word leaped to mind as when she'd first seen Black Magic. *Magnificent.*

"What are you doing here, Miss Timberlake?"

Mesmerized by the sheer pleasure of looking at him, she didn't realize at first that he'd spoken. She dragged her gaze from his broad chest to his eyes. It would have been better if she hadn't. A wolf's predatory gaze couldn't have startled her more.

Unable to speak, let alone breathe, she licked dry lips. That brought his gaze to her mouth. Where it stayed. A muscle ticked in his jaw. Was he thinking about kissing her again? She shivered at the thought and wished he would close the distance between them, take her in his strong arms . . .

Blinking several times, she swallowed hard. "I . . ." Her voice squeaked.

"It is unwise to venture out in the dark, Miss Timberlake."

Endless seconds ticked by. Her downward glance found the wooden instrument, then lifted to him again. "I heard your flute."

He frowned. "I thought I was camped far enough away that the sound would not bother you."

"Oh, it didn't. It was quite lovely, really."

Camped far enough away. Her brow furrowed. "Why aren't you in the bunkhouse?"

His lips kicked up on one side. "Have you ever smelled a bunkhouse?"

No, she hadn't. She tilted her head questioningly.

"I would prefer a polecat's scent." A smile lit his remarkable eyes.

"Surely not." She paused as her own smile came. "You're joking."

He shook his head and pushed away from the tree. "No. The odor of a passel of men cooped up together can be . . . unpleasant." Moving as stealthily as the animal he reminded her of, Walker strolled toward her.

Unsettled by an inexplicable quiver of anticipation, Samantha stepped back and caught her heel. Walker leaped the last few paces separating them.

The next thing she knew, she was crushed against the wall of his chest. Heat like she had never known radiated from him. Each time he touched her, she marveled at how big, how powerful he felt. Walker held her upright with ease, and after a moment he looked down as she looked up.

His mouth was inches from hers, and remembrance of his firm lips weakened her knees. She heard not a sound except the words galloping through her head. *Kiss me again.*

When he didn't, Samantha's gaze traveled upward. His eyes glittered with that unholy light and searched over her face while he seemed to fight a battle within. She wished she could read his mind. His tense body thrummed so strongly that she could feel it. Then his lids shuttered halfway as he released her and stepped away.

"Go back to your house, Miss Timberlake."

Disappointment squeezed her heart. She felt sure . . .

Walker leaned down, flipped open his saddlebag and drew out a shirt. As he stood, she realized what he'd said. He'd dismissed her as he would a child.

"I think not. Since I'm here, where is my horse?"

"Safe." He pulled the shirt over his head, thrust his arms into the long sleeves, and unbuckled his gun belt. Without turning around, he began unbuttoning his trousers. His gaze challenged her.

Samantha lifted her chin and stared him straight in the

eye. "That's not good enough, Walker. I want you to return Black Magic to me . . . tomorrow."

Try as she might, she couldn't stop her wayward eyes from lowering to his strong hands as he drew aside the opened placket of the trousers. Before he shoved the tail end of the shirt into the opening, she glimpsed lighter skin and dark hair. It was too hot to wear longjohns, and Walker wore no small clothes, either.

Her cheeks warmed. She had changed Guy's nappies when he was a baby, and she'd been raised around randy horses, but a man was . . . different. Flicking her gaze away from the tantalizing unknown, Samantha drew in a shallow breath. Silence reigned for several seconds; then she heard the click of his gun belt as he rebuckled it around his waist.

"I cannot bring your horse in one day, Miss Timberlake, even if I would bend to your will."

That rankled. "Blast it, Walker. Who do you think you are?"

He pinned her with an enigmatic expression. "You do not want to know. You would not like who I am, Samantha Timberlake."

Chapter Seven

The seed of guilt planted by Aunt Mattie germinated and flourished in Samantha's head. Holed up in her father's office, she pored over his ledgers. It was all there, everything she needed to know about horse trading. Hiram hadn't always received money for his horses. Sometimes he'd traded for labor, other times for hay or grain.

She discovered where steer meat for the family's table came from, too. Money appeared to be in short supply at the Butcher ranch. Five horses over the past four years had been swapped straight across for slaughtered beeves dressed for cooking or jerking.

A smile lit her eyes at the thought that her father had doubtless come out better than his neighbor on those deals. She'd heard beeves on the hoof went for sixty dollars a head up north. Course, they had to be trailed to the railhead to get that kind of money. But cash for even a saddlebroke horse rarely topped forty dollars.

She was drifting, her eyes unfocused on the precise writing and neat columns in the ledger, when men's voices gradually intruded on her thoughts. Samantha dropped the pencil she'd been unconsciously tapping on the blotter, rose and stepped to the window. Brushing aside the lace curtain, she spotted Holden Walker.

He stood in the center of the clearing. A horse circled around and around him, tethered on the end of a long lariat. Surprised he would lunge the animal outside the confines of the corral, she watched. He certainly had a gift for handling horses.

Kissing, too.

Astonished at the unbidden thought, she scolded herself. She didn't know if he was gifted or not. C. J. had stolen a kiss when she was about sixteen. She remembered it as awkward and downright slobbery. That had been her sole experience until Walker came along.

"Hold up there." Uriah's voice carried on the hot wind.

It seemed the horse divined what Walker wanted, for it stopped as if confronted by a ten-foot wall. With his back to her, she hadn't seen him tug on the rope, but surely he had.

Oscar and Baker stood with Uriah. Guy played in the shade by the barn. She scanned the clearing, thankful she didn't see C. J. Her lip curled with distaste. One Butcher at a time was plenty to bear.

Uriah approached Walker and said something. Samantha couldn't hear the exchange, only the indistinct rumble of Walker's deep-voiced reply. The sound washed over her, and goose bumps rose on her arms.

"You would not like who I am."

What Walker had meant by that she didn't know, but gazing at him now, she disagreed. He stood a head taller than Uriah and Oscar. He moved . . . gracefully, if one could describe a man that way. A man with broad shoulders, narrow hips, and long, muscled legs. Powerful, but, oh, how gentle he could be.

She liked what she saw, how he handled the horses, how

he'd held her. How he'd kissed her . . . twice. Quiet and reserved, he nevertheless got on well with Oscar and the other men. Walker was especially patient with Guy. She liked the man far too much, perhaps, but she didn't know him. Not really.

Her lips tingled as if remembering the feel of his firm ones. Her stomach contracted, a pleasurable sensation that radiated through her. She shivered.

"Samantha, have you seen Guy?"

She started, glancing over her shoulder at Aunt Mattie in the doorway. Her gaze returned to the window so her aunt couldn't see the flush heating her cheeks. Thoughts of Walker affected her more than she wanted to admit.

"He's out front," she said.

As Mattie walked into the room, Samantha faced her.

"You're looking at your father's ledgers. I'm glad." A faint smile lifted Mattie's lips.

Samantha smiled back. "You made it clear I wasn't doing my job." She shrugged. "You were right. There's far more to managing Timberoaks than herding horses from one place to another, or breaking them."

Mattie moved around the desk and scanned the ledger entries. "Your father was a meticulous man, Samantha. I suspect you'll learn as much about running the ranch from his books as you will from dealing with the men. You already know there's plenty of labor to get the job done."

Samantha's eyes dimmed at the memory of the last time she'd seen her father in this room, at that desk. "He made it look easy, didn't he?"

"I suppose," Mattie said, then strolled back toward the door. "He put in sixteen-hour days, though, so I don't recall that it was easy. Routine, perhaps, but the work had to be done, day in, day out." She looked Samantha in the eye. "I know there were times right after your mother died that he wanted to give up, but he didn't. Somewhere deep in Hiram was the sure knowledge that he needed to build a lasting monument to Elizabeth's life, to his. He passed that legacy to you."

"Now it's my turn," Samantha said quietly, moved by Mattie's words about her parents.

"Yes. And if you have half the backbone he had, you'll get through these next months and years. You'll overcome obstacles, even the Butchers." Her lips pursed with distaste. "You'll get past all of it and be stronger. Or you won't," she said flatly.

"I can't let Pa's work fall to ruin, Aunt Mattie." She smiled ruefully. "It took a bit of prodding, but I understand what you meant the other day. I know what you're telling me now."

"I hope so." Mattie paused, eyes narrowed; then her mouth trembled into a weak smile. "And if you choose not to marry, I'll understand. God knows, C. J. is no prize."

Samantha rushed forward, her hand extended entreatingly. "Oh, please, I'm sorry for my hateful words to you that day. I knew the moment I leveled the accusation that it wasn't true. It's just—"

"I know. I miss him, too." Tears glistened in Mattie's eyes.

Remorse squeezed Samantha's heart. She wasn't the only one dealing with loss. She'd do well to remember that. Clearing her throat, she changed the subject.

"You wanted Guy?"

"I've been remiss of late with his studies."

"I'll get him." Samantha arched a brow. "He'll probably balk."

"Won't be the first time. Tell him to come to my room."

Moments later Samantha approached the men in the clearing. Walker had returned to gentling the horse. She could stand all day and watch, not only for the pleasure of how he accomplished taming the animal, but simply to admire his subtle grace.

Uriah and Oscar turned as she neared. Baker cast a wide smile.

"There ya are," Uriah said.

His blue eyes swept her length, then lingered on her breasts. She glanced at Oscar. Was she the only one who noticed Butcher's . . . distasteful interest in her?

"C. J. says you've made yerself scarce for a few days, Samantha."

Avoiding him, as I do you.

"Yes," she said. "I've been studying Pa's ledgers." The minute the words were out of her mouth, she wanted to bite her tongue.

"Have ya, now?" Uriah's expression changed to one of speculation. "Maybe I'll take a look and help ya."

"That won't be necessary." The last thing she wanted was Uriah's "help." If she could keep the financial information to herself, she'd feel more in control.

"Well—"

"Guy," she interrupted. "Aunt Mattie wants you in the house."

Hunkered down shooting marbles, he looked up.

"Time for your studies."

"Aw, Samma, I don't wanna—"

"You heard me. If you went to a regular school, it would be every day."

"I don't wanna—"

"Guy! Stop arguing. One of these days we may find a teacher and erect a schoolhouse nearby. You wouldn't want to be the dunce, would you?"

His expression thoughtful, Walker drew in the horse. She didn't know what she'd said that had captured his attention, but his piercing gaze unnerved her.

"Awright," Guy said grumpily, then scooped up his marbles and marched toward the house.

"In her room," Samantha called after him.

Walker's enigmatic gaze followed her brother. With longing? Regret, maybe?

"Ya seen this here feller workin' horses, Samantha?"

She looked at her neighbor and composed her features, hoping she could manage a pleasant exchange. Uriah had never been anything but cordial to her. Still, there was that occasional glance, sometimes a touch, that put her teeth on edge.

"Yes, I have. Extraordinary, isn't it?"

"I ain't never seen the like. He gets the job done in half the time, 'pears to me."

"Walker sure learned this old dog a new trick or two," Oscar said.

"I can show you how to work them as I do."

Samantha wasn't sure to whom Walker spoke because his glance passed from Oscar to her and back. Not to Uriah, though, which pleased her. One day Uriah and C. J. would be off the ranch. The less they knew about Timberoaks's operations, the better.

"I'll use the stock you train, young feller," Uriah said.

Alarms fit to deafen clanged in Samantha's head. Use Timberoaks's stock? Without paying for it? Was Uriah the man Walker had warned would take her horse? Her inner turmoil must have been telegraphed to Uriah, for he hurriedly explained, "I mean, next time I buy one o' yer horses, I'll want one Walker's trained."

"Well, sure," Oscar chimed in. "He's gonna be mighty busy the next few weeks. We got a couple dozen head needs work. Ain't all of 'em sold, neither. Afore summer's gone, we need a bunch close by for winter sales. C. J. went out with Grogan and some o' the boys to do some roundin' up."

Samantha's breath hitched with relief. C. J. could be out on the range for days, which explained why his father was here. But Uriah had a ranch of his own to run. Surely he wouldn't hang around every day as C. J. had.

"Where do you want this horse penned?" Walker asked. "He has worked enough today."

"South pasture," Oscar said. He looked at Samantha. "You got time to show him the way?"

"I can find it on my own," Walker said.

He spoke so quickly, she wondered if he didn't want her along. Ride with Walker, just the two of them? Her pulse beat a tattoo.

"Prob'ly could, but I need ya back here afore the day is spent, if'n ya know anythin' about shoein'." Oscar cocked his thumb at Baker. "He ain't half bad at the job, but he's still learnin'."

"That's a fact," Lemuel drawled.

"I know how to shoe," Walker said with obvious reluctance.

"Good. Samantha, bring back that spotted mare with the hoof that's split. And you," Oscar jabbed a finger toward Walker, "find that cussed stallion runnin' down thataway. If'n ya can get a lasso on him, bring him in. If not, run him off again. He's a pistol, that one. Wants to steal ever' mare we got."

Well, she'd wanted Oscar's help and she had it, but not once did he ask her to do a task. He simply assumed she would.

Oscar glanced at Uriah. "You an' me got some jawin' to do. Let's get a cup o' mud." He strode toward the bunkhouse, expecting the man to follow.

Seeing Uriah fall in step with the foreman as meek as you please tickled her. Instead of seething at Oscar for telling her what to do, she bit back a laugh at his high-handed manner.

Holden kept pace with Samantha, even though the trailing horse balked a time or two. The recently gelded animal was likely sore, and some horses were more easily trained than others. This one would take a couple more sessions on the lunge line.

Ahead of him, Samantha's lithe body swayed in the saddle. He found it impossible to concentrate on the business at hand. His mind wandered where it should not go.

Kissing her had been a mistake. Now he knew the feel

of her slender body pressed to his, the taste of her, the smell of her arousal. Innocent, timid . . . at first. Then passion, evidently new to her, even wondrous, had driven her to mindlessly accept his roaming hands, his lips, his tongue. . . .

He suppressed a groan. There was more, much more he wanted to taste, to feel, to give. When he thought of the way she had melted at his kiss, he fought mindless need himself. His gaze riveted on the jeans stretched taut across her bottom.

He wanted her naked in his arms, his hands free to explore her smooth flesh, his mouth free to taste, to pleasure her—and himself—when he sank into the softness between her thighs. His body responded painfully to the thoughts. He bit down and tasted blood. Served him right.

Ahead, Samantha slowed, then guided her mount to the left before drawing to a halt. She looked over her shoulder as he rode up next to her and reined in. The gelding kept going until Holden tugged on the rope.

Kicking his left foot out of the stirrup, he bent his knee to casually lay his foreleg over the gray's withers and leaned forward. Elbow resting on the saddle horn, he prayed the Spirits would take pity on him and shrivel his telltale arousal . . . quickly.

Rather than look at her, he scanned the area before him. "This is a pasture?" Not a fence in sight.

"That's what we call it." She pointed. "There's water down among those trees. Between the grain the men bring twice a week and the water, the horses pretty much stay put."

It worked, apparently. Holden counted a dozen head grazing the knee-high grass in the open field. More could be hidden beneath the trees.

"Look!" She pointed again.

Two foals raced across the flat, kicking up their heels, nipping at each other. His grin matched Samantha's. The gelding chose that moment to yank on the rope. It slipped though his fingers before he tightened his grip and was nearly unseated.

"Ho!"

A laugh gurgled from Samantha while he struggled to find the stirrup and hold the horse. To prevent a fall, he stood in the right stirrup until his groping toe slid into the dangling left one, then plopped back against the cantle. Knowing his own mount would hold still, he dropped the rein and rubbed his shoulder. Damnation. The jerk had pulled a muscle.

"May . . . maybe you bet . . . better release him before you end up on your no . . . nose in the dirt."

He scowled at her laughter. "You would enjoy that, would you not?"

"Oh, come on. Don't be so serious." Her smile, white teeth flashing, lit up her face. "It would be funny if *I* fell in the dirt, Holden."

The sound of his first name on her lips caught him unaware and zinged through him like notes from his flute. His breath hitched. Unable to resist her merriment, he, too, smiled.

"Follow me." She kicked her horse and flew down the slight incline. Her hat tumbled behind her, but the leather tie held it against her back. Golden hair uncoiled from atop her head, spread across her shoulders and glinted in the sunlight.

The breath he'd managed to draw in moments ago left him in a whoosh. Vivid images of her lying beneath him, her hair spread across his blankets, his fingers tangled in the silken strands, caused his groin to tighten once again. He brushed his hand over his face. Another groan of frustration escaped.

Moments later, he spurred his gelding down the hill, knowing in his gut he would follow her into the bowels of the white man's hell. But if she ever discovered who he really was, he would plunge into that hell alone. The laughter he had heard, had seen light her eyes, would disappear. She would doubtless look upon him with fear. Maybe . . . hatred.

Butterflies swooped in Samantha's stomach. She drew in a shaky breath. Holden Walker was too handsome, especially when he smiled. She'd coaxed that smile from him, then regretted it because she wanted . . . more. More of what, she wasn't sure, except . . .

Another kiss? Oh, yes. That would be heavenly.

Reining her mount near the trees, she slid from the saddle and waited as he pounded toward her, the gelding in tow. Moments later, Walker slipped down from his horse. Trailing the rope across the gray's rump, he began to coil the hemp, slowly drawing the gelding toward him.

"Come," he cajoled in a deep voice.

Apparently the horse recognized authority when he heard it, for he trotted forward and stopped directly in front of Walker. He unhooked the lead from the headstall, but kept a grip on the leather next to the horse's jowl.

He glanced at Samantha. "Which is the dominant mare in this herd?"

"Huh?" What an odd question. "I don't know what you mean."

"Every herd has a dominant mare, Miss Timberlake. If you wish this gelding to graze here, he must be introduced to the mare who will or will not allow him to stay."

She blinked once, twice, and shook her head. "You're kidding, right?"

Sometimes this man surpassed strange. Downright loony. She'd recently heard that word for the first time and thought it perfectly described some of the things Walker said and did.

"No," he replied, obviously serious. "It is true, but you are apparently unaware of that."

"You bet. There're"—she turned, scanning the horses she could readily see—"maybe a half-dozen mares here."

She shrugged. "They get along just fine as far as we know."

"How many horses have you lost from this area?"

"Holy moly, Walker. I don't know. Some, of course, but that's inevitable. Plus, that stud is around here somewhere."

His lips kicked up in a half smile. "So, he is blamed for stealing the stock that may have run afoul of a mare."

This time she threw up her hands. "You *are* nuts!"

That earned a full-fledged grin from him. Even his eyes sparkled. "I have been accused of that, yes. But watch and learn, Samantha Timberlake."

He unbuckled the headstall and released the gelding. The animal stood stock still for a moment, staring at Walker, then shook his long head. Finding himself free, he wheeled and galloped away, but not far.

"Make yourself and your mount comfortable," Walker said. "This may take a while."

The gelding ran toward a clutch of mature horses, slowed to a trot, then stopped. Every single horse in the pasture jerked up its head and eyed him for several seconds before returning to cropping grass. The two foals found their mothers and nuzzled them to nurse. One allowed it; the other did not. She ambled away, lowered her head and began to eat. The foal followed, but she kept a step or two ahead of him.

As if testing the waters, the gelding sidled closer. The mare had placed herself between him and the other horses. She raised her head, stared at him a moment, then ran at him, her ears back. He veered off, and the other horses ran the opposite direction for a short distance.

"That is the dominant mare in this herd," Walker said.

"So? What difference does that make?"

"If she takes it into her head to run him off, she will. A lone horse on the prairie is vulnerable to all kinds of danger. He would not last long without the safety of numbers."

Samantha *tsk*ed at that, then reined her horse toward a stand of trees. Walker followed on foot, his horse on his heels without being led. Dismounting, she loosened the cinch. Walker had been right, and now she wanted to watch what happened next. She dangled her hat from the saddle horn and ran fingers through her hair.

Her mount lowered his head to eat, as did Walker's. He stepped to the animal's side, fished in his saddlebag, and brought out a spyglass. She blinked in surprise. Walker seemed prepared for every eventuality.

"What are you doing?"

He pointed his chin to the south, then looked through the glass in that direction. After several seconds, he handed her the small telescope. "There is a stallion below the crest of that far hill. Is it the one Oscar is worried about?"

It took a moment to spy the animal. Though his coat was rough and dirty, he was recognizable as a golden palomino, the troublemaker several of the men had tried to get a rope on over the past couple of months.

She lowered the glass, handed it back to Walker and nodded. He sat, knees bent, resting his elbows on them to steady the scope, and assessed the stallion. Moments later, he shook his head.

"What would Oscar do with him if I caught him?"

"Break him, of course. We can always use a good stud, and that one is wily and smart."

Walker shook his head again. "I think not. Both hocks are capped, and I think he has a bowed tendon on the right foreleg. He may be smart, but his legs are weak."

"What? How do you know?"

He again thrust the glass toward her. "Take a look."

She did. And while she scrutinized the horse, Walker described more of his bad points: short-coupled, narrow-chested, and long-eared like a mule.

"From the look of his legs, I suspect his hooves are soft. His coat is dull under the briars and dirt, and he is thin, so his teeth are probably bad, too."

Samantha lowered the glass, amazed at Walker's observations. "You saw all that in the few seconds you studied him?"

"Of course. Perhaps Oscar has never been close enough, or does not have a telescope, for he would see the same things. The stallion would sire poor foals. He should be run off or shot."

Samantha's stomach clenched at his matter-of-fact words. Shoot him? No. "A bullet sounds cruel, Walker. Run him off, but don't kill him."

Walker's eyes shuttered. "There are worse things than death. Far better to shoot him than let him starve, Miss Timberlake."

That might be true, but she'd rather have the stallion take his chances. When she remained mute, Walker sighed and stood.

"I will do as you wish." He glanced around, then looked down at her and frowned. "You will be alone if I run off the stallion."

"So?" Good grief, she knew every inch of Timberoaks land. She wasn't about to get lost on the way back to the ranch house.

"It is not safe for a woman alone on the prairie."

She stood and glared at him; frustration coursed through her. "Look, Walker, I'm tired of having every man on this ranch treat me like a child. I own this place now. I intend to manage it, too, without a man questioning every move I make, every word I say."

If she thought her tirade would get a rise out of the enigmatic man, she was sorely mistaken. He simply looked at her, and maybe, just maybe a glint of admiration flickered in his remarkable eyes. And something else.

Realizing what it was, she found it hard to acknowledge the helpless fear she'd felt when C. J. had trapped her. "I appreciated your help." Did she have to spell it out? Apparently so, for he remained mute. "Okay, maybe I wouldn't have escaped C. J. that day, but he's not here now."

A faint smile curved his lips, but he said nothing. His

point made, he didn't have to. He only gave her that haphazard two-fingered salute against his hat brim, then mounted and rode away.

She watched as his gelding picked up speed. Simultaneously, Walker released the coiled lariat on his saddle and prepared a loop. He would doubtless swing it to spook the stallion into running far and fast. Her gaze followed him until he disappeared over the rim of the hill. The sound of pounding hooves diminished, replaced by wind soughing in the trees.

Sighing, she strolled over to sit beneath the trees and returned her attention to the gelding's progress. After a moment, she grinned.

Sure enough, that old mare had the new horse at bay. He stood a good fifty yards from the herd. Though grazing like the rest of them, he repeatedly raised his head and whickered, as if asking permission to go closer. The mare didn't respond at all.

She seemed to ignore him, continuing to eat.

Walker had said this might take a while, and now she was beginning to believe it. But she couldn't sit here all day, no matter how pleasant it was in the shade. She would have to find the mare Oscar had mentioned and head back. No telling how long Walker would be gone.

Rising, she started toward her horse, which had drifted near the ribbon of water. She sucked in a startled breath and halted midstride. Her heart did a flip-flop.

C. J. stood across the stream, covered in dust and tired-looking from riding since sunup. His glance flicked past her in the direction Walker had gone.

"I see that drifter left ya by yer lonesome, Samma." A smirk curved his lips. "Ain't it lucky I come along."

Chapter Eight

Stepping back, Samantha scowled to hide the frisson of trepidation that sliced through her. "C. J., how long have you been standing there?"

"Long enough." His mouth thinned. "You fancy that no-'count drifter, don'tcha?"

"That's absurd."

"If'n ya mean I don't know what I'm talkin' about, yer wrong. I got eyes, Samma. I saw how ya wuz lookin' at 'im."

She blinked, astonished by his observation. Had her expression betrayed her feelings for Walker? "I'm not sure what you think you saw, but you're wrong about my feelings for Walker, or any man, for that matter."

"Me in partic'lar, huh?"

He actually looked hurt. Or was she seeing something that wasn't there? If she could hurt him, that made C. J. vulnerable, even pitiful. How could she dislike someone she pitied?

"This conversation is pointless," she snapped, annoyed with her thoughts.

Her horse separated them. While the animal cut steers

from a herd at the mere pressure of her knee, he never had respected her whistle. She'd have to walk toward the odious man to reach her mount.

C. J. fiddled with a lucifer stuck in his mouth. His shoulder propped against a tree, he appeared relaxed. She knew he wasn't, knew he would lunge at her if she got close enough.

Playing for time, she asked, "Aren't you supposed to be with Grogan and Old Henry hunting for horses?"

"Yeah. But I got tired o' trailin' after them two." A smile twisted his lips. "Figured I could bring in a couple horses from this pasture and nobody'd be the wiser."

"What?" Samantha planted her hands on her hips. "Most of these horses are broken and ready to ride. Some already carry Timberoaks's brand."

"Is that a fact? Well, I'll have to be careful which ones I pick, won't I?"

Samantha glanced around and wished with all her heart for Walker to reappear over the hill. How far would he chase the stallion?

She looked back at C. J., and her heart beat a nervous tattoo when she realized he'd stepped closer. It wouldn't take much for him to cross the narrow stream. Her heart thudded. The breeze had died, and not a bird chirped.

"Ya know, Samma . . ." He flipped away the spent match. She flinched. His voice sounded loud in the unnatural quiet. "Paw 'spects us to marry up."

"And you always do as your pa says," she sneered.

"The hell ya say! I don't, not by a long shot."

"Will you let it go?" It would be unwise to raise C. J.'s hackles further, so she made a supreme effort to keep the loathing out of her voice. "I won't marry you. I don't intend to marry at all."

" 'Less'n that drifter asks ya."

She shook her head violently. Still, thoughts of Walker lingered: his big body and strong hands, his soft lips, his powerful presence.

She forced a denial. "No. I told you . . ."

Abruptly, he lunged. Caught unprepared, she tripped and fell backward, landing so hard it took her breath. In the next instant, C. J. pinned her to the ground.

Head back at an angle, she found she couldn't even swallow. The leather strap of her hat cut across her neck until she couldn't breathe, couldn't swallow.

"Look at me." C. J.'s hot, tobacco-stench breath blasted over her chin and lower face.

"I . . . my hair . . ." Caught beneath her, the long hair held her head immobile.

He levered himself up a few inches to allow her to raise her shoulders. She reached to ease the strap from her throat, and lowered her chin to take shallow breaths.

His lips curled in a smirk of triumph. "I been wantin' ya for a long time, Samma. Now I'm gonna have ya."

"No."

"Paw wants us hitched, and if'n I takes ya, you'll have to marry up with me."

"No!" She screamed this time, planted her heels and bucked in an effort to dislodge him.

Her movements only settled his lower body against hers. She could feel his member nestled between her thighs. His enlarged member. She shuddered, then stilled.

Talk to him.

"I don't think this is what your father had in mind. We shouldn't be . . . together before marriage."

He laughed, his breath washing over her entire face this time.

Shifting her eyes, she glanced in the direction Walker had gone. *Please ride over that hill. Now!*

A chuckle rumbled in C. J.'s chest. "He ain't comin' back quick-like, Samma, and we's gonna have a little party afore he does."

Her eyes snapped to his face. "Like hell. Get off me right now!"

He laughed again and reached for the top button on her shirt. Panicked, she raised a hand and slapped him.

His head snapped to the side. Then, ever so slowly, it came around until his narrowed eyes looked directly into hers, promising retribution. "If'n that's the way ya want it, that's the way it'll be, Samma. Ya don't want it nice, I can be rough."

She flailed her arms, dug her fingers into the ground, and planted her heels again. Lifting with all her might, she squirmed and writhed. C. J.'s heavy body didn't budge.

Panting, she collapsed—until she felt his clumsy fingers working the buttons on her shirt. "Clarence James Butcher, if you do this, I swear to God on high, I'll kill you."

He slapped her—hard.

Tears as hot as her abused cheek burned in her eyes, and she closed them. She bit her lip, but refused to cry.

Then C. J. spoke fast, spittle spraying over her cheek and ear. "Goddammit, Samma. Don't make me hurt ya. We can have a fine time, but ya got to coop'rate."

"Not as long as I draw breath."

"Look at me, dammit."

Determined to thwart him any way she could, Samantha refused to open her eyes. "I hate you, Clarence James Butcher. I will until the day I die. Go ahead. Do your worst. But I'll never say 'I do' before a preacher. Not for you."

She opened her eyes to see his face when she delivered her final ultimatum. "Not ev—" The word died on a gasp. Her eyes grew round as saucers. "Dear God," she said on a strangled sob, her attention focused beyond C. J.

"Dear God," she said again. "Look behind . . ." She couldn't get another word past dry lips.

His brow crinkled. "What?" He leaned on his elbow and glanced over his shoulder.

"Holy shit!" Rolling off her, he sprang to his feet. "Where the hell did they come from?"

Samantha heard the fear in C. J.'s voice as she pushed slowly to her feet. He couldn't be more afraid than she. Her eyes riveted on first one man, then shifted to another and another—six in all.

Comanches!

Holden could have caught the stallion easily, but he kept his mount at a steady lope. The wild horse maintained his distance, his labored breathing proof of his poor condition.

Only the strong survived the harsh Texas prairie. Though Holden knew that, he found himself loath to put a bullet through the animal's head. It would be kinder to the horse, but Samantha's shocked response to that solution remained uppermost in his mind. For her sake, he would wait. For a while.

When the stallion returned, and he would, Holden would shoot him. With any luck, Samantha would not be around to see it or to hear the report of his rifle.

He paused and pulled his blue-and-white neckerchief over his mouth and nose to block the worst of the hot wind and choking dust that flayed his face. Up ahead, the stallion also slowed, then stopped. At that same instant, a hawk screeched overhead. Holden looked up. The bird flew so low, he heard the flap of wings. His eyes narrowed. The majestic bird soared straight up, then banked into a dive directly at him, only to level out and fly straight over his head.

A challenge? It flew in the direction from which Holden had ridden, then circled back toward him—ascending in a spiral, all the while calling as if communicating with him.

At that moment Holden understood the white man's expression: *It felt as if someone walked over my grave.* He shuddered.

Danger.

He scanned the ground he had covered. No dust devils. Nothing moved. He scowled. If the Spirits were trying to tell him something, he failed to understand the message.

Samantha's face flashed in his mind's eye. He had not wanted to leave her alone.

As she had pointed out, she rode as well as a man. She was on Timberoaks land. C. J. Butcher presented the only threat to her, but today he rode with Grogan and Old Henry.

For many seasons Walks in Shadow had listened to the voices in his head. Now, Holden Walker turned troubled eyes to the palomino in the distance. Disgusted that he was seeing danger where none existed, he shook his head as the hawk disappeared over the horizon.

Nudging the gray, he swung the rope over his head. "Yah!" he yelled and galloped toward the stallion. He plunged down a hill, across a meadow, up a slight incline, then down the other side. He rode hard, pushing his mount and the stallion. The rope whipped over his head. "Yah!"

In the distance the stallion ran full-out, up and down rise after rise. Silhouetted against the sky at the top of a higher hill, the horse veered beyond sight. Holden rode on, sure he must have pushed the animal five miles from where he had left Samantha. Far enough.

Slowing the gray as he, too, gained the top of the hill, he drew in sharply. A dust cloud in the swale below caught his eye.

Holden dropped his arm and began coiling the lariat, watching two wranglers haze several horses in his direction. As they neared, he recognized Buddy Grogan and Henry Sullivan.

Mournful, soft music had long been range tradition to quiet herds, whether horses or steers. Despite his snaggle-teeth, Old Henry was good on the mouth organ.

"Yo-ho," Grogan called, and waved when he spied Holden.

He yanked his bandanna down and waited, watching the men herd the horses. It took a moment to realize why trepidation claimed him. C. J. Butcher was not with them.

Holden circled down. "Need any help?" he asked when he met Grogan.

"Naw. Me an' Henry got it under control. No need to hurry the stock and get 'em riled. Ain't got that much farther to go anyhow." Grogan swung his rope in a steady circular pattern, his horse plodding along.

Holden frowned, reliving his sense of danger—the hawk, Samantha's face. "I thought Butcher rode out with you."

Grogan threw him a glance. "He took off a couple hours ago. Ain't seen 'im since."

Alarm stilled Holden in the saddle; then he swung his head to stare at Grogan. "A couple of hours?"

The wrangler nodded. "C. J. ain't worth the powder to blow him to hell. Not when they's work to be done. He diddle-daddles wors'n any squaw I ever did see."

Holden stiffened at the comparison. Indian women of Walks in Shadow's acquaintance worked hard from sunup to sundown and beyond. But he could not defend his people to this white man or any other.

Besides, his concern lay elsewhere: Samantha.

"I will leave you to your work, Grogan."

Not waiting for a reply, Holden spurred his horse away. In seconds the well-trained gray stretched into a flat-out run.

Danger. The word clanged in his head.

Why had he not listened to his inner alarm earlier?

Samantha swallowed convulsively, but produced not a trickle of moisture to ease her dry throat. She'd experienced fear with C. J. Now she knew terror. Her fingers clutched the coarse fabric of her trousers. Her innards quaked so hard that she expected to shatter.

"Samma."

She jumped at C. J.'s whisper.

"Keep 'em lookin' at ya and I'll run for help."

"No!" She couldn't suppress the frantic timbre in her voice.

Her wide eyes shifted to the still-as-stone Indian before them. Though not as tall as Walker, the well-muscled savage topped her by a few inches. Close to six feet, she'd guess.

His black-as-pitch eyes slowly assessed her length, then returned to her face, settling on her hair. His interest caused her to shiver so violently that even her teeth clicked. Scalps decorated the lance in his strong hand. One white-blond, several in various shades of brown, but none golden like hers.

He raised an arm circled by a wide silver bracelet above his elbow and pointed at C. J. "Car . . . lence?"

He directed the question to her, his fathomless eyes narrowed on her face.

"Car . . . lence?" she croaked right back.

What did he want? And why did the six men stand rooted to the ground? Every story she'd ever heard about raiding Indians told of screaming demon savages who rode down on unsuspecting folks.

Another spoke to the man she suspected was the leader. He shook his head once, the feather swaying in his scalp lock. Whatever the exchange, the five Indians ranged behind the tall one didn't like it. All of them spoke at once, and the two who carried bows raised their arms and shook them, snarling like dogs at C. J., then at her.

"*Suvate!*" the leader snapped.

Although she didn't know the word's meaning, the other Indians quieted, sullen to a man. Still, they didn't challenge him further when he turned back to her.

"Car . . . lence?" he asked again.

"What the hell's he sayin'?" C. J. whispered.

She threw a disgusted glance his way. "How should I know?"

"Well, I ain't waitin' to be scalped, Samma."

Never taking her eyes from the Indian, she muttered, "Don't be a fool. You think they'll let us leave?"

"Ain't got no choice if'n I slip behind this tree and disappear."

"You're not a ghost. Besides, our horses are out of sight, C. J."

The Indian took a step toward her. Samantha swallowed hard.

"Car . . . lence?" he persisted, the lance tip pointed at C. J.

Realization finally penetrated her fogged brain. She glanced at C. J. "I think he's asking your name."

"Huh?"

Confused, she frowned at the Indian and nodded once. His lips thinned in what passed for a smile.

At the same moment, C. J. made a break for it. Simultaneously, the lance tip swung in her direction and stopped a hair's breadth from her throat. The two Indians holding bows nocked arrows in a flash and let fly. She felt the hot air stir as the arrows whistled within inches of her on either side. Behind her a strangled cry rent the air.

She closed her eyes, willing herself to stay upright. Though she disliked C. J., she didn't wish him dead at the hands of these savages.

She whirled to see him lying facedown on the ground. Both arrows had found their marks. Their shafts still quivering, they were buried in the backs of both his thighs. He groaned.

A terrified cry ripped from her. "C. J.!"

Strong hands clamped her upper arms. Held immobile by the two Indians flanking her, she couldn't go to him.

Bows now angled across their broad backs, the two savages passed her and stalked toward the fallen man. Each clamped a foot on one of C. J.'s calves, reached down to grip a shaft and ripped the arrows out.

He screamed as his head reared off the ground. Then he collapsed, mercifully unconscious.

But the horror didn't stop. They hauled up his limp body as another Indian led his pony near them. Grunting with the effort, the two men lifted C. J. and flung him over the saddle, belly down. Blood soaked the lower half of

C. J.'s trousers. Quicker than Samantha could blink, one Indian tied C. J.'s hands to his feet so he couldn't slip off. Then the savage started across the stream, leading the horse. The other two followed.

"No!" she wailed, kicking at each of her captors. "Where are you taking him?"

Renewing her efforts, she leaned to one side and bit one captor's wrist. He grunted, but didn't release her. On the contrary, his grip tightened, cutting off her circulation. The Indian on the other side grabbed a hank of her hair and jerked her head back. Her neck snapped so painfully that she saw stars. But unlike C. J., she wasn't blessed with unconsciousness.

The man holding her hair snarled something in his guttural tongue. A knife flashed into her vision. In that instant she knew her fate.

"*Suvate!*"

Her head bowed backward, she couldn't see him, but she knew the leader's voice.

Both captors yelled something, and the knife hovered near her forehead.

"*Suvate!*" the man ordered again, then spewed a string of Comanche.

Her hair was suddenly released, and her head snapped forward. Vertebra ground and she closed her eyes against the pain. The leader's long fingers curled around her chin and jerked up her head. A rainbow of colors flashed behind her closed lids. She bit back a groan as pain shot down her neck into her back.

He spoke again—endlessly.

She opened her eyes. The lance tip waved within inches of her face, back and forth, back and forth. Mesmerized, she tracked the motion. Still held by the other two, she knew escape was impossible. She flinched when the leader released her chin and reached for her hair.

Oddly gentle, he lifted a handful, then trailed the tresses through his fingers as he withdrew his hand. All the while he spoke to his companions. The hands imprisoning her arms eased. Three pairs of obsidian eyes stared at her, the expressions on their faces . . . curious?

"Sa . . . man . . . ta," the leader said clearly.

The meaning of his garbled utterance hit her. Knees wobbly, she shook from head to toe. "How do you know my name?"

Heaven help her, she didn't want to find out. Staring into his dark eyes, she saw . . . humor. His mouth softened almost to a smile.

Feeling the grip ease on her arms, she wrenched herself away and took a quick backward step. Surprised when they didn't grab her again, she stiffened her spine.

"C. J. Clarence." She pointed the way the other Indians had gone. "Where are they taking him?"

The leader might not have understood the words, but he understood her gestures. Expressive eyes hard, he raised his arm, then brought it down in a chopping motion. A shaft of sunlight glanced off the silver armband. He shook his head and covered his mouth with a cupped hand. His meaning was clear. *It's none of your business. Shut up.*

Perhaps madness ruled her, but she argued further. "If you don't release him, C. J.'s father will search till his dying day. And when he finds you, you'll die."

The Indian wagged his head as if he understood. Then he shrugged as if her threat didn't matter.

Panic reclaimed her as she glanced over her shoulder for her horse. She must escape and ride home as fast as she could. At this very moment, C. J. might be dying at the hands of the savages who'd led him away.

The Indian seemed to divine her thoughts. He barely uttered two quick words, and his companions seized her again.

"Let me go!" She kicked one in the shin, aimed at a more vulnerable spot on the other and missed, but her attack did not a particle of good.

The leader brought her up short when he grabbed a

hank of her hair and jerked up her head. He leaned close and spoke slowly. She still couldn't understand his garble.

"Release me!" she screamed right in his face.

He blanched, then stood tall. The oddest expression claimed his face. Had she not known better, she'd have described it as remorse.

Without warning, his arm shot forward. Pain exploded in her jaw. Dimly, she realized she'd bitten her tongue and felt herself slowly falling backward. No, not falling. The Indians were lowering her to the ground. *How odd.*

Darkness.

Chapter Nine

Holden leaned forward, pushing the gelding ever faster. Though the horse covered the ground in long strides, Holden felt he moved at a snail's pace. Ignoring the hot wind that stung his eyes, he searched the terrain, alert to any movement out of the ordinary.

Nothing. He scoffed at his unfounded alarm. Still, the feeling persisted. He damned the Spirits for the mixed blessing of his insight. Today he could not read the signs accurately, only knew something was wrong.

Damnation, he had not realized how far he had chased the stallion. An eternity seemed to pass before he finally crested the last rise and looked down on the south pasture.

He jerked the gray to a halt, then patted his withers when the horse tossed his head in protest. "Easy."

He swept off his hat and brushed his forearm across his sweaty brow. Clamping the hat back in place, he fished the glass from his saddlebag. Peering through the telescope, he slowly inspected the entire area. A blackbird flitted from limb to limb near the stream where he had last seen

Samantha. He trained the glass on each horse. One foal grazed peacefully. He could not see the other, which was doubtless hidden in the trees.

Lowering the scope, he concentrated on the sixth sense that had served him so well for so long. Still there. The indefinable presentiment that something was amiss. He stowed the glass in the saddlebag, then spurred his mount.

A hundred yards out from the line of trees, he dismounted. With inborn caution he led the horse as he walked toward the stream, still hidden from view. Inspecting the ground as he went, he paused when he came to beaten-down grass. He squatted on his haunches, absently stripped off his gloves and stuffed them in his back pocket. Horses' hooves had cut grass stems and mashed them into the ground. But other lighter-tread prints claimed his attention. He rose and moved on, eyes trained on one indentation after another. Moccasin prints.

C. J. did not wear moccasins; Indians did. He knelt again to take a closer look. One clear impression showed the lacing knotted at the base of the heel. Comanches.

Had Samantha left before the braves arrived? He knew the members of Two Horns's band, but there were others he did not know. Regardless, his Indian brothers would simply view her as a white woman ripe for the taking.

Rising, he counted the few horses he could see. There had been a dozen or more earlier, but that meant nothing. He reasoned that several had drifted beneath the trees out of his line of sight.

Ever more cautious, he approached the scrub oaks and listened. The only sound was the faint rustle of swaying grass and leaves clicking in the breeze. Birds twittered now and then, which told him they were not alarmed. He crept downstream several yards before encountering the trickle of water.

A branch cracked. Immediately he saw a horse twenty yards away, head down, placidly eating. He dropped the reins so his own horse could drink and graze while he searched the area.

Glancing from side to side, he decided to head upstream since the faint breeze was in his face from that direction. If Indians lingered about, his scent would be carried away from them.

He had not gone far when he stopped midstep and sucked in a breath. Something . . . He heard it again. A moan? Leaning over, he wove his way into the trees, seeking a measure of cover to approach the spot whence the sound came.

Nothing could have prepared him for the fear that bolted through him when he saw her. Samantha lay sprawled on the ground, still as death. Earlier caution forgotten, he sprinted toward her, oblivious to the branches pulling at his shirtsleeves, slapping his face. He slid to a stop. His gaze swept her length, then he dropped to his knees.

"Samantha," he whispered past dry lips.

A red bruise marred her chin, and God of the white man, three buttons on her blouse were undone. His breath hitched, fear coiling through him like an insidious snake slithering close by. He glanced past her waist. Her jeans were undisturbed. Surely she had not been . . . He would not take the thought further.

Hesitantly, he pressed his fingertips to the pulse point at the base of her throat. When she moaned, he snatched his hand back. Afraid to touch her, equally afraid not to, he slid his hands under her shoulders and lifted her close to his chest.

"Samantha, wake up. What happened?"

The hunger to hold and protect her ran strong. Reluctantly, he eased her away, then brushed tendrils of hair from her temple. Cinnamon-colored lashes several shades darker than her golden hair lay thick on her cheeks. A dusting of freckles splashed her small nose. Unable to resist, he leaned to feather a gentle kiss on her well-defined lips, warm but unresponsive in her semiconscious state.

"Samantha."

A shudder shook her form as her eyes opened, though at first she did not see him. Then her eyes focused.

"No!" She lashed at him, her nails raking his cheek. "Let me go!"

She bucked in an effort to break free of his arms. He held her tightly and grabbed for her flailing arm, her fist aimed at his face.

"Easy. It is Holden."

"No!"

"Samantha! Stop it. I will not hurt you."

Stilling, she blinked, her eyes filled with so much terror that tears burned his own. Her gaze focused on his face, and in the next instant she lunged up and wrapped her arms so tightly around his neck he could not move.

"Oh, God! Holden, they took him!"

Took him?

New horror slammed into his gut so hard that he felt as if an iron horse had rolled over him. Little Spring . . . Guy. Had he followed them? The boy turned up in the most unlikely places.

Shaking as uncontrollably as she, he felt a world of anguish fill his heart. He doubted the People would harm Guy, but finding him would be like looking for a spoonful of water in the desert. He eased her arms from around his neck so that he could see her face. How had she escaped capture? "Samantha, the Indians took Guy?"

"No! C. J. They took him away. Arrows."

Relief swept through him, leaving him so weak he nearly dropped her.

"We have to find him. Holden, they'll kill him! They knew his name. They—"

"Wait! Slow down. Are you all right? That is the main thing."

"No. It's not. Listen to me! The Indians took C. J." She shuddered in his arms.

Holden pressed his fingers against her lips. "Please, Samantha. Are you all right?"

She shook her head as if to clear it. "Yes," she whispered, and in a thready voice, asked, "They . . . left me here?"

Holden eased back to sit, but he could not bring himself to release her. He cradled her against his chest, his heart thundering. He swallowed.

"I found you unconscious. Tell me what happened."

"They took—"

Again, he cupped his palm over her mouth to stop her babble. "From the beginning."

She winced. He snatched his hand away, realizing the slight pressure pained her already bruised chin.

"Sorry."

She explored the area with a tentative touch. "He hit me!"

Rage sizzled through him, much of it directed at himself for not being there to protect her. "C. J.?"

"The Indian. I thought I'd wake up . . . somewhere else." She frowned in bewilderment.

"Tell me what happened." Impatience roiled together with simmering rage.

Samantha shifted to sit up, hugging bent knees. Reluctantly, he released her.

Her gaze became unfocused as she remembered. "After you left, C. J. showed up. He tried . . ." Glancing down, she spied the undone buttons on her shirt and with shaking fingers did them up again. "He said that if he . . . took me, then we'd have to marry." An almost imperceptible shudder shook her.

"The son of a bitch!" Holden resisted the urge to draw her back into his arms. But right now, the last thing Samantha needed was a man's touch.

"We fought." She went on as if he hadn't spoken. "And then . . . I looked up, and they were there. We hadn't heard them." She shivered. "There were six of them."

He understood her disjointed explanation. "Indians?"

"Yes. C. J. wanted to run for help."

"He what?" Holden could not believe his ears. The sniveling little . . .

"I . . . Well, he didn't, of course." Tears shone in her dark eyes. "He tried, and they shot him in the legs."

"I heard no gun reports."

Samantha shook her head. "Arrows. Two of them shot him in . . . both legs. He fell." She gazed up at him. "They jerked out the arrows." After a moment she wiped her eyes. "Then they tossed him over his horse and left."

C. J. had attacked Samantha. It mattered not to Holden if they killed C. J. Butcher. "That is all?"

"All?" She looked confused. "Uh, no. The Indian, the leader, asked me C. J.'s name. He kept saying 'Carlence.' "

Holden shook his head, as confused as she. "His name?"

"Yes. It took a while to figure out that's what he wanted. When I understood he was saying 'Clarence,' I nodded."

Holden went utterly still. That hated name. The man had been right in front of him all this time? He clasped her arms. "His name is Clarence?"

"You're hurting me."

Dropping his hands away, Holden did not apologize. Instead, he pressed for an answer. "His real name is Clarence?"

"Yes! Clarence James." She frowned. "What's so important about his name? The Indian was so insistent. Now you—"

"What did this Indian look like?"

Samantha scrambled to her feet. "We sit here talking while those Indians haul C. J. off God knows where. We have to find him, Walker. He was injured. They'll kill him for sure."

Holden followed suit, towering over her. "What did he look like?"

"What do you think he looked like? A Comanche. Lord in heaven, Walker, haven't you heard a word I've said? I don't like C. J., but we can't leave him with them."

When he didn't move, she scowled, then glanced around. The only horse in sight was his own.

"I trained him. He will not let you mount." He planned to take her back to the ranch, but not until she answered his question.

She sighed. "He was tall. Not as tall as you, but . . ." She raised her hand and rested straight fingers against her upper forearm. "His hair hung to about here, and he wore a feather." She paused, worrying her lower lip. "And there was . . ." Clamping her fingers around her arm just above the elbow, she continued, "He wore a wide silver arm bracelet."

Swift Arrow. Curse the Spirits!

The desire to find and kill the hated Clarence had seethed inside Walks in Shadow for so long. Now, Swift Arrow would probably kill the vile man long before he could get his hands on him!

With lightning speed, he scooped Samantha into his arms, strode to his horse, and plunked her on the saddle.

"What are you . . . ?"

He swung up behind her. In two strides, the horse stretched into a gallop, headed toward the ranch.

"Walker, you're going the wrong way!"

"No. I will leave you where it is safe, then I shall find your Clarence."

She slammed her fist into his shoulder awkwardly. "He's not *my* Clarence. But he doesn't deserve to die at the hands of . . . Holden, I don't know how long I was unconscious. Don't you see? We need to see which way they've gone so we can get help."

"Do not worry."

He refrained from telling her Clarence Butcher was a

dead man, either at Swift Arrow's hand or his own. But his next words sent her into mute shock.

"I know the Indian you speak of."

Samantha rested against Holden's hard thighs, her back braced by the sturdy wall of his chest. She sighed with relief, ignoring the wind that buffeted her as the horse carried them to the protection of the ranch, to Aunt Mattie. Oh, how glad she'd be to see her aunt.

She felt safe in Holden's embrace, though she shouldn't. His unsettling words came back to haunt her. He knew the Indian. How? He'd warned her she wouldn't like who he was. Were the two connected?

And Aunt Mattie had said that Walker might not be the simple wrangler he seemed. That was a certainty after seeing how he gentled horses.

She stared at his hand holding the reins in front of her, the other resting on his thigh next to hers. Big hands, gentle hands. Not like . . . She shuddered again, reliving the way C. J. had clawed at her clothes, held her down.

Holden slid his free hand across her midriff and pressed her more closely against his body. He spoke above the noise of the horse's pounding hooves. "No one will hurt you."

She angled her head, but could only see his chin. Realizing he must have felt her shiver, she was astonished he'd divined her thoughts. Before she could think further, distant hoofbeats echoed a counterpoint to those of Holden's gray. He reined in as several horsemen came over a rise into view.

Oscar rode the mustang he favored, followed by several ranch hands. Next to him, Uriah Butcher kept pace. A cloud of dust preceded them, enveloping the whole troop as the men slowed, then stopped several yards away from Holden and Samantha.

Dear God, it wouldn't be easy to tell Uriah that Indians had kidnapped his son. But before she could utter a sound, Uriah's gaze settled on her bruised face. Then he scowled at Holden.

"What the hell ya done to Samantha?"

Walker's body tensed. "I am taking her to the ranch."

"After you beat 'er up?"

"Ain't no call for that, Uriah." Oscar stepped in smoothly. "Don't make no sense a'tall that he'd hit her, then bring her home."

"All we got is *his* word he was takin' 'er home."

"You have mine, Mr. Butcher. I have a tongue and can speak for myself."

"Your horse showed up at the barn, Samantha," Oscar said, his tone reasonable, though all the while he inspected her from head to toe. "We was worried, so we come out lookin' for ya."

"Your son is enjoying the hospitality of Comanches, Butcher," Walker said.

Samantha gasped. She'd intended to tell Mr. Butcher of his son's peril, but not so coldly.

Uriah's blue eyes rounded, then narrowed. "I sent Clarence out with Grogan and Sullivan. 'Less'n Injuns got the drop on three crack shots, which ain't likely, yer a lyin' son of a bitch."

"He isn't lying," Samantha said quickly, hoping to defuse the flinty anger that emanated from Walker.

"Samantha—"

"It's true, Mr. Butcher," she interrupted. "C. J. found me in the south pasture. He and I were fi . . . talking." No need to tell Uriah Butcher now that his son had tried to rape her. He wouldn't believe her, and she didn't want Oscar and the others to know. "They . . ." Should she tell him C. J. had been arrow-shot? "Six Indians took him away."

"And left you? That's a load of bull!"

"I know it sounds crazy, but"—she shrugged—"it happened." If she lived to be a thousand, she'd never understand why she had been spared.

"While you question Miss Timberlake, your son moves

farther away, Butcher," Walker said. Again, his voice fairly dripped ice.

"That's a fact," Oscar said. "But none of us is trackers. I don't know if'n we can find 'em."

"I will," Walker said.

Samantha believed him; his steely conviction was unmistakable.

He took over as if born to lead. "One of you take Miss Timberlake on to the ranch. The rest of us will backtrack."

He certainly did everything with ease. But she didn't intend to be left behind.

"We have wasted too much time as it is. I'll ride with you," she insisted.

Walker slipped his hands beneath her arms, lifted her as if she weighed no more than an empty duffel bag, and swung her out to land on her feet next to his horse. Without a word, he wheeled the gray and started back the way they'd come.

At the same time she cried, "Wait!"

Oscar agreed with Walker. "No, you ain't goin', Samantha." He glanced around and spoke to Daniel Arbuckle. "Y'all take her home," he ordered.

Daniel hired out on Timberoaks. His pay supplemented his folks' meager subsistence on a dirt farm a couple hours' ride southwest. The foreman knew that what they would encounter when they found C. J. could be mindshattering to such a young boy. Uriah and two other men took out after Walker.

"Oscar—" Samantha began.

"I ain't gonna listen to it. Your aunt would have my hide if'n I let you ride along. Besides"—he leaned down and caressed her cheek, his rough fingers trailing over the bruise on her chin—"looks as how you come out on the short end o' the stick. Y'all need to let Miss Mattie take care o' that."

She had no chance to protest further. Oscar spurred his

horse into a gallop. Left standing in the dust, she propped her hands on her hips and seethed with frustration. If she'd had her own mount, they'd have played billy-blue-blazes leaving her behind.

"Uh, Miss Samantha?" Daniel questioned in a croaking voice. "Y'all wanna climb up behind me?"

No, she didn't, but what else could she do? A wicked thought occurred to her. . . . She usually didn't snoop into other people's lives, but with each day that passed, with each encounter, Holden Walker became more mysterious. While he was gone, maybe she should have a look around his camp. . . .

Mattie sat on the porch churning butter. Bengy lay stretched out, his long back pressed against the wall. The moment Samantha and Daniel came into view, Mattie rose, strode off the porch, and met them halfway across the clearing.

Over by the barn, Lemuel Baker straightened from shoeing a gelding's back hoof. Guy was with him and started toward her, too, but the black man caught him by the collar. Samantha heard his voice, but what he said to Guy was indistinct.

"Dear heaven, where have you been, Samantha? We were worried sick when your horse ambled in without you."

While she spoke, her aunt's dark eyes assessed her as she slid from behind Daniel and landed on her feet. Mattie saw her bruise, stepped forward and raised her hand, but stopped short of touching the swollen jaw.

"That looks angry. What happened?"

Again faced with her earlier dilemma, Samantha hesitated to say anything before Daniel. She shook her head, then turned to the young man. "Thanks for the ride. Maybe Lemuel can use your help."

"Yes'm." Daniel dipped his head in assent and reined off toward Baker and Guy.

"Come," Mattie said, taking Samantha's arm.

She went, relieved to be home. Mattie passed the butter churn and Bengy without a glance, and steered Samantha through the house to the kitchen.

"Sit down while I chip some ice for that knot on your chin." Mattie plucked the ice pick from a nail shoulder-high on the wall, raised the icebox lid, and made quick work of piling chips on a spread towel.

It was then Samantha began to shake. She'd managed to face Oscar and Uriah. She'd ridden home behind Daniel and held herself together. Now that she was safe, now that she could give herself over to her aunt's care, she couldn't stop reliving the fear. Tears stung her eyes as Mattie turned toward her, folding up the ends of the towel.

"Oh, dear." Mattie stepped close and pressed Samantha's head to her breast. "Let it out, honey; then we'll talk."

Wrapping her arms around Mattie's waist, Samantha gave in to wracking sobs. Mattie's gentle hands stroked her hair. She cooed as if Samantha were a distressed baby. When at long last the sobs diminished to sniffles, Mattie pressed a square of linen into her hand.

She tucked fingers beneath Samantha's chin and lifted. "Do you want me to hold the towel?"

Samantha sucked in a shaky breath. "No. I can do it." She picked up the little bundle. Unprepared for the jolting sting when the cold cloth touched the bruise, she cried out. "Ow! It's sore."

"I should imagine so," Mattie said. "Would you like a glass of lemonade?"

"Later, maybe." She withdrew the towel a few inches, and with her other hand carefully fingered the swollen area. "The ice stings like the dickens. Is the skin broken?"

Mattie sat and leaned toward her for a close look. "No. But I won't be surprised if that bruise darkens the whole side of your face. Did you fall?"

Samantha shook her head. "He socked me."

"Who?" Mattie asked, bewilderment painting her features.

"The Indian."

Mattie's voice rose. "What Indian?"

"There were six. But that really wasn't the worst of it."

"I beg your pardon? Good grief, Samantha, you faced six Indians? What could be worse? How did you escape? Heavens, child . . ."

Mattie's questions came faster than Samantha could think.

"Tell me what happened. From the beginning." Walker's gentle, coaxing voice rang in her head. That was what she needed to do for her aunt. She hitched in another breath and gingerly laid the wet towel against her aching jaw.

"You know I took a horse to the south pasture and Walker went along to run off that rogue stallion. After Walker left, C. J. showed up."

"I thought he had gone out with Grogan."

"So did I. So did Uriah. Anyway . . ."

She found it difficult to relate what C. J. had tried to do. In halting words, she finally got it all out, ending with waking to find Holden leaning over her.

"I woke up thinking he was the Indian."

Mattie rested her hand on Samantha's shoulder, and gave a squeeze. "Honey, I'm sorry you had to go through all that." She shook her head. "As for C. J., I never thought he could be so . . . vile. Your father would have shot him."

In one way that was a comforting thought, but in another, Samantha felt sorry for C. J. She'd be the first to say he had been despicable toward her, but no man deserved capture and torture by Comanches. She cringed.

"Uriah must have gone into a rage when you told him about the arrows."

Samantha shook her head. "I couldn't tell him that, Aunt Mattie. Walker told him."

Her brow crinkled, recalling the wrangler's spiteful-sounding words. Okay, so Uriah had jumped to the wrong conclusion. Naturally it would gall a man to be accused of something he didn't do, but . . .

"Walker didn't spare Uriah's feelings one bit."

Mattie didn't comment. Instead, she reached for the towel. "Here, let me chip more ice. It's already melted. That bruise is probably feverish."

While she replenished the ice chips, Mattie said, "I'm going to heat water for your bath. Then you should lie down for a while."

"No. I'm all right."

"Of course you are," Mattie said dryly. "Nevertheless you're going to rest until supper. I won't hear further argument, Samantha."

An hour later, wearing a clean nightgown and tucked between crisp sheets that smelled of sunshine, Samantha welcomed sleep. She was exhausted, heartsick about all that had happened to her, to C. J. Her last thought before drifting off was that as soon as she could slip from the house without Aunt Mattie being the wiser, she would find Holden Walker's camp. Time to snoop.

Chapter Ten

"We're movin' too goddamn slow, Walker. While you diddle-daddle checkin' fer signs, Clarence and them Injuns is God knows where by now."

Holden had come to the end of his tether with Uriah Butcher. He fixed Butcher with unblinking eyes. "You think you can do better"—he swept his arm in invitation—"go right ahead. The Indians bait us."

"Whatcha mean by that?"

Remounting, Holden took a moment to answer. For four hours they had followed the trail of Swift Arrow and his companions. Somehow his blood brother had known that he would be the tracker. The signs Holden followed were reminiscent of years past when the two men practiced tracking each other.

"The signs disappear, then reappear. The Indians want us to follow."

"Ya leadin' us into a damned trap?" Uriah asked.

"No."

Oscar reined his mustang ahead of Uriah, kicking up a

cloud of dust that settled on already gritty hands and faces. "Walker, if ya think we'll fall prey to Injuns, maybe ya better knock off trackin'. I ain't puttin' Timberoaks men in that kind o' danger."

"The hell ya won't!" Uriah grabbed Oscar's arm and pulled him around in the saddle. "He said he ain't. I'm callin' the shots on Timberoaks, and I says you and yer men work for me. It's my son out there, and by God, y'all are gonna help find 'im!"

Butcher's outburst got about as much response from Oscar as it would have from a fence post.

Holden spoke into the silence. "If they wanted a slave, they would have taken Miss Timberlake. The Indians wanted C. J. Butcher."

"That don't make no sense." Uriah's face reddened with frustration.

He had lived on the range for forty years. It stood to reason he had seen his share of brutality by Indians and white men alike. Uriah's agitation telegraphed itself to the horses, which began to shuffle, tossing their heads and mouth bits. Each man kept a tight rein to avoid a horse bolting.

"They mean us no harm," Holden said in a level, calm voice. "I repeat my offer. Track if you can do better."

Fear shone in Uriah's eyes. He might have been a bully, but like most men, he put great stock in his son. His only legacy would be his son who lived on after him.

"Naw. But, dammit, git on with it, and quit this infernal stoppin' ever' turn in the trail. Jesus Christ, Walker, them Injuns'll disappear if'n we don't hurry up an' find 'em. And Clarence . . ."

Uriah did not finish his obvious bleak thought.

Darkness halted their search. Holden knew he was on the trail, but Swift Arrow's dim sign meant he would have to endure Butcher's muttering until daylight. Without complaint, Oscar and the other Timberoaks men unsaddled their horses, chomped some hardtack, bedded down and did not stir until daybreak.

As light strengthened, Holden lay with his head propped on his saddle and listened for familiar morning sounds. Quiet reigned. No wind, not a leaf moved. Not a single bird twittered a morning greeting. Unnatural quiet such as this made him uneasy, but now he waited for . . . he knew not what.

Sitting up, he looked about. This peculiar stillness meant something or someone lurked close by. Still, he felt no alarm. Careful not to disturb the sleeping men, Holden stood, then turned in place, searching for . . . what?

A ranch hand snorted in his sleep. Uriah turned restlessly as he had done all night. Walker's intent gaze passed over each man, then rescanned the surrounding terrain. Tall grass stood like a sea of bayonets in the early dawn. They had bedded down in the open, but near a few scrub oaks with scraggly undergrowth cloaking their trunks.

Holden's inspection slowed as he looked into the shadows beneath the oaks. His roving eyes skittered back to . . . a face. Dark skin, dark eyes, black hair. White teeth appeared when the mouth curved into a smile. Swift Arrow.

Neither man moved. Swift Arrow raised his arm, palm facing Holden, and stepped out of the foliage. Grim-faced now, in sign language he pointed Holden in the direction he should go.

Holden knew in that moment that he had been denied the vengeance that had kept him going for so long. Swift Arrow signaled that he, Bubbling Water's blood brother, had stolen vengeance from her adopted brother.

For endless seconds cinder-black eyes stared into green-gray ones. Then, in a few deft motions, the Indian he had known most of his life said good-bye. Swift Arrow might as well have hit him over the head with an ax. As surely as the Spirits breathed life over the land, he had seen his friend for the last time. Even worse, the quest that had kept him connected to Two Horns and his band for the past five years was finished.

His heart thudded painfully as Holden realized that, to the People, Walks in Shadow was no more.

He squared his shoulders. He had spent years relearning to be a white man. Now he would devote his time to Little Spring . . . and Samantha. A faint smile lifted his lips. Oh, yes. He wanted her, but should he claim her?

"Somethin' wrong?"

He looked over his shoulder at Oscar. The foreman kicked off his blanket, stood and stretched. The others yawned and scratched, slow to climb to their feet after a night on the hard ground. Again, glancing toward the trees, Holden bit back a gut-wrenching sigh. Swift Arrow was gone.

"As soon as everyone is ready, we will go this way." He pointed toward the spot where his blood brother had stood moments ago.

Oscar came level with him and peered into the trees. "You seen signs thataway?"

Holden nodded, strode to his horse and began tacking up.

Other than occasional mutters under his breath, Uriah was surprisingly quiet this morning. His eyes appeared unfocused, as if seeing something no one else could. His motions mirrored the other men's, but clearly his son occupied his vision.

Though certain his group would not encounter Swift Arrow's party, Holden nevertheless remained alert for any eventuality. Traveling at a walk, he was struck once again by the eerie quiet, as if nature were holding her breath.

Unease crept over him. His scalp tingled beneath his hat; the hair on his nape rose. His breath quickened. He was sure that Swift Arrow had already reaped revenge; it remained only for them to find C.J.'s body. Had he not sought death for the man who violated Bubbling Water? So why this reluctance to go on?

"What's the holdup? Y'all lost the sign?"

Uriah rode up next to Holden, who had unconsciously allowed his mount to stop. Ignoring Butcher's terse questions, he studied the area. He spied several large birds perched high in a tree up ahead.

Uriah followed his gaze. "Vultures!" he whispered. "Ya think . . ."

The unfinished question hovered in the air. C. J. had been in Indian hands since yesterday afternoon. Uriah had to be scared spitless about what they would find.

"Wait here. I will ride ahead and take a look," Holden said.

"Don't think so," Uriah argued. "We's been slow enough as 'tis. I ain't hangin' back like some lily-livered kid."

"Suit yourself," Holden snapped. He nudged his horse and rode on.

Unprepared did not adequately describe Holden when he first saw C. J. Butcher's body. Aghast, stunned, horrified—all these—and sickened.

"Jesus God!" Oscar exclaimed in a whisper next to Holden.

On his other side, Uriah made a strangled sound. Then, "Nooo," ricocheted through the trees like the wail of a locomotive's whistle.

Holden heard retching behind him and fought to keep down his own bile. Uriah dropped from the saddle, suddenly an ancient man. He shuffled toward his son's prone body, blubbering as if demented. The sight alone would have been enough. He collapsed on the ground within inches of . . .

The Spirits knew Walks in Shadow had sought retribution against the man who'd violated Bubbling Water. He would have gut-shot him, then made sure Clarence Butcher knew why before he bled to death. But this . . .

Holden swung his leg over his mount and lowered himself to the ground in slow motion. He need not go closer to see the slashes of dried blood on the man's chest. Carved in crude letters on pale flesh was the single name: *Clarence*.

Unable to pronounce the name, Swift Arrow had remembered how to write it. Holden recalled that evening before the campfire when he had unconsciously drawn those same letters in the sand. His blood brother had traced them.

Holden steeled himself to look at C. J.'s dead face. Lifeless, open eyes stared at the sky. But what had him fighting the urge to vomit were C. J.'s severed genitals, which spilled from his blood-smeared, open mouth.

Uriah rocked next to C. J.'s body, his face awash with tears. "Why? Why?" he repeated over and over in a barely audible whisper.

"Jesus have mercy," Oscar said as he, too, reluctantly stepped down off his horse. "I ain't never seen the like, Walker."

"Vengeance is harsh." He now knew why Swift Arrow had broken off further contact. Walks in Shadow had raided often after becoming a warrior, but he never sanctioned torture, and certainly not brutality such as this.

"Vengeance?" Oscar turned questioning eyes on him. "Ya think the Injuns what did this knew C. J., and . . . Jesus! Vengeance? For what?"

"Not my son," Uriah blubbered. He swiped a hand across his runny nose. "Not him," he cried, heartbroken.

It took several heartbeats before Holden could concentrate on Uriah's all but incoherent words.

"Dammit, boy, what was ya doin'? How many times I told ya to keep yer eyes peeled?"

Too busy causing Miss Timberlake grief, Holden thought. But it would serve no purpose to tell Butcher that now.

"Me. Why'n't they capture me?" Uriah bent double, arms wrapped across his stomach. "Me! I've lived my life."

Reluctantly, Oscar stepped forward. Holden understood. But C. J.'s wrists and ankles would have to be untied from the stakes driven in the ground. They would have to lift that mutilated body and give the departed man a decent burial.

"Come on, Uriah. We got to bury yer boy."

He whipped his head around, his tear-streaked face screwed into a snarl. "No!"

"We'll carry him home," the foreman persisted.

Butcher extended his hand toward Oscar in a beseeching manner, tears still flooding his face. "Why'd they carve him up like that? Why'd they cut off . . ."

"Indians make the punishment fit the crime," Holden said quietly.

"Crime?" Uriah gazed up at Holden. "My boy never done nothing to no Injuns. He steered clear of 'em just like I taught. . . ."

Butcher seemed to retreat into another world. For several seconds he swayed back and forth, transfixed. Suddenly he speared Holden with horror shining in his eyes. "It can't be," he whispered, then screamed, "It shoulda been me! Dammit, I did it."

Holden stilled.

Oscar put a consoling hand on the man's shoulder. "Come on, now. The boys and me will . . ."

Uriah shook off the gesture. "Ya ain't listenin'. Them Injuns kilt the wrong man! It was me found that Injun gal way back—"

"Uriah!" Oscar glanced up at Holden. "Think he's losin' his mind?"

"No, I ain't."

Oscar frowned and scratched his chin. "What you sayin', Uriah? They killed C. J. 'cause o' somethin' you done to a Injun girl?"

Quieter now, though tears still crawled down his cheeks, Uriah stared at his lifeless son. He spoke as though C. J.

could hear him, "I'm sorry, boy. God, I'm sorry. She was alone that day." He shrugged. "Hell, Clarence, wasn't like she was worth anythin'. Sure weren't worth this." His tears splashed on C. J.'s body. "Just a little Injun gal. No bigger'n a runt." His gaze unfocused, Uriah rocked back and forth, back and forth, as his words faded to nothing.

Oscar blinked and blinked again, then frowned at Holden. "He thinks C. J. was killed because he . . ." Oscar shook his head. "Jesus. Uriah's sayin' he raped a Injun girl, Walker. He thinks . . ."

For several seconds Holden forgot to breathe, transfixed by the man's confession. But Bubbling Water had called him Clarence. How could this be?

"He was," Uriah insisted. "Why ya think them dirty redskins carved my name into the boy's chest? 'Cause that little bitch told 'em. Goddammit, I thought she died. I left her—"

Abruptly, he stopped speaking to stare at Oscar's horrified expression.

"Jesus in heaven," the foreman exclaimed. "You sayin' you raped a Injun girl and left her to die?"

"Your name is Uriah," Holden said.

"Course it is," he snapped. "My middle name. Clarence Uriah Butcher. Like my paw afore me, Clarence Perkins Butcher, and his paw afore him, Clarence Josiah Butcher."

Poleaxed, Holden narrowed pale eyes on Uriah. "It is a family name?"

"Yeah, and it got my boy kilt." Uriah turned back to that boy, the evidence of his horrible death, and began blubbering all over again.

More than stunned by this turn of events, Holden looked around the little clearing. He noted the few Timberoaks hands still mounted. Oscar appeared stupefied, and disgusted by what Uriah had confessed.

Realization hit Holden. Though alive, Uriah would carry the heartache, the guilt, for the rest of his days. Because of his actions, his own son lay dead.

Greater vengeance than his own death? Perhaps. Holden had no son of his own, but he loved Little Spring like a son. If he caused the boy harm, it would eat at him forever.

Holden cocked his head to one side, listening to an inner voice. *Vengeance.* In that regard, Swift Arrow had satisfied his own sense of honor. Now, long-held hatred eased from Walks in Shadow's heart. The Spirits had exacted revenge on Clarence Uriah Butcher far better than he ever could. Holden flexed his shoulders, a terrible weight lifted from them.

Aunt Mattie hovered like a protective mother hen. It was late afternoon the next day before Samantha finally escaped the house. "I need to be alone for a while," she insisted. "I promise not to go far." In truth, though she would never admit it, she was a little afraid after the horrors of yesterday morning and her baffling escape from the Indians.

Walker and the men had not returned the past evening. Though that didn't bode well for C. J., it suited her purpose. She glanced up through the leaves overhead. Dusk would be upon her in an hour or less, and she had yet to find Walker's camp. She knew she'd headed in the right direction, so she must have passed the spot. It hadn't taken her long the night she'd found Walker and his magical-sounding flute, and she'd been on foot then.

Looking in all directions, she sighed, patted her horse, and mumbled, "At this rate I'll be old and gray before . . ." Her searching gaze skittered to a halt on a blanket-wrapped bundle dangling from a tree limb not twenty feet away.

Well, no wonder she'd missed it. Other than this cache obscured by leaves above eye level, there was no evidence whatsoever that Walker had camped here. The fire pit had been obliterated, the surrounding ground brushed clean of footprints. Leaves and twigs were scattered helter-skelter, maybe by the wind.

She dismounted and tied her horse on a loose rein to a tree. Hands propped on her hips, she gazed up at the parcel, wondering how heavy it was ... and how to get it down. Walker had tied the rope around the trunk well out of her reach.

Frowning, she looked for a log to stand on, and spied her horse. Remounting, she rode over and worried the knot that had tightened on itself because of the bundle's weight. When the slipknot gave way, the rope whirred through her hands. The bundle crashed to the ground with a clank. Her horse shied. She clamped burned palms on the saddle horn.

"Ouch!" She waved smarting hands in the air, then looked dolefully at the reddened flesh. Thank goodness they weren't bleeding; the skin hadn't broken.

Once again she secured her horse, then knelt to work on a much more cleverly tied knot. She noted the way it was fastened so she could retie it when she was done. He'd never guess that someone had rummaged through his things.

With the blanket corners folded back, she found the source of the clanking sound: tin cookware. But what caught and held her attention was the same bow she'd seen once before, along with a quiver that held half a dozen arrows. She froze. The image leaped to mind of arrows just like these imbedded and quivering in C. J.'s legs.

Hesitantly, she pulled one out, and couldn't help but marvel at the craftsmanship; she sighted down its length. "Straight as an arrow." A little laugh bordering on hysterical erupted. Unlike the lethal, iron-tipped arrows the Indians had shot into C. J., this one had a bone tip ... a blunted bone tip. Now that was odd.

Carefully replacing it, she picked up the bow. Though it was horrible in its use, again she admired the work that had gone into it, the wood polished to smooth perfection. Her stroking hand stilled. Too small for a full-grown warrior to use, this weapon had been made for a child.

Her breath hitched. Was Walker married? A stab of pain in the vicinity of her heart was so real, it made her gasp as she stared at the lovingly crafted weapon. Did he have a son for whom this bow was intended? That might explain the blunt tip.

For endless seconds she sat, unseeing and aching. She felt . . . loss? It couldn't be. Holden Walker didn't belong to her. He was a drifter—a good wrangler, yes—but a drifter nevertheless. Besides, regardless of the kisses he'd bestowed upon her, he had said nothing about how he felt. She shivered, reliving with vivid clarity those reckless moments in his arms.

Shaking her head, she clamped parted lips together. Nonsense! There was nothing between her and Walker, so why even think about it? Taciturn, even rude at times, he remained a total stranger.

She couldn't stop thinking about him, though. A scowl wrinkled her brow. What was he doing with a handmade bow and arrows? Of Comanche workmanship, unless she missed her guess.

Her eyes widened at a nerve-shattering thought. Had Walker lived with Indians? His words came back to haunt her. *"I know the Indian of whom you speak."* Had he been captured as a child? *"You would not like who I am."* An involuntary shudder shook her. Had he killed white men?

"Who are you, Walker?" she murmured. With his possessions spread before her, there was no time like the present to find out.

Casting care aside, Samantha began picking through the cooking utensils—nothing unusual—his clothes, a book. She paused and opened it, smiling when she saw it was one of those hilariously untrue accounts of how the West was settled by impossibly brave, never-miss-a-shot cowboys.

A second book puzzled her beyond measure. A child's grammar book. Why would Walker carry this? Unless . . . If he truly had lived with Indians for many years, maybe he'd needed it to learn proper English. It would certainly explain the precise way he spoke.

"What are you doing here, Holden Walker?"

A falling leaf brushed her face. She yelped, sure Holden had touched her, caught her unaware. Shivering as her dread eased, she focused her scattered thoughts on her missing horse.

She didn't care what fine point Walker had put on it when he'd said the animal might be taken from her, nor was she mollified by the exchange of gold. Darn it, he'd taken her horse, and she had yet to find out where. That thought sent her back to look further through his belongings. Maybe she'd find something that would tell her where he'd taken the stallion.

As she searched, she found more and more evidence that Holden Walker was not what he seemed. She began to believe he really had lived with Indians, especially when she spied the length of soft hide she'd seen on the blanket before. Unless she missed her guess, it was a loin cloth. Next she pulled out a pair of denims and exposed well-crafted moccasins as well as a strip of intricately beaded leather. To decorate a shirt? Or a wife's dress?

Pausing, she looked up, eyes bleak. Her heart ached, and she fought against the spill of useless tears. *Face it, Samantha, you've fallen in love with the man. If he's already married, and with a child to boot, he will never return your love. And yet, he's here without his family. Why?*

A gust of wind lifted her hat from her head. Reaching for it before it sailed away, she leaned on her other hand to keep from falling onto Walker's belongings. With an odd little sound something broke beneath her steadying hand.

Now Walker would know that someone had been rummaging in his things. Too late, she carefully lifted a pair of long johns and found a tintype, facedown. One corner had snapped off.

"Oh, no."

Gingerly, she picked up the pieces and tried to fit them together. Annoyed at her clumsiness, she turned over the photograph—and stopped breathing. A woman's solemn face stared at her.

This time she was unable to master the tears that stung her eyes. The woman was the loveliest Samantha had ever seen. His wife? Seated, the woman appeared petite and elegant. An abundance of lace ruffles framed her oval chin and spilled down the front of a form-fitted bodice. Beautifully coiffed hair detracted not one whit from large, solemn eyes. One hand lay relaxed in her lap; a closed fan was clasped in the other.

Feeling ungainly as a newborn calf, Samantha took slow breaths and blinked time and again to dry senseless tears. She might have fallen in love for the first and perhaps the last time in her life, but Walker was spoken for. Tears would change nothing.

A shiver tingled down her spine when she recalled how masterfully he'd held her. How glorious his lips felt upon hers. His wife was pretty, no doubt about that, but she must be crazy. If Holden Walker were *her* man, he'd play billy-blue-blazes leaving her to languish someplace while he wandered off God knew where.

Shaking herself out of her wishful but meaningless thoughts, she looked up. Startled by the darkness almost upon her, she realized Aunt Mattie would probably be frantic before she got back to the house. She set to work replacing Walker's possessions as she'd found them. As nearly as she could remember, anyway. Perhaps he wouldn't notice the broken tintype.

"Yeah. When goats purr."

Well, it could have been damaged during his travels, couldn't it? She arranged the two pieces together, then covered them with the long johns. Certainly the photograph could have broken many times over—even when he'd hoisted the cache into the tree. It was a consoling thought, even if she didn't really believe it.

A rustling noise stopped her cold. She peered into the trees. The sound came again, followed by a rabbit hopping into view. Whiskers twitching, he assessed her with his beady little eyes, then sprang away. She closed her eyes with relief and swallowed to alleviate a dry mouth.

Galvanized to action, she folded the blanket's corners as she'd found them. Frustrated that she couldn't recall exactly how Walker had tied the knot, she did her best, then started hauling on the rope to lift the bundle.

"Did you find what you look for, Miss Timberlake?"

The bundle crashed back to earth when her benumbed fingers sprang from the rope. *Dear God!* Not one sound had warned her. Walker was back, and he'd caught her snooping.

Dreading the encounter, she turned to face the man who had every right to think the worst of her. She hadn't taken anything. Still, her actions spoke no better of her than did his when he'd spirited away her horse.

What excuse could she give? Unable to find her tongue, she looked into his compelling eyes. Unsmiling eyes.

"Again I ask. Did you find what you look for?"

Chapter Eleven

Caught! Samantha couldn't utter a sound. The sight of Holden's magnificent chest kept her tongue hopelessly tied. His bare chest.

He'd bathed in the river. Trailing ends of slicked-back hair dusted his shoulders. Water rivulets slowly inched down over rounded muscles, caught in dark hair, glistened like trails of diamonds. She wanted nothing more than to sip the water from his sun-browned skin.

Holy moly!

"I . . . I . . . ," she stammered.

She stepped back as he moved toward her with the grace of a dancing stallion. He paused, looked down and dropped his shirt and hat atop his blanket-wrapped possessions. Strands of wet hair caught in beard stubble on either cheek as he looked up, pinning her with unreadable eyes.

Her insides fluttered. "I . . . I . . . ," she stuttered again when the insane thought swam into her head that she'd like to catch his wet hair on her fingers and tuck it behind his ears.

"I shall change my question, Miss Timberlake. You found something?"

"No!"

He cocked his head and surveyed the heap near his feet. "No? All I own in this world is wrapped in that blanket. Perhaps if I knew what you wanted, I would gift you with it."

Walker propped a shoulder on a tree trunk, crossed his arms over his muscled chest . . . and smiled.

Her heart thudded and her fingers clenched as she wondered about his smile. It looked . . . mischievous. Downright wicked. What was he thinking?

"C. J.," she said. What had happened to the man she'd known her entire life? Maybe the change of subject would distract Walker.

He stared at her for several seconds before he spoke. "He is gone. To his maker." Walker's lips thinned. "Perhaps to hell."

Samantha sucked in a breath. "Dead? No! The Indians . . ."

Holden Walker could be hard as rock. And yet, she had experienced his gentle side. When he'd held her, kissed her, she'd floated in ecstasy. When he'd dealt with Guy, he was understanding, sensitive.

"You do not want the details. His death was . . . unpleasant. After what he tried to do to you, he deserved it."

Tears of remorse sprang to her eyes. "I didn't want C. J. dead. Yes, what he tried was despicable, but he failed. I've heard enough talk about the Indians." She shuddered. "He didn't deserve to die."

Some indefinable emotion passed over Walker's face. *Regret? For what?* "Mr. Butcher must be grief-stricken."

This time there was no mistaking Walker's reaction. "Do not feel sorry for him. He deserves to suffer."

"Holy moly, Holden, the man's lost his only son."

"Perhaps."

"There's no perhaps about it. C. J.'s brother died when he was four years old."   .

"Hmm," Walker murmured, his expression enigmatic. "You were not there, Miss Timberlake. I promise you, Uriah Butcher brought this grief on himself."

"I don't under—"

"Enough. You have not answered my question," Walker interrupted, straightening away from the tree and starting toward her.

Intimidated by his purposeful stride and determined gaze, she panicked. She spun around and ran. Her hat went flying, but she didn't care. *There's no excuse for snooping.*

She should have known her cowardly retreat would spur him on. Within five yards, Walker's arm circled her waist. He yanked her backward against the wall of his chest.

"Running away . . . again?" His warm breath tickled her ear and cheek.

In the next instant, he whipped her around. Dizziness thrummed in her head. As he clasped her in his strong arms, every one of those taut chest muscles she'd admired moments before pressed against her.

An unholy light gleamed in his incredible eyes, as if lightning shone from them. "Father of the sun, I should never touch you," he muttered. "And never . . ." He swooped down and captured her lips with his own.

His sensual onslaught turned her bones to mush. She leaned into him, lost in his glorious embrace, marveling at his soft lips, the way his exploring tongue dueled with her own. A faint yearning cry issued from her throat as she wrapped her arms around his neck and pressed closer, wanting, needing . . . more. Oh, yes. Holden could go on kissing her forever!

He cradled her head in one big hand, his fingers tangled in her hair. The other explored her spine, her shoulders, teased down her side. His palm grazed the side of her breast. She shivered with anticipation.

He pulled her closer still, the intimate portions of their

bodies nestled so she could feel his need. Moments or an eternity galloped by. She didn't know which, didn't care. This was heaven.

Suddenly, he wrenched his mouth away and tucked her head beneath his chin. "God of the white man. I should not do this."

God of the white man? She chilled as if a bucket of ice water had been dumped over her head. She lurched back out of his arms and kicked him in the shin.

"How dare you," she seethed. "You, a married man, and with a child!"

Confusion etched his features. "Married? A child? What say you?"

"That! The way you speak. Who are you? I saw her likeness. And the bow. You made it for your son, didn't you?" She spat the jumbled thoughts in rapid succession, appalled at her own behavior. How could she succumb to his charms?

"You are mistaken."

"I'm not blind, Walker. I saw—"

"A likeness of a good friend."

"Men don't carry mementos of a *friend!*"

"I do. She is a . . . teacher."

She pounced on his hesitation. "You're lying."

Before she had time to react, he was upon her again, clasping her arms in a firm grip. She swung her leg to kick him, but he was ready this time. Stepping aside, he pivoted on the other foot, lifted her straight into the air and whirled around to set her down on her feet with tooth-jarring force.

"I can play your game for hours, Samantha. Settle down and we shall talk."

"Talk! I don't care what you have to say. You are nothing but a . . . a deceiver. You abandon your wife and child. Then you make inappropriate advances toward me. Release me!"

He did. Her mouth agape, she watched the exasperating

man turn his back on her and walk toward his belongings. Darkness had arrived, but she could see him well enough when he squatted, untied the bundle and flipped open the blanket.

She felt guilty as the dickens when he lifted the tintype and corner fragment. He looked over his shoulder, eyes reproachful, then brought out the bow and quiver. He sat back and crossed his legs, Indian fashion.

"I do not lie, Samantha Timberlake. You wish to know who I am. . . ." Resignation mixed with sadness in his voice.

Okay, perhaps he hadn't outright lied, but he had by omission. Uneasy, Samantha approached him, then circled to sit on the opposite side of the bundle. It would be dangerous to get close again. She peered into the trees where her horse had joined Walker's. The gelding was near enough that she could run and mount, maybe before Walker could react.

He apparently divined her thoughts. The corner of his mouth kicked up in a derisive smile.

Again, Walker picked up the tintype and fitted the two pieces together. Fortunately, the break hadn't spoiled the image. Samantha was thankful for that, but she squirmed, discomfited. From the way Walker stared at the photograph, she could not believe the woman was a mere friend.

"She taught me to read and write."

"You've carried that photograph since childhood?"

"No. Three years."

"Three . . . ? So recent? You're saying you didn't learn until you were grown?"

"True."

"But, why? Weren't there any teachers where you lived? Surely your mother or an aunt could have schooled you."

"I had none."

"You are an orphan?" That could explain his reserve.

"You might say that."

"Walker!" Aggravating man. He spoke in half-truths or not at all.

"English is unspoken by my people."

A large migration of Germans had moved into Texas. Was that what he meant? She shook her head. It didn't make sense. The few Germans she had met spoke English. Many with an accent, yes, but all were well versed in the language of their adopted country.

Walker laid aside the photograph and picked up the bow. His actions sent a chill through her. Again, the vision of arrows protruding from C. J.'s legs overwhelmed her. She could no longer avoid the truth. "You were raised by Indians." Her voice dropped to a whisper. "Weren't you?"

"Ha," he murmured, then lifted his gaze from the bow to spear her with those incredible wolf's eyes. "Yes. From two or three circles of the seasons."

"What?"

"Years, Samantha. Four seasons mark a year for my people."

Why couldn't he say it in plain English the first time? His fingers stroked the weapon, reminding her of his hand on her body moments ago. Thrusting away the lascivious thought, she took this opportunity to study him: his sable hair, now dry, his muscular physique. Walker's skin was naturally a shade or two darker than hers, but he owed the bronzed hue to the sun's relentless rays.

"Your people." She frowned. "You are as white as I, Walker. Indians may have raised you, but you're not of their blood."

A faint smile lifted his lips. "I am not as I seem."

Where had she heard that before? Aunt Mattie. The woman was so intuitive.

"Here"—he tapped his chest—"I am Indian."

"Did they teach you to gentle horses?"

"Comanches do not teach as the white man does."

"Comanches?" The word barely made it past her dry

throat as a nerve-shattering thought took root. "You know the Indian who socked me, the men who killed C. J."

Walker looked up and again gazed at her without speaking. Then he raised his right arm. It took a moment to understand what he intended her to see. A white scar slashed across his wrist.

"My blood brother," he said gravely. "You would not be here if Swift Arrow was not known to me. You would have disappeared into the *Llano Estacado*."

The dawning revulsion in Samantha's eyes reinforced what Holden had feared in his heart. His eyes were light, his skin much like that of the white man's. But inside, where it counted, he was Comanche. He wanted this woman, but it could never be. She despised him right down to her soul.

Samantha stood and wrapped her arms around her torso in a protective gesture. He expected her to leave. He would not stop her, he thought with bleak resignation. But she did not.

Instead, she walked away a few steps and gazed into the darkness.

Turning back, her expression thoughtful, she asked, "What about your son?"

His upbringing was damning, but further truth would cement her revulsion, possibly spawn hatred. His heart turned over at the thought, but he had already reached another painful decision about what he must do. Telling her now would only reinforce his commitment to that course of action.

Perhaps it was for the best.

"I have no son." He studied the bow still clasped in his hand. "It is for my nephew."

"How can you have a nephew if you've been with Indians since . . . ? Unless you married one."

He shook his head. "Little Spring is my adopted sister's son. She . . . Bubbling Water . . . died."

Though he spoke of an Indian, Samantha was painfully familiar with the death of a loved one and reacted with compassion.

"I'm sorry. How did she die?"

"The white man's measles took her to the spirit world."

Hesitating over his reference to the spirit world, she nevertheless persisted. "And the child?"

"He . . ."

Walker rose and paced away from Samantha. Taking a deep breath, he jammed his fingers into the back pockets of his trousers, and looked up at the stars glittering through the leaves. Telling the truth about the boy was the hardest. But what did it matter now? He had decided to leave . . . without Guy.

"Little Spring had seen more than one full circle of seasons when he was given to white people."

"Given."

He heard her approach. Turning, he looked into her troubled eyes and steeled himself to continue. "A white man violated Bubbling Water. Little Spring is half white. Swift Arrow did not agree that the white man will one day destroy the Comanche, but our chief listened. Little Spring would have surely died if I left him with the People."

Samantha's eyes rounded with shock. "You abandoned a child?"

Abandoned? He had never thought of it that way. It had broken his heart to leave Little Spring, but he had vowed to come back for him. And he had. But now he could not reclaim the boy. Little Spring had become Guy Timberlake.

Girding himself against the inevitable, he strode past Samantha, picked up the bow and quiver and thrust them into her hands. "Give these to Guy for me."

Confusion painted her features. She frowned. "Why would . . ." Understanding bloomed in her eyes. "Guy is the boy you abandoned! My God, Holden, how could you? What if Pa had taken him to Austin? God only knows what would have happened to him if my father had put him in the orphanage there." She stared at him, horror-struck.

"Bubbling Water assured me of your family's kindness."

"How would she know?" Samantha's brow smoothed. "Now I remember. That poor girl. Good heavens, she was little more than a child when Pa . . ." Her eyes rounded in astonishment. "She was Guy's mother?"

He nodded.

"Guy is an Indian?"

Anger such as he'd never experienced shook him. Why had he thought Samantha would be different from other white people? "He is half white, Miss Timberlake. Little Spring will not cause you grief because Bubbling Water gave him life."

She shook her head as if he'd slapped her. Her anger soared equal to his. "Now just a cotton-pickin' minute, Walker. Guy is my brother by everything but birth. If his mother was Indian, that's no skin off my nose. Aunt Mattie will feel the same. So climb down off your high horse."

His emotion shifted from seething anger to relief so quickly that he felt tears sting the backs of his eyes. He had not misjudged the Timberlakes. And Samantha? God of the white man, he wanted nothing more than to scoop her up and carry her away to love her . . . forever.

She stomped right up to him and slammed the bow and quiver against his chest. "I won't give these to Guy. He wouldn't know how to use them, and people might wonder. We Timberlakes protect our own." She glared at him. "Now I know why you're here. You came to take him away, didn't you?" Giving him no time to answer, she snapped, "You can't have him."

It was true. He had known for a long time, but it did not stop his heart from breaking. As the white man, Holden Walker, he was exactly what Samantha had believed him: a deceiver, perhaps, and a drifter. It was his lot in this life. His choice. No ties, no loved ones to come home to after a long day in the saddle. No woman to love until she was breathless and could not see straight.

"I want my horse." Though pain dimmed her eyes, she persisted. "Then I want you gone, Holden Walker."

When he returned the stallion, he hoped to see her once more. He would make a point of seeing Little Spring, if only from a distance. Then he would honor Samantha's demand. His gaze met her dark, troubled eyes, roamed over her face to memorize it. The curve of her stubborn jaw, the sensual bow of her lips. The wealth of shining hair.

Both pieces of his cracked heart shattered. "Ha," he agreed softly.

Chapter Twelve

Misery filled her heart and simmered in her mind, cloaked her like a burial shroud. She'd sent away the man she'd fallen in love with. Tears clogged her throat and dampened her cheeks. She dashed them away with the heel of her hand.

Slumped in the saddle, she let her mount mosey at his own pace toward home. He knew where to find the feed bin. The soft *thump, thump* of the horse's hooves stilled crickets' chatter in the grass as they passed. An owl hooted to her left.

Samantha felt the air stir over her head, heard the faint flap of wings. Then, from ahead and to the right, the owl hooted again. Or perhaps another one answered the first's call. Yips from a pack of coyotes floated in the air, signaling a meal run to ground.

Not until the leaves on a low-hanging branch brushed the top of her head did she remember her hat, forgotten near Holden's camp.

It was plain crazy. How could she love this man? A horse

thief. A man who had lived with Indians. Well, she couldn't hold that against him. Indians were people, no matter the color of their skin, their uncommonly violent ways. White men could be, often were, as violent.

But, above all, how could she love a man who had abandoned a child? Okay, so he'd come back. She hadn't pursued the matter enough to find out why he'd done such a thing. He'd said something about Indians dying at the hands of white men.

And, to make matters worse, how could he so callously consider ripping Guy away from her, from Aunt Mattie?

Yet none of that mattered. Not when it came to her wayward heart. Not when her body ignited at his touch, needing . . . whatever a man and a woman did when they made love. She didn't know exactly what the all-consuming heat in her body would lead to, but she'd wanted so desperately to find out.

With Holden.

The murmur of distant voices intruded upon her reverie. As she broke from the trees onto open ground, she was startled to see lights blazing from every window in the house. The bunkhouse, too. What in the world was going on?

The voices belonged to Aunt Mattie and Oscar, who stood on the porch, backlit by light that flooded through the open door. Her horse picked up his pace; the sound of his thudding hooves filled the night.

Aunt Mattie and Oscar broke off their conversation. Both stepped off the porch and started toward her. Oscar stopped, hooked a thumb on his gun belt, stuck a toothpick in his mouth and waited. Her aunt kept coming. Her ramrod-straight back and relentless march reminded Samantha of a soldier.

When they met halfway across the beaten ground, Mattie stopped and planted fisted hands on her hips. Her blazing eyes pierced Samantha as surely as the arrows had C. J.

"Uh-oh," she muttered to herself, and reined in.

If looks could kill, Aunt Mattie had just reduced her to the dust the Bible said all must return to. Her aunt didn't utter a sound.

Cowed by her scrutiny, Samantha said, "What?"

"What?" Mattie hissed and fell silent again.

Shifting anxiously from the discomfort of her aunt's unwavering anger, Samantha cleared her throat. She didn't need this. Whatever this was. She needed to be alone.

"Where the devil have you been?" Spoken low, each word was delivered like a bullet—Aunt Mattie had found her voice.

"Where . . . ?" She couldn't tell her aunt she'd been with Holden Walker, held in his strong arms—where she wanted to be again.

"Samantha Rose . . ." She braced herself for the lecture that always followed the use of her full name. "It has been dark for two hours." Mattie swept her arm. "Look around you."

Samantha did, realizing for the first time that it was pitch-black, and had been . . . well, a long time.

"We've got every man out looking for you. How could you be so thoughtless, girl? If you were younger, I would tan your bottom within an inch of your life for worrying—" Tears filled her dark eyes as Mattie cut off her own tirade.

But Samantha could finish the sentence without further prompting. ". . . worrying me, Oscar, and every man on this ranch half to death."

Samantha dismounted, now adding remorse to her other misery. She knew her aunt's anger stemmed from fear . . . and love. She'd been there a time or two herself due to Guy's harebrained antics.

"I'm sorry. I don't know what else to say."

As she awaited whatever else her aunt might throw at her—after all, she deserved it—Mattie surprised her. She crushed Samantha against her.

Despite her aunt's diminutive frame, Samantha found it difficult to breathe within Mattie's fierce clutch. Her entire body atremble, Mattie Crawford was nevertheless much stronger than she looked.

"Oscar told me the sad news about C. J., and when you didn't return, I . . . Oh, God, Samantha, if anything happened to you or Guy, I'd—"

"Shh," Samantha soothed, returning the embrace. "I'm sorry. I didn't realize it was so late. Please, Aunt Mattie, don't take on so. I'm all right." Debatable words, but she wouldn't reveal that to her aunt.

Stepping back, Mattie fished a square of linen from her pocket and quickly swiped at her nose. Turning, she said, "Oscar, please take Samantha's horse and bed it down. I want her inside right now."

Oscar tossed the toothpick to the ground, closed the short distance and took the reins from Samantha's hand. He said not a word, but reached over and squeezed her shoulder. She wasn't sure if it was a reassuring gesture to gird her for the possibility of Aunt Mattie's further tongue-lashing, or a thank-God-you're-all-right sign.

It didn't matter.

Samantha simply thanked her Maker for both of them. The love of these two, combined with Guy's, was all she could look forward to now that Holden was gone. Her heart constricted at the thought, but she pushed it aside and circled an arm around her aunt's shoulders to urge her forward.

"Let's go in."

After calming Mattie as best she could, Samantha climbed the stairs to bed. Looking at it from six ways to Sunday, it had been a hellish couple of days. Exhaustion seeped into her bones.

Fumbling with the buttons on her blouse as she headed toward her room, she wondered if the anguish she felt at losing Holden would fade one day. She consoled herself with the thought that she would see Holden again—at least once. Surely he would bring the stallion to her. A sad smile curved her lips when she remembered the gold nuggets hidden beneath her unmentionables in the bottom of the armoire. She'd return them to him, no more questions asked.

When she entered her room she heard a . . . sniffle? Frowning, she turned in place and listened. There it was again. No light appeared beneath the closed door to Guy's room across the hall, but she was sure that was where the sound came from.

Rebuttoning her blouse, she crossed to open the door a crack. The room was dark. Aunt Mattie had said Guy was asleep. Apparently not, for the sniffling sound came again, much louder this time.

"Guy?" she whispered and pushed open the door.

A dark shape hurtled toward her, and Guy launched himself at her. Startled, she closed her arms around him.

"Holy moly! Guy, what on Earth?"

She twisted, slamming her back against the doorjamb to keep from sprawling backward into the hall. Guy was not tall for his age, but he was sturdy. His arms circled her so tightly that she stretched her neck to relieve the pressure. His legs clamped around her torso at the waist, like a bear cub clinging to its mother for dear life.

"Where wuz ya?" he wailed. "I wuz so scairt, Samma! Aunt Mattie look'ted all over and cou'n't find ya. Oscar said, Oscar said . . ." he babbled.

"Stop, darlin'. I'm fine. I went for a ride and lost track of time."

Still sniffling, Guy pressed his runny nose against her throat. "I wuz scairt somethin' awful."

So much for keeping things from the boy. He hadn't been safely asleep as Aunt Mattie had thought. He'd heard every fear-induced word she had uttered to Oscar.

"I'm sorry, Guy. Please . . ." She didn't need to hold

him. He was plastered against her. "I . . . can't breathe, sweetheart." She pushed on his knees, but his vicelike grip didn't budge.

Staggering the few steps to his bed, she eased onto the mattress. "Come on," she coaxed. "I'm here safe and in one piece. You're drenching my shirt."

That seemed to get through to him. Lifting his head, he sat back slightly, his arms looped over her shoulders.

Guy drew in a shuddering breath. "I'm sorry."

She smiled as she wiped his face with the tail end of her shirt. With her other hand, she smoothed the unruly midnight hair from his forehead. "Don't be. It was my fault for worrying you and Aunt Mattie. I won't do it again. I promise."

Though he'd mastered his sniffles, tears still swam in his light blue eyes. As her own eyes adjusted to the darkness, her gaze followed her hand's brushing motion as she again slicked back his hair. Straight, thick hair, and black as the depths of a cave. When taken with his copper-hued skin, it was evident Indian blood coursed through his veins. Why hadn't anyone seen it before? Because the truth was bizarre.

Indians stole white children. Not the other way around. Of course, they hadn't stolen Guy, but an Indian child left on a white man's doorstep was . . . well, unheard of. The few men she'd seen of mixed blood had unfailingly been ostracized by white society. Disparagingly referred to as "breeds."

Shame washed through her when she realized she'd thought of them the same way. Now she faced a boy she considered a brother, a boy of mixed blood. Comanche blood. Plain and simple, she loved him. If anyone ever found out . . . She shook her head. No one would learn the truth from her. Not even Aunt Mattie.

"Where wuz ya?" Guy's voice quavered. He swallowed hard to control it.

"I rode into the woods. It was . . . quiet there. Peaceful, you know?" She smiled reassuringly.

"Um." Guy frowned for a moment, then leaned forward and rested his head against her breast. His stubby fingers clutched at her shirt, but he didn't overwhelm her this time.

Samantha sat for some time simply rubbing Guy's back, her thoughts veering to Holden Walker. She remembered the first time he'd seen Guy. How intently he'd stared at him. Called him "Little Man." A play on the boy's Indian name, Little Spring.

There had been times she'd caught Holden looking at Guy with . . . what? Sorrow, maybe. He'd missed years of Guy's life. She wondered how the man had kept his distance, had hidden his feelings. She didn't doubt that Walker loved this boy. It must have ripped his heart asunder to leave Guy here when he was young. At the time they'd guessed the baby to be a year old, maybe a bit more, because he could say a few words, some unintelligible. One had been "Unca." Comanche? Or had Holden taught him the English "uncle"?

Ever so slowly, Guy's body relaxed. His head felt heavy against her breast as he succumbed to sleep. Like everyone else, he was exhausted. He should sleep the night through. Other than repeatedly rubbing his back, she sat unmoving for several minutes until she was certain he wouldn't wake.

He still wore denims and a shirt. She eased off the pants, then covered him with a quilt. Though the room was now warm, as morning approached the air would cool. As she brushed a kiss on his forehead, a thought came to her. She stared at his sleeping face.

Her brow wrinkled as two and two began to add up. Bubbling Water had been raped by a white man. Had the Indian, Swift Arrow, believed that C. J. was the culprit? She shuddered at the thought, aware that it could be true. He would have been a young man, but it would have made no difference. C. J. had been ready to rape a woman he'd known all his life; he would have thought nothing of forcing himself on an Indian.

Then there was Holden's perplexing remark about Mr. Butcher. *"He deserves to suffer."*

As she eased Guy's door closed and crossed to her room, she realized she'd been kidding herself about giving Holden's gold to him without further conversation. She wanted answers to her questions.

As Holden approached the bunkhouse, a faint lightening in the Eastern sky heralded the new day. He cocked his head and listened to the horses shuffling in the barn. Smiling faintly, he heard indistinct voices behind the door before him. Probably the men were breakfasting before heading out to work. He raised his hand to knock but paused.

He scanned the distance between where he stood and the main house, then looked down at the hat in his hand and wondered if Samantha was awake. His body tightened at the mere thought of her lithe body beneath a quilt, warm and welcoming. Maybe not. He was sure that Samantha was a virgin.

Holden longed to teach her how to welcome a man, to school her in the art of lovemaking. He longed with a near physical ache to awaken the passion he knew simmered beneath her surface. No woman could respond to his kiss as she had without possessing unbridled passion. His gaze darted over the house's facade, from one upstairs window to the other. Was she abed in one of those rooms?

Absently, he raised his hand and knocked, his attention still on the house. If wishing would make it so . . .

Light flooded over him. He squinted at the man silhouetted in the doorway.

"Mornin'," Oscar said affably. "Come on in. We ain't movin' too smartly today."

Holden smiled at the foreman's appearance. Wearing a sleeveless undershirt half tucked into unbuttoned trousers, he stood on lily-white feet. One sock dangled from his hand.

Holden looked past the foreman. Grogan's scrawny, unclad lower legs dangled off the side of one bunk. A man above him lay prone, his head propped in one hand, in no hurry to crawl from his bed. Old newspapers littered the walls. Doubtless the men who could read had fingered the papers until they were tattered and faded.

"Whatcha got there?" Oscar looked pointedly at Samantha's hat.

"I found it . . . on a corral fence post," Holden lied and handed it to Oscar.

"Coffee's brewin'," the foreman said.

Holden could smell it. Inviting, but he declined the invitation. "I stopped by to say I am leaving for a few days. I have . . . business to attend to." No need to tell Oscar he would bring Samantha's stallion back. The foreman would learn of it soon enough. Holden didn't think Oscar Dupree would be pleased when he learned of the particulars. If he learned them.

"Leavin'? I'd planned to brand them broncs Grogan brought in the other day."

Branding was not a chore Holden enjoyed. He had done his share since his return to the white man's world, but it would never set well to put a red-hot iron on an animal. He wished there was another way to show ownership in this world. It made no difference to the Indian. They, and he while in their midst, stole branded horses as readily as unbranded.

"You comin' back?" Oscar asked.

"Yes, but probably I will not stay for long." The foreman frowned, but before he could speak, Holden continued. "That empty one-room place down by the creek. What is it used for?"

Oscar glanced over his shoulder, then stepped outside and closed the door. "Ain't used for nothin' now. Baker used to sleep there. Hiram said he'd never heard of a negra's skin color rubbin' off on a white man just 'cause he lived with 'em. He moved Baker in here." Oscar smiled faintly and waved his hand in the general direction of the bunkhouse behind him.

"I see," Holden replied thoughtfully. Too bad he had not had the chance to know Hiram Timberlake. He must have been quite a man. "Would Miss Timberlake be willing to rent it?"

Oscar barked derisively, "Who'd want it?" He looked up at Holden. "You?"

"No. Perhaps a friend of mine might find employment in this area. A schoolteacher."

Oscar's eyes widened. "We ain't had nobody willin' to stick around these parts to teach the few young'ns needin' learnin'."

"Miss Mattie mentioned that Guy could use some schooling."

Oscar laughed. "Well, he could, that's for dern sure, but don't know if he'd take kindly to bein' cooped up in a schoolroom. Besides, they ain't that many folks willin' to pay the price for a man to do nothin' but teach."

Holden wasn't surprised Oscar jumped to the conclusion that the schoolteacher was a man. And he would not tell him otherwise. Not now. Oscar would see for himself soon enough.

He would offer to pay the first year's salary in advance, to ensure Lillibeth a place to work. And he would help clean up the small place. It already housed a bed and shelves for storage. A rusted water pump stood outside the back door of the one-room dwelling.

Oscar scratched his belly and speared the gnarled fingers of his other hand through sparse, sleep-tousled hair. "I'll speak to Miss Mattie. Never know," he said, shrugging. "They might be tickled to have him. Samantha don't give a lick about nothin' but horses, and Miss Mattie is busy as all get-out."

Holden didn't doubt that Miss Mattie was busy. Besides cooking and cleaning, she cultivated a good-sized garden, and Guy helped with the weeding. But he wondered if

Samantha Timberlake's thoughts were always and forever centered on horseflesh. His own flesh rose, tightening his jeans. No. Last night Samantha had thought of—wanted—something else. What he longed to give her.

Chapter Thirteen

"Here's your hat, Samantha. Best you not leave it layin' around."

Samantha stared in astonishment. "Where did you find it?"

"I didn't. Walker give it to me earlier this mornin'."

"You saw him?" He had been here talking to Oscar? Holy moly, what had he said?

"Leavin' yer hat on a fence post is a good way to lose it, girl."

Relief flooded her. So Walker had apparently not divulged the details of their conversation of the previous night.

"That young feller don't stay lit in one spot very long. Said he'd be back, but he had some business somewheres." Oscar shook his head. "Sure coulda used his muscle this mornin'."

He did leave! Her heart plummeted. But what could she expect? She'd told him to. He'd better return, though . . . with her horse.

A vision of Holden standing in the twilight, his bare chest gleaming with water droplets, assailed Samantha. Heaven help her, she would see him half dressed in her dreams forever.

A few feet away, Guy came out of the barn trailing Grogan, who led a horse. Turning at the sound of hoofbeats, she spied Uriah Butcher approaching much too fast. He veered toward the barn and pulled up, sending dust over everyone. The tethered mare pranced. Grogan said something but his words were drowned out.

"Dammit, Clarence, what ya doin' here?" Uriah bellowed.

Samantha and Oscar exchanged perplexed glances as Uriah dismounted and stalked toward Guy.

Before she or Oscar could react to his mystifying question, Uriah grabbed Guy by the arm and yanked him so hard that the boy yelped.

"Ain't I told ya to tell me where yer headed? I'm a mind to beat the shit out of ya!"

Galvanized by his violence, Samantha charged toward the two. "Stop that, Mr. Butcher. Take your hand off Guy."

"Guy, hell. Clarence . . ."

Oscar passed Samantha as if she stood still, and clamped a restraining hand on the older man's arm. "What in hell ya think yer doin', Uriah? Let that boy go."

"I told Clarence—"

"That's Guy!" Samantha shouted.

"It ain't . . ." Uriah's eyes clouded with confusion as he released Guy's arm and glanced around as if he didn't know where he was. He looked down at Guy, who peeked from behind Oscar's protective body. Bewildered, Uriah said, "Where's Clarence? I been lookin' ever'where and I can't find that no-account this mornin'."

Oscar looked at Samantha, as confused as Uriah; then his brows lowered in a frown. "Uriah, he ain't here. Don't you remember? We buried yer boy."

"No. He . . ." Uriah's eyes darted every which way.

"Come on, man, let's have a cup of coffee. Sounds like ya need it." Oscar clasped Butcher's arm. With his other hand, he gave Guy a little shove in Samantha's direction. "Take him inside," he said out of the side of his mouth.

She didn't have to be told twice. She scooped her brother into her arms as if he weighed no more than a chicken. Had Mr. Butcher lost his mind? She vowed to keep Guy far away from him.

"Why'd Mr. Butcher call me Clarence?" Guy asked. His voice shook with every jarring step Samantha took as she hastened into the house.

"He's a bit . . . addled, sweetheart. Don't pay him any attention."

As he slid out of her arms to his feet, Guy rubbed his arm. "He squeezed'ed awful hard. It hurt." Tears swam in his eyes.

She knelt in front of him, brushed his hand aside, and rolled up his sleeve. "No bruise, sweetie. He didn't mean it. Mr. Butcher is just upset."

"Why?"

Should she tell him the truth? He'd hear it anyway, and it would be better coming from her than someone else. Maybe.

"What's going on?" Mattie stood in the parlor doorway, a dust rag in her hand.

"Mr. Butcher called me Clarence," Guy said.

Mattie's eyes darted from Guy to Samantha.

"He doesn't seem to remember what happened to C. J."

"What happened to C. J.?" Guy's little brow puckered.

There was no help for it. He would have to be told the truth, but Samantha hesitated, glancing imploringly at her aunt for guidance. And, bless her, Mattie grabbed the reins.

"Come into the parlor, honey." Beckoning Guy forward, she turned and strode back into the room to sit on the sofa. She patted the cushion next to her.

He crawled up beside her, his look expectant.

"Honey, you know how I told you your pa has gone to be with the Lord?"

Guy nodded in solemn assent. Samantha leaned a shoulder against the doorjamb to listen. Better her aunt explain the unexplainable. Samantha would probably botch the telling.

"Well, although he was a lot younger than your pa, C. J. has gone to be with the Lord, too."

Maybe, Samantha thought, then castigated herself for the unkind thought that C. J. more likely had descended into hell.

"Why?"

Mattie fumbled with her apron, obviously wrestling with how much to tell the child. She breathed deeply and plunged in. "You know how we always warn you not to stray away from the house? C. J. did, and he ran into Indians."

"Injuns?" Guy's blue eyes rounded like silver dollars. "He saw Injuns?"

"Yes. They took C. J. with them, and he . . . died."

"You mean they kilt him? Like Pa said they used to?"

"Yes," Mattie said, as honest as she could be without going into detail, for which Samantha blessed her.

"But why?" he persisted.

Mattie shook her head. "I don't know, honey. Sometimes men are mean and sometimes they aren't. You must always mind what you're told. Never stray far from the house."

"I won't, Aunt Mattie. I promise I won't."

Mattie gave him a hug. "There's fresh cookies cooling on the kitchen table. Go help yourself. Two. No more."

"Okay. Cookies!" His face alight with pleasure, Guy scrambled off the sofa and sprinted past Samantha, his boots clattering loudly on the bare floor. How quickly children recover, she thought, their minds slipping like quicksilver to pleasant thoughts. Sweets. The heavenly smell permeated the house.

In the silence that followed, Mattie looked up at Samantha. "What do you mean, Uriah thought Guy was C. J.?"

"I think Mr. Butcher's lost his bearings. He scared me almost as much as he did Guy. He was so . . . so demented."

"Where is he now?" Mattie rose and strode to look out the front door.

"Oscar took him to the bunkhouse. For a cup of coffee." She smiled tremulously. "What would we do without Oscar?"

"I don't know, dear, and I don't want to find out. He's solid gold, and priceless to the operation of this ranch." Mattie smiled. "He's more family than hired hand, and that's a fact."

Samantha agreed. Since her father's passing, she had called upon Oscar's strength more than she cared to admit. One day she hoped to take the reins and run this place. But not yet, she told herself. Uriah Butcher's menacing image plagued her mind. Technically he still managed her ranch. Now that he seemed to be crazy, maybe he wouldn't make his presence felt.

The man she longed to have next to her was gone. She breathed a sigh of gratitude for Oscar, the bulwark who stood foursquare on Timberoaks soil.

"You're out of your mind!" Alarm fairly shimmered in Lillibeth's golden eyes.

Exhausted from hard riding, Holden slapped his dusty hat against his pant leg. He had covered the distance to Waco in a day and a half instead of three full days, with night rests thrown in. He felt an urgent need to return to Timberoaks. To Samantha.

Once assured that Black Magic had been well cared for, though the stallion was skittish from lack of handling, he had come directly here. Now Lillibeth had her back up, unwilling to consider his proposal. He would have to change her mind somehow. She did not belong in this brothel. But convincing her of that fact would prove difficult.

"No. I am quite sane, Lillibeth. Do you have anything to ease a parched throat?" he asked, changing the subject. He needed time to marshal his arguments. He kicked himself for not foreseeing Lillibeth's fear.

"Yes. Of course." She turned to the bureau.

As she lifted a decanter, he said, "Water, not liquor."

She set down the crystal container and lifted a frosted metal pitcher. Her small teeth worried her bottom lip as she poured the cold water into a glass. "Here you go." Obviously distracted, still mulling over what he had said, she looked everywhere but at him.

"May I sit down?"

"Of course, Holden. Make yourself at home."

Not what he wanted to hear. The tone implied that this was her home and would be for as long as she drew breath. Not if he had anything to say about it. Lillibeth deserved more, a better life. He was here to see she got it, and he would not leave Waco without her.

Seating herself on the sofa as far from him as possible, she frowned into his eyes. "I could no more move onto this . . . Timberoaks ranch than I could take wing, Holden. What if they found out who, what I am?"

"What you are is a decent woman, a fine teacher. You will be a good schoolmarm for Guy Timberlake and the other youngsters in the area."

Lillibeth surged up off the seat. The light fragrance she wore drifted to his nostrils. She paced away a couple of feet, then turned back and swept her hand downward in front of her body. "Have you looked at me, Holden? Really looked at me? Dear God," she wailed. "I wear scanty gowns. I wear paint on my face. I pleasure men every day and night of the week."

Holden's gaze roamed over her petite but luscious curves. The black-and-pink striped gown she wore was colorful, but not as revealing as those he'd seen on others, and the paint on her fine features was negligible. He could not argue the last point. Holden had firsthand knowledge of Lillibeth's talents. But they had no bearing on her ability to be a fine, caring teacher.

He shook his head, then quaffed the remaining cold water. Setting the glass on the small table near his elbow, he relaxed against the sofa back and cocked an ankle over his opposite knee. "Soap and water does wonders on paint." His lips curved in a faint smile when she *tsk*ed at the remark. "You can wear different clothes, Lillibeth. As for your other argument, who is to know about your past employment?"

"Anyone who passes through. A saddle bum, for heaven's sake. You."

"I would never reveal your past. Is that what frightens you?"

"I'm not frightened!"

He chuckled at her defiant response, her ruffled feathers. "Could have fooled me," he murmured.

She returned to the sofa, a cloud of satin settling around her like a nest. Hands clasped in her lap, she implored, "Holden, listen to me. I would be mortified if the women there discovered my past. Here, everyone knows. I'm immune to it in this town."

Tears sparkled in her eyes. Immune she was not, even if she wanted him to believe so.

She went on relentlessly, "I've suffered hateful glances, cold shoulders. But to go through it again . . . Think how those women would react if they knew a whore lived in their midst."

Holden clapped his hand across her mouth. "*That* you will not call yourself, Lillibeth," he said sternly, then lowered his hand. "You are one of the most honorable women I have ever known. How you have been forced to make your way is beside the point. Look to the future." Before she could demur, he continued. "You can and you will leave this place. If I have to carry you over my shoulder, you are going to Timberoaks."

"Oh, Holden." Her breath hitched as she took a deep breath and searched his features. "Why are you so determined about this?"

It was his turn to fidget. His long fingers picked at grass that had speared into the seam of his trouser leg as he had cantered over the prairie. He had never given Lillibeth a full account of his life. She'd figured out on her own that he had lived with Indians. That he was more redskin than white in heart and mind. Especially when he had first arrived on her doorstep.

She did not know about Little Spring and Bubbling Water. After the way Samantha had reacted, the dismay in her eyes, he did not want to see the same expression in Lillibeth's. Though that response would not be as gut-wrenching to him as Samantha's, still, he liked Lillibeth, and wanted to remain her friend.

"Holden?" she coaxed.

He sighed. "Miss Timberlake has a young brother. He's a . . . special young man. He needs schooling every day, not as he is now taught."

"And what does that mean?"

"A special boy, or how he is taught?"

"Holden!" she snapped, sounding like the schoolmarm she was meant to be.

He could not avoid saying more than he wished, he supposed, but he managed to tiptoe around his personal involvement. "Miss Timberlake is a horsewoman, first, last and forever. She will not close herself into a room long enough to properly teach the boy. His aunt is far too busy to teach him often." He glanced to see if she believed him. It was the truth, as far as it went. "There are a few other families scattered about with children. I believe they will bring their youngsters to you if you are employed by the Timberlakes." He added another half-truth. "Besides, I have already said you would come."

"You what?" Lillibeth's eyes rounded as she half rose off the sofa before settling back, agitated as the dickens. "You had no right to do that, Holden."

He grinned. He could not help it. Whether she liked it or not, he had her corralled. He knew from her response that she would go. Unwillingly, perhaps, but she would go.

She missed him.

Overwhelmingly.

Samantha wanted to kick herself, but there it was. Holden Walker had stormed into her life as swiftly as a blue norther raged over the prairie. And just as unexpectedly, he had captured her heart.

A horse thief, for heaven's sake.

"Can I go down to the creek?"

She jumped at Guy's sudden appearance in the barn, where she purposely kept herself busy mucking out stalls. Not a chore she enjoyed. She avoided the odious labor whenever possible. Baker or one of the other hands usually wielded the pitchfork she now lifted filled with heavy, wet straw that more than one horse had used as a privy. Her nose wrinkled and her eyes burned at the pungent odor wafting in the air.

Straightening, she leaned against the upright handle clasped in her hand. "That's quite a ways from the house, Guy. Can't you find something to do closer to home?"

"Aw, Samma, I ain't been fishin' for a long time. Ain't seen Mr. Butcher for a long time neither."

True enough, and Samantha thanked the Lord for that. He hadn't been back to the ranch since his irrational episode four days before.

"Please," Guy begged, his blue eyes hangdog sad.

She fought back a smile. He could charm a pack of starving coyotes out of their dinner. Well . . . "Did you ask Aunt Mattie?"

"She's busy," Guy replied.

Nothing new in that regard, Samantha thought. But

should she allow her brother to scamper that far without Aunt Mattie's say-so? Of course, that was handing off the responsibility that she should assume. With her hand at the small of her back, she stretched. Maybe she should take a break and go with him. She'd worked like a demon for days. Shaking her head, she forced away the reason for her hard work because it only led to thoughts of mesmerizing wolf's eyes.

"Samma?"

She sighed. Persistence was Guy's middle name. The stream really wasn't that far. "I suppose it will be all right. Wait!" she cried when he spun around to leave. Groping in her pants pocket, she drew out her father's pocket watch, which she'd been carrying. Ten-thirty. "You come back at twelve. If you don't answer the dinner bell, I'll come looking for you, young man."

"Geez, Samma, I won't hardly get my line in."

She waited and didn't relent.

He frowned, but reluctantly agreed. An hour and a half to fool around at the river should be plenty of time to get soaked, all part of the fun. And these warm days would soon draw to a close. The past couple of evenings she'd donned a coat to night-check a near-to-foaling mare. The chill definitely heralded fall, and if the coming winter brought anything like the last, it would be a long, cold season. Though rare, it might even snow.

Would Holden move into the bunkhouse then?

*Tsk*ing, she again bent to her task. He probably wouldn't stick around long enough. The woman in the tintype, whom he undoubtedly knew intimately, would entice him away from Timberoaks . . . from her. Samantha's heart constricted, but she doggedly speared straw and dumped it into a wheelbarrow.

Stop wishing for what can never be.

Chapter Fourteen

Late the third day out from Waco, Holden champed at the bit. Doing so would not make the miles fly any faster beneath his mount's hooves. Not a chatterer, Lillibeth had proven capable of handling the two-mule team that drew her wagon along the road, leaving Holden too much time to think. Mile after mile the only sounds were the creak of saddle leather and harness, the rumble of wagon wheels over hard-packed ground, the occasional *scree* of a bird.

Disjointed thoughts—regarding Guy, seeing Lillibeth settled on Timberoaks—always circled back to Samantha and her response to him. Lord of the white man, he so wished to be the first to explore her passions, to bring her to fulfillment, to love her as fully as he envisioned.

Envision he did.

It took little imagination to picture Samantha wearing nothing at all. The times he had held her in his arms, though she was soft and yielding as he expected a woman to be, her body had been taut with desire. Her skin, much lighter than his, would surely turn rosy with heat, and her nipples . . .

He pictured them as dark rose rather than brown-tipped, and large. When they were pressed against his chest, he nearly went mad with the need to caress them, take them into his mouth, circle each with his tongue, nip them, suckle . . .

He groaned.

"Are you all right?"

Lillibeth's question dropped him like a stone from near heaven to the dust-clogged road and the hard saddle. He shifted uncomfortably and glanced at his companion.

The reins were held tightly in her small, gloved hands. The tendons in her forearms were taut from long hours of maintaining control of the animals. He noted the westering sun; he must find a suitable place to stop for the night. Alone, he would have ridden straight through, but he could not ask that of Lillibeth. Driving a wagon lengthened the trip another full day from riding solo on horseback.

Had he been alone, he would have arrived at Timberoaks sometime yesterday. "I am fine," he finally said, "but we must stop before long."

He searched the broken terrain ahead. Dry hills undulated in every direction, some topped with scraggly trees, others bare except for scrub growth or rocks. Recognizing their location, he pointed to the southwest.

"There is a narrow stream in the gully past the next hill. We will camp there for the night."

Lillibeth bit her lip as she surveyed the area ahead, then glanced skyward. "It won't be dark for another hour. I can go a bit farther if you wish."

"Past this area we will find no water until midday tomorrow. The animals need it."

She smiled. "And us?"

"That too." He grinned back.

If he had to choose a traveling companion, he could not ask for better than Lillibeth. No complaints, even though she must have been hot and uncomfortable. Her poke bonnet, once-white shirtwaist and dark skirt wore a coating of fine dust kicked up by the mules.

When Holden asked Lillibeth to pull up, she looked around the clearing. He shrugged when her roaming gaze settled on the trickle of water. "The stream usually runs deeper." He shook his head and laughed at her skeptical glance. "Sorry, no bath tonight, but you can wash off the top layer." When she did not respond, simply gazed longingly at the nearly nonexistent stream, he added, "Barring problems, we will arrive at Timberoaks tomorrow evening."

His announcement did not have the desired effect. Instead of thinking about the luxury of a bath, she looked worried. He had assured her she would be accepted, that everything would work out, but she still harbored misgivings. She now looked the part of a respectable woman, yet until she met the people on Timberoaks, further assurance was pointless. So, rather than try, he settled the stock, then gathered up a small bundle of fallen branches for a fire.

Lillibeth paused in her efforts to extricate a pouch of foodstuffs from the wagon. "Is it safe to light a fire, Holden?"

Neither had spoken of threats until that moment, and he did not know exactly what to say. Danger lurked everywhere in Texas. If not from marauding Indians, then from cutthroat white men willing to kill a traveler for nothing more than a tin of coffee; throw in snakes, scorpions, coyotes and the occasional bear . . . Safe? No. But her concern centered on Indians and he knew it.

"I have seen no sign of Indians, Lillibeth. It is safe enough."

"No sign . . . What do you look for?"

"Several things, but unshod hoofprints are a first sign."

She tilted her head and asked gravely, "Indians are the least of your fears, aren't they?"

"Hmm," he responded noncommittally, and continued to lay the fire for coffee. Finished, he stood and stared at her steadily. "Lillibeth, you are more apt to be struck by a snake than harmed by Indians . . . when I am with you."

She paled and glanced down, her eyes searching the ground in every direction. "Snakes. Good heavens, I hadn't even thought of them."

"Sorry. I should have said nothing, but you seem afraid of something that is not a true threat." He relieved her of the sack. "Come, we will eat before it is dark; then you should bed down on the wagon seat."

"That's why you suggested I sleep up there the past two nights, isn't it? Snakes," she said again.

"And other varmints that crawl on the ground."

She planted her hand on her hip. "Holden, you can stop right there. I don't need chapter and verse about . . . everything!"

He grinned, pleased he had sent her fears in a safer direction.

An hour or so later, Holden gazed up at the night sky. Tomorrow he would see Samantha again. His body quickened at the thought. Wishful thinking.

"Holden?"

He glanced over his shoulder, surprised to hear Lillibeth's voice. She had made no sound for the past fifteen minutes. He had thought her asleep after the grueling day on the trail.

"Yes?" His night vision as keen as ever, he saw her sit up on the wagon seat.

"Would you like to talk about it?"

"I do not know what you mean, Lillibeth."

"Who is she?"

"Who?"

Even with starlight the only illumination, he saw her golden eyes flash with amusement. She chuckled as he walked toward her.

"The woman who has you tied in knots."

He stopped next to the wagon. "There is no woman."

Again she laughed, then shook her head. "Do you forget

who, what I am, Holden? I know frustrated desire when I see it."

Did others see it as well? No. He had honed his impassive expression to reveal nothing of his thoughts. Two Horns had been an excellent teacher in that regard. Watching the chief deal with members of the band or Indians from other bands had taught him to hide his emotions.

"You are mistaken," he lied in an effort to forestall Lillibeth's probing.

"I don't mean to pry, Holden, but I think talking might help. Maybe you see obstacles that don't exist."

They are there all right, he thought. *I am more Indian than white. I am a horse thief in her eyes. And I abandoned a child, for which Samantha damns me most of all.* Disturbed, the horses and mules snuffled. He peered into the darkness beneath the trees where he had tethered the four animals. Black Magic nodded his head as if irritated, then stretched his neck and nipped the rump of Holden's gray. A whinny of pain erupted from the abused horse.

Thankful for a reprieve from Lillibeth's astute questions, he strode over to the stock and walked between the two animals. With a comforting hand on the gray's rump, he looked at the black and spoke quietly.

"Settle down, my friend. We have not much farther to go. Then you can kick up your heels . . . in a corral," he added.

The black didn't seem to like that. He stretched his neck, teeth bared for another bite, aimed at Holden this time. Raising his hand, Holden butted his palm against the animal's soft muzzle.

"None of that." He chuckled.

Black Magic pulled back, raised his head as far as the rope would allow, and rolled his eyes. Apparently this human was not intimidated by his big, sharp teeth. Holden laughed outright. Slowly, he raised his hand to rub the horse between twitching ears. Black Magic stood stock still. Then a shiver rippled his sleek coat, as if the gentle gesture pleased him.

Holden knew it did, but to be on the safe side, he untied the rope that secured the horse to the tether line. Leaning into the muscled shoulder, he pushed the horse back, then led him away from the gray and the mules and tied him to a tree.

He caressed the long neck. "Sleep, my friend. Tomorrow you will be home."

Would that he could take comfort in that thought. He had no home and probably never would. He glanced over his shoulder and sighed in relief to see Lillibeth stretched out on the seat. He hoped she had fallen asleep. Her questions hit too close to the truth of raw need he could not control.

Samantha leaned back, a rope gripped in both hands, her booted feet planted in the dirt. She kept tension on the lariat while Oscar did the same on the other side of a mare as Grogan placed a hot iron on her rump. She whinnied with pain, lifted first one front hoof and then the other in an effort to break free.

The moment Grogan removed the iron, Samantha relaxed a fraction, her gloved hands on fire from gripping so hard. Actually, she hurt right down to her toenails and was as dirty as she had ever been. *Idiot.* In an effort to forestall thoughts of Holden, today she'd offered to help brand the ten relief mounts they planned to keep on Timberoaks. One more and they'd be finished. At least, she would be.

Eight days, and no word from Holden. If anyone was counting. It was time she came to terms with his departure. And before she killed herself with heavy labor. Wasn't likely he'd return. Distracting herself with chores didn't work, anyway. No matter the activity, her mind still swirled, continued to berate her for sending him away.

She licked her dry lips. When Oscar stepped forward to release his rope, she did the same.

"One more." Exhaustion made his voice tremble. He gave the mare's rump a smack.

Off she went, crow-hopping and grunting her displeasure. Baker and another hand hazed her toward the horses that milled in a second corral, waiting to be herded out to pasture. That Samantha wouldn't do. The day was almost spent, anyway. It would be dark in an hour or so. Just enough time for a much-needed bath before supper. She lifted her hat, brushed a sleeve across her forehead, felt dirt grind on her skin before she clamped the hat back in place.

Too late, she realized it didn't make a bit of difference who or what Walker might be. Nor did she care that he'd stolen her horse. Even his abandonment of Guy was a moot point, since the boy was safe at Timberoaks. She *tsk*ed at herself for constantly thinking about the man.

"Well, I'll be. Would you look who's here," Oscar said.

One hand against an aching back, she groaned at the effort to turn around and look in the direction of Oscar's interested gaze.

She stilled. Her heart thudded.

He's back!

Excitement swept through her as she focused on the man loping next to a wagon. Even from so far away, she had no doubt that it was Holden Walker. Few men rode with such grace and ease.

A smile lifted her lips when she saw Black Magic behind the wagon. Holden had kept his promise.

Beside her, Oscar frowned. "Who's that with him?"

For the first time, Samantha's gaze shifted to the wagon driver. This time her heartbeat skipped. "A woman?"

"Looks like." Oscar scratched his whiskered jaw. "Wonder who she is?" His frown deepened. "Ain't that your black, Samantha?"

"Looks like," she parroted through dry lips. Holden had brought a woman here? His woman? Had he gone back for . . . ?

He'd said he had no wife. A new acquisition? Dread shivered through her.

"You got somethin' to tell me, girl?"

Samantha looked sideways and caught Oscar's speculative expression directed at her. Could he know? Had he read her mind? Nervously, she asked, "Like what?"

"The horse. What's the deal here?"

The horse. Not the woman. She sighed mentally. Well, this surely was the lesser of two evils. No hope for it. She had to tell Oscar the truth. "I didn't turn him loose. Holden took him away for fear Uriah or C. J. would claim him."

"Addle-headed," Oscar snapped. "Nobody would take that horse from you, Samantha, not with me here to stop 'em."

Oscar didn't have to argue his worth to her.

Her gaze snapped back to the couple coming closer and closer. She frowned. Maybe she *should* tell Oscar that Holden had stolen the horse. Serve the arrogant bas . . . man right.

If Oscar knew the manner in which Holden had taken Black Magic, he'd probably throw him off the ranch. But now Holden had the horse in tow. Besides, in the past days she'd come to the conclusion she didn't want the man gone. She wanted . . .

Don't think about what you'll never have.

She flipped back and forth between half-truths, but her seething mind circled back to one burning question: *He had the nerve to bring his woman here?*

If she was honest, she had to admit nothing much had passed between them but a few kisses. Still, that didn't stop the anger from building.

Her eyes narrowed on the woman again. She couldn't make out her features shaded beneath a poke bonnet.

So she waited.

As Holden drew to a halt, his eyes bored steadily into

hers. She couldn't glance away. He looked wonderful, compelling, dangerous. A faint smile lifted a corner of his mouth.

"I have brought your horse, Miss Timberlake."

His honey-toned voice flowed over her. As though it were nothing, huh? So male! Struck dumb by her body's reaction to the sight of him, she could say nothing.

Fortunately, Oscar filled the void. " 'Bout that stallion, Walker. You mighta discussed it with me afore you led 'im off. Where'd you have 'im stabled?"

"Waco." Holden's eyes remained fixed on Samantha. "He has been well cared for."

"That ain't the point," Oscar groused.

Reluctantly, Walker shifted his attention to her foreman, breaking the mesmerized trance that held her. Her gaze snapped to the woman. While Oscar and Holden talked, Samantha had an opportunity to study her. The lady didn't flinch, her perusal equally avid.

Though travel stained, she looked far fresher than Samantha, and that galled her no end. Golden eyes peered from beneath the bonnet's brim; a faint smile lifted her generous lips. Grudgingly, Samantha acknowledged that she was a beautiful woman. The same one she'd seen in the photograph. Small, dainty even, she had well-balanced curves in all the right places.

A friend.

Right. Samantha nursed a giant helping of skepticism.

"Hello." The woman's smile widened to show even white teeth.

"Sorry." Holden spoke to his companion, then to Samantha. "Miss Timberlake"—he nodded—"Oscar Dupree, this is Lillibeth . . ."

"Gentry," she supplied, but not before Samantha noticed Holden's hesitation.

Holy moly, he didn't know her last name? Or was she lying? Maybe her name was Walker. With effort, Samantha smoothed her brow and nodded. "Ma'am," she replied stiffly.

Served him right. Served them both right. Lillibeth Gentry, whether that was her real name or not, had to be . . . well, several years older than she. Older than Holden, too, by golly. Again, reluctant honesty surfaced. *But she sure is pretty.*

"Please, call me Lillibeth. 'Ma'am' sounds so formal."

She'd meant it to. *Respect for age.*

"Oscar, Miss Gentry is the teacher I told you about."

Out of the corner of her eye, Samantha saw Oscar's mouth drop open. At the same time, he snatched off his hat and crushed it to his chest. The only word to describe her foreman's expression was "smitten." She stopped just shy of a snort at his calf-eyed gaze.

"It's a real pleasure to meet you, ma'am . . . Miss Gentry."

"And you, Mr. Dupree. Miss Timberlake," she added with a nod and the sweetest smile.

Samantha ground her teeth. "I don't recall hearing about a teacher."

"I do," Mattie said.

Samantha jumped and whipped around. She hadn't heard her aunt approach. Ever faithful Bengy, his tongue lolling to one side, flopped at Mattie's feet the moment she stopped.

"Miss Gentry, this is Miss Crawford." As he spoke, Holden dismounted, and with no effort at all, reached up, circled Lillibeth's waist and swung her to her feet beside him. The top of her bonnet reached only to the middle of his chest.

Samantha jammed grubby fingers in her back pockets. Not only did she feel as if she'd been smeared with pig wallow, but she felt awkward and gangly as well. And why hadn't someone discussed this schoolmarm business with her? Timberoaks belonged to her. Would that fact never get through the thick heads around here? Well, not her aunt's, of course.

Mattie stepped forward and extended her hand. "Oscar said you might settle in this area. You're interested in the one-room place down by the creek?"

"I . . . think so," Lillibeth replied with a tremulous smile. "Holden told me you have a boy who needs schooling. Perhaps there are others. . . ." Her musical voice trailed off.

"Maybe, but we won't discuss this standing out here," Mattie said. "Oscar, you'll help Mr. Walker with their animals and the wagon?"

"Yes'm," Oscar said, his enamored eyes still fastened on Lillibeth as if he couldn't bear to look away.

"Come inside." Mattie beckoned to Lillibeth. "Supper will be ready soon." She glanced at the men. "Mr. Walker will likely be more comfortable eating in the bunkhouse, but you will eat with us."

"Oh, no!" Lillibeth exclaimed.

Samantha's sentiment exactly, but she couldn't say a word. Ever gracious to women, and especially since she'd traveled for several days, their guest would, of a certainty, receive a bit of pampering, Mattie Crawford–style.

On the other hand, Mattie had been wary of Walker from the start. Apparently that discomfort still haunted her, Samantha thought.

"I don't want to put you out," Lillibeth continued. "Holden and I will camp somewhere. We have for the past three nights, and—"

"Nonsense," Mattie interrupted. She wouldn't hear another word of protest as she started for the house, drawing Lillibeth with her. Bengy dragged himself up and lumbered after them.

Halfway there, Mattie paused. "Samantha, you'll need to bathe before supper. You'd better come to the house now."

Thank you very much, Aunt Mattie. I'm not a child.

She darted a glance Holden's way. Though he didn't look at her, she suspected it took studious effort not to, for she could see the side of his face well enough. His smiling face.

"Oscar," she snapped in an effort to bring him out of his gaga trance.

"What?" Reluctantly, he fixed his dark eyes on her.

"Do you need my help with that last mare?"

"Nah." He clamped his hat over tousled hair and glanced at the tall wrangler next to Black Magic. "Soon's Walker stables your horse and them other stock, he can join the last fracas of the day. We been brandin' mares." He jutted his chin in the direction of the one horse remaining in the corral. "She's jittery as a rickety old chair. Maybe you could settle 'er afore we lay on a hot iron, now that yer here," he added with a wry smile.

"Of course," Holden said.

"Y'all go on, Samantha. You been at it all day."

That she had, and if her burning hands and aching back were any indication, she needed a long soak in the tub. Besides, she intended to don her best shirtwaist and skirt before she sat down at the table with Miss Lillibeth Gentry. Her aunt wouldn't need to tell her this time.

Again, Mattie called to her. "Find Guy before you come in."

"Yes, ma'am."

Chapter Fifteen

"I ain't goin' to no school," Guy asserted as Samantha walked into the kitchen.

"You will if I say so, young man." Mattie's expression stern, she scolded Guy, then winked at Miss Gentry.

Fast friends already, Samantha thought dourly, then berated herself for being mean-spirited. It got mighty lonely out here in the middle of nowhere. Mattie Crawford was no different from any other woman who found herself surrounded by men with only an occasional woman to talk to.

"Samantha, I thought you'd fallen in, child."

"I'm not a child, Aunt Mattie." She strode to the table, pulled out her chair, and caught herself before she flopped down on the seat in a childish manner.

"It's only an expression, Samantha."

"Well, I'd appreciate it if you'd refrain from using it from now on."

Mattie's brow creased, then cleared. "Of course," she said in a placating tone. Then she stretched out her arms, her hands open for Guy and Miss Gentry to clasp. "We'll say the blessing, then eat before dinner gets cold."

A backhanded slap if Samantha had ever heard one. Okay, so she'd soaked longer than she should, but at least she now felt halfway human. She tamped down her foul attitude, took their guest's and Guy's hands and bowed her head.

"Lord, for the food we are about to receive, we give thanks. Use this bounty to strengthen our bodies to serve Thee better. And thank You for Lillibeth's fellowship at our table. Amen."

She liked Lillibeth Gentry.

Hard as she tried not to, that feeling persisted as Samantha headed up the stairs for bed. Lillibeth spoke with cultured words and voice. She laughed easily, and she'd charmed Guy despite his reluctance.

That did not mean, though, that Miss Gentry had convinced him to attend any school she might set up in the little house by the stream.

Obviously Aunt Mattie wholeheartedly favored the idea. It would relieve her of the guilt she carried because she didn't spend near enough time teaching Guy his basic reading, writing and arithmetic skills. There were only so many hours in a day, and she filled each to the brim with house and garden chores. Of a certainty, Samantha admitted to herself, she helped her aunt not at all.

She lit the lamp in her room, then began to disrobe. A faint noise from the front bedroom gave her pause. Though Lillibeth was small, the floor creaked beneath her light step. Aunt Mattie had insisted their guest sleep in her father's room, their only spare bedroom, whether Samantha liked the notion or not.

His room couldn't be kept as some sort of shrine. But it was so hard to accept the fact that her father was gone and life continued without him.

There was one benefit to having Lillibeth tucked up in the house: she knew Walker slept alone.

Where did that come from? "What difference does it make?" she muttered. *None.*

She paused again to stare at her image in the armoire mirror. Jealousy rode her hard and she didn't like it. Holden Walker could sleep with or marry—she realized with a pang—anyone he chose. *If he has his druthers, he's bound to pick a lovely, dainty woman like Lillibeth Gentry over the likes of me.*

Her gaze dropped to the floor of the armoire, a reminder of the gold tucked beneath her folded clothes. "The low-down sneaky cur!" She winced at her feeble effort to put him at a distance with those words. They no longer worked.

Holden hadn't stolen Guy, which was doubtless his reason for returning to Timberoaks in the first place. She pressed a shaking hand against her pounding heart. Thank God he'd had a change of heart. It didn't bear thinking about; how shattered they all would have been had he taken her brother. Then, too, he'd kept his promise and returned Black Magic.

So she should give back his gold. Tonight. Now.

Rather than give herself time to think about the real motive behind her actions, she replaced her blouse and skirt with trousers and a long-sleeved shirt, stomped her feet into boots, and scooped up the nuggets. She paused in the hall just short of slamming the door. Wouldn't do to alert Aunt Mattie of her intention to go to Walker in the middle of the night.

To give back his gold. *That's all,* she lied to herself as she tiptoed down the stairs.

The lace curtain in an upstairs window twitched sideways. Lillibeth gazed down on the figure striding toward the barn, her white blouse like a torch in the dark night.

Samantha Timberlake was a force to be reckoned with. She didn't intend to challenge the young woman, but Holden would certainly have his hands full.

He had not discarded all his predatory instincts, but would he use them to claim this girl? Or would he slink away like a wounded animal and remain an outsider in the white man's world, not realizing he already fit into that life?

No doubt about it. He wanted Samantha Timberlake.

A smile kindled in Lillibeth's eyes as she watched Samantha stop at the corral, where the black's coat gleamed in the starlight. After a moment, the horse ambled oh-so-slowly toward the woman's outstretched hand. But he stopped out of her reach and nodded his head as if carrying on a conversation.

Lillibeth couldn't tell if Samantha spoke. After several moments, she moved on toward the barn. Then, in short order, she reappeared leading a saddled mount. The faint *clip-clop* of the shod hooves drifted to Lillibeth's ears, but it was quiet enough that those who slept would not hear. It wasn't until Samantha reached the edge of the clearing that she mounted and nudged the horse into a fast walk. Horse and rider disappeared into the trees.

Lillibeth spread the curtains and lifted the sash. The lace panels billowed, and the mingled fragrances of roses, jasmine and mustard weed rushed in on the gentle breeze. The smell of rain drifted on the wind as well. They were in the last throes of a terribly dry summer, and even a sprinkle would be welcome.

Discarding her robe, Lillibeth climbed into bed. Even though she had surmised Samantha didn't want her in the house and in this bed, contentment seeped through her when her head nestled into the soft pillow. After sleeping on the wagon's bench seat for three nights, she thought this luxury felt like heaven.

She stacked her hands beneath her head and stared at

the ceiling. Could she live here and start a school? If anyone discovered her past life, she'd become a pariah. Gracious to a fault, even Mattie Crawford would change her
tune if . . .

Lillibeth sighed. No use borrowing trouble. She'd wait
until she saw how the drama between Holden and Samantha played out. If Holden moved on, maybe she should, too.

She grinned, recalling the way sparks had shot off
Samantha when they'd first arrived and the girl got a look
at her. Lillibeth knew Holden liked her, admired her even,
but his heart belonged to Samantha. The girl, unfortu-
nately, didn't know that yet. Discerning Holden's reserva-
tions, Lillibeth wondered if the younger woman would
ever understand.

Remembrances marched through her mind. The first
time she had found Holden in her room. Lord in heaven,
he'd scared her so much that her teeth chattered, until his
smile appeared. A beautiful man, she'd decided, and that
feeling had never changed.

Her heart had remained frozen while she'd "plied her
trade" in that god-awful room over the saloon. Until that
night.

They had made love.

Yes, love.

Holden Walker was a remarkable lover. He gave far
more than he took, and she had succumbed to his gentle
hands, his glorious mouth. For weeks he had appeared like
a phantom and taken her to heights she'd never imagined.

Then, with a shyness that belied his boldness in bed,
he'd asked her to teach him to read and write.

The lovemaking had gradually ceased over the next six
months, then stopped altogether. Their relationship had
shifted in his mind if not in hers. She'd become a teacher,
rather than a body for him to pleasure and from which to
draw satiation.

To say she missed that closeness, the heights of sexual

arousal, was an understatement. Perhaps she'd fallen a little bit in love. She smiled sadly into the darkness, remembering. . . .

Her further attempts at seduction had been a lesson in futility. Holden had come once a week to learn how to read and write, with the single-mindedness of a starving bear looking for honey.

Lillibeth chuckled. "Would that young Guy were as eager to learn as Holden," she murmured.

When she quit work and came upstairs ready to call it a night, he'd been there, books spread over the sofa, pencil in hand, and bearing the expectant expression of a hopeful child. Holden had devoured every book she owned, from *McGuffey's Reader* to Shakespeare.

And then he'd come no more.

She hadn't seen him for almost a year when he'd turned up to ask this last favor. Now she understood why the horse's care had been so important to him.

His heart belongs to Samantha Timberlake, and she doesn't even know it.

Lillibeth stifled a frisson of regret. "Ridiculous," she muttered. Her infatuation with Holden had been just that: simple infatuation. Soul-deep love had never been a part of the friendship that developed between them. His feeling for Samantha was that deep, though, all-consuming. If only he'd admit it.

Closing her eyes, Lillibeth pictured Samantha's face, her eyes trained on Holden this afternoon. Gladdened by the sight of him, yet a tad fearful—maybe of her own feelings. Possessive, too.

"The girl wants you, Holden."

She reopened her eyes and whispered into the darkness, speaking to her friend as she might to a younger brother. "Take that valiant though terrifying step, Holden. Unlock your heart for her to see. Or you'll never have her."

* * *

A light breeze lifted Holden's damp hair. After an invigorating dip in the river, he had donned buckskins. He stared into the yellow and blue-white flames, which flickered and danced. Absently he lifted a cup to his lips and savored the smell, the taste of strong coffee. He was not hungry.

Not for food, anyway.

Flexing tense shoulders, he set down the cup and picked up a stick to stir the few short logs. They popped and hissed as flame licked over the dry wood. His nerves felt brittle, as if the fire raced though him rather than the logs.

He would move on after he got Lillibeth settled. Seeing Samantha, steeling himself not to touch her, put such a strain on his willpower and, yes, his heart, that he feared his resistance could not last long. But resist he must.

Holden Walker had nothing to offer her, and Walks In Shadow was no more. He glanced down at his attire. His loin cloth and the knife given to him by Two Horns were all that he had left of his years with the People. His lance and bow, even his sacred war shield, had been left behind.

Two weeks before he departed with Little Spring, Two Horns had offered him the pick of the captured horses, but not his war pony. No. Holden had gifted the Appaloosa to a young warrior. In only a few days, he had trained the gray he now rode.

His leave-taking from the village seemed only yesterday. He remembered Two Horns's grave words of farewell, Swift Arrow's stony expression when the chief lifted Little Spring into Walks in Shadow's arms. The ring of people staring at him as if he had lost his mind.

Perhaps he had.

Holden lifted the cup and swallowed half the coffee, scalding his tongue. Ignoring the sting, he relived that slow walk out of the village. Not a soul wished him well, and neither did they keen his loss. More than a mile from the encampment he had paused at Bubbling Water's grave. The band would move on. Her last resting place would be lost.

Pain twisted his heart, wringing it as one would a cloth at the river.

He never looked back. If he had, he doubted he could have gone through with it. He shrugged, uncertain whether he had done the right thing, even now. The worst, however, was yet to come: once again leaving Little Spring with the Timberlakes.

But now he could no more take Guy away from Samantha than he could deny this deep urge to have her in his bed, in his life. Besides, Guy did not remember his uncle, nor his life as an Indian child. No, the boy would not thank him. Except for the brief moment of confused recognition Guy had experienced that first day, he had said no more.

Holden sighed.

Somewhere behind him a twig snapped, then another and another. He stilled, listening. A horse approached.

Fire-blinded, he lifted his gaze and stared into the darkness to allow his sight to adjust as he rose. Excitement skittered through him, for he knew even before she came into view who it was.

Samantha reined in the slowly plodding horse and simply looked at Holden for endless seconds. She said nothing.

Holden's pulse quickened with desire he could not deny. His heart pounded while he devoured this vision before him. She wore no hat, and her unbound hair was draped around her shoulders like gold shot through with fire. His fingers itched to spear through those tresses, feel them slip through his hands, yield to his touch as would the rest of her lithe body.

Her fathomless dark eyes mirrored the flames that danced behind him. Then she slowly dismounted.

"What do you here?"

Not until she blinked in confusion did he realize he had jumbled the words the way he had when he first learned to speak English.

He sucked in a steadying breath and corrected himself. "Why are you here?"

She didn't answer. Instead, she looped the reins over a tree limb, then turned and took a few hesitant steps toward him.

"It is late. You should be in bed."

The instant the words left his mouth he regretted them. *Lunatic!* Visions of her lying abed leaped to mind. He could no more halt his imaginings than he could stop breathing.

What did Samantha wear to bed? Lillibeth and the other women he had bedded wore garments made to lure a man: silk or satin nightgowns that slithered through his hands when he removed them, snagged on his callused palms.

He did not think Samantha wore such, nor could he picture her wantonly lying naked. No. He pictured her in virginal white cotton buttoned up to her throat and down to her wrists. He groaned inwardly, visualizing her body beneath the soft folds of material. Full breasts, taut, silken thighs, the triangle of . . . He shook his head.

"It is late," he said again, his voice rough.

"I brought your gold."

She fished in her trouser pocket, which only added to his tension. Samantha stepped closer, her arm extended. He raised his hand, and as she dropped the nuggets into his palm, the tips of her fingers touched his skin. Heat sizzled through him. He closed his fingers, capturing her hand.

Alarm, followed by something he could not define, chased across her face. She offered no resistance. Her dark eyes searched his—wide, questioning. But she did not jerk her hand away.

"You could have kept the gold."

Samantha's gaze skipped from his eyes to their joined hands and back again. He moved a half step closer. Her breasts rose on an indrawn breath. And the man in him knew. She had come here for more than she pretended. Did she want the same thing from him that he longed for from her?

Unwise. Unwise. Let her go. Let her go.

The litany drummed in his head, but it was as if his hand had a mind of its own. He drew her a step closer. One more and their bodies would touch. God of the white man, he wanted to do more than touch her body.

The desire to make love to her raged through him. *Unwise* again echoed through his mind, but he could no more release her than he could sit on the curve of a waning moon. Roses and her own womanly fragrance danced on the breeze. Her scent tickled his nose. Consumed his senses.

"Samantha?" Did she know what he asked of her?

Without warning, she rose on tiptoes and kissed him. A closed-mouthed, unpracticed kiss, but it so astonished him that he went utterly still. She broke the kiss and stared up at him with unblinking eyes.

"Why did you kiss me?"

Her cheeks rouged prettily. "A . . . thank-you for returning my horse."

"Your only reason?"

She refused to answer.

"We had a bargain."

She shook her head. "*You* voiced a bargain that I did not agree to." She sounded defiant.

Amused, he realized that was true, but he never went back on his word. In time she would understand that. *No,* he told himself sternly. There would be no time for her to learn more about him. *Remember, soon you leave Timberoaks.*

A series of losses throughout his life haunted him. He did not remember his white parents, but surely as a three-year-old child he must have grieved.

Since the day Bubbling Water breathed her last, the ache had never left his heart. His adopted sister had been sweet, kind and aptly named. Laughter bubbled in her expressive black eyes until the final day when she passed into the Spirit World.

Cut off from the People, he had also relinquished any claim he ever had to Little Spring. Now he would ride out of

Samantha's life. Right or wrong, he wanted, needed to have her, but he gave her a chance to leave. He stepped back, dropped his hands to his sides, and pocketed the nuggets.

"Go home, Samantha. You play with a fire you do not know exists."

Her brow furrowed as she glanced around, uncomprehending. "There's no fire."

He again clasped her hand and flattened it against his chest. "Feel that?" His heart raced like a herd of buffalo running through brush.

Her gaze darted from their joined hands to his eyes and back again. "Yes," she whispered. Capturing his other hand, she copied his action against her breast. "My heart races, too."

Chivalry only went so far. He was not made of rock. Still, he hesitated, clung to sanity. For a certainty she had never been with a man. Surely she would regret it if he took her virginity.

He had never made love to a virgin. A daunting thought. Could he bring her the fulfillment every woman deserved her first time? Yes, for Samantha he would. Or die trying. His desire leaped at the challenge.

"You would tempt a corpse," he murmured.

Of their own volition, his arms encircled her, drew her against his frame. He felt her breasts jiggle when she stifled a chuckle at his words. He lowered his head and kissed her. Though she was pliant in his arms, he asked her to open her mouth. She did, without hesitation.

Night sounds receded before the rush of blood in his brain, his ears: rustling leaves, the creak of tree limbs, their horses' disquiet. All swept away, replaced by feelings. Her soft lips yielded to his, her mouth wet and warm; their tongues tangled.

His hands moved over her back, down her sides. One hand paused at the side of her generous breast. He cupped it. His thumb brushed over the nipple, which beaded instantly. Frustration shortened his breath. He wanted her naked . . . now. Beneath him . . . now. He wanted to be inside her. . . .

He groaned.

Slowly.

Lowering both hands, he cupped her derriere and brought her lower body up against the juncture of his thighs. She trembled, but did not pull away. Did not break the kiss. He felt her breath quicken in his mouth, heard the tiny sound of need she made in her throat. Exciting and different from other women he had bedded.

It sang through his senses, heated him to flame. Her slender fingers tangled in his hair as he walked backward, drawing her with him, never breaking the kiss. Not even for one second could he bring himself to let her go.

He followed her down as he lowered her to his blanket, arranging his length half over her, half to her side. Then he did as he had wanted to do from the first moment he saw her on the porch all those months ago. He speared his fingers into her hair, sifted the tresses through his hands. As soft as he had imagined. He wound the abundance around his fist, effectively anchoring her beneath him.

His other hand worked on her shirt buttons. In seconds he parted the fabric and brushed his palm over her velvet skin. Slanting his mouth one way and then the other, he devoured her responsive lips. His fingers found and fondled her breasts. Anticipating tasting each one, he teased first one and then the other to readiness.

Samantha began to move beneath him in the age-old cadence she did not yet understand. Little gasps puffed from her mouth into his as her desire quickened. He reached between them to unbutton her trousers. Slipped his hand inside and caressed her taut stomach. Lower. The sounds of his own need mingled with hers.

As his fingers found the tiny bud of desire, he murmured against her mouth, "Open your eyes, Samantha." He pulled back, wanting to see her responses.

Her hands clasped his shoulders in near desperation. "Don't leave me."

He needed her with all-consuming fire . . . and joy, he realized with wonder. Leaving was the last thing he would ever do, but he never got the chance to tell her.

She cried, "You make love to Miss Gentry. Make love to me!"

Joy died in one disillusioned blink. The fire fizzled as if extinguished by thrown dirt. Holden's hands fell away and fisted next to her shoulders. Despair and desolation seethed through him.

What had he been thinking? Young, inexperienced, Samantha was not the type of woman he bedded. *Make love?* Did she know what the word meant? More importantly, did he? Love had never been a part of his lust-filled couplings. Not even with Lillibeth. He did not deserve to make love to Samantha.

She looked bewildered as he sat up, stood, and straightened his buckskin shirt. She lay unmoving, exposed to his roving eyes as he forced his heart to stone.

"What's wrong, Holden? I wanted . . ."

"A stud."

Harsh, but he had to hurt her to save her from making a terrible mistake.

"Wh . . . what?" She slowly sat up. With shaking hands, she pulled the shirt together to hide her glorious breasts from his eyes.

"Go home, Samantha."

The hell of it was, he understood her curiosity. But if he took her virginity and then walked out of her life, she would rage against him. He would be forevermore an uncaring drifter in her eyes. He grimaced. Kind, that word "drifter." Saddle bum, more like it. Had he not told himself only moments before that he would move on? That he would never be good enough for her? If he did this, he would hate himself far more than she ever could.

She extended her hand in supplication, and crystal tears shimmered in her eyes. "Holden, please."

"Leave," he growled.

If she did not, he feared he would take her like an animal.

Samantha stood and began to straighten her clothes, obviously confused. "What happened? I don't understand."

He forced himself to walk away into the darkness that had always felt protective.

Until now.

Chapter Sixteen

For the past nine years Lillibeth Gentry had worked night hours, except for the occasional late afternoon when a man accompanied her to the single room she called home. Her only source of pride dwelt in the fact that Sid Henshaw boasted the highest-priced whore in Waco.

Well-read, Lillibeth longed to call herself a courtesan, for she hated the word "whore" as vehemently as Holden did. But honesty forbade it.

Of course, she'd had regulars, but the succession of men through her life were legion, their faces a blur. Actually, she thanked God for that blessing. Had she remembered each one, despair would have brought her to her knees long before.

Since her work extended into the wee hours of morning, Lillibeth was not an early riser. When a shrill whistle jolted her awake this morning, her unfocused eyes gazed at the unfamiliar ceiling. Several seconds passed until her wits returned and she realized where she was.

Turning her head on the soft pillow, she stared at the

ticking clock. Her heart pounded in cadence with the time-
piece. She placed a hand on her chest in an effort to calm
her agitation.

The next whistle brought her straight up in bed. Her
gaze snapped to the window she'd left open, then zoomed
back to the clock. "Seven o'clock."

The middle of the night in her former life, but not on a
Texas ranch. If she was to assume a mantle of respectability before the ranch hands, Miss Timberlake and Mattie
Crawford in particular, she'd best learn to awaken early
and be ready to work, whatever the task.

Even through the closed door, she could smell bacon,
the heavenly scent of freshly baked bread. Tossing off the
covers, she strode to the window and flicked aside the lace
curtain. A half dozen men rode off in different directions,
and then she saw the reason for the whistles.

Quite a—what did they call it? Clutch? No. A remuda
of horses milled about, strung out in a haphazard line.
Two men, one near the head of the column, the other adja-
cent to the last horse, flapped coiled ropes against their
legs. The trailing rider whistled, and every horse picked up
its pace. Dust flew over men and beasts and billowed
toward the house, the open window.

Lillibeth slammed down the sash before the grit entered
the room, then turned in a near panic. *Get dressed.
Quickly.* Past time to be downstairs. Miss Crawford probably already thought she'd lolled in bed far too late.

After hasty ablutions, Lillibeth raced down the stairs,
then slowed and composed herself to walk into the
kitchen. Relief filled her to find only Miss Crawford at the
sink washing a heavy iron skillet, her back to Lillibeth.

"Good morning," she said with more than a little trepidation in her voice. The next few minutes could seal her
fate: to remain on Timberoaks or be sent packing.

Miss Crawford turned with a welcoming smile. She laid
the skillet on the drain board, then motioned toward the
stove. "We don't stand on ceremony, Lillibeth. Help your-

self to coffee. The cups are in the dishsafe to the right of the stove."

Somewhat relieved by Miss Crawford's relaxed manner, Lillibeth poured the much-needed coffee. No way would she escape some sort of interrogation, no matter what Holden had said. And rightly so.

"I've saved a plate for you."

"I'm sorry to have slept so late, Miss Crawford."

As Mattie approached with a covered dish, she frowned. "We'll have none of that, Lillibeth. As I told you last night, it's Mattie."

"Oh, yes." Lillibeth smiled as she removed the towel from the food. Fluffy scrambled eggs covered half the plate; strips of crisp bacon and two thick slices of bread overflowed the other side. She inhaled deeply. Breakfast had always been her favorite meal, but . . . "There's far too much here, Mattie. I couldn't possibly eat all this."

"That's the leftovers. Eat your fill and Bengy will lap up what's left." Mattie grabbed a cup of coffee for herself and settled across from Lillibeth. "Guy scooted out this morning before he ate his usual four eggs." She paused to blow on the steaming brew, then took a sip. "He probably thought you would sit him down at this table today to begin studies. But that's a bit premature, I think. I'm not sure you'll want to stay after you see the shack intended for you."

Crunching the delicious bacon, Lillibeth waved dissent. "I think it's far more likely you'll ask me to move on, Mattie. I haven't taught a group of youngsters in years."

Lillibeth knew she was opening herself to a wealth of difficult questions, but she had vowed to tell the truth. At least partially. Better to settle the matter now than wait for a later day when leaving would be harder yet.

"Oh?" Mattie's dark eyes, so similar to Samantha Timberlake's, sparked with interest. "You lived in Waco? What did you do there?"

Very carefully Lillibeth laid the fork aside and sat back in the chair. "I worked for an . . . individual in Waco."

Mattie took the bait with ease. "A private tutor?"

Naturally she would think that was what Lillibeth meant. "How interesting." She cocked her head. "I haven't been to Waco in years, but we do hear of folks over that way. Maybe I know your employer."

Lillibeth's gaze roamed over the older woman's handsome, strong features. Though not what one would call pretty, Mattie was striking, with expressive dark brown eyes, a firm jaw and a wealth of black hair generously sprinkled with silver and done up in a double braid. No, this upright woman would not know Sid. She'd probably cross the street if he approached.

"Sidney Henshaw." She followed that truth with a lie. "The Henshaw children have left the nest. My services were no longer needed."

"Henshaw." Mattie's teeth worried her bottom lip. "No. Don't think I've heard of the family."

Thank God. A premature sigh of relief escaped Lillibeth. She braced herself for further questioning.

"You were born in Waco?"

She shook her head. "I'm not sure where I was born."

"Pardon?" Mattie's brow creased questioningly.

Here was safe ground. "My first remembrance is of Sister Margaret Mary slapping my fingers with a ruler. The Sisters of Charity in St. Louis raised me at the orphanage."

"An orphan? One wonders what this world is coming to. Were you ever told about your parents?"

Again Lillibeth shook her head. "A note was pinned to my clothing when I was found. 'Lillibeth Gentry' was all it said." Before Mattie could ask another question, she went on. "When I was old enough to do the orphanage's shopping on market day, I made inquires at the courthouse. Only one Gentry lived in the county, an old man in his midnineties."

All true, thank heaven, which gave Lillibeth a modicum of confidence.

"How did you become a tutor?"

"Sister Kathleen taught me, right along with a few paying pupils brought to the school by wealthy St. Louis patrons. Later, I took over teaching some of the orphanage's younger students before accepting a position in a private residence."

And that was where she had to leave the whole truth and nothing but the truth. No way could she tell Mattie that Mr. Bradford had made advances upon her. When Mrs. Bradford found out, she'd blamed Lillibeth and promptly ejected her onto the street. After the lurid stories spread by the vile woman, Lillibeth couldn't find other employment in St. Louis. She'd had a devil of a time getting enough back wages to board the first stage traveling west and sustain herself a few days in the rollicking town of Waco.

Where she'd met Sid Henshaw. Lillibeth could not, would not, reveal the rest. She pushed back her chair, anxious to put a stop to further questions. "Would someone be kind enough to show me the way to this dwelling Holden told me about?"

Mattie walked with Lillibeth toward the front of the house. "Let's see if Samantha is still in the office."

After discovering Samantha already gone, Mattie returned to her chores while Lillibeth continued outside. She found the young woman talking to Mr. Dupree. With some relief, she spied Holden lifting the latch on a corral gate.

"Holden," she called and hastened toward him. Distraught at the half-truths and outright lies she'd told, she barely noticed the smile that erupted on Mr. Dupree's craggy features.

He whipped off his hat. "Ma'am," he said.

She gave him a friendly nod and glanced at Samantha, prepared to do the same. Instead, she blinked at the hard stare the girl leveled at her. Obviously, Samantha Timberlake did not want her here. Well, she'd deal with that later. Anxiously, she strode on to the one person with whom she could be entirely open and honest.

Without a second thought as to how her actions would appear, Lillibeth slid her arms around Holden's waist and settled against his hard frame. His strength made her feel safe.

Clearly surprised, he hesitated a second before wrapping his arms around her. The bridle in his hand slapped her backside. "What is wrong?" His voice, low and quiet, stilled the jitters in her stomach.

She leaned back slightly and looked up. Concern painted his handsome features. A tremulous smile curved her lips. "Nothing, really. I just underwent Mattie Crawford's interrogation. I'm feeling a bit disoriented."

"Unkind, was she?"

A nervous laugh clogged her throat. "No. That's the hell of it, Holden. I lied through my teeth, by omission if nothing else, and I'm sorry for it. I think she believed every word."

Holden looked over her head. His eyes dimmed for a second as he murmured, "I know how you feel."

She turned in his arms and looked over her shoulder. Oscar Dupree had mounted a spotted horse, but Samantha Timberlake still stood in the middle of the clearing, her dark eyes riveted on them. Only then did Lillibeth realize what she had done. How her actions might appear to this woman who, without a doubt, loved Holden.

Glancing up at his set expression, she decided she didn't regret it. These were two people made for each other. Might be time she put her talents to good use. Time to get Samantha Timberlake so jealous that she'd come to her senses and make the first move. Lillibeth doubted Holden ever would.

Turning back to him, she reached up and pulled his head down to plant a kiss at the corner of his mouth. From where Samantha stood, it would look like she'd kissed him squarely on his expressive lips.

Abruptly, he lifted his head and frowned at her. She smiled at his confusion, confident his hat brim screened his expression from the woman looking on.

Clearly baffled, he jumbled his words. "Why for you kiss me?"

"Oh, no reason. Perhaps to thank you, my friend."

Lillibeth looked over her shoulder in time to see Samantha stomp off toward the barn. She grinned.

That went well.

She had changed her mind.

Lillibeth Gentry was a conniving . . .

Samantha paused inside the door and leaned against the wall. Tears welled when she pictured Holden the past night. How could he do that? How could he come so close to making love to her, then kiss Lillibeth this morning?

Brushing away the tears, she stifled a sob. Her own fault. She'd been the one to practically throw herself into his arms. Now she remembered how reluctant he'd been. But, then, he *had* kissed her. She shivered, almost feeling his callused hands on her sensitive skin. He'd caressed her with such skill, such tenderness. And all the while . . .

Lunging away from the wall, away from painful thoughts, she went straight to the saddles hanging on wooden forms to keep them aboveground and dry. Her horse's bridle was looped over the saddle's horn.

She ripped her gear from the form and muttered to herself, for no one could hear. Lemuel Baker would doubtless be along to muck stalls, but right now she could seethe and curse, if she was of a mind to. And she was. Oh, yes!

Her father would have washed out her mouth with soap for such colorful language. But he was no longer around.

"Lillibeth Gentry and Holden Walker can take flying leaps into hell. He's a liar and a . . . a cheat. No wife. Ha!"

Well, maybe he told the truth in that regard, but their actions before God and everybody certainly spoke to the contrary.

She wrenched open the gate to her mount's stall and dropped the heavy saddle with a clank. He danced back when she charged in, her boots kicking up loose straw and dust, the bridle ajingle dangling from her fingers.

He'd have none of it. He ground his teeth and presented his shoulder to her. She reached for his neck, but he turned farther into the corner of the stall.

"Stop that. I only want to bridle and saddle you, you consarned jughead."

He blew and raised his head out of reach, backed a few steps and whipped around, giving her his rump.

Samantha glared and planted fists on her hips. "What the devil is wrong with you this morning?"

"Perhaps you should approach him more gently."

She knew that liquid voice. Lord, did she ever. Glare still in place, she swung to face Holden. His blasted woman stood there too, taking it all in. Her small hand was tucked possessively in the crook of Walker's arm, and a smile lit her golden eyes.

Pretty and delicate and . . . Dammit! She winced. Her language had deteriorated to the point that surely Pa was turning in his grave.

"I don't need lessons from you about how to handle horses, Holden Walker. I'll thank you to keep your notions to yourself."

He shrugged. "If you do not lower your voice and slow your motions, you will still be here at noon."

He was right and she knew it. Still . . . She drew in a breath and turned to the horse. Slowly this time. And when she spoke, she did so in a reasonable tone.

"All right, fella, no more nonsense from you."

It worked, of course. The horse stood as docile as you please while she brushed him down, saddled and bridled him. All the while Samantha could feel Holden and Lillibeth's scrutiny. Neither said a word until she had finished and began to lead the horse from the stall.

Childish, she knew, but she couldn't help herself. She looked up at Holden. "Satisfied?"

He simply smiled. Which sent goose bumps all over her. *Damn the man.* Samantha glanced at Lillibeth, and got an enigmatic smile for her pains. *Damn her, too.*

"Oscar disappeared before I could speak with him," Holden said. "If you see him, would you tell him that I will work the mare in the corral later today? Right now I am taking Lillibeth to see the little house he said she might rent."

Oh, he did, did he? The first she'd heard of it. Oscar took far too many liberties. *And that's a load of bull, Samantha Rose. Come down off your high horse.* Without Oscar's assistance since her father's death, she'd have sunk.

Rather than snap off Holden's head again, she tried to be civil. "He probably followed the men herding the horses out to pasture. If I see him, I'll pass on your message."

"My thanks." Holden turned, Lillibeth still on his arm, and strode out of the barn.

Samantha rested her forehead on her mount's warm neck. She sighed, silently whipping herself for being a shrew. A bitter brew to swallow, but she had to admit that Lillibeth Gentry had done nothing to her. Nothing but capture Holden's heart. And long before Samantha had ever laid eyes on him. Her own heart constricted.

Lillibeth had said not one word just now. She didn't have to. Her actions spoke volumes. From the moment she'd seen Lillibeth's portrait, Samantha had known Holden Walker was spoken for.

She rode out alone, ambled aimlessly. She put off finding something to do, while her mind constantly returned to the night before. Holden's soul-consuming kisses. His hands. Lordy, he'd set her skin to burning. Her insides smoldered like hot coals. Her breasts and . . . lower.

Why had he stopped? What had she done wrong?

"You make love to Miss Gentry. Make love to me!"

Those words had been her undoing. She'd reminded Holden of the woman possessively grasping his arm this morning.

"So what does that make you, Samantha Rose?" she murmured.

A wanton woman, that's what. Uncaring, in Holden's eyes, how or to whom she gave her virginity. Maybe he had done the honorable thing, stopping before they both did something they would regret.

He, staining his relationship with Lillibeth, and she . . .

Would she have regretted it today?

Samantha reined in her mount and sat motionless. No. She would have felt gloriously fulfilled. Even if he intended to marry another, she had given her heart to him. That thought flayed her as nothing else could.

"It isn't fair," she mumbled, tears burning her eyes.

But what did fairness have to do with life, with love? Not a cotton-pickin' thing. She would live the rest of her life with an empty heart unless she convinced Holden otherwise.

She gasped. What nerve! Besides, how could she compete with Lillibeth's beauty? Why in heaven's name would Holden pick her over that tiny, vulnerable-looking woman? And yet . . .

At that moment, Samantha's eyes focused on Guy's red agate marble, lying against a rock. She frowned. What on earth was that doing here, a half mile from the house? She dismounted and knelt to pick it up, then rubbed a thumb over her brother's prized shooter.

Aunt Mattie had made a pouch from a flour sack so Guy could carry his marbles everywhere he went. It was unlike him to misplace them, this marble in particular. A Christmas present from Pa.

She looked around, her brow still creased. This was a long way for him to have wandered. Scanning the ground, she swiveled full circle, but saw nothing else untoward. Only hoofprints. Not unusual.

Guy had been told to stay close. And what had he done? She shook her head. He was a growing boy, but still a boy. One who'd apparently defied Aunt Mattie's directive. Again.

Samantha decided to deliver a few choice words to her brother upon her return. Rising, she dropped the marble into her pocket and patted it for good measure. Maybe she'd withhold the marble from Guy for a few days. Serve him right. A good object lesson for his carelessness, but mostly a way to teach him to think twice before disobeying.

Before she went back to the house, though, she needed to check a young mare due to drop her first foal. First foaling could be tricky business.

Fetching her father's watch from her trouser pocket, she checked the time. About right. The pasture was only another mile or so. She'd be back in time for lunch. As she sank her boot into the stirrup, a thought hit her like a slap in the face.

Darn. Lillibeth will be there for lunch. And I'll have to be civil.

Chapter Seventeen

Her timing couldn't have been better. As Samantha approached home from the north, she heard the clang of the dinner bell. Passing one of the bigger oaks shading the rear of the barn, she noticed one of Guy's circles drawn in the dirt. They were everywhere he found a shady spot to ply his skill at the game of marbles. She rode into the center corridor, and while she dismounted, Lemuel Baker came out of a stall, propped a pitchfork against the wall and smiled.

"Don't know 'bout you, but I's hungry as a b'ar."

Samantha nodded, returning his smile. "Me too. I took a look at that gruella-colored mare."

Lemuel's sweaty brow creased. "Ever'thin' okay?"

"Yes, but she's taking her own sweet time about dropping her foal."

"Them young mares is a trial, that's fer sure."

Lemuel headed toward the bunkhouse. Samantha unsaddled and gave her mount a slapdash rubdown. She couldn't smell dinner over the pungent odors in the barn, but she imagined she could. Which made her ravenous by the time she walked into the kitchen.

Pork roast. A welcome change.

"Lordy, it smells like heaven in here, Aunt Mattie."

Samantha hung her hat on a peg and pumped water to wash up at the sink. Her usual efficient self, Mattie set a big bowl of green beans on the table next to a larger bowl of carrots and potatoes. The roast's mouthwatering fragrance steamed into the air. Though only four would eat, the entire crew of the ranch could have eaten. They'd have leftovers for supper, and maybe even some at lunch tomorrow. No one could ever say Mattie Crawford set a skimpy table.

"It's you, me and Guy today. Lillibeth is still at the shack with Mr. Walker," Mattie said.

The reference to their guest turned Samantha's stomach sour. She bit back a shrewish remark, but not before Mattie's sharp eyes glimpsed her expression.

Laying the plates around on the table, she said, "You have a problem with Lillibeth being here. I want to know why."

Her back to Mattie, Samantha said, "You're imagining things."

"I'm not one to imagine things. Now tell me what sticks in your craw."

"Nothing, really. It's just . . ." She couldn't tell her aunt about last night. She couldn't reveal her improbable feelings for Holden Walker. For some reason, Aunt Mattie didn't like him. Too strong a description, perhaps, but something about Holden didn't set well with her aunt.

"I hope you're not letting your feelings run away with you."

How does she do that? Her aunt appeared to read a person's mind at every turn.

"Mr. Walker is a drifter. I know that without being told."

There. She'd reinforced Mattie's belief without committing herself. She'd have to rein in her wayward heart, anyway. Holden didn't love her and he never would.

Mattie changed the subject. "Did you see Guy? I sent him out a couple hours ago to weed the garden after he brought in the eggs. Haven't seen hide nor hair of him since."

Should she tell her aunt about Guy's disobedience? No. She'd handle it herself. Tension left her body as she dried her hands. "If he's in the barn, he kept his head down."

Mattie pursed her lips. "Look again. I swear, that boy will be the death of me. He's either pestering me about something to eat, or he's off God knows where when I want him. You'd think he'd come running when he heard the dinner bell."

"You're sure he isn't upstairs?"

Mattie planted her hands at her waist. "Why in heaven's name would he be in the house on a pretty day like today? Besides, I'd have heard. Guy may slip around outside, but he's no lightweight on his feet when he's upstairs."

"Maybe he's in the bunkhouse with Cookie."

"Dinner is getting cold. Stop maybe-ing me to death and find him."

Samantha spread her hands. "Okay. Okay."

She couldn't find him in the barn. Samantha climbed the ladder and checked the hayloft to make sure he wasn't funnin' with her. At the bunkhouse, Cookie answered her knock with a dripping spoon in his hand and gave her a blank stare when she posed her question.

From the middle of the clearing, she called at the top of her lungs, "Guy!"

A covey of startled birds fluttered noisily from a tree, but her brother didn't answer. Had he gone fishing without permission?

Samantha strode to the backdoor and spoke through the screen. "I'll have to check the river, Aunt Mattie. That little cuss isn't close by."

Not waiting for an answer, she took off toward what she'd referred to as the river, in truth a stream little more than five feet wide and no deeper than her knees in the dry season. Sometimes during the winter, though, it raged fast and deep in places.

The farther she walked, repeatedly calling Guy's name, the more she fumed. "Darn it, young man, I should tan your britches when I find you."

Ducking a low-hanging branch, she straightened and looked in both directions along the stream. No sign of him. Then again, Guy had never disappeared like this.

Samantha frowned, chewing her lip. A bird twittered above her. She glanced up, and the thought came that Guy might have gone as far as the shack. He'd known Holden and Lillibeth were headed there today. That meant she had to walk nearly a mile, but she didn't know where else to look. Darn it!

Striking out at a good clip, she swiped aside tree branches in her path, muttering under her breath about dinner getting cold, and Aunt Mattie's ire when they returned. The litany throbbed in her head, and then she irrationally transferred her vexation to Holden.

Take your lady and leave.

It was a selfish wish, of course. Guy and several of the neighbors' children would benefit if Lillibeth opened a school. Would Holden stick around, too? Probably. Her heart did a flip as she stumbled over a rock outcrop. How could she bear to watch those two together?

"Like I'll have a choice," she muttered.

As she neared the shack, sweat streamed down her face from her walk. A walk that had grown brisker as she tried to outdistance her thoughts. Her shirt clung to her, damp with perspiration. She heard the pounding of a hammer before she spied Holden's and Lillibeth's mounts. The horses placidly cropped knee-high grass that had sprung up around the long-neglected structure.

Holden's gray jerked up his head and peered in her direction. His ears scissored and his nostrils flared. Recognizing that she presented no threat, he returned to eating. Smart as a wary beaver, that horse.

Though she'd made no noise, Holden suddenly appeared in the doorway, hammer in his right hand, his left thumb hooked over his gun belt. *Talk about wary.*

He watched her approach with narrowed eyes, sober and intent. Her stomach did a flip every time he looked at her with that stillness about him. As if he knew her thoughts, felt her heartbeat.

She cleared her throat and approached the doorway, willing away her nervousness at seeing him. "Is Guy inside? I've looked everywhere for him. Aunt Mattie is holding dinner for us."

"No," Holden said.

Lillibeth appeared at his side. The petite woman's hair wasn't perfectly coiffed this afternoon. Wisps straggled helter-skelter from her upswept chignon. Dirt smudges marred her forehead and right cheek. Samantha bit back a nasty smile. Sweat rings stained the woman's bodice under the arms.

Then Holden's negative reply slammed into her head. "Not here? Where could he be? It's not like Guy . . ." Her eyes widened with anxiety when another, more ominous thought clattered into her brain. Her lips trembled. "Surely not. He hasn't . . ."

Holden stepped toward her and clasped her upper arm. "What is wrong? You look . . . What is wrong?" he asked again.

She drew in a shaky breath. No. Mr. Butcher hadn't been seen near Timberoaks for . . . what? Five days? He wouldn't harm Guy. Would he? Her eyes round as dollars, she couldn't think clearly as she looked at Holden.

He dropped the hammer in the dirt and grabbed her other arm, none too gently, and shook her. "You are frightened about something. What it is?"

Samantha barely noted Holden's backward question. "No. It's foolish of me."

Holden's eyes bore into her. "I will decide if what you are thinking is foolish."

Worried, she didn't bridle at Holden's take-command attitude. *Maybe he can* . . . "While your were g-gone, Mr. Butcher s-sort of went out of his head." Ice water seemed to trickle through her. So very cold.

"Loco?" he snapped. His fingers bit into her arms. "Like how?"

"Holden, ease up. You'll hurt her." Lillibeth put a restraining hand on his forearm.

All her senses riveted on Holden, Samantha felt his vise-like grip loosen, but he didn't let her go. She didn't want him to. This man could help her. Help find her brother. Holden might have left Guy here at one time, but he'd come back. The man loved him as much as she did.

His voice mellowed a bit. "Tell me, Samantha. Now."

Before she had the chance, Lillibeth thrust a dipper in her hands. "Here. Drink this, Miss Timberlake."

Samantha gulped the cold water, and Lillibeth placed a rickety chair behind her.

"Sit before you fall down," she ordered, then looked up at Holden. "She's definitely frightened about this Mr. Butcher, and you won't get it out of her by scaring her more."

Holden jammed his fingers inside his gun belt.

Samantha brushed an unsteady hand over her forehead, and concentrated on his face. It was the only reassuring thing she could hang on to while her insides churned.

Slowly, she began, "The day after you left, Mr. Butcher rode in mad as could be, yelling at Guy." She blinked, recalling the scene. "He y-yanked Guy off the ground, berating him something awful. He . . . he thought Guy was C.J."

A muscle twitched in Holden's jaw. His eyes gleamed as if a fire had been lit behind them, but he said nothing.

"I hope I'm wrong. But maybe . . . I can't find Guy!" she cried. "Maybe Mr. Butcher . . . took him."

Without a word Holden whipped around and disappeared into the shack, then returned carrying his tack. "You ride double back to the ranch with Miss Timberlake, Lillibeth," he said over his shoulder.

"No. I'm going with you." Samantha leaped after him.

Again, Holden said nothing, ignored her as he threw a blanket over the gray's back, followed by his heavy saddle.

"He's my brother, Holden. I'm going with you. If he's . . ." She didn't want to let herself think that Mr. Butcher would harm Guy, but the remembrance of how he'd bruised her brother's arm freshened in her mind.

Lillibeth stepped in smoothly, snagging Holden's sleeve as he fitted the bit into the horse's mouth. "Listen to her. He's a child, Holden. He'll need someone who loves him when you find him."

Holden rounded on Lillibeth, his eyes blazing. "I do! He is my . . ." He bit off the rest of what he'd intended to say.

"Your what?"

"Nothing," he snapped, and slapped the last buckle into place. "I must go. The trail will grow cold."

Samantha went around the couple, sank her foot into the stirrup and mounted the horse behind Holden's saddle before he could stop her. She glared down at him. "I'm going, Holden. Get that through your thick head."

Lillibeth gave her the sunniest smile Samantha had ever seen. "Bravo. Give him a dose of his own stubbornness. Do him a world of good." She fluttered a dainty hand. "Not to worry, Holden. I'll find my way back to the ranch."

All right, she liked this woman. Despite her relationship with the brooding man who mounted before her without further argument. She would come to terms with them—and herself—later. Now, Guy was all-important.

She nearly toppled backward off the horse when he put spurs to the gray's sides. Clinging to Holden's shirt, she pulled herself upright again and hugged his lean torso. He said not one word.

Samantha's anguish was centered on her brother. Holden's tense body told her his was, too.

As Holden's gray pounded into the clearing that surrounded the ranch buildings, one sweeping glance confirmed Samantha's fear. Everyone except Lemuel Baker and Aunt Mattie was off working. Though she longed for more help, she figured she and Holden could manage. She slipped from his horse. Holden must be a good tracker. He had to be.

"Lemuel," she yelled, "saddle my horse."

A muffled, "Yes'm," drifted from the barn.

As she sprinted toward the house, she heard Holden's horse start away. In midstride, she pivoted and bellowed, "Holden Walker, you stop right there!"

He did.

"I told you I'm going with you."

"And I told you, the longer we wait, the colder the tracks grow."

Samantha fished in her shirt pocket, then extended her hand.

Holden nudged his horse toward her. When he got close enough to see what rested in her palm, his brow creased. "A marble? What—"

"Guy's shooter. He never goes anywhere without it."

"So? I still must find the tracks—"

"I found this, Holden. I know where. You don't. Won't it save time if we begin the search from there?"

"Yes," he fairly snarled just as the screened door slammed.

"Samantha, what's going on?"

A sick dread filled her. Slowly, she approached Mattie, then paused, laid a hand on her shoulder and squeezed. "Guy's missing, Aunt Mattie."

"No, he's—"

Again, Samantha raised her hand and opened her fingers so her aunt could see the marble.

"Guy's agate," Mattie murmured, worry dawning in her dark eyes.

With a nod Samantha pocketed the marble. When they found Guy, she'd return it immediately, not keep it as she'd planned. He hadn't carelessly left it lying beneath the tree. Something had happened to him.

"Oscar will want to help, Samantha."

Bless her. So like Mattie Crawford to jump from mindless worry to planned action, but Oscar would not be the answer today.

Samantha shook her head. "All the men are off somewhere. Holden and I will find him." Before dropping her arm, she again squeezed her aunt's shoulder, this time for reassurance.

Mattie looked at Holden. His horse pranced in place, Holden's impatience telegraphed through his hands on the reins.

He nodded. "We shall find him, ma'am. Soon."

Giving him a long assessing look, Mattie said nothing. But as Lemuel led Samantha's horse from the barn, she finally spoke: "I thank you in advance. I know you'll bring my boy back safely."

Holden touched his hat brim in salute, then looked at Samantha. "Show me where you found the marble."

Together they rode to the tree. Holden glanced back toward the barn, which was visible in the distance.

"You could have pointed to this spot. It would have saved time."

"Five minutes' delay while Baker saddled my horse will make no difference."

"Maybe. Maybe not," Holden snapped. He dismounted to scan the ground more closely.

His terse words shot a prickle of foreboding through Samantha. As she watched Holden cover the area with care, she told herself again and again, *Mr. Butcher's crazy, but he won't hurt Guy. He won't.*

"North, toward his ranch." Holden leaped into his saddle and took off like a shot.

As they rode, Samantha spied another of Guy's marbles, then another. Suddenly Holden veered off the road to the Butcher place and headed more westerly across open country.

"Where are you going? The ranch is—"

"The trail leads this way," he called over his shoulder. He continued at a canter, his eyes trained on the dirt beneath him.

Samantha looked down, too, but saw not a darn thing unusual. Hoofprints pitted the land everywhere in this area, along with those of cow, and tracks left by bear, cat, and rabbit. A long list. How could Holden identify specific tracks? How didn't really matter. As long as he found Guy.

Unharmed.

Near dusk Holden reined in for the fifth time and picked up another of Guy's precious marbles. "The boy is leaving a trail. Clever."

Samantha added the blue marble to the growing stash in her pocket. She felt inordinately pleased that Holden recognized her brother's ingenuity. *Holden loves him, too. I know he does.*

"Where might Butcher head, Samantha? There is not much out here."

She chewed her bottom lip, secretly pleased that this taciturn man had asked her opinion. Turning in her saddle to look in all directions, she voiced the only idea that came to mind. "We are on Singletree land. Mr. Butcher has line cabins just as we do. He runs a lot of cattle."

Holden's eyes narrowed as he watched the last sliver of sun sink in the west. "Do you know if there is one in this direction?"

"No. But it would be a logical place to take Guy, wouldn't it? If he took him home, Guy would surely make a fuss. Mr. Butcher's men would know something was up."

"You think he is logical?"

"Not the last time I saw him."

"Loco men do not reason, Samantha."

Frustration ignited inside her. "Do *you* think he's taken Guy home?"

"No."

"Then why are we having this conversation?" she cried.

"To know what I face with this man."

A shiver slithered down her spine. When they found Mr. Butcher, challenged him, there was no telling what he might do to Guy.

Chapter Eighteen

Clarence Uriah Butcher is a dead man.

Holden buoyed himself with that thought. He should have killed Butcher the day he discovered the man had violated Bubbling Water. The day they had found C. J. dead. But no. His reasoning that Uriah Butcher would suffer more by living left a bitter taste in his mouth now.

Vengeance had been Walks in Shadow's to impose. He never should have veered from that path, even if he had hanged for it. Had he killed the man that day, he and Samantha would not be searching for the bastard right now, searching for Little Spring.

Not Little Spring.

He glanced at Samantha. She rode next to him, her face knitted with worry. Guy now belonged to her, to Timberoaks and the white world. Indian blood coursed through his veins, but because of the life he had lived, the boy was no longer Little Spring.

Intently studying the ground beneath his horse's belly for several yards, Holden again saw the faint hoofprint he

now identified as the left foreleg of the horse Uriah had
ridden at a gallop.

A lone coyote's howl sounded from the east. Taking
stock of the daylight left to them, he drew rein. Surely he
would find the bastard before Guy had to spend the night
away from Timberoaks.

Holden had no idea how the boy was dressed, but he
doubted Guy wore a coat. It had been too warm for one
that morning. But the nights grew cool as soon as the sun
went down. He glanced skyward. That time had already
passed.

"Why are we stopping?"

"I must walk if I hope to see trail in the gloaming."

"But that will slow us down," Samantha wailed.

"Better slow than to overlook a turn," he said gravely.
Signs could be followed in darkness, but it tested the met-
tle of the best tracker. Fortunately, there would be a moon
tonight.

"We must hurry, Holden. Mr. Butcher is crazy. There's
no telling what he might do to Guy."

Holden paused, looking up at her. "What have you not
told me?"

"He might hurt Guy worse than the last time."

His gut clenched. "And that means . . . ?"

"He bruised Guy's arm that day."

"Bruised."

"He yanked him up off the ground, wrenching his arm.
It's a wonder he didn't break it."

Could be worse, yes. But if Butcher mistook Guy for
C. J., he would not maim him for the hell of it. Even a loco
man prized his son.

Holden shook his head. He could only do his best, no
matter how much he wanted to hurry. Patience had served
him well in the past; it would have to now. He scanned the
ground again and found another print, which gave him the
direction to walk.

When he moved on, it was several minutes before he heard Samantha's horse's softly thudding hooves behind him. And something else. Pausing again, he raised his hand to stop her. When she stilled, he listened. Faint and indistinct, a man's voice carried in the night from . . . somewhere.

"What—"

"Shh!"

He tilted his head and turned in a slow circle . . . and then he saw it. A glimmer of light off to the west. Unnatural light since the sun had already sunk below the horizon.

"Holden . . ."

A second time he raised his hand. And this time he placed a finger over his lips. He motioned for her to dismount. She did, and walked up next to him. He hiked his chin in the direction he wanted her to look.

Her face the picture of hope, her voice a mere whisper, she leaned close. "You think it's them?"

He shrugged. "Could be Butcher's men having a smoke before they turn in."

"Please, God," she murmured.

Holden understood her plea. He reached for her reins and led the two horses himself. Samantha stumbled in the dark behind him. He turned, again placing his finger across his lips.

"All right!" she mouthed.

"Damn . . . I told . . . to . . ."

Disjointed words carried in the night. Definitely Butcher's voice. Holden breathed a sigh of relief. Maybe premature, but at least they had found the bastard. Now he would check the lay of the land before moving in.

"Do it again!" Butcher ordered.

Holden circled behind a rock outcrop. He looked over his shoulder. Damnation. Where had Samantha gone? If she barged into an unknown situation, she might cause more harm.

Hampered by the two horses, horses that needed to be kept quiet, he glanced around quickly. Nothing but brush met his eye. It would have to do. He led the animals away from the line cabin where Butcher's voice was still audible. Yanking on a bush, he found it anchored by roots and quickly tied both horses, then backtracked to where he had last seen Samantha.

Bent at the waist, he cautiously headed in the direction of Butcher's harangue. He heard Guy's plaintive reply.

"I did just like ya said!"

"No, ya didn't. Ya ain't got the sense God gave a snake, boy. Put that gun back together and do it right this time."

Holden's brow crinkled. *Put the gun together?* As he mulled those words, he spied Samantha crouched behind a pile of rocks. Her light shirt gleamed in the night like a beacon, even though the moon had yet to rise. Beyond the protective rock screen, the light Holden had spied earlier flared skyward. Kerosene scented the air.

Without a sound, he eased up behind Samantha. As he clamped a hand over her mouth, he simultaneously pulled her back against his chest.

She bucked against him until he hissed in her ear, "We need a plan before confronting him."

Rather than have Samantha stumble backward and alert Butcher to their presence, Holden whipped her around and pushed her ahead of him, back the way they had come. He did not stop until he figured they could talk without being heard.

The minute he halted, she swung around and glared at him. "I wasn't going to do anything until you returned. You didn't have to scare the liver out of me."

Oh, how he loved this woman's fire. How he wished he could have her forever. But right now he needed to save young Guy from Butcher's clutches.

"Fine. But I did not know that. Did I?" he challenged right back.

"I'm not stupid, Holden."

"No. You are worried about your brother. And worry causes us to lose our heads."

Samantha settled down immediately, her expression changing from anger to worry in a heartbeat. "You're right. I'm . . . sorry. What do you suggest?"

"Your choice of concealment was good. We shall return there. I do not know if Butcher will let us enter his camp, but if he does not . . ." The sentence dangled as Holden wracked his brain for an idea.

"Let me confront him," she said eagerly. "He won't expect me. Shoot, he won't figure anyone's going to come along here."

"No."

"He won't expect me, or—"

"No, it is not a good idea for you to—"

"Do you have a better idea?"

Actually, all of a sudden he did, and she would be pleased that he was simply enlarging upon her plan.

She must have seen his expression change, for she entreated him to continue by spreading her hands. He drew her down to the ground. Marking an *X* in the dirt, he showed her what he had in mind.

"This is Butcher and Guy. You and I will split up. I go this way, circle around and come in behind him. You will go this way." He drew another *X* that put her on the trail leading to the cabin from the direction of Butcher's ranch.

In the darkness he could barely see her face, but he caught the lift of her lips when she smiled. "I thought you didn't want me to confront him?"

He shrugged. "Once I am positioned behind him, there will be little time before I move in." He looked into her eyes. "Nothing will happen to you or to Guy."

For mesmerizing seconds they gazed at each other.

"My promise," he murmured.

She swallowed and licked her lips. His gaze settled on her mouth, a luscious mouth he longed to taste; then he looked into her eyes again. Samantha dropped her gaze first.

"Okay." Her voice shook. "Do I say anything?"

"Not unless you have to. But wait until I am positioned before you show yourself. And do not walk too close, Samantha."

She frowned, but didn't argue. "I won't be able to see when you're ready."

She started when he raised his hand, cupped it beside his mouth and made a wild turkey sound.

Her eyes rounded. "How did you do that?"

"My people learn to bird-speak when young."

Off in the distance, a turkey answered. A real turkey.

Samantha clamped a hand over her mouth to stifle a laugh. "How will I know it's you?"

Rattled, he was not sure himself. The hen had surprised him as much as Samantha. "I will make sure you see me. Besides, Butcher may not be hostile. He may welcome you."

Sure he will. And invite me to sit for a cup of tea while he's at it! She crouched behind the rocks, watching Holden's shadow merge into the darkness as he made his way to the other side of the clearing.

"No! How many times I gotta tell ya?"

Samantha's attention settled on Mr. Butcher and Guy as the demented man grabbed the gun stock from her brother's small hands.

"Like this," Butcher said, fitting the stock to the cylinder. He handed it back to Guy. "Now, do it again."

Seated before the open door of the shack, Guy hunched in the dirt, his profile to Samantha. She could see smudges on his cheek and suspected he had been crying. Right now, though, he glared at Mr. Butcher before accepting the gun pieces. Then he set to work.

Why Butcher demanded that Guy do this, Samantha didn't know. Perhaps he figured since men must clean their weapons on a regular basis, Guy needed to know how to break down his gun and put it back together again. That was the only thing that made sense to her.

But Guy was still a boy, for heaven's sake. Yes, he knew how to shoot. So did Samantha; she carried a rifle when she rode out. But other than the handgun her father carried in his belt, Hiram had kept other firearms he owned locked in a cabinet in his study. Time enough for Guy to learn how to handle and take care of a gun when he grew older.

From the corner of her eye she saw movement in the trees behind Butcher. Her gaze snapped back to the tableau in the circle of light, afraid the man had also seen Holden. At that moment, Butcher's hand snaked forward and cuffed Guy across the face.

"No! Dammit."

Without thought, Samantha lunged up and stepped into the clearing. She checked herself at once, Holden's words of caution jumping to mind, but too late. Butcher had seen her.

He frowned, probably light-blind for a second. He sputtered, "Wh—What the hell ya doin' out here, Cora Sue?"

Cora Sue? Stock-still, Samantha blinked. Mr. Butcher had mistaken her for his dead wife. She had been a careworn woman no more than an inch over five feet, with mousey blond hair. She'd never worn trousers like Samantha's. No one with a lick of sense could confuse the two. Besides, Cora Sue Butcher had been dead more than ten years.

"Samma?" Guy's voice quaked across the distance.

She put up her hand to silence him, her attention glued to Mr. Butcher. She had no idea if Holden was in striking distance and dared not look. Dared not alert this insane man that danger lurked behind him.

Butcher appeared not to have heard Guy, for he stood and beckoned Samantha forward. "Git yer ass over here, Cora Sue. Guess I'm gonna have to teach ya another lesson."

Samantha had a good idea what kind of lesson he had in mind after seeing him strike Guy. She didn't move. Not until Butcher started toward her. She raised her hand to forestall his movement.

Oh-so-slowly, she stepped forward. "I'm coming."

Reasoning that he couldn't do much to her, she walked to within two feet of him. Without warning, he hauled off and slapped her so hard that she saw stars. Unbalanced, she flew sideways and landed in the dirt.

"Samma!" Guy cried.

For a second she thought she might lose consciousness. When the faintness passed, she stiffened her arms to lift herself. Out of the corner of her eye, she saw Holden Walker's avenging form.

"Butcher!"

The shorter man whirled to face him.

Holden had let the slap to Guy pass because he was not in position. Then Butcher had nearly taken off Samantha's head. Now, his gun leveled, Holden stalked toward the man he wanted to see dead more than he wanted to take his next breath.

In the next instant, several things registered in his brain. Butcher's sudden fear as he stared down the barrel of Holden's .44. Guy's race toward Samantha. Her wide eyes staring, not at her brother but at him. Pleading . . . ?

For what? That he allow this vermin to live?

Could he cold-bloodedly cut down Butcher with Samantha and Guy there to see . . . and remember?

All this whirled through his mind in that split second he cocked the repeater and fired . . . twice.

Butcher screamed and went down.

The gun reports echoed . . . echoed . . . echoed over the prairie for long seconds.

Then silence.

Chapter Nineteen

Samantha barely had time to push herself to a sitting position before Guy flung himself at her. His arms wrapped tightly around her neck; his legs anchored around her waist in a grip she couldn't have dislodged if she'd wanted to. But she didn't.

"You all right?" both asked simultaneously.

"Uh-huh," Guy blubbered into her neck. "He hit me too."

"I know, sweetie. I'm sorry."

In the next instant, she was pulled up from the ground, and Holden's protective arms held both her and Guy. "I promised you would not be hurt, but you were."

"We're okay, Holden. Is he—"

"Son of a bitch!" Uriah screamed, cutting off her inquiry and answering her fearful question.

Holden hadn't killed him.

No matter what he had done, Samantha didn't want her neighbor dead at Holden's hands. In a fraction of a second he had winged Mr. Butcher, handling the .44 with such speed that his ability with the weapon amazed her. The smell of spent gunpowder burned her nose.

"My hand! My knee! Damn you. I'll kill you!"

"Come. I will see the two of you to Timberoaks," Holden said over Butcher's threat.

She pressed a hand against his chest. "We must treat his wounds, Holden. He could bleed to death." As she spoke, she looked at Mr. Butcher, propped on one elbow in the dirt, his face screwed into a mask of pain. And well it should be.

"My God, his hand and knee are shattered."

"The punishment fits the crime."

She frowned with incomprehension.

"He will never hit another person with his right hand, Samantha," Holden said grimly. "And he will be unable to sit a horse for a long while."

Guy peered past her shoulder as he hitched in a breath. "What'sa matter with 'im, Samma? He scairt me again."

Giving her no time to answer, Holden said, "Come." He clasped her arm this time.

"We can't leave him like this."

"Yes, we can. You are going home." He tugged her along.

"But, Holden—"

"Goddamn you! Come back here, you son of a bitch."

"Holden—"

"I will see to him after you and Guy are safe at home,"

See to him? What did he mean? Come back to finish the job? She shook her head. Of course not. If Holden had intended to kill Mr. Butcher, he would have with his first shot. Those bullets had not gone willy-nilly. Each one had hit the mark intended. That she was sure of. Still, she argued.

"We can't leave him lying out here so . . . crippled. The smell of blood could bring . . . no telling what."

"Fine," Holden snapped, then turned on his heel and stalked toward Mr. Butcher.

Uriah flopped on his back, raising his good arm protectively. "Get away from me."

Ignoring his cowering, Holden cupped him under the arms and dragged him, none too gently, toward the line shack.

"Jesus Christ!" Butcher ground out through a grimace of pain.

Samantha knew he must be in agony, but she turned her back and pressed Guy's head against her shoulder. Her young brother had already seen enough.

"Walker! Walk—" The slam of the door cut off Uriah's words.

In the next instant, Holden took her arm again. He led her away; Mr. Butcher's obscenities grew fainter as they walked toward the horses. She guessed she'd have to be satisfied with that. At least he would be out of the elements until Walker got back to him. Then what?

Holden said not a word during the three-hour ride home. Hours in which her brother lolled off to sleep. Far stronger and more capable of handling the boy's weight than she, Holden took him up before himself.

Several times Samantha relaxed enough to doze, then jerked upright when her eyes closed of their own volition.

She absently rubbed her temple and cheekbone, vowing never again to range close enough to be on the receiving end of Mr. Butcher's fist. The fact that he would never again hit someone with his right hand might slow him down a bit, but he still had his left.

Perhaps she should feel guilty, but a half smile of satisfaction lifted her lips. Mr. Butcher wouldn't sit a saddle for a while. Maybe a long while. Bully that he'd always been, it wouldn't look manly if he appeared at Timberoaks in a buggy. Even if she kept her mouth shut about tonight's events, she doubted Guy would. He'd spread the tale to anyone who'd listen how Holden Walker had got the drop on Mr. Butcher.

At long last she saw light from the ranch glimmering over the treetops, and was not surprised that a golden glow spilled from every window and door in the house and bunkhouse.

As they rode into the clearing, Oscar spurred his horse toward them. "The boy okay?" he asked when he got close enough to see Guy cradled in Holden's arms.

Guy pushed himself up and squinted toward the house as Samantha answered, "Tired, but okay."

"Where'd ya find him?"

"Mr. Butcher made me go with 'im." Guy rubbed sleep-drenched eyes.

"Miz Mattie is fit to skin a polecat," Oscar said. "Ya best get the boy over to her right away, Walker."

Oscar reined his horse around and fell in next to Samantha, his dark eyes scanning her from head to toe. "You all right?"

She gave him a weak smile. "Tired."

"What's the matter with your face?"

Her hand came up to her cheek before she thought. "Nothing serious."

"He hit her," Holden said.

"That son of a bitch!" Oscar exclaimed.

"Guy!" Mattie ran toward them. "Give me that boy!"

Holden didn't have to be told twice. Guy more or less fell into Mattie's waiting arms. And as he'd done with Samantha, he clung to his aunt like a woolly cub.

Mattie glanced up at Holden, then without a word turned and trudged toward the house, staggering a bit under Guy's weight. Samantha stepped down from her mount, feeling oddly at loose ends. Then she looked up at Walker.

"Thank you." It was little to say, but the gratitude in her heart couldn't be expressed in words. He'd found and rescued Guy in record time. And, thank God, he hadn't killed a man to do it.

He didn't acknowledge her thanks. With an ache in her heart, she knew Holden would move on. Leave Guy to them. A boy he loved as much as she did.

"Holden?"

Samantha jerked her head around at the feminine voice. Lillibeth. Holden's woman. She closed her eyes. Rather than witness their reunion, she threw the reins in Oscar's direction, uncaring whether he caught them. She passed Lillibeth without a glance.

Holden sat his horse, watching Samantha as she practically ran from him. On the ride back to the ranch, time and again he had caught her surreptitious glances. Fear? Disgust? Sometimes his superlative night vision was a curse rather than a blessing.

He knew not exactly what she thought, but rage had sprung up in him when Butcher slapped her. His pistol discharged before he realized he held it. He shrugged inwardly. Untrue, perhaps. He did have the presence of mind to pull his shots.

After Butcher's abuse of Guy, Holden did not doubt that the man was as crazed as a rabid coyote. Rabid animals were shot for two reasons: to protect humans and to put the animals out of their misery. Now he regretted his impulse to let the man live.

"Holden?"

He glanced down where Lillibeth's small hand lay against his knee.

"Are you all right?"

"Sorry," Oscar said. "Didn't think to ask that myself."

Holden shrugged. Physically he was fine, but his mind . . . his heart . . . Against all common sense, he had fallen in love with Samantha Timberlake. He shook his head at the futility of that emotion. She feared him now more than before.

"I am fine. But I must return to Butcher."

"Where is he?" Oscar asked.

"At one of his line shacks. He is . . . injured."

Oscar stared at him, saying nothing.

"I shot him."

"Oh, Holden." Tears sprang to Lillibeth's eyes.

"He lives. I will take him to his ranch."

"Want some help?"

"No." He did not want Oscar around to hear his little talk with Butcher before he took him home. Holden knew he must leave Timberoaks, leave Samantha, but before he did, Uriah Butcher would understand that if he ever returned to Timberoaks, Holden would not spare him a third time.

He looked into Lillibeth's compassionate eyes. There was no reason she could not remain here. As painful as it might be to hear about Samantha—when she took a man into her heart, into her bed—Holden would know, for he vowed to correspond with Lillibeth. To know exactly what transpired at Timberoaks after his leave-taking.

Glancing up, he gauged the hour by the gunmetal-colored sky. By the time he got back to the line shack, dawn would have brightened to full day. He patted Lillibeth's hand, still lying on his knee.

"I will return later."

She stepped away.

Oscar touched his hat brim. "Y'all watch yer back, Walker."

Samantha stood at the parlor window and watched Holden ride away. A frisson of fear flashed through her. She knew where he was headed. Did Mr. Butcher have another gun in the line shack? Holden had dragged him inside, but had he taken the time to check? Even one-handed, Uriah Butcher could doubtless handle a rifle or pistol.

"Stay safe, Holden," she murmured. "Don't walk in blind."

Floorboards creaked overhead, followed by steps on the

stairs. She turned as Mattie gained the bottom landing. "Is Guy asleep?"

"Yes. He's worn out." Mattie paused, her brow crinkled. "What happened out there, Samantha? Is Uriah . . ."

Samantha shook her head. "Holden shot him, but he's alive." Crippled, maybe, but still able to cause her grief.

Mattie took that information in stride. As though shooting a man were an everyday occurrence, she changed the subject. "You should get some sleep, too." She looked out the window. "Where is Mr. Walker?"

"He's gone back to take Mr. Butcher to his ranch. He needs . . . tending."

"I should have thanked him for bringing Guy home."

Samantha remembered his taciturn manner when she had done so. "He doesn't want our thanks, Aunt Mattie. He doesn't want a thing from us. From me," she added softly.

Mattie caressed Samantha's cheek. "Oh, dear, you didn't heed my warning." She missed a beat as tears welled in her eyes. "Sometimes we have no choice, do we? Love is given before we realize it."

Samantha dashed away, biting back a sob. Pounding up the stairs, she repeated all the reasons why she shouldn't love Holden Walker. *He's more Indian than white. He abandoned a child. He must be a gunfighter! He couldn't handle a pistol that well if he weren't.*

And he's in love with Lillibeth Gentry.

Unmindful of Guy asleep across the hall, she slammed the bedroom door, flung herself across the bed and twisted the coverlet in her fist. It did no good whatsoever to tell herself all that. None of it mattered. Not to her heart.

She loved him.

Fatigue lay like a blanket over Holden. It had been a long night. He eased out of the saddle and tied his mount to a bush. Sage stung his nostrils. Rain would be welcome, but the air promised another warm, dry day. While stripping off his gloves and looping them over his belt, he listened. The occasional bird twitter, faint scrabble of passing small animals, squirrels' chatter told him nothing untoward was afoot. He thanked the Spirits for that.

Once he had a talk with Butcher and carted him home, nothing would hold him here. He had reached the conclusion that it would be best for all if he collected his belongings at Timberoaks and simply lit out.

Initially, Lillibeth might put up a fuss. No fool she, he knew in his gut she had already discerned his ill-advised feelings for Samantha. Lillibeth would understand his need to move on.

Lifting his hand, he brushed his mount's soft muzzle. The horse nodded, mouthing the bit. "Thirsty?"

Holden loosed the strap of his canteen from the saddle horn and shook it. Not much, but it would wet the gray's whistle until he could get him to a stream. Uncapping the container, he took a single swallow for himself, then poured the remainder in his hat.

While the thirsty animal slurped up the meager offering, Holden gave him a last reassuring pat, then clamped the hat back on and walked in the general direction of the line shack. Now, in daylight, he could move quicker, though caution prevailed.

Had any of Butcher's men found him? Butcher was a loudmouth and a bully when he thought he could get away with it. And because he was a substantial landowner, he got away with it more often than not. Still, Holden doubted he inspired loyalty in his men. But none of that meant Butcher's ranch hands would take kindly to Holden. They did, after all, collect pay from Butcher. That alone sometimes inspired fealty.

Finding himself near the rocks Samantha had used as a shield during the night, he paused and listened again. Nothing. He edged past the rocks and searched the area around the line shack. Other than Butcher's horse in the small enclosure at the side of the building, nothing breathed.

Ever more cautious, he approached the door. Inside, he heard a clink. Apparently awake, Butcher moved around a bit. Pulling his gun, Holden grasped the latch, pulled open the door and stepped inside. If Butcher lay in wait for him, he could do nothing about the seconds it took for his eyes to adjust to the dim interior.

He was in luck.

Across the small room, Butcher had propped himself against the wall and attempted to load a rifle with one hand. Fortunately, he had not accomplished the task.

"Forget it." Holden drew the door closed behind him.

Butcher glared at him, his mouth thinned to a line. "Get outta here, you son of a bitch. Ain't you done enough?"

Holden strode across the floor and yanked the firearm from the man's hand. "Maybe. Maybe not." He slid the rifle toward the far wall. "You will not need that."

Butcher put up his good hand to ward off a blow.

"I have no intention of slugging you. Not yet, anyway." He picked up the one chair in the cabin, swung it around and straddled it backward, facing the man he considered the vermin of the earth. "We will talk."

"I ain't got nothin' to say to you."

Holden thumbed his hat back. "Correct. You do not. But I have plenty to say to you, old man."

"When my boys shows up, yer a dead man, Walker."

Absently, Holden stroked the barrel of his six-shooter. "I doubt they will help you, Butcher. If they try, I doubt they will succeed."

Fear passed over the man's features before he masked his thoughts. He did not have to say anything. His expression had shown Holden all he needed to know. It would be a miracle if any of Butcher's hands even showed up.

"Did you really think you could get away with kidnapping Guy?"

"Who?"

"No games, Butcher. You may be loco at times, but right now you know what I am saying."

"I ain't loco. Whatever give you that idea?"

"For starters, mistaking Guy Timberlake for your son. C. J. is dead, old man."

Butcher's fevered eyes dimmed before he ducked his head. "I know. Them damned redskins is gonna pay."

"For your vile act? I do not think so."

"I didn't do nothin'! They killed my boy for no good reason."

Holden stood, grabbed a fistful of Butcher's shirtfront and lifted him as if he were a featherweight. The sudden movement caused the injured man to grimace with pain. Holden jarred him down on his feet.

"Goddamn!" Butcher gritted through his teeth.

"You want more, old man? I can break the rest of your limbs. Give me half a reason."

"No! Jesus, Walker, put me down."

Holden pushed the coward against the wall and let him slide to the floor. At the last moment, Butcher put out his good hand to slow his fall. He gasped for breath.

"No lies. A few years back, you raped an Indian girl and left her for dead." Holden knelt and stuck his face close to Butcher's. "She did not die. She lived to tell the tale."

"You don't know nothin'. You ain't no Indian."

Holden smiled coldly, noticing that Butcher did not deny the charge. "You would be surprised. But this is not what I have come to speak of." He regained his seat. "You have ridden onto Timberoaks for the last time. Show your face there again and I will kill you. That is my word."

"Now just one damn minute. Hiram wanted me to manage his place, and I'm gonna do it!"

Shaking his head, Holden holstered his gun. "I believe Mr. Timberlake wanted Oscar Dupree to manage for Miss Timberlake until she can manage on her own."

Or marries.

Holden had heard enough talk to understand what Timberlake's will stipulated. He could not bring himself to believe that Samantha's father would have put her future in this man's hands. No. When he wrote the stipulation about a ranch manager, he had thought his trusted foreman would be in charge for as long as his daughter needed his assistance.

"Send word to the judge who appointed you. Tell him your services at Timberoaks are"—Holden's eyes ranged from Butcher's useless hand to his shattered knee—"more than you can handle. That he should ask Oscar Dupree to take over."

"You think I'm crazy? Jesus, Walker, Samantha will marry . . ." He paused, frowning. "Well, not my boy." He looked up, a crafty expression in his eyes. "We'll have the best damned spread around if'n I marry her."

Holden thought he had been angry before. The rage that now claimed him burned fire-bright. As he lunged up, the chair tipped to crash on Butcher's injured knee.

"Holy shit!" the man screamed. In the next instant he clamped his mouth shut.

Holden's gun jammed against his forehead square between the bastard's eyes. Fear washed through Butcher, lit his eyes. Holden smelled the warm urine that puddled beneath the man. How he kept from pulling the trigger, he would never know.

Voice low, Holden narrowed his eyes and spoke in measured words. "If you again fail to listen when I speak, I will put you out of your misery here and now."

As still as a startled rabbit, the older man fixed his gaze on Holden.

"I say again, you will never ride onto Timberoaks. You will steer clear of Samantha, her brother, everyone who works for her."

"It's a free country. I can go—"

Holden cocked his gun. Butcher stopped as if his throat had been cut.

"You have a death wish, old man?"

"N—n—no. Don't—"

"Repeat after me, Butcher. I will not go near Samantha Timberlake, her family, or any of the people who work on Timberoaks."

"Huh?"

"Too much to remember? Try."

Butcher swallowed hard; his Adam's apple bobbed up and down. "I ain't gonna bother Samantha."

Holden said nothing, only arched an expectant brow.

"I ain't gonna go over to Timberoaks."

"And Guy?"

"He ain't worth a lick o' salt. He needs—"

Holden rammed the gun barrel hard against Butcher's forehead. His finger tightened on the trigger.

"Wait! He ain't worth it nohow. I won't talk to him neither."

For long seconds Holden did not move, kept the pressure of his gun between Butcher's eyes. Could he believe this man? Probably not. So his earlier plan would have to work. If anything untoward happened, Lillibeth would let him know.

But by then, undoubtedly, it would already be too late.

Chapter Twenty

Samantha had lingered in her room that morning in the hope that she wouldn't come face-to-face with Lillibeth. When she'd finally gone downstairs, Aunt Mattie informed her that Lillibeth was already at work in the little shack. Probably with Holden's help. She'd grimaced at the thought as she tried to down a few bites of breakfast.

Now, pausing in the wide doorway as her eyes adjusted to the dimmer light inside the barn, she heard her brother's exasperated voice.

"Ya gotta watch, Lemuel!"

Guy stood halfway down the corridor, looking toward a stall across the much-trodden dirt. At that moment, Lemuel Baker's head bobbed into view inside the stall.

"I gots work to do, Guy. This here stall don' muck itse'f."

Samantha didn't have to be told what Lemuel was doing. The barn always held its own mingled odors: straw, oats, dirt and urine. The last odor was strong this morning with Lemuel stirring up the bedding straw.

She glanced back at Guy, who stood ramrod-straight.

For the first time, Samantha noticed a short, bent stick thrust into his belt.

"It'll only take a minute."

"Awright. Show me so's I can gets back to ma job."

"He yelled, 'Butcher!' and marched up to him." Guy took three deliberate steps, then yanked at the stick. But it caught on the leather.

"Dern it!" he exclaimed, more exasperated than before. When he fumbled the stick loose, he pointed it at Lemuel. "Kapow, kapow! Two shots quicker'n a rattlesnake strikes, he shot Mr. Butcher."

"Fast, huh?" Lemuel feigned the awe that Guy undoubtedly desired.

"Yeah! Mr. Butcher fell screamin', 'Son of a bitch.'"

Samantha's eyes rounded at the expletive coming from her young brother's mouth.

"He was so fast!" he continued. "I'm gonna learn how to shoot like that someday."

At that dire prediction, Samantha found her tongue. "Not likely, young man."

Guy jumped at the interruption and swung to face her, the stick still extended. "Yes, I will. Walker'll teach me."

"That's *Mr.* Walker to you. And, no, he will not teach you to shoot. We only use guns for protection, Guy."

"Well, Walk . . . Mr. Walker was protectin' me and you, wudn't he?"

In a way Guy was right, but be darned if she'd admit it. "He could have shot at the ground and missed Mr. Butcher. The shots alone would have stopped him."

"No—"

"I'm not going to argue the point, Guy. If you persist, I'll tell Aunt Mattie, and she'll lock you in your room if need be."

His lower lip protruded. "She cain't keep me locked up forever." Defiance burned in his pale blue eyes.

"Guy!"

"Miss Samma's right, boy. No need larnin' shooter's

ways here on this ranch. Ya already knows how to shoot snakes and such. That's all a body needs ta know. 'Sides, ya ain't larned to be up early enough to get ahead o' yer auntie."

Samantha shot a grateful glance at Lemuel. Though shunned by many because of his skin color, he was a good person, with common sense and loyalty to Timberoaks that went bone-deep. In fact, more than most white men possessed.

Guy had ducked his head and dropped his arm to his side. He still held the stick, but his boot toe swirled in the dirt. Lemuel's words had chastened him.

"Now, boy," Lemuel went on smoothly, "I could use yer he'p. Get a halter and take that thar mare outta the next stall. Day's gettin' old and I gots other things ta do when I finish this muckin'."

Suppressing a smile, Samantha stepped in to give Lemuel the opportunity to show her brother a thing or two. "I'll take out the mare while Guy helps you."

Lemuel picked up on her suggestion quicker than the striking rattler Guy had mentioned. "That's a fine idea, Miss Samma. That short-handled shovel you used to use is 'round here somewheres. Wudn't you about his age when yer paw showed you how to work in the barn?"

"Aw, Samma, I—"

"Yes, I was, Lemuel." She leveled an innocent expression at her brother. "Get the shovel off the back wall and start to work."

Guy lowered his gaze and let his shoulders slump. "Yes'm," he mumbled and dropped the stick. Slowly, he scuffed off toward the back of the barn, shortly returning with the shovel in hand.

Lemuel's white teeth flashed in a smile. He winked at Samantha before bending out of view to his task. Guy joined him in the stall.

"Fill that shovel 'bout half full. When you is bigger and gets a set of muscles on ya, then y'all can scoop up more."

She went into the tack room and picked up the bridle that fit the mare. Returning to the barn, she passed the stall where Guy worked. He struggled to get the shovel's bowl under the wet straw. Over his bent back, Lemuel offered her an amiable smile and another wink.

As she saddled the mare, then mounted, she recalled the speed and ease with which Walker handled his gun. Her stomach clenched at the thought that Guy might learn to shoot with such deadly precision. She was grateful for Walker's assistance, but one man on the ranch that fast with a six-shooter was one too many. Trouble plagued men like that. Worry would follow her every waking moment if her brother gained such a skill.

How had Walker learned to shoot so well? And more importantly, why? Did he hire himself out? He could have easily killed Mr. Butcher. But, she consoled herself, he hadn't.

She reined in next to the corral where the black stood by the fence. He tossed his head and crow-hopped away from her. How could Walker show such patience, be so gentle with a horse, yet shoot a man with no apparent compunction?

It doesn't matter. You love him, fool that you are.

Lillibeth chipped at the paint streaked on the windowpane. Whoever wielded the brush long ago had been careless about where the paint landed. Laying the file aside, she stared dolefully at her red palm. She needed a better tool or gloves or she'd soon have no skin left on her hand. Two blisters had already appeared; one seeped.

Well, shoot, she could take till Christmas to get that paint off the window. She'd do something else for a while.

Christmas. Would she be here that long?

Glancing around the sparsely furnished room, she couldn't help hoping. Just a little. She'd liked Mattie Crawford from the moment they'd met. She figured in time Samantha would come around.

Lillibeth knew what stuck in the young woman's craw. Would it help if she told Samantha she didn't love Holden? That he most certainly didn't love her? Perhaps Holden loved her in a sisterly way, but not in the sense that bothered the stubborn girl.

She smiled.

Lillibeth had no doubt that "stubborn" was Samantha's middle name. Between Holden and that young woman . . . *Oh, my. Sparks will fly if they will allow themselves to acknowledge their love for each other.*

She picked up the broom, swept the dirt and paint shavings sprinkled below the window. Her thoughts roamed to Oscar Dupree. Pausing, she rested on the broom handle. Now there was a man who piqued her interest. Mr. Dupree stood a half head shorter than Holden, but that put him closer to her height.

By no stretch of the imagination could he be considered handsome. Not even by his mother. But within his dark, lined, lived-in face, he possessed the most beautiful chocolate-brown eyes. Kind eyes that stared at her with admiration.

She winced and shook her head, pushing the broom with a vengeance. *If he or Mattie Crawford ever finds out about your recent profession, you'll be a pariah, Lillibeth Gentry, and don't you forget it.*

It took a moment to identify the faint noise that interrupted her thoughts. Stepping to the door, she scanned the clearing, then caught sight of Holden as he rode toward the cabin. In no apparent hurry, he allowed his mount to amble.

With his head tipped down, she couldn't see his face for his hat brim. His shoulders were slumped, the reins held slack in his hand. He looked as if he dozed in the saddle, the picture of exhaustion. No doubt he was exhausted, but she wondered if that tiredness stemmed from lack of sleep, or if it wasn't as much mental. A betting woman would put her money on the latter.

The gray halted at the hitching post of its own accord. A moment later Holden roused himself with a shake of his head, swung his leg over the back of the horse and dismounted. He hadn't seen Lillibeth yet. Absently, he patted the gray and said something in a low voice she couldn't hear. Then he removed the saddle.

When he turned toward the shack, the saddle in both hands, he spied her. Never in her life had Lillibeth seen such an expression of desolation. He struggled to compose himself, his lips curved in a halfhearted smile, but his eyes remained as bleak as winter skies.

"You are here early." He walked toward her, carrying the saddle with ease.

"I've been working about an hour." She searched his face. "Are you all right?"

"A long night."

"And?"

She stepped back and allowed him to enter the small dwelling. He tipped the saddle on its horn and fork in the corner of the room, then straightened. "You have been busy. It is coming along."

"Stop this annoying habit of avoiding my questions, Holden. What have you done about that vile man?"

"I did not shoot him again, if that is what you want to know. I did nothing but talk to him."

*Tsk*ing, Lillibeth narrowed her eyes. "And?"

"Butcher preferred that I leave him where he was. I rode to his ranch and alerted one of his hands that he needed assistance."

She continued to look up at him expectantly.

Holden sighed. "I ordered him never to come to Timberoaks again. If he does, I *will* kill him."

"Why didn't you?"

Holden ignored her pointed question and started past her. Lillibeth shot out a hand and gripped his arm. "Why didn't you?"

Still silent, he stared out the door, refusing to look at her.

Since he didn't answer, she expressed her own thoughts on the subject. "You didn't want to taint Samantha Timberlake's opinion of you. If you killed that horrible man, she might hate you."

Not by the flicker of an eye did Holden respond. The man might as well be made of marble.

Vexed, she stopped just short of stamping her foot. "You've got rocks in your head, Holden. She loves you. She could never hate you."

He looked down at her, bleakness again dimming his eyes. "It is questionable as to who has rocks in the head."

"Against my better judgment, I've allowed you to bring me here to attempt to set up a school. I don't consider myself a courageous person, Holden, but if I can take this chance, why can't you talk to Samantha?"

"Talk is pointless, Lillibeth. I will move on soon."

"To where?" Men! Such pigheaded creatures. Why couldn't he just admit he loved Samantha?

"I do not know where I will go," he finally replied. "It makes little difference. I will find a job trailing cattle or handling a remuda."

"And maybe drift into trouble along the way with that fast gun of yours. Holden, it's time to settle down. Here. With Samantha Timberlake."

He shook his head, walked over to the window and scooped up the file she had used earlier. His back to her, he began to scrape the paint.

Samantha sat on the bank of the stream not far from Holden's camp. She'd frittered away the entire day riding aimlessly. Only once had she seen Oscar, Grogan and another hand. They labored in the heat, knocking together a new pen. She'd kept her distance. She couldn't work up enough gumption to help them or anyone else today.

As she chucked a small pebble into the water, Aunt Mattie's words rose fresh in her mind. *"Love is given before we realize it."*

"So true," she muttered.

Common sense had deserted her. From the get-go she'd known Holden was a drifter. If he'd lived with Comanches for years, he'd surely killed white men and women. That should frighten her.

But it doesn't.

He'd left Guy here and not looked back for more than five years. His way of protecting Guy, perhaps, but to her it seemed a misguided way. Thank God her father had taken the boy in and treated him like a son, made him her brother.

Around and around her thoughts went. But her needs kept coming to the fore. She wanted Holden's strength to support her. She wanted his help with the ranch. She wanted to experience his innate gentleness.

The memory of his hands caressing her was so vivid that heat, then cold shivered through her entire body. She rubbed her upper arms as she ducked her head to rest her forehead on her knees.

You want him to love you as you've come to love him.

That wish made her as addle-witted as Mr. Butcher.

She fought against seeing Miss Gentry in her mind's eye, but lost. Holden would never choose her rather than that lovely woman. She opened her eyes and stared at her bare feet, the hems of her denim trousers. Lord knew, she had balked at every effort, every argument Aunt Mattie had made to instill her with ladylike ways.

In the quiet, her horse nickered. Startled from her reverie, Samantha's gaze shifted to the water. An image danced on the wavering surface. Her breath stalled.

Dead-still, Holden watched her from across the stream.

Chapter Twenty-one

"What do you here alone?"

Holden's archaic English again reminded her that he had lived apart from white people. Still, it made no difference in how she felt about this man. Contrarily, inexplicably, she found him more endearing for it.

"I'm on Timberoaks. I usually ride alone."

"And you may find trouble as you have before."

She shook her head rather than answer. Images marched through her mind. The day C. J. had disappeared; the day C. J. attacked her. Holden was right, of course, but she wouldn't admit it.

He strode into the stream and advanced toward her, oblivious to the cold water lapping his knees and filling his boots. He held his spurs in his hand, the reason why she hadn't heard him. She looked up and down the stream, but his horse was nowhere in sight. Probably tethered at his camp.

He stopped in front of her. She curled her bare toes in the dirt, uncomfortable as his remarkable eyes scanned her length. He had not yet taken Lillibeth to wife, and that gave her guarded hope that he might . . .

"Put on your boots and head home, Miss Timberlake. Darkness fast approaches."

"Miss Timberlake? Why so formal?"

Instead of answering, he leaned down, gathered her boots and socks in one hand and thrust them against her knees.

"Go home."

"No." Excitement ignited inside when she noticed his hand trembled ever so slightly. Did he find it unsettling to be alone with her? Brazen though the feeling was, her desire that he make love to her flashed through her like quicksilver.

"Damnation, woman! It is dangerous for you to wander alone. Put on your boots, and I will see you home."

"No."

Holden clasped both her arms and jerked her up. Even through fabric, he could feel the warmth of her flesh beneath his hands. Hands that shook. She stared into his eyes, searched them. Asking . . . ?

When he realized what she desired from him, he dropped his hands and stepped back. It would be a mistake to have Samantha. But he had not reckoned on her determination or his own weakness.

She closed the distance between them and set both hands on his waist, fingers curled in his belt loops. Hot irons could not have seared him more.

"Holden," she whispered.

His undoing.

With a silent curse, he clutched her against his frame, swooped to claim her soft lips. Lips that instantly parted. Tongues met, tangled, tasted, savored for long drugging moments. His hands moved restlessly up her back, down to her buttocks, then pressed her lower body into his arousal.

"Yes." Her warm breath puffed into his mouth.

God of the white man, he wanted this woman like no other. He felt her tug at his shirt, pull it from his trousers;

then her hands caressed his bare flesh. Flames singed wherever she touched, licked through him like a prairie fire.

"Samantha," he gasped as her knees buckled. He followed her down, sprawled over her slender body. In seconds, without even realizing it, buttons gave beneath his shaking fingers, opening her shirt. Then his mouth was on her nipple, first one and then the other, licking, sucking, greedy for more, much more.

Another "Yes!" exploded from her lips, her hands as busy as his as she worked to remove his shirt.

Little sounds of frustration erupted when he did not help. His fingers slid to her waist, undid her trousers. In seconds the denim parted. Then he was on her petal-softness, his fingers finding wetness. She was ready! And willing. Oh, so willing. He could not believe his luck, nor the swiftness of her response.

He heard material rip as she spread her hands and arms wide beneath his shirt, determined to have him as bare as she. He eased up and shrugged out of the shirt, then kissed her senseless again as his hand returned to pleasure her.

His arousal swelled painfully behind the stiff fabric of his own trousers, but he would not stop now. She was so close.

Her hips bucked as he slipped his finger inside. In seconds he felt her softness contract around his finger, while his thumb worked the hard little nub. Then she shattered in his arms, gasping with the release that was upon her in the next instant.

He pulled back enough to watch the rapture on her lovely face. Cheeks aflame, eyes squeezed tightly shut, she panted, tossed her head from side to side. Mindlessly her nails scored his back as wave after wave claimed her.

He gritted his teeth as her contractions around his finger nearly made him spill inside his pants. Not yet. He would have her, and she would fall apart a second time. All he had to do was endure a few minutes longer. Then his seed would fill her.

He stilled when the import of that thought sank in. Dropping his forehead to hers, he took a shuddering breath. And then what? Move on? Ride away, never to see her again?

Maybe fill her belly with a bastard?

She had finally stilled. Though she trembled, her hips had stopped bucking against his hand. Her chest rose and fell with labored breaths. He withdrew his hand from her softness, then brushed tousled hair from her forehead.

As her breathing slowed, the smile on her lips shone in her lovely eyes. "That was . . . extraordinary, Holden."

She moved her hips fractionally. He knew she felt his hardness when her smile widened.

"You haven't . . ."

Levering himself up, he rolled to sit next to her and speared unsteady fingers though his hair and down to rub the back of his neck. No, he had not, and he would not. But that did not seem to make a difference to his raging blood and engorged member.

"Holden?" She touched his back.

He flinched, then lunged to his feet, bringing his tattered shirt with him. As he shrugged into the ruined garment, he looked down at this woman he had come to love. He had nothing to offer her. He could no longer work for her. Not when he would be tempted to take her at every opportunity. Even now, despite his resolve.

A drifter he was; a drifter he would remain.

Slowly, Samantha sat up. "Holden?" When he didn't respond, she rose and stood in front of him. "What? Why are you—"

"I am leaving Timberoaks." The words were wrenched from him, almost a snarl. "Get dressed so I may see you safely home."

Emotions flickered in her eyes as clearly as words on the page of a book.

"Why?"

Bewilderment.

"You can't leave."

Denial.

"I wanted . . ."

Hurt.

"But you didn't, did you?"

Shame. *No! Never shame.* Not hers. "This was my doing, Samantha."

"Was it?" She leaned, scooped up her own shirt and donned it. With fumbling fingers, she did up the buttons, stuffed the tails into her waistband, and swiftly fastened her trousers as well. Then her eyes narrowed. "A game?"

Anger. He refused to deny it. Better anger than shame. "Come." He pointed the way to her tethered horse.

She gave a quick shake of her head. "I can find my way home without your help, Holden Walker. Leave if you must." She started past him, then stopped and glared. "But don't come back. Guy belongs to Aunt Mattie and me."

Guy? What did this have to do with Guy? Though he would not enlighten her, he had already made that gut-wrenching decision. Let her believe the worst of him; he had it coming.

She mounted, reined into the trees and never once looked back. The last glimpse he had of the woman he loved was of her straight back, head held high as she rode away from him. For the rest of his days, he feared he would remember the look in her lovely eyes, the hurt and shame.

Sorrow like none he had experienced clenched his chest. He brushed fingers over his eyes.

Tears?

No, he never cried.

Seven days had passed since Samantha had last seen Holden. She'd survived each day by rote, and managed to hide her shame and embarrassment from Oscar and Aunt Mattie. How, she didn't know. But they seemed unaware that she had thrown herself at Holden Walker and come out the loser. Just as well he hadn't made love to her. If he had . . .

"Stop it," she mumbled. Allowing desire to flood her senses every time she thought about him would do no good. *Allowing? Hah.* As if she had control over herself in that regard.

He'd made it perfectly clear he didn't want her. But, God in heaven, how it hurt. And now he was gone.

"Samantha." Her aunt's voice drifted up from below.

Opening the door, she called, "Be right down." She grabbed her hat and fur-lined coat from the peg and went down the stairs. She found Mattie at the front door opening a letter. Oscar stood cocooned in a heavy coat. Two days before, the weather had abruptly turned icy cold.

"What?"

Mattie looked up, fingers busily ripping open an envelope. "Oscar brought this. A Ranger, of all people, dropped it off for us. It's from Judge Crocker."

Now what?

Loath to read a further pronouncement likely to make her life more miserable, Samantha waved away the proffered paper. "Read it to me," she said wearily.

> To Miss Samantha Timberlake and Miss Matilda Crawford:
> I've received notice from Uriah Butcher that he can no longer manage Timberoaks. It seems he has suffered an injury.

An injury? Mr. Butcher had that right, but she didn't believe the maiming would have kept him off Timberoaks without Holden's threat.

> Since I know of no one in Waco whom I can ask to perform this task, I must now appoint your foreman, Oscar Du—"

Mattie's eyes flicked to Samantha, then to Oscar.

Holy moly, had she read the letter herself, she could have burned it. Judge Crocker would never have been the wiser. Well, it made no difference now, and probably wouldn't have anyway. Her father's lack of faith in her ability still rubbed her raw, but she would have felt guilty as the dickens if she'd done something that devious. Shrugging, she said, "Finish it."

> *I must now appoint your foreman, Oscar Dupree, to guide you in the management of the ranch until further notice or until Hiram's stipulations have been met.*

Which won't be anytime soon, Samantha thought dourly. Not the marriage part, anyway. She'd fallen in love with the wrong man, and would not put herself into a similar predicament again. She'd never marry now.

> *If Mr. Dupree is unable to perform this duty, please contact me, and I shall make other arrangements.*
>
> *Your servant,*
> *Judge Hazlett Crocker*

"Our servant?" She huffed derisively. "That's a good one."

"Samantha."

She turned at the sound of Oscar's voice. He waited, hat in hand.

Before he could continue, Mattie asked, "Are you willing?"

He assessed each one of them for long moments, turning his hat around and around by the brim. Finally he shrugged. "Guess so. If'n that judge ain't gonna name Samantha to run Timberoaks, I'll help her out. Just like I been doin'. Maybe he shoulda not got Uriah involved a'tall."

"That's settled, then," Mattie said. "Right, Samantha?"

She worried her lip a moment. Dwelling on her father's stipulations would gain nothing but anger. "Yes," she finally said. "I'm grateful for your help."

"No call for that, girl."

Briskly, Mattie said, "Fine. Now that's out of the way, what were you about to say a moment ago?"

"We got a situation . . ." He gulped, then went on in a reedy voice . . . "Needs handlin'."

Samantha glanced back to see what Oscar's attention had focused on. *Should have known.* Lillibeth Gentry floated—and darn it, she did seem to float—down the stairs.

Pausing on the last step, Lillibeth glanced from one to the other. "Sorry. I didn't mean to interrupt. I'm on my way to the cabin to set up for students." She grimaced. "That is, if any youngsters choose to come to school."

"Oh, they will," Mattie assured her. "I've already heard from several folks interested in your school."

Samantha wished not a single child would show up. But then she rebuked herself for the uncharitable thought. "Oscar?" she prompted.

He ducked his head and rubbed the back of his neck, then looked up. "Got them twenty head o' horses ready to take to Carter tomorrow. Problem is, I cain't leave, and there ain't nobody to trail 'em the five days to his place."

"I can," Samantha said.

"No, ya cain't. Five days, Samantha. Didn't ya hear me? You don't know the way, and 'sides, it's turned mighty cold."

"What does that have to do with anything?"

"It's a norther, girl. You'd freeze if'n ya got lost. 'Sides, Carter won't deal with no skirt."

Samantha rolled her eyes. "Why am I not surprised?" She thought a minute. "We can send Grogan or Lemuel."

"Grogan cain't read nor write, and Lemuel is a black man."

"Oh, for heaven's sake!"

Oscar grimaced. "That's the way of it, Samantha. Carter's a dyed-in-the-wool South Carolinian. Since the war, he don't truck with no negras. Runs 'em off if'n they come near his place."

Sighing, Samantha ran fingers through her loose hair. "What do you suggest, then?"

"Well, that's the problem. Cecil and Lefty took off a few days ago. Don't know when they'll be back. So they's nobody can take the stock that far and deal with Carter."

"A price wasn't set when he ordered the horses?"

"If they was, I ain't found nothin' in writin'. Yer pa mostly handled stuff over a handshake. Ya know that."

She did. And that was what made her position so difficult. Men dealt that way, between each other, but not with a woman. Darn it!

"Might I make a suggestion?" Lillibeth asked.

Samantha started. What could this lady know about horse dealing? Before she could respond, though, Mattie did.

"Of course. What do you have in mind?"

"Holden could do it."

"Walker? Oh, no. He left here without looking back. He's a drifter, for heaven's sake!" Samantha couldn't help the shrillness in her voice. The nerve of the woman!

"Precisely," Lillibeth said. "He may even have worked for this Mr. Carter." She looked into each person's eyes, stopping at Oscar. "He knows horses. And he's as trustworthy as the day is long. I believe he would do it."

Samantha exploded. "He's not here. Doesn't want to be here."

"Samantha, would you hush a minute?" Mattie said. "Do you know where Mr. Walker is, Lillibeth?"

Her aunt's reasonable tone put Samantha's teeth on edge. This was too much. "It makes no difference. He's not welcome here."

She might as well have kept silent, since Lillibeth answered without flinching. "He's in Waco."

Lillibeth Gentry knew where he was, but she didn't. That hurt far more than Samantha cared to admit. The misery that swept though her must have shown in her eyes, because Mattie's brow crinkled speculatively.

"What do you mean, Mr. Walker isn't welcome here?"

"Well, he"—she squirmed—"left. He made it perfectly clear he didn't want to work for Timberoaks." Though not precisely true, it was the only explanation she could come up with. It didn't work.

" 'Perfectly clear.' What did he say?" Mattie turned to Oscar. "Was he adamant with you when he said he was leaving?"

Of course Walker would have spoken to Oscar. Hired by her father, nevertheless he worked for Oscar, the foreman.

"Well, he didn't say much. When a man says he's leavin', I don't press 'im."

"Do you think he'd come back and help a while?" Mattie persisted. She glanced at Lillibeth. "I'm not doubting you. I'm just, well . . . I don't know. But if you and Oscar think he'd be willing, perhaps it's for the best." She eyed Samantha. "What do you think?"

No. But what could she say to make that point clear, yet not alert her aunt to the real problem?

"I repeat, he's not here. You said the stock is ready to move tomorrow, Oscar."

"Well, yeah. But I don't have nobody to send, so don't make no difference if'n we was to wait for Walker." He smiled shyly at Lillibeth. "Yer right. Walker is a top-notch hand. And he dealt fair and square with me."

Gathering self-control around herself like a protective shield, Samantha said, "If you feel strongly about it, go ahead. Ask him."

Ambivalence wracked her. Hope that he might come back. Hope that he would not.

Chapter Twenty-two

Wrapped in his hip-length leather coat, hat tipped over his eyes, Holden sat on the porch of the house where he had taken a room. Balanced on two legs, his chair leaned against the wall. He mulled over his priorities. Look for a job, for one. The loss of Samantha and Guy left him at loose ends. Try as he might to deny it, his heart remained with them on Timberoaks.

"Get your black ass outta here!"

Thumbing up the brim of his Stetson, Holden looked across the street and down three doors. A burly man backed into the street from Gilbert's Hotel. The desk clerk dogged his retreat. Holden frowned, knowing full well the cause of the altercation. What fool man of color would walk into a Waco hotel and expect to get a room?

"I jest—"

"I don't care what you *just*. Your kind ain't wanted here."

"Well . . ."

The chair's legs met the floor with a thud as Holden recognized the man. What was he doing in Waco? He stepped off the porch and strode across the street.

"If'n you'd jest answer ma question, mister."

"There ain't no feller by that name stayin' here." The clerk flapped his hand. "Now get afore I call the sheriff."

"What is the problem here?" Holden demanded when he came within ten feet of the men. The burly man turned. Lemuel Baker.

"Walker," he said, relief plain in his voice and face. "I been in ever' hotel in town."

"You know this boy?" the clerk asked.

Anger sizzled through Holden as he glared at the clerk, a half head shorter than Lemuel Baker. "Yes. And Baker outgrew 'boy' some years back."

The clerk had the sense to realize he'd raised Holden's ire. His face reddened, he said sheepishly, "Well, you know what I mean."

"I do," Holden snapped. Then he turned his back on the man. "What brings you to Waco?"

"You."

He blinked. "Me? Why?"

"I got this here letter from Oscar." Lemuel fished a crumpled paper from his shirt pocket beneath his coat.

Holden scanned the single sheet. His breath caught when he read the signature. Not Oscar's.

Mr. Walker,
    We don't know what took you from Timberoaks. But we find your services invaluable, and ask if it would be possible for you to return at least for a few weeks? Oscar is shorthanded and needs someone with your experience to trail fifteen horses up north to Martin Carter's ranch.
    We realize this is an imposition. But if you have not found other work, please consider our request. Mr. Baker is prepared to wait if you need a few days to settle matters.

Yours truly,
Matilda Crawford and Samantha Timberlake

Miss Crawford had penned the note, but he hoped it had been with Samantha's knowledge. That she had allowed her name to be added. After all, did not "we" mean the two of them made the request?

Hope. A fool's emotion.

Stuffing the paper into his own pocket, he asked, "Why does Miss Crawford ask me to deliver horses that Oscar or you could handle?"

Lemuel smiled thinly as he looked over Holden's shoulder. The hotel man had disappeared. "I ain't the right color." He shrugged. "And I cain't read. Mr. Timberlake done ever'thin' on the up-an'-up, but no writin', I guess. Oscar's athinkin' Mr. Carter'll want somethin' in writin' now that he's dealin' with womenfolk."

"He is probably right." Holden raised a brow. "Oscar does not read or write?"

"Oh, sure, but nobody else can that's left."

"Left?"

"Couple hands lit out the day after you hit the trail. Don't know when they'll be back. Oscar's takin' over managin', so he cain't leave fer that long."

Satisfaction settled inside Holden. Thank the Spirits. No problem with Butcher. At least, not at the moment.

"Carter's spread is north?"

Lemuel scratched above an ear. "Yeah. Oscar says it'll take five days to herd the stock up there."

"One way?"

"Yep. Mr. Timberlake sold horses all over Texas. Once't, he drove twenty head all the way to El Paso. We was gone three, maybe four weeks. If'n Miss Samma's gonna make it, she'll have to do that, too. Cowmen want good stock, and we's got some a the best."

Dust billowed around them as a wagon lumbered past. For a moment, the creak of harness and grind of wheels made conversation impossible. Holden glanced skyward and closed his mouth on grit. Why waste time on questions? Whether Samantha herself had asked for his assistance made no difference to him. He would help her even if it meant traveling across the country to do it.

The day was half over, but he could be well along the trail by nightfall if he gathered his gear and lit out now. Then he remembered Lemuel.

"You probably need to rest. We can start in the morning."

The man snorted. "Where'd I find a place in this town to lay ma head?"

Little did Baker know that Holden understood his problem better than other white men. A few years before, had he entered Waco wearing his usual apparel and paint, he would have been shot on sight.

"Where is your horse?"

Baker tipped his head. "Edge a town. They's a little valley yonder where I tied 'im to a tree."

Holden toyed with the idea of taking Baker with him into the boardinghouse, but decided not to put this fine man through more degradation. "I will gather my gear and horse and meet you in fifteen minutes."

"Then y'all'll come? Miss Samma didn't think ya would."

Holden turned away and grimaced. Doubtless, she did not want his help. Apparently she lacked other choices, though.

Oh, yes, call me a fool.

Samantha hunched deeper into her coat. Absently, her gloved hand rubbed Black Magic's withers. For the second time she'd decided to ride the black for work, and what a pleasure he was. Comfortable gaits, and spirited, but a gentle animal. Still a bit skittish, he needed more training before she'd feel sure of him. And he of her. Horses weren't so different from people, it seemed. Trust went both ways.

She scanned each of the horses corralled for the drive to Martin Carter's ranch. Oscar had explained that months ago her father had singled out the individual horses intended for Mr. Carter. All were healthy and would give a good day's work to the cowhands who claimed them. This norther had caught them unawares. It was doubtful that Carter would start a herd north to a railhead anytime soon, but he expected the stock delivered just the same.

She nudged her mount with her knee, but he remained anchored. She grinned. He still needed the additional signal of turning his head with the rein, which she did and again nudged him, this time with her heel. He responded, and they ambled around to the far side of the makeshift corral to check the depth of water in the old round tub.

Earlier, she'd had to crack a sheet of ice with her boot heel so the animals could drink. Miserable cold. She tilted her head back to look at the lowering sky. Dreary as the dickens. It would probably snow if those clouds carried moisture.

He won't come.

Unbidden, the thought of Holden slammed into her mind. Keeping remembrances of him at bay didn't work for long, she thought with disgust. Of course, he wouldn't return. Hadn't she told him not to?

Aunt Mattie had shown her the note before giving it to Oscar. Samantha hadn't fussed that her name had been added to the signature line. A crafty woman, Mattie Crawford. But not one to pry unless given the opportunity to ask uncomfortable questions. By not saying anything, Samantha believed she'd been craftier. She smiled without humor.

Casting a last look at the horses huddled together for warmth, she assured herself all was well with the stock, then turned her mount toward home. As she rode up from the south pasture directly into the wind, her cheeks grew numb. She reined in, worked her neckerchief up over her nose, and kept riding. Her eyes smarted from the cold.

Maybe Oscar was right. Not because she was a woman, though. Driving the horses to Martin Carter's place in this weather would challenge the best of men. Though, if they, if she, asked Holden to make the trip, shouldn't she bear the misery as well?

Pitiful, Samantha.

Drumming up paltry excuses to be near him certainly didn't say much for her pride. Holden loved Lillibeth. Why couldn't she accept that and get on with her life?

Because he'd left the woman here. If he truly loved her, wouldn't he have taken her with him? Wouldn't he have married Lillibeth by now? Instead, he'd ridden away . . . from both of them.

She sighed to clear her muddleheadedness, and peered into the distance with teary eyes. Thankful, she spied the roof of the barn. Shortly the other ranch buildings came into view. Coffee. Throat-scorching, stomach-warming coffee was what she needed.

Forget Holden Walker.

It had been—what?—maybe five days since Lemuel had left for Waco. She snorted at her attempted mental deception. She knew exactly how long he'd been gone. Four and a half days.

She gave another sigh, this one of relief as she rode into the barn. The cold chilled her to the marrow, but the walls cut the wind. Blinking back wind-produced tears, she dismounted, patted Black Magic's rump, then lifted the stirrup out of the way to remove the saddle.

"What for y'all been out in this cold, Miz Samma?"

Startled, she nearly swallowed her tongue. Gripping the saddle horn, she swiveled toward the sound of Lemuel's voice. His white teeth glimmered from inside a stall.

"Good grief, you scared the liver out of me!"

That brought a chuckle. "Sorry. Ya been ridin' the black," he observed unnecessarily.

She took a breath to ease her racing heart, then laughed too. "Yes. He needs work, but he's a joy to ride."

"Surely ya ain't been joyridin'."

"No. I went to check the horses meant for Mr. Carter." Disappointment washed through her. She'd been right. Lemuel had returned alone. Holden—

"Hello, Miss Timberlake."

She stiffened as he spoke from behind her. Her heart again raced out of control. Grip tight on the saddle horn, she looked over her shoulder.

God in heaven, he looked wonderful, tall and deceptively big in his heavy coat. She met those remarkable wolf eyes. Even in the cold, he appeared relaxed, comfortable.

"I didn't think you'd come." She was proud that her voice didn't quake at all.

"You asked, Miss Timberlake." He tilted his head. "After our last encounter, I knew you must need a hand rather badly. So I came." He shrugged. "Besides, drifters can always use the pay."

Her own words thrown back hit her squarely in the chest. She should have expected it. Instead, she'd dared hope. . . . Rather than let him see how he affected her, she removed her saddle and spoke over her shoulder. "See Oscar. He'll tell you what needs to be done and when."

Silence was the only response; a second later she heard the musical *chink, chink, chink* of his spurs. She watched him walk out of the barn, felt her insides disintegrate. *Crack, crack, crack.*

Tears threatened, and she asked tiredly, "Lemuel, I know you must be exhausted, but would you rub down Black Magic and feed him for me?"

"Sure 'nuff. Y'all get outta this cold."

There was cold, and then there was *cold*. One she could escape; the other encased her heart.

Chapter Twenty-three

Samantha paused outside the barn when she saw Holden and Guy squatting, looking under the porch. Guy reached for something, but came up empty-handed.

His voice carried on the brittle air. "What's the matter with 'im?"

"Let me try," Holden said.

In a moment, he dragged something out, then stood, drawing her brother to his feet at the same time. "I am sorry, Guy, but he is dead."

Bengy lay at Holden's feet. Eyes wide, Samantha sprinted toward them.

"Oh, no." She clamped a hand over her mouth.

"Naw. He's just sleepin'," Guy insisted.

Holden put his hand atop her brother's head. "No, little man. He now runs in the Great Beyond."

A tear streaked down the boy's cheeks. "But he was okay yesterday. Ya think he got too cold?"

"Maybe. But he had grown old and tired."

"I . . ." Guy looked up imploringly, first at Holden, then at Samantha.

She laid her hands on his shoulders. "Mr. Walker's right, sweetie. Bengy lived a long life for a dog." She gestured to the already stiff body. "See how gray his muzzle is?"

Guy sniffled and wiped his sleeve over his nose. "Ya think he's with Pa?"

Oh, God. She bit back tears and glanced at Holden. He shook his head ever so slightly in commiseration, but said nothing.

"I don't know if dogs go to heaven." She spoke around a closing throat. "But if they do, I'm sure he's perched at Pa's feet right now."

Mattie stepped outside. The screened door slapped shut. "What's . . ." Her gaze found the cause of the sadness evident on three faces. "Bengy."

Guy leaped onto the porch, wrapped his arms around her waist, and buried his face in her midriff. Automatically, Mattie brushed his tousled hair, her gaze on their beloved pet.

Samantha remembered years back when Guy had first begun toddling outside. He'd played with Bengy, crawled all over the patient animal. But the dog really belonged to Mattie. She might not have wanted the stray in the beginning, but he'd latched on to her every step.

Mattie's breath clouded in front of her face. "Mr. Walker, he'll need burying. One of the men—"

"I will do it, ma'am. Where do you want him?"

Mattie exchanged a sorrowful glance with her niece, and Samantha answered for her. "Up by Pa, I guess. I hope the ground isn't too frozen to dig. I'll get a shovel if you'll carry him."

Holden squatted, then rose with the big dog's body cradled in his arms, the seventy-pound animal balanced as if no burden at all. His spurs *chink*ed as he walked away,

"I'm goin' with 'em," Guy said.

Mattie squeezed him as if to prevent his going, then patted his head. "You do that, honey. And say a little prayer for him, will you?"

Guy's head bobbed assent.

When Samantha entered the barn for a shovel, Lemuel carried a second one, and between the two men, they had a hole dug in no time. At the foot of her pa's grave. Lemuel reached to drag Bengy into the hole, but Holden stayed him.

He strode to the barn and returned with a blanket. His blanket. Spreading it, he motioned for Lemuel to help lay Bengy in the middle of the shroud, then covered the body before lowering it into the hole.

He knelt by Guy. "You may throw in the first dirt if you wish, little man."

"Just like Samma did for Pa?"

Holden nodded. "Your prayer will not go unheard for your faithful friend."

Guy scooped up a handful of dirt, then trickled it through his fingers as he muttered something. "Do you think Bengy is in heaven, Mr. Walker?"

Standing back, Samantha hitched a breath when Holden sat next to Guy. Lemuel filled the hole while Holden spoke in low tones to her brother.

"Heaven? Maybe."

Guy leaned against Holden's side. Held-back tears trickled down Samantha's cheeks when Holden hesitated, then slowly wrapped an arm around her brother's small form. In her heart, she knew Holden loved the boy, and now, finally, he had the opportunity to touch him, give comfort.

"Indians believe every living thing possesses a spirit," Holden continued. He looked up at the overcast sky. "Father Sun nourishes Mother Earth. She nourishes plants for man and beast." He gestured toward the grave. "Bengy now runs on young legs in the Great Beyond. He tires not. He runs on soft earth. Lies on green grass. Laps cool, clear water. He will never know hunger as his spirit continues forever. Your pa is blessed with that undying spirit, too."

Enthralled by his words, Samantha stood perfectly still. Distant and closemouthed most of the time, Holden possessed a faith that went soul-deep. Though raised by Indians, he'd survived to be a gentle man where it counted. In his heart.

Closing her eyes, she wished . . . In that instant, she vowed to accompany him to Carter's ranch. Despite the cursed weather, she *would* have time alone with Holden. Dared she hope he could come to love her as she loved him?

That evening, after Guy had gone to bed, she announced her plan. And, not surprisingly, Mattie erupted in a firestorm of objections. "Absolutely not! It's too cold, Samantha. Mr. Walker would be hampered worrying about you. You'd slow him down. Besides, it's unseemly for a young woman to go off alone with a man."

She might have known that would be one argument. "He brought Lillibeth Gentry here."

"Miss Gentry is—"

"Unmarried. You saw nothing wrong with the two of them traveling together."

". . . a mature woman—"

"And I'm not?"

"Would you let me finish, young lady?"

Makes no difference.

"Mr. Walker and Miss Gentry are longtime friends, Samantha. Almost related, you might say. They appear much like brother and sister, or cousins, maybe."

That set Samantha back on her heels. "He's not courting her?"

"Of course not. She's taken with Oscar."

"Oh, Aunt Mattie! Oscar practically salivates over her, but I've seen no indication she's interested in him."

"Good heavens, Samantha. What a crude way to describe Oscar's feelings."

She ducked her head. Her aunt was right. Still . . .

Grudgingly, she apologized, then returned to her plan. "We're off the subject, Aunt Mattie. I am going along to Carter's ranch. By golly, those horses belong to me. Martin Carter may not deal with me, but I can sure as fire listen to what he says to Walker." She shrugged. "Call it a . . . learning experience."

Mattie sighed and rubbed her temples. "Honey, you're my niece. Mr. Walker—"

"You don't like him."

"That's not true. I don't know the man well enough to like or dislike him. But he's . . . Samantha, I fear you're going to be hurt. You're . . . oh, what's the word? Enamored, I think. He's a drifter." Quickly she inserted, "I don't mean that disparagingly." Mattie laid her hand atop Samantha's. "You're right. The horses do belong to you. And you belong on Timberoaks. 'Pride goeth before the fall.' It's good to be proud of yourself and Timberoaks. But too much could be your undoing. I think Mr. Walker has more than his share of pride."

"What are you getting at?"

"Because he has worked far and wide, he has no roots; it's doubtful he ever will. You come saddled with a ranch. And I mean that in a good sense, Samantha. Look at it from his perspective. He doesn't have a thing to offer you that compares with Timberoaks."

"I don't want anything from him other than . . ." She paused, unwilling to voice her fondest desire.

"His love," Mattie finished quietly.

She chose her words carefully, unwilling to let her aunt know Holden had lived with Indians and abandoned Guy long ago. "There's another side to Walker. You should have heard him answering Guy's questions about heaven. Beneath that sternly quiet exterior, he's a gentle man, Aunt Mattie."

Dark eyes intent, Mattie stared at Samantha for several heartbeats. "It's too late, isn't it? You've already fallen in love with him."

"I won't deny it."

"He won't welcome you."

Her nerves scraped raw by that simple statement, Samantha rose and poured two cups of coffee. What did Aunt Mattie mean? The offer of her heart, or her company on the trail? Returning to the table, she slid one steaming brew before Mattie, then reseated herself.

She sipped the coffee to hide her turmoil, and chose to believe Mattie spoke of the trip. "It doesn't matter if he wants me along or not. My horses are to be sold. If I'm there when Mr. Carter deals with Walker, he'll . . . Well, maybe he'll get used to the idea, and it won't be the last Timberoaks stock Martin Carter buys."

Samantha felt secure in these arguments. Unless she learned to bargain with ranchers—male ranchers—she'd never keep body and soul together. Timberoaks would decline and the hands would have to be sent on their way. Her father might have foreseen these problems, but it was up to her to overcome them.

You'll have ample opportunity to talk with Holden, her maddening inner voice said. *You'll bed close together at night. Who knows what may come of ten days alone with him?*

During the long restless night, Samantha would close her eyes, nearly succumb to sleep, then jerk awake and peer at the clock. Sometime after midnight, snow began to fall. Oh, yes. The ride promised to be miserably cold. If she didn't follow close on Holden's trail when he departed, she'd doubtless be lost within hours.

That was her plan. To follow him, staying out of sight until near nightfall. By that time, they'd be too far along the trail for him to send her back. Particularly if the snow kept up most of the day. Like it or not, he'd be stuck with her.

At three-thirty, she gave up the futile effort to rest and rose from tousled, knotted covers. After shivering into long johns, a flannel shirt and jeans, she pulled on two pairs of socks. But not boots. Too noisy. She straightened the bed and gathered extra clothes. Later, she'd stuff them into saddlebags.

Guy didn't know of her plans. No way would he be allowed to go, but if he knew, he'd doubtless put up a fuss. She'd leave the telling to Aunt Mattie after she and Holden were long gone. Pausing at the door, she suddenly realized a note should be left so no one would worry about her.

Though hardtack would have been perfect for the trip, it was not an option in Mattie Crawford's kitchen. Samantha tiptoed around to gather biscuits, a few apples, coffee, canned beans. She fished in the bottom of the dishsafe for an old coffee pot. Found a tin plate, a knife and spoon.

She nearly dropped her teeth when the top of the coffeepot clattered to the floor. Too close to the table's edge, she'd brushed against it. Holding her breath, she listened. When the overhead floor didn't creak, signaling Guy had wakened, she sighed with relief, bent and picked up the lid.

Wind and blowing snow clawed at her hat when she stepped out the back door. Noiselessly setting down her saddlebags, she pulled her neckerchief loose, tied it over her hat, then knotted the bandanna under her chin.

She walked toward the barn, nothing but a shadow looming ahead of her. Her own muffled bootsteps and the wind were the only sounds in the snow-covered world. She eased into the barn and made her way to the stall where Holden kept his horse.

Already gone.

More speedily than ever before, she saddled the mare she usually rode. Black Magic was not the horse to ride on this trip. At the last minute, she remembered blankets. Lordy, she'd freeze without them. Rummaging in the dark tack room, she found two already rolled and tied them behind the cantle.

An hour later, she despaired of ever finding Holden. For sure, she'd headed in the right direction. Hadn't she? Snow blew directly into her face, blinding her. Then, over the wind, she heard a horse whinny, then another. Dismounting, she crept forward and stopped behind some trees.

Peering around a trunk, she saw him standing not more than thirty yards away. All fifteen horses, sixteen counting his mount, stood around him. She blinked, wondering why he had stopped. Then she watched as he tied first one horse to another, then another, and linked them behind his gray. Two columns trudged behind his horse when he remounted and moved on, their heads bent before the wind.

Of course. It made sense. In this storm he couldn't herd the horses ahead of him. If they spread out, he'd lose sight of them. The dark images ahead were a boon to her in the blowing snow. She could see the cluster without crowding Holden's back, without alerting him to her presence too soon.

Later, Samantha found herself hungry and tired from the tense ride. Her one consolation, that the snow had petered out to no more than a few flakes, had also forced her to drop back in case Holden looked behind him. Now she followed the tracks in four inches of snow covering the ground.

Assured she wouldn't lose him, she dismounted, removed her gloves, and rummaged in her saddlebag. Finding a second bandanna, she covered her nose, mouth and chin. Only her eyes peered between her hat brim and the protective cover shielding her windburned face. By the time she pulled on her gloves again, her fingers were red and numb.

Famished, she climbed back in the saddle. When would he stop to eat? Surely he wouldn't travel all day without nourishment or rest for the stock. Though they didn't move quickly, he'd kept up a steady pace. These thoughts clamoring in her head, she looked down at the tracks, rounded a rock abutment, and found herself not thirty feet from the line of horses. Fortunately, Holden was nowhere in sight. Perhaps he was behind the stand of trees up ahead.

Cautiously backing her mount behind the rocks, she swung down and sneaked a peek. She hoped he'd stopped to eat. Tensed against the cold for so long, she felt wobbly. She had to get something in her stomach.

Before she could move or entertain another thought, an arm circled her shoulders, yanking her backward so fast that the breath whooshed from her lungs. She crashed against unyielding muscle and bone.

A knife blade nicked her throat.

A low voice rasped in her ear, "You court death, hombre."

Chapter Twenty-four

The instant the words left his mouth, Holden realized whom he held.

Samantha!

He would know her scent anywhere. It haunted his dreams.

Sheathing his knife with one hand, he whipped her around with the other. "What do you here?"

She stared up at him, wide-eyed. Those eyes. They were all he could see of her face. Her quick breaths fluttered the bandanna over her mouth. He had scared the daylights out of her. And rightly so.

"I could have killed you!"

Still, she made no reply. He grasped her upper arms and shook her.

She jerked free and stepped back. "How did you know I was here?"

He answered in scathing tones. "I knew not it was you. But I knew of your presence before the snow let up."

"You couldn't have."

He just looked at her. After a moment, she ducked her head and yanked down the bandanna that covered most of her face, then glanced back up, eyes aglitter.

"I nearly lost you a couple times."

"You should not be here."

"Don't tell me what I should or shouldn't do, Holden Walker." She pointed her thumb over her shoulder. "Those are my horses. I need to know what transpires between you and Martin Carter."

"You trust me not?"

"Oh, for—"

"You ask me to deliver this stock, but you trust me not?"

"Hush!" she snapped. "Of course I do. I just said, I want to be there while you and Carter negotiate. Is that so unreasonable? One day I will be forced to deal with this man and others like him. I'd better learn how."

He could not argue with her. She had every right to be present when her stock was sold. He would move on. . . . *Do not think of that now.*

Her horse nudged her back, and she staggered into him. Automatically, his arms circled her. Her hat brim jabbed into his sternum, then bent downward over her eyes. She struggled to push away, but he held tight. And wished to the Spirits he did not have to let her go.

Resigned to the fact that it was too late to send her back, he set her away and drew a steadying breath. With her so close for the next few days, he would live in what the white man called hell. Tight and aching from the contact, his body called to hers. But he must not touch her. Not again.

He strode past her. "Come. We will eat before we again take to the trail."

The man would try the patience of a saint. Samantha glared at Holden's back where he knelt beside a small fire he'd kindled on this, their second stop of the day. They'd bed down until dawn. Maybe. She remembered how relentless he'd been on the trail after their meager lunch.

When he'd wordlessly unsaddled his horse and staked the others, she figured he intended this for their night camp. His throat might have been cut for all the conversation they'd exchanged. Not that it mattered. Her scintillating conversation would consist of no more than agonized groans. She couldn't find a spot on her that wasn't sore. How the devil did the man go on hour after hour?

Sighing, she lifted leaden arms and pulled the saddle from her horse's back. Her strength a laughable commodity, she let the saddle slip from frozen fingers and thump onto the sodden ground. *Great.*

Holden rose and turned to face her. A frown marred his handsome features. "Not there. Bring it closer to the fire. It will get colder before sunup."

"Bring it closer to the fire," she mimicked under her breath as she slowly bent to grasp the saddle horn. Did he think her an idiot? She would sit in the blasted fire if she could. With luck, her frozen limbs would thaw by Christmas. Even her rump was numb, but only partially from cold.

For the past few years, Samantha had prided herself on her ability to keep up with the men who worked for her father. If need be, she rode from sunup to sundown. But not in this cold. She'd certainly never been forced to sit like a knot on a log for ten or twelve hours without a break. All right. One, she admitted dourly.

She'd refused to check the pocket watch she carried for fear Holden would catch her at it. As daylight waned, her one consolation was that the wind had died to a gentle breeze sighing through the trees.

She dragged the saddle along the ground to within a few feet of the fire, plopped down next to it, keeled over and rested her weary head on the seat. *Sleep. My kingdom for uninterrupted sleep.*

The next instant, hard unyielding hands hauled her to her feet. "You will freeze to death, Samantha. Besides, you must eat. It has been a long day."

All wide-eyed innocence, she asked, "Really? I hadn't noticed."

He let go so abruptly that she staggered back a step. The quick motion pushed a groan through her lips before she could squelch it. She glanced up at his face. If she hadn't known better, she'd swear a smile flitted across his mouth.

"Do you wish to share my meal, or did you bring your own grub?" he asked.

What was the use? Belligerence would get her nowhere. Hunger won out. "I have biscuits, apples, a few cans of beans, and coffee."

"Well?"

"Well, what?"

"I am fixing beans, but I did not bring a coffee pot. We may share if you wish."

Good heavens, that was the most he'd said all day. Share? If he was willing to cook, he'd get no argument from her. "I'll dig out the coffee pot." She glanced around. "Water?"

He pointed behind her, then turned to his own saddlebags and began to pull out fixings for their meal.

Two hours later, unable to relax, Samantha lay rigid, her muscles tensed against the cold. Holden didn't seem to share her problem. Head resting on his saddle, hat tipped over his eyes, he slept, or so she assumed since he hadn't moved after draping his gun belt over the saddle horn.

As she had done, he had spread one blanket on the cold ground, another over him. Also, as she did, he wore his coat. Which was a major part of her discomfort. Like trying to get comfortable in a straitjacket.

Once again she flipped over. Frigid air seeped beneath her blanket, curled around her stiff legs. She shivered.

"Go to sleep."

Samantha froze, startled by Holden's command. So

much for his sleeping. The beast. She said nothing, refused to acknowledge she'd heard him.

It seemed that no more than an instant had passed when she felt a hand shake her shoulder. She batted it away, then groaned. That simple movement had surely cracked her bones.

Her eyes popped open. Holden's face hovered over hers.

"We ride soon," he said. Behind him, stars flickered in the arc of dark sky.

She blinked. Ride at night? "What time is it?"

"I know not."

"What do you mean, you don't know? Don't you carry a watch?"

"Time matters not. Eat, then we ride."

She smelled coffee. How long had he been up? He rose and left her. She felt drugged, and so sore she didn't know if she could move a muscle, let alone get up, eat, and then mount her horse.

But she'd brought this misery on herself. It would be a cold day in hell before she'd complain. A grin cracked her chapped lips. *You've arrived!*

Mustering resolve, she sat up and bit back another groan. It took longer than she'd thought possible to toss back the blanket, then lumber to her frozen feet. Needles stabbed at her booted toes, then pricked up her legs.

A low fire flickered in the circle of rocks Holden had arranged the night before. Steam curled from the coffeepot's spout. A surprisingly good cook, Holden made excellent coffee. Strong enough to walk from the cup to her mouth, but oh, so welcome. First, though, she needed some seclusion.

A few minutes later, shaking from the cold, she pulled up her trousers and rebuckled her belt. It wasn't fair. Men didn't have to practically disrobe to relieve themselves and freeze their tails off in the process.

Silence reigned as she ate. Afterward, finding the narrow stream frozen over, she scoured the plates clean with sand, doused the fire, then saddled her horse. Holden had checked each horse's hooves, and had been long since ready to ride. She kept her mouth shut. Refused to give him the chance to chide her for holding him up. She *had* cleaned up the breakfast mess.

Except for lack of snow and no wind, thank God, the endless day promised discomfort like the day before. The temperature didn't rise one bit. If anything, it was even colder.

As he had yesterday, Holden ignored her. She frowned at his straight back for the umpteenth time and vowed tonight would be different. She'd force him to talk while they ate. *Why wait?* Nudging her mount to a faster walk, she rode up next to him. "I could handle some of the horses if it would help."

"No need."

She glowered at his profile. Exasperated, she said, "Look, Holden, I know you can lead all fifteen with no assistance, but I'm here. Why not put me to some use, for heaven's sake?"

"You should not be here."

"We're not going over that again!"

He shrugged, looked straight ahead and said no more.

Discouraged, she gave up the effort to converse, but her gaze lingered on those broad shoulders. *Holy moly, the man is . . . beautiful.* A big man to start with, Holden looked larger, more menacing in his heavy coat. Menacing. Incongruous, that thought. He might be big and sturdy as a tree, but he was gentle when he . . .

She closed her eyes and allowed her horse to slow, dropping back to ride beside the linked stock. Images and feelings leaped to mind. His big hands caressing her breasts, her ribs. The heat that had swirled in her belly. Ecstasy. Even now, that same heat settled between her legs. She shivered.

The first time Holden kissed her . . . Coming on the heels of C. J.'s unwanted advances, Holden's kiss had overwhelmed her for a moment, but then delicious warmth simmered through her. And she yearned for more, much more. Unconsciously she shook her head. Not to be, though. Not then.

"Don't hurt my sister!" Guy, her protector. A smile curved her lips.

Guy liked Holden. He hadn't at first. Hadn't trusted him. But after their talk by Pa's grave, her brother clearly held the man in much higher regard.

For Holden that had to be rewarding. He'd said little. No surprise there, she thought wryly, but he did love Guy. He considered himself the boy's uncle, but maybe his love ran as deep as that for a son. If Holden's gentleness was any measure, he'd suffered when he'd left the little boy unprotected that rainy night, with only the hope strangers would care for him.

Despite her musings, she couldn't escape the bone-weariness and breath-snatching cold. It took what little strength she had to stay in the saddle and follow Holden as docilely as the stock. Grimacing, she tucked her free hand between her arm and body, seeking warmth for the gloved fingers. She vowed the taciturn man would not hear her complain.

Samantha would be the death of him. He did not know how much more he could take of her stoic silence. Yet he had forced her to it by his refusal to talk. Still . . . He stayed ahead of her, but that did not relieve him of the feeling her dark eyes were boring into his back. Add her mere closeness and his body remained in a constant state of half arousal.

Yes, the death of him.

Long after dark, on their third night-camp, he listened to her sighs, her restlessness, her inability to get warm enough to drift off to sleep. Only one way to remedy that.

But it would kill him. Sure she was unaware of his wakefulness, he watched her from half-closed eyes beneath the brim of his black hat.

After an hour, he could no longer stand her misery and flipped back his top blanket. On silent feet, he walked the few steps that separated them, leaned down and scooped her into his arms, blankets and all.

A surprised, perhaps alarmed, "What?" rushed from her. "What are you doing?"

"I need to sleep, Samantha. You do, too. We will share body heat."

When she bucked in his arms, he nearly dropped her.

"We certainly will not!"

He lowered her to his blankets and lay beside her, held her down as he arranged their blankets over them. "We will."

Before she could object further, he pulled her into his arms and nudged her head against his shoulder with the heel of his hand. In a roughened voice, he ordered, "Now sleep!"

Samantha's agitated breathing signaled her apparent shock at his high-handedness. But, no fool, she did not move away, did not move at all. The relief of their shared body warmth was immediate.

Big mistake. With her lithe body tucked next to his, now he could not sleep. But what choice did he have? Samantha was near perishing from fatigue and cold.

His member pulsed with desire; his body flamed. She certainly should be warm enough now. He bit back a moan, closed his eyes tight and prayed for strength.

Yes, Samantha might very well be the death of him.

Chapter Twenty-five

Nestled into Holden spoon-fashion, her head pillowed on his muscular shoulder, Samantha felt warmth seep through her almost immediately. By degrees, her body relaxed. She sighed.

"You are uncomfortable?"

"No," she murmured. "Uncomfortable" hardly touched what she felt. But hadn't she longed for this? To be embraced by Holden?

She wanted more. His love.

Be satisfied, she told herself. A couple of days remained on their northern trek. Then they must travel home again. Who knew what might come of this closeness? His hard body pressed to hers . . . it was enough. For now.

She smiled and drifted off to sleep.

Sometime during the night Samantha turned. When she wakened she faced Holden. His arms still clasped her; his leg draped over her hip drew her intimately close.

Tilting up her chin, she stared into his beard-roughened face. His wolf-eyes focused intently on her.

"Good morning," she whispered. Without a second thought, she raised her arm, curled her hand behind his head and pulled him toward her. She kissed him with all the longing in her being.

Her heart soared when he deepened the kiss; his tongue swept inside her parted lips, taking, giving. She felt his arousal at the apex of her legs. Then he jerked away.

"Holden," she breathed on a contented sigh.

He shook his head and would have sat up, but she tightened her hold around his neck. "Make love to me," she ordered boldly. "You want to. I know you do."

"Not wise," he said in the rough tone of the night before.

"What does that mean?"

He reached back and pried her fingers from his neck, then rolled to sit next to her. Chill air swept over her, but her attention remained riveted on his profile.

He gazed into the distance. "You deserve a man who will marry you, Samantha. A man who will give you more than I can. Who will not leave you."

"Yes, I want to get married." She rose to sit next to him. "I want to have children, have a man who will help me with Timberoaks."

Tight-lipped, his jaw set, he nodded in agreement but said nothing, eyes averted.

When he didn't speak again, she pressed him with questions. "What do you think I want that you can't give me? Why must you leave?"

He swiveled his head and impaled her with those remarkable eyes. "You know who, what I am. A drifter all my life. Not by choice in the beginning, but it is the way of things for me."

Startling her, he pushed her to her back, then laid a hand on her stomach. In a grating voice, he asked, "Should I fill your belly with a child, Samantha? Take my pleasure, then abandon you?"

She searched his face, hoping to see his stern mouth soften. "Why must you leave?" she repeated.

He grunted as if disgusted, then drew away from her again. "You do not listen, woman. My life is what it is. I have nothing to hold me in one place, nothing that belongs to me to give a white woman."

"White woman? What about an Indian woman, Holden?"

That silenced him, but not for long. "Indian women have their own lodges, other possessions gifted to them by their fathers. They expect a mate to hunt for food and protect them from danger. That is all."

Samantha smiled tentatively. "You accuse me of not listening, but do you hear yourself?"

His brows knitted together in consternation.

Not giving him a chance to argue, she said, "I have my own lodge gifted to me, as you put it, by my father. Furnishings for the house. Horses and other stock. You want to hunt? No one will stop you." She laid a hand on his sleeve. "You have already protected me, Holden."

He shook his head even before she finished, and deliberately clasped her wrist to remove her hand from his arm. "It is different . . ."

Horses' whinnies sliced the still air. In an instant, Holden jumped to his feet and ran toward the animals. They plunged against the restraining ropes. Pointed at the sky, his pistol reported twice in rapid succession.

"Whoa!" He reached for the first horse in line. The animal reared. "Whoa," he coaxed as he ducked beneath a bay's neck and grasped the headstall of a third animal. Unmindful of hooves crashing around him as the horses plunged in fear, he sidestepped two mares, which slammed into each other.

Had he not moved, he would have been crushed, Samantha realized as she untangled her feet from the blankets. She sprinted after him and added her quick hands to snag lead ropes and quiet the frightened animals. "What . . ."

A hissing whistle sound rent the air before she finished the question. A cougar stalked the horses, and Holden had disturbed its breakfast search. The cat had to be close. Frantic, Samantha looked about. Then she saw the creature, poised to leap.

"Holden! In the tree! Behind you!"

His gun on the rise as he pivoted, Holden fired off a single shot. Claws unsheathed, forelegs outstretched, the cat shuddered in midair, then its body cartwheeled downward from branch to branch. Tree limbs snapped and popped, snagged at the animal's fur until the lifeless body hit the ground with a thud.

"Whoa!" Holden called as he whipped around, holstered his gun and again grabbed for leads.

Samantha lunged forward, managed to grasp one mare's dangling rope. She clutched a freed gelding's halter. He dragged her backward. The lead in her other hand ripped across her palm until she increased her grip.

She didn't know how long it took—a minute, five, ten—but by the time the horses quieted, Samantha was warm as a hot biscuit. And exhausted. Trembling, she leaned against a tree and brushed her hair from her forehead.

Only then did she feel her stinging palm. Looking at her raised hand, the flesh mangled, she groaned. Blood oozed.

"You are hurt." Holden set his hands on her shoulders, and scanned her forehead. "Blood."

"On my face?" She brushed the back of her injured hand across her forehead. "I guess I smeared it there."

He clasped her wrist when he spied her bloody palm. "Your hand. Come." He didn't give her a chance to refuse.

She stumbled behind him until he again set his hands on her shoulders and pressed her down on the bedding. In moments he produced clean cloths and—she cringed from the anticipated sting—iodine.

Holden said nothing as he ripped one cloth into strips,

then soaked another with canteen water. Kneeling before her, he washed the bleeding flesh, more gently than she expected.

As his head bent toward her, Samantha's senses filled with his essence. A manly fragrance that was all his own, overlaid with leather and something wild. Indefinable. As elusive as trying to describe the smell of sun-dried linens. She inhaled sharply, enjoying the moment, his ministrations forgotten.

Glancing up quickly, he misinterpreted her indrawn breath. "I'm sorry if I hurt you, but I must clean the wound."

"No. I mean, you didn't hurt me."

His brow creased. Clearly he didn't believe her.

The horses shuffled, still agitated by the dead cat's proximity. Holden ignored them. Since he'd moved so quickly earlier, gun blasting before she could even rise to help, she wondered about his indifference. Then her gaze fell on the cougar. In the center of its throat, one neat hole oozed blood.

Intent on cleaning her wound, Holden was unaware she observed him. His sable hair hung to his shoulders. She resisted the urge to brush away strands that caught on his dark beard stubble.

She'd heard somewhere that Indians plucked out every last hair on their faces, even on their bodies. Holden's friend, Swift Arrow, didn't even have eyebrows. Holden didn't embrace that practice. Obviously, he shaved and had done so for a long time.

She didn't know how adept he was with a bow and arrow, but the way he handled a gun boggled the mind. Her gaze strayed to the cat again. And he hadn't even aimed.

She sucked in a startled breath. "Ooow!" Blinking sudden tears, she blew on her hand; an on-fire, orange-stained hand. Holden had poured iodine directly on the torn flesh.

"Sorry." He quickly laid a piece of folded cloth over the

wound, then bound it with the strips he'd torn for that purpose. "Be careful pulling on your glove."

Gritting her teeth, she shook her hand in a vain attempt to stop the stinging heat.

Their departure from camp came later than usual. Samantha nursed profound disappointment at the interruption in their conversation. Damn that cougar! Holden resumed their relentless pace and his annoying habit of ignoring her.

She endured the cold nights alone. He didn't offer to share his bed again. The only time he came near her was to clean and dress her hand. Though the operation was accomplished in silence, she allowed it. It forced him to hold her hand.

Pathetic, Samantha.

Frustrated, she fumed the rest of the trip to the Carter ranch.

Shortly after eleven o'clock the fifth morning out, Samantha stared at the precise, unmistakable handwriting on the bill of sale Mr. Carter handed her. Her father's bold signature left no doubt that he'd negotiated the sale last spring, months before his death.

Oscar had known and collected the correct number of geldings and mares listed in the sale. She'd failed to question her foreman. And, most damning, she'd found nothing in her father's papers to this effect. How well had she looked? Surely Pa had penned something regarding the sale.

Her cheeks warm despite the bitter cold, she glanced at the wiry man before her, his hazel eyes crinkled in a perpetual squint against sun-scorched prairie. Even today when the overcast sky boded rain, perhaps more snow.

"Ever'thin' in order, Miss Timberlake?"

"Yes, Mr. Carter. I didn't realize you and Pa had already handled the details."

"Hiram never left nothin' to chance. Me and him got along just fine in that regard." He grinned a mouthful of prominent teeth. "Weren't nobody better at horse-tradin' than your pa. He wrangled three dollars a head more outta me for them young mares." He sobered. "Sure sorry to hear he's gone."

"Thank you," she said, still unable to accept her loss.

Carter jammed his fingers in the pockets of his jeans and tipped his head toward the corral where the horses milled. "Well, if'n your hand'd put a couple o' them geldin's through their paces, I'd like to see them work."

Her hand?

Holden? She didn't think of him in the same way she did Grogan and the other hands. But judging from his actions toward her, she'd better start.

Holden needed no prompting. Employing his usual ground-tie method, he dropped the gray's reins and walked forward to speak to Carter. "I can use my saddle, but maybe you have one you would rather I use."

"Sure 'nuff. Shorty!"

Shorty, all six-two of him, appeared in the barn doorway. "Yeah, boss?"

"Bring my double-cinch rig out here." Half a head shorter than Holden, Carter looked up at him, then scanned his lean frame. "Actually, I don't ride that rig 'cause the seat's too roomy for me, but it should fit the bill for you, young fella."

Holden relieved the hand of the heavy saddle and strode to the corral gate.

"Ride that paint first," Carter ordered. "Looks like he's full o' piss and vinegar." The older man's cheeks reddened. "Sorry 'bout the language, ma'am. Ain't usually no lady 'round to hear me cuss 'cept Ma, and she's used to it."

Samantha smiled. "So am I, Mr. Carter. I've heard worse."

A huge smile on his face, he propped crossed arms on the corral's top rail and, in the age-old stance of cowboys, settled a booted foot on the bottom one. Samantha followed suit.

Holden rode with his usual grace. Each horse responded without hesitation: sidestepped, backed, whirled, showed bursts of speed, and slid to stops that sent dust into Samantha and Mr. Carter's faces. Several ranch hands paused to watch. Holden side-circled and overhead-circled ropes to prove the horses wouldn't spook. He obliged the rancher by riding three horses before the man nodded, satisfied they had delivered well-behaved working stock.

The silence unbroken between them, Holden stood off from Samantha while they waited for Carter to return from the house with the promised bank draft. She had no idea what Holden thought, but she felt a bit foolish. Her so-called reason for accompanying him had evaporated. There had been no bargaining needed between the men.

Mr. Carter had spoken to her as an equal, though. She was as grateful for that as for the valuable information he'd provided. Apparently ranchers didn't use cash. When she returned home, she vowed to take a *very* close look at her father's books to see if that was how he'd handled the financial transactions on Timberoaks.

Samantha bit her lip in thought. Now, she must either go to Waco or send someone else to deposit the bank draft. She couldn't justify another ride with Holden.

She masked a smile. They still had the ride home.

Chapter Twenty-six

Listless from lack of sleep, Samantha dragged off her hat and dropped it on the bank of the small stream they had camped near last night. Or rather this morning. At well past midnight, Holden had finally called a halt to their relentless hours in the saddle. They'd arrive home later that day, probably around noon. What had taken five days going north would be cut to three and a half days going south. Every bone in her body knew it.

She shrugged out of her heavy coat and lay prone to dunk her face into the stream. Jerking back, she squelched a yelp. Icy! But it might wake her enough to climb back into the saddle after precious few hours of sleep.

She wiped her face with a bandanna and contemplated her failure to seduce Holden. *A tempting siren you're not, Samantha Rose.* She rolled to sit cross-legged.

For starters, the weather had turned warmer and dashed her hope of crawling between Holden's blankets to share body heat. She stared at the coat heaped next to her. Yeah, the weather was cold enough to welcome its warmth, but not as frigid as it had been four or five days ago. Even her rope-burned hand hadn't cooperated. She glared at its reddened skin. It had healed far too quickly for her purpose.

About ten feet from her, a jackrabbit hopped to the stream. Hardly breathing, she turned her head to watch him dip his whiskered snout into the cold water. A squirrel scolded somewhere behind her, and the rabbit jumped straight into the air. Back feet pumping before he hit the ground, he ran toward her, then somersaulted to reverse direction when he scented her. She chuckled. Amazingly agile, wild critters.

A squirrel upstream chittered in answer to the first. Birds trilled. It was as if someone had set off an alarm. Time to rise and shine! She leaned back, braced on her hands, and looked up between the branches. The sky brightened before her eyes. Another clear day.

Holden was probably champing at the bit to hit the trail. Well, let him wait. If he was so all-fired anxious to get back to Lillibeth—the only reason she could think of for this hard ride—he could go on alone. She knew where she was, more or less. Somewhere on the north boundary of the Butcher place.

Sitting forward, she hunched her shoulders and wrapped her arms around her middle, a protective motion. Every time Lillibeth crossed her mind, she cringed at her own pitiful attempts to distract Holden. Not only pathetic, but downright sinful. If the man loved Lillibeth, what right did she have to throw herself at him? He was spoken for.

She glanced downstream in the direction of their camp. Seeking privacy, she'd walked far enough to be out of sight and earshot. If he should call for her, which she seriously doubted, she didn't think she'd hear. On a good day, a half dozen words passed between them. The man sure could be closemouthed and distant when he wanted.

She shrugged into her coat and picked herself up. *You*

can't win him, so you might as well make peace with the life dealt you. She had the ranch, which she loved. *But it's not enough.* Forlornly she dragged herself back to camp.

Voices?

Samantha stopped, listened. Who . . . Not Holden. More strident, grating. Mr. Butcher? Remembering their last encounter, alarm spiked through her, and her breath shortened as she slowed her pace and soundlessly eased toward camp.

"Who ya ridin' with?" were the first clear words Samantha heard.

"No one," Holden lied.

Samantha peered between sparse tree trunks. Uriah, dead ahead, faced about three-quarters away from her. It would take but half a turn of his head to see her.

"Then who's that thar horse belong to? I know you ride the gray."

"A Timberoaks horse. I am using it for packing."

Mr. Butcher rested his weight on his good right leg, the other supported by splints. He scanned the camp; she did the same. Holden had already picked up his bedroll and saddled the gray. She blinked. His gun belt hung from the saddle horn.

Surprise didn't begin to explain her reaction. That gun belt was the last thing he took off at night and usually the first thing he buckled on each morning. He must have left it there while he took care of morning needs.

Her breath stuttered to a halt when she saw the rifle in Butcher's hand. He waved it at Holden's belongings. "If'n you is travelin' alone, who belongs to this gear?" He pointed the gun barrel at her saddle, poised above her bedroll as a headrest. Right where she'd left it.

Holden shrugged.

"Ya stole this stuff, saddle tramp." He spat on the ground, then leveled the rifle directly at Holden, who stood a good fifteen feet from his own weapon.

A chill raced through Samantha at the expression on Butcher's face. Malicious. Evil.

"I can shoot ya for a horse thief."

His words sent her eyes darting in search of a weapon. Her rifle lay next to her bedroll.

Holden again said nothing, only nodded as if in agreement. Wearing his heavy coat, he stood perfectly at ease. He might be prepared to face death, but Samantha certainly wasn't ready for him to die.

Spying a broken limb about five feet away, she eased back. Stopped when Uriah turned directly toward Holden. Then, using the moment to advantage, she stooped and snatched up the branch. About four and a half feet long and three inches in diameter, it would be strong enough for her purpose, she prayed.

She gripped the branch in both hands. Could she knock him on the head from behind? Uriah went right on talking while she took one stealthy step forward, then another and another.

"Maybe I oughta lame ya like ya done me. Could shoot yer gun hand, too. Yer left-handed as I remember." He laughed cruelly.

How could Holden hold his tongue? He surely had seen her, but not by an eyelash flicker did he reveal her presence.

"No," Butcher said conversationally, "think I'll blow ya to hell and get it over with, you son of a bitch."

Click.

Samantha tossed caution to the wind and screamed, "No!" Breath labored, frightened tears streaming down her cheeks, she charged forward and swung the branch like a club to catch him on the back of the head. At the last moment, Uriah turned. The cudgel smashed his cheek and sent him flying sideways. The rifle jolted from his grip and hit the ground with an ear-shattering *kaboom!*

As if in a vacuum, sudden stillness enfolded her. She

dropped the limb and stared at Butcher's prone form. When she looked at Holden, he took an unsteady step and turned to face her. Odd. Why had he turned away?

She shook her head, then hesitantly approached her neighbor. She grasped his shoulder and turned him over. Vacant, open eyes stared skyward, his mouth slack. A fist-sized, bloody rock lay by his temple.

"My God." She fell to her knees. "He's dead, Holden. I killed him." She began to shake and couldn't rise to save her soul.

"An accident," Holden said in a strained voice.

Her eyes rounded in horror. "But I killed him."

Holden approached slowly. "It was not intentional. We must go."

"We can't leave him like this."

Holden nodded once. "We can and we will. A message can be sent to Butcher's ranch."

"What message? Just thought we'd let you know, folks, Uriah is dead. You'd best bury him."

"A message will be devised. Let us be gone from here. I must see you safely home. Now." He turned and retraced his steps to his horse.

Samantha's mouth gaped at his apparent unconcern. True, Mr. Butcher was evil. His actions in the past weeks had scared her, and moments ago he'd have shot Holden without a second thought. Still . . .

Holden hauled himself up, slumped for a second, then straightened. His face carved granite, he ordered, "Saddle up."

She did. No choice, really. Neither of them had a shovel. Before mounting, she covered the body with her bedroll. Useless if wolves or coyotes nosed around, but the best she could do. That Holden didn't appear to care one way or the other bewildered her. He didn't even pause to gather the rest of his few belongings.

As the day warmed past noon, he kept a slow but steady

pace. She ought to be thankful. She didn't think she had the strength to keep up if he pushed the way he had the previous days. Riding in front of her, his head nodded. And he was quiet. No surprise there.

It gave her time to think about the horror they'd left behind. Maybe Holden was right. She certainly hadn't meant to kill Mr. Butcher. If he hadn't fallen on the rock, he'd have a super goose egg, but he wouldn't be dead.

Nearing home, she nudged her horse up on Holden's left. Though not asleep, he didn't acknowledge her presence. He simply rode on, face strained, color oddly pale. As tired as she, no doubt. His fault, by golly. He'd set the pace.

They arrived in time to hear the dinner bell. As they broke into the clearing, she spied Aunt Mattie on the porch. Guy sprinted toward the house from the barn. Oscar followed at a leisurely walk, and Miss Gentry rose from the rocking chair on the porch.

Guy saw them first. "Samma!" He changed direction as everyone else looked their way. Even from a distance Samantha saw her aunt's posture straighten. Oh, boy, was she in for it. She'd left a note, but there would be hell to pay anyway.

The closer she got, the more sure she was of the tongue-lashing to come. Eyes narrowed, her aunt looked like she'd bitten into something sour.

"We're back," Samantha called, hoping to forestall the inevitable.

"Yep," Oscar said. He also knew trouble brewed. "Everything go all right?" He looked up at Holden, who'd reined in but sat still as a post. Standing opposite Samantha on the off-side of Holden's horse, the foreman frowned. "What's wrong?"

Dismounting, Samantha broke in before Holden could respond. "It was awful. Mr. Butcher . . . God help me, I hit him when he would have shot Walker, and he . . ." She looked at her aunt and burst into delayed tears.

"Tried to shoot Mr. Walker?" Incredulous, Mattie stepped forward to take Samantha's arm. "Uriah?"

"I hit him with a tree limb," Samantha blubbered, "and he . . . and he fell on a . . . rock." She wiped her nose on her sleeve. "Oh, Aunt Mattie, he's . . . dead!"

"Oh, child." Mattie enfolded Samantha in her arms.

"I killed him!"

Guy's arms circled her waist from behind. "Don't cry, Samma. Don't cry!"

"It was an accident, dear," Mattie soothed.

Samantha wagged her head. "It doesn't make any difference! Don't you understand? He's dead because I hit him!"

"Holden?" Lillibeth said at the same time Oscar asked, "Walker?"

If he answered, Samantha didn't hear. Now that the dam had broken, she couldn't stop sobbing.

"Where'd it happen?" Oscar asked.

Turning from her aunt's welcome comfort, Samantha again raked her sleeve over her runny nose. "We camped on the north of his ranch last night. He . . . came on us this morning. I was at the river." She paused and looked to Holden to continue the story, but he appeared to be off in another world.

"Why don't you both come inside," Mattie interjected.

At that invitation, Holden's horse ambled forward as if he intended to leave.

"Holden?" Lillibeth questioned again, and grabbed his near rein.

Holden's body toppled toward Oscar, whose eyes rounded as he braced to catch the falling man.

"What the . . . ?"

Samantha ran to help the foreman break his fall. Much bigger than Oscar, Holden hit the ground hard and rolled to his back, unconscious. His coat flapped open.

"Holden!" Samantha and Lillibeth screamed at the same time.

"What's wrong with him?" Samantha asked.

"Jesus God," Oscar said. "Look! He's covered in blood." Elbowing Samantha aside, he said, "Let's take a look."

Samantha gasped. The entire right side of Holden's shirt and trousers was soaked. "Oh no, oh no! He's been shot. He didn't tell me! Why didn't you say something?" she cried into Holden's still face. "You had to get *me* safely home? You idiot!"

"Samantha." Mattie tugged at her arm. "Let's take him in the house."

Though reluctant to leave his side, Samantha allowed her aunt to pull her up. Baker and several other ranch hands had arrived during the commotion. The largest man in the group, Baker kneeled down, slid his hands beneath Holden and lifted him without help.

"This way." Mattie headed toward the house.

Three nights later, Mattie sat beside Mr. Walker's bed and sponged his perspiring brow and chest. Still delirious, he mumbled in his restless sleep. He batted at the cool cloth as she wiped it over his broad shoulders.

"Stay . . . wake . . . Samantha . . . home . . . safe."

Not until he'd repeated the disjointed words over and over did she'd finally figure out what he meant. He thought they still rode toward the ranch, and he meant to see Samantha safely home.

Pausing in her ministrations, she sat back and bit her lip in thought. Even delirious he pursued his duty to Samantha. Admirable. And unexpected. She winced. When he wakened, she'd thank him. No matter how self-reliant Samantha thought herself, Mattie knew, as apparently did Mr. Walker, that her niece's impulsiveness could lead to all kinds of trouble.

When he moaned, she bushed his thick hair back from a sweaty brow. "Oh, honey, you needn't fret. You got Samantha home safely."

The door opened on silent hinges. Mattie looked up and smiled at Lillibeth, here to relieve her from the vigil she'd kept. "How is he?"

"His fever has broken, but he's still unconscious."

"Samantha . . . safe," Holden said again.

Mattie dipped the cloth in a bowl of cool water and reapplied it to his chest. "I think he's about to surface, though. Ever since I checked his wound, he's been restless." She rubbed the cloth over his beard-stubbled chin, then chuckled when he again pushed at her hand. "I don't think Mr. Walker is used to being cared for."

"Probably not." Lillibeth took the chair on the opposite side of the bed. "Is the wound clean? No festering?"

"Yes. Thank the Lord. I'm more than grateful for Oscar's ability, too. I couldn't have dug into this man's side the way he did." Her hand shook as she remembered the blood that spilled over the kitchen table's oiled cloth. As soaked as his shirt and trousers were, she was amazed he'd had any left to shed.

Oscar had probed until he found the bullet. Lodged next to a lower rib, the bullet's impact had cracked the bone. Lemuel carried Mr. Walker upstairs after the crude surgery. Since then, the two women had taken four-hour shifts day and night to watch over him.

Though Samantha railed at Mattie, she'd been adamant. It was improper for a young woman to tend a man in this situation. Recalling Samantha's indignant argument, she smiled.

"And why not? He's unconscious, for heaven's sake!"

"You're unmarried, dear. There may be moments of . . . immodesty while we care for Mr. Walker."

"You've never been married, Aunt Mattie!"

"That's true, but I've had some experience tending injured men."

Samantha's dark eyes flashed. "I changed Guy's nappies when he was little. I've seen—"

Mattie laughed. "There's a bit of difference after a man matures, Samantha. Now don't argue with me."

"Lillibeth is helping."

Mattie rolled her eyes. "Lillibeth is a grown woman whom I barely know. I have no say over her conduct, but I do yours, young lady."

"But—"

"No buts. Besides, I promised your father I'd look after you. He wouldn't allow you to tend Mr. Walker. Would he?"

Samantha'd *tsk*ed with disgust at Mattie's straitlaced comments, but she couldn't argue against the last one. Hiram would have surely banned Samantha from the sickroom. And Mattie knew without a doubt that Samantha's interest in Walker went beyond friendship, beyond the concern of employer for employee.

After listening to him for the past hour, though, she wondered if her first impressions of the man had been premature. Evidently, he was far more trustworthy than she had given him credit for. He could have bled to death in his determination to see Samantha safely home. That attitude flew in the face of her assumption that he was no more than a drifter who'd hightail it at the first opportunity. As Coleman Sheridan had so long ago, she thought with a pang of heartache.

Lillibeth interrupted her thoughts. "You need rest before the day begins. I can manage now."

"How well do you know him?"

Lillibeth averted her eyes and plucked the cloth from Mattie's hand. Cautiously she said, "As well as he will allow. Holden is not one to talk about himself."

"I've gathered that from watching him work. Other than the first day he arrived, he never offers his opinion unless asked."

"That's Holden," Lillibeth said noncommittally. What could she say that would not reveal her own situation?

"Do you know where he's from, anything about his family?"

"No. I . . . think he's an orphan."

Mattie watched Lillibeth's hand gently apply the wet cloth to his muscled chest.

"Probably so. But he gets along with children. Guy has taken to him."

Remembering the few times she'd lain with Holden, a wistful smile curved Lillibeth's lips. Unlike other men she'd entertained in her profession, Holden had not rutted on her. He'd made love. She'd experienced pleasure with him when she thought those feelings long dead.

"Holden is an uncommonly gentle man, Mattie."

Mattie's eyes rounded in disbelief. "Gentle? He wears his pistol like a gunslinger."

"But doesn't use it unless necessary."

"How do you know that?"

Nerves jangled by Mattie's questions, Lillibeth licked her lips and steadied her hands before she wrung the cloth again.

"Home . . . safe," Holden murmured. His legs moved restlessly beneath the quilt.

"Because he's a man of honor, Mattie. It may not be your concept of honor, but Holden has his own code. I taught him to read and write."

"Really? I didn't realize you'd known him so long."

"Five years. It's not uncommon for men to grow up illiterate."

Holden mumbled something unintelligible. Mattie's gaze riveted on his face. "That sounded like—"

Lillibeth nodded. "I think Holden lived with Comanches for many years."

Chapter Twenty-seven

Samantha sat on the side of her bed and glared out the window. Today she would judge Holden's condition for herself. No matter what Aunt Mattie said. According to Lillibeth, he'd said little when awake yesterday, and wouldn't acknowledge pain when she changed his bandage, but his eyes spoke otherwise. She'd assured Samantha that his wound was healing nicely, though.

"With no help from me," she muttered, pulling on her boots. Coat and gloves in hand, she stepped into the hall.

She planned to work Black Magic after checking on Holden. If she didn't, Holden's excellent training would go out the window, and he'd have to start all over. If he stuck around long enough, that is. Somehow she must convince him to stay, even if that meant watching him marry Lillibeth one day.

She unclenched her hands and opened his bedroom door. Lillibeth dozed in a chair. Beyond, Holden lay still, eyes closed, covers tucked across his chest. Ever so softly she shut the door behind her and studied the man she'd so foolishly fallen in love with. His muscled arms lay close to his sides, long-fingered hands limp. She shivered, remembering how once those hands had caressed her breasts. Deliberately pushing that thought from her mind, she stepped forward, touched Lillibeth's shoulder.

Golden eyes sleepy, she smiled and whispered, "I wondered when you'd visit."

I'd have been here every minute if not for my aunt. Fearing Lillibeth might misread her hostility, she forced the thoughts away. It wasn't Lillibeth's fault, and if anyone deserved to care for Holden, it was the woman he loved. "Is he okay?"

"Resting. He still wakes disoriented, but perhaps that will pass today. He's strong and healthy." She cocked her head questioningly. "Would you sit with him a few minutes? I need to visit the privy. Has Mattie brewed coffee?"

Samantha nodded. "I smelled it. If it's not ready, it soon will be."

Lillibeth rose. Samantha took her place. "Do I need to do anything?"

"No. Other than give him water if he wakes. He needs fluids after so much blood loss." She paused, hand on the doorknob. "I won't be long."

"Take your time," Samantha said to the closing door. Her gaze rested on Holden's face. He looked so vulnerable lying there. Maybe everyone did when asleep, but this man had never shown a single weakness in the months she'd know him.

She longed to clasp his hand, but feared it would disturb him. "You could have bled to death." Tears glistened in her dark eyes. "I'd want to die if you had, Holden," she whispered.

She hadn't felt so even when her father died. Her heart thudded painfully. *The two most important men in my life have occupied this cozy room.* Each in his own way had protected her. And as sure as she would live out lonely days on Timberoaks, Holden would abandon her as her father had.

Despair shook her whole being. "Pa had no choice, but you do."

Confident that she could speak her mind while he was unconscious, she continued. "I love you." Unshed tears clogged her throat, roughened her speech. "Stupid, huh?"

His fingers curled. Samantha watched him for several quiet minutes, fearing he might be waking, might have heard her confession, but his eyes remained closed and he didn't stir again.

"You said you would move on. Now I know why." She sniffed and wiped her nose. "I can't dislike her, Holden. Lillibeth is so nice. But . . ." In a tiny voice, she asked, "Why can't you love me instead of her?"

A moment later Lillibeth returned. "I'm in hot water." She chuckled.

"Why?"

"Your dear aunt isn't pleased that I left you alone with Holden."

"Oh, fiddle-faddle. Let her stew." This overprotectiveness had gone on long enough. Holden was no threat to her reputation. Who in blazes cared, other than Aunt Mattie, if she slept with the man? No one!

Except Lillibeth. Guiltily, her eyes darted to the woman she'd come to like in spite of everything.

Let them be, Samantha, she ordered herself. Anxious to get out of the room, away from Lillibeth and Holden, she rose. "When he wakes, tell him I'm working Black Magic today. I don't think he would want the stallion's training to suffer."

At Lillibeth's nod, she left as quietly as she'd come.

Moments later, Lillibeth set the coffee on the night table. Maybe the aroma would wake him. He needed to get up today if possible. Her cursory appraisal of him halted at his hand.

His fisted hand.

Surprised, her eyes flicked to his face. *He's awake. Why is he pretending sleep?* She frowned and glanced over her shoulder at the door Samantha had just closed.

Lillibeth allowed a moment to pass, then softly said, "She's gone, Holden. You can open your eyes."

He did, but instead of looking her way, he stared at the ceiling, brow knitted. She remained silent. Let him tell her what troubled him . . . or not. Probably the latter.

At long last, he asked, "Where are my clothes?"

"In the top bureau drawer."

"My gun?"

"Beneath the left side of the bed."

"Leave me. I will get dressed."

"And do what?"

"I must leave Timberoaks today."

Unbelievable! He had to be weak as a newborn pup. But arguing with him would gain nothing. Let him make the discovery for himself.

"I'm not going anywhere, Holden. You think you can get up, dress, don your gun belt and walk out of here? Fine. Do it. With my blessing." That was a lie, but he couldn't know that. "I am, however, curious as to why a fire has suddenly ignited under you." Secretly she believed the reason had just walked out the door.

Reaching for the coffee cup, she settled back to enjoy the brew herself. And watch the show. Unkind, perhaps, but it was past time Holden understood he wasn't invincible. Most people learned that at a far younger age. Apparently, he never had.

The School of Hard Knocks is in session. She suppressed a grin. *Final examinations are coming up!*

He struggled to sit. His deep breaths sent pain piercing through his side, but determination won. Braced on an extended arm, he turned accusing eyes on Lillibeth but, as promised, she did nothing.

His head swam. Though consciousness had eluded him too often for several days, he needed to muster the strength to leave Timberoaks.

Love? Did Samantha truly believe she loved him? Her feelings could not possibly be so deep.

Gratitude, maybe, for his part in rescuing Guy. He had worked Black Magic and taken her horses north, but those chores were nothing more than his job; Oscar could have done as well.

Samantha believed his heart belonged to Lillibeth. He glanced sidelong at her. Perhaps, in a grateful sort of way. Lillibeth was not, would never be, the love of his life. Not like . . .

He clamped down on those wayward thoughts. Only heartache lay in that direction, for her and for him. Samantha needed a man with nesting instincts. Definitely not him.

As far back as Holden could remember, the tribe had moved twice a year. He had always enjoyed exploring new places, new hideouts he and Swift Arrow found for their endless games or for honing hunting skills. That was the only life he knew: nomadic. He liked it that way. Yes, he assured himself.

He could not still the little voice in his head. *You lie.*

And when he thought about walking away from Samantha and Guy, another ache blossomed in his chest, higher this time, and knife-sharp.

Tossing back the covers, he gritted his teeth and slowly slid his legs to the edge of the bed. Another blizzard of pain blinded him when he lowered his feet to the floor.

Although it injured his pride to do so, he gave in and asked for assistance. "I will need help to stand, Lillibeth."

She nodded. "And to walk this floor at least once today. But I won't help you dress. It will take a few days for you to regain enough strength to leave."

Even though he wanted to deny her assessment, she was

right. He opened his eyes and this time took a shallow breath.

"You have my shoulder to lean on for a day or two, as well as—"

"Not Samantha's."

". . . Miss Crawford's."

He blinked, surprised that the little woman might help him. She did not trust him. With good reason, he admitted. Had he stuck to his original plan, he would have snatched Guy and taken him away. . . . Where? Not to the People. Little Spring was no more. Walks in Shadow would never return to the tribe.

Lillibeth broke into his thoughts. "Well, are you ready to do this before Mattie relieves me?"

Holden looked down. He had no small clothes like those that covered his lower body, so they must have belonged to Mr. Timberlake. Scanty cover, but they would have to do. Besides, Lillibeth knew his body. Heat blossomed in his cheeks when he realized Miss Crawford probably did too. As an Indian, he would have thought nothing of stepping from his lodge naked. But he had lived among the white people long enough to feel differently now.

Anger surged through him each time he realized he had adopted a bit more of the white man's beliefs. He lunged up. Mistake! Agony lanced through him. Sweat beaded his brow and washed his chest.

"Are you crazy?" Lillibeth cried as he toppled toward her. Staggering beneath his weight, she somehow kept him upright. She wrapped her arms around his torso—could do nothing else—even though her arm pressed against his bandaged side. "Holden, if this opens your wound again, you have no one to blame but yourself."

Pain ricocheted from his side to his head, then hammered its way straight down to his toes. It was a moment before he could utter a sound. "True. But I need to walk," he gritted through his teeth.

"All right." She puffed as if she had run a footrace. "Give me another second or two."

She gingerly pulled her arms back and pressed her small hands against his chest. He leaned against them like a slanted timber.

"Take a couple steps toward me."

He shuffled a minuscule distance, then paused to breathe shallowly. God of the white man, his bare feet were iron-weighted.

"Can you make it to the wall?"

"I will," he vowed, then wondered how his legs would carry him that far. Weak did not begin to describe the helplessness he felt.

Shaking from the effort, he reached for the solid wall with both hands. Once he found support there, Lillibeth scooted behind him and wrapped her arms around his sweat-slicked torso, careful that her right arm rode above the bandage.

His lungs burned as he tried to suck in air without increasing the pain in his side. He still must return to the bed, he thought morosely. At that moment the door opened inches from his hand. Miss Crawford yelped in surprise at finding him so close, staring down at her.

Her dark eyes rounded in astonishment. "Are you crazy?"

Lillibeth laughed. "My exact sentiment."

"I must . . . regain strength. Walking . . . helps."

"Falling on your face won't," Mattie snapped. "Here." She took command and clasped his upper arm. "Lillibeth, take his other arm so we can at least get him pointed in the right direction."

Though both women were strong, their small statures worked against them. He nearly pitched forward as they turned.

"Wait!" Mattie widened her stance and eased Holden's arm over her shoulders. "You too, Lillibeth."

He had trouble putting one foot in front of the other.

But they finally wrestled him a few steps, pivoted, and then all three fell backward across the bed.

Mattie leaped up, bristling. "Look at you." She pointed at the bandage. "That little exercise opened your wound. It's bleeding again!"

No doubt, he thought, but could not get past the pain to answer. And that might not be the worst of it. When they fell, he swore the rib weakened by the bullet snapped. But he was too busy thanking every god he had ever prayed to that he was about to pass out. In the next instant, blessed oblivion claimed him.

"Men! I swear they don't have a lick of sense," Mattie blustered. She rounded on Lillibeth. "Why did you let him do that? You knew—"

"Let him?" Lillibeth shot back. "Have you ever tried to stop a wall of raging flood water?" She sniffed indignantly. "Once you know Holden better, you'll discover he does exactly as he pleases, when he pleases."

Mattie backed down, her expression contrite. "Sorry. You're absolutely right. That was uncalled for. Let's get him settled and take a look at the damage."

Chapter Twenty-eight

Samantha made it a priority to stay away from Holden for the better part of the next week. Until she heard he planned to leave, possibly today. Brow creased in muddled thought, she leaned down to clean Black Magic's front hoof. He shifted ever so slightly, nudging her shoulder. She slid her right foot out to a wider stance, so the stallion couldn't knock her over.

"Easy, boy. I'm almost finished." The horse reminded her of a grumpy man, irritated at having his sleep disturbed.

Why, if Holden intended to leave today, did Lillibeth plan to remain at Timberoaks? She didn't understand Lillibeth any better than she did Holden. Boy, if he were in love with *her,* he'd play billy-blue-blazes riding out of her life!

"But he doesn't love you! So stop thinking that way, Samantha Rose," she muttered, frustrated by her futile wish for things that could never be.

"You talkin' to me, Miss Samma?"

Oh dear, she'd forgotten Lemuel at work in the next stall. "Uh, no. Just . . . telling Black Magic to behave himself."

"He's an ornery one, that's fer sure."

She heard the smile in Lemuel's voice. The big black man was amiable and kind almost to a fault. All their hands were. And every one of them worked like the ranch belonged to him rather than like hired help. Her father and Oscar had, over the years, hired the best men available. Some of their success came from the two men's abilities to measure a man and his worth. One day she hoped she'd possess that same insight.

After just a few words had been exchanged, her father had hired Holden: a man who worked hard, who minded his own business but knew what had to be done and did it, oftentimes without being asked.

She had fallen in love with him. And now he was leaving to find work elsewhere.

When she closed her eyes, Black Magic sensed her loss of concentration, and again leaned into her. Yelping, she scrambled to keep her feet. "Darn you!" She whapped him on the shoulder.

Lemuel chuckled as he watched her from the stall's doorway. "Give 'im an inch and he'll take a mile, Miss Samma."

She laughed. "That's for sure." This time she patted the stallion's shoulder affectionately. He whiffled as if it was his due.

"Hello, the barn!"

Startled, Samantha glanced toward the front door, then to the back, where a man stood outside in the weak winter sun. A chill slithered down her spine and she shivered. "Yes?"

He dropped his mount's reins and stepped closer. A sudden gust of wind whipped his long duster around his legs. Even with his hat square on his head, his face shadowed by the brim, she could still make out light, gleaming eyes in an abnormally pale face.

Laying the hoof pick on top of the stall fence, she

walked toward him. Lemuel stayed put, a comforting presence.

"What can I do for you, mister?"

"I'm looking for Hiram Timberlake."

Already aware he was a stranger in these parts, she felt even more unsettled by his request. "My father passed away last summer."

He removed his hat and tipped his head respectfully. "Sorry to hear that, ma'am."

"I'm Samantha Timberlake."

She could see him clearly now, his thin snow-white hair mussed by the wind. Though it shouldn't have mattered, his appearance further alarmed her. *An albino!*

"I'm looking for a man. I was told he works for Timberoaks."

At that, Lemuel's sturdy presence edged up behind her. "What man?" she hedged.

"Name's Walker. Hear he trains horses."

"You trying to steal my hired hands?"

"Not exactly."

The wind caught his duster and folded it back from his right side. A six-shooter every bit as long and menacing as Holden's rode the man's hip. And then she knew. A Texas Ranger. From what she'd heard, they were often as vicious as the outlaws and Indians they sought.

He noticed her attention on his gun, donned his hat and, with his left hand, pulled the duster closed. "I need a word with him if you might tell me where to find him."

"Mr. Walker is—"

"Here." A low, familiar voice spoke behind her.

Samantha spun around. Holden, wearing his heavy coat and carrying a bedroll, sauntered the length of the barn toward her, his remarkable eyes riveted on the stranger.

"Hawkins, isn't it?" he asked amiably.

Her gaze raced over him. From his steady pace, one would never know he'd been near death a week before.

Mattie had sponged the bloodstain from his coat until only a faint, dark smear remained. His gun holster protruded an inch or so below the coat's hem.

Her heart sank. He was leaving . . . now. And there wasn't a thing she could do to stop him. She darted a glance at Lemuel, praying he might somehow help her. But the big man paid her no mind, his attention focused on the albino who, though still in sunlight, had stepped closer.

"You know me?"

Holden's lips turned up in a half smile. "Know of you."

Hawkins returned Holden's smile, equally wry. He nodded. "Best we have some privacy for what I have to say."

"We keep no secrets on Timberoaks."

Samantha blinked at her aunt's timely arrival and take-charge attitude. Lillibeth followed right on her heels. Both women had thrown shawls around their shoulders, but Samantha knew they provided little comfort against the chill wind blowing through the barn. Neither seemed bothered. She glanced at the Ranger and nearly laughed aloud.

His light eyes darted from woman to woman, to her, to Lemuel, and lastly to Holden, his startled expression priceless. Samantha heard Hawkins's exasperated sigh.

But Aunt Mattie wasn't finished.

"Lemuel, take the gentleman's horse, please. The rest of you come to the house. The coffee's on, Mister . . ."

"Hawkins, ma'am. Asa Hawkins." He hesitated, shifting on his booted feet. "You the new owner of Timberoaks, ma'am?"

"No. That would be Samantha. I'm her aunt, Matilda Crawford."

"Well, then . . ."

"We extend hospitality to one and all, Mr. Hawkins."

That wasn't exactly the truth, but Samantha didn't disagree. Instead, she glanced at Holden and found humor glinting in his eyes. He had certainly found out that no one, absolutely no one, deterred Mattie Crawford from her chosen course. Whatever that might be.

"You've no doubt ridden for hours this morning. You can use a cup of coffee." It was not a question.

"Uh, yeah, I guess so." Hawkins surrendered to Mattie's determination.

Like Holden, the man was twice Mattie's size. He could easily ignore her directives. Samantha bit the inside of her lip. But he wouldn't dare. No one would.

Mutely, Lemuel held out his hand. Frustration plain on his face, Hawkins walked farther into the barn and handed over his horse. "He could use some water."

Lemuel nodded. As he turned to lead the horse into the stall he'd just mucked, Samantha spied the grin on his face. She looked away quickly, afraid she'd laugh out loud after all.

Mattie pivoted and walked sedately toward the house. Lillibeth cast a worried glance at Holden, then joined her. Behind them, Hawkins fell into step with Holden, and Samantha brought up the rear.

Samantha's mind raced. What did this man want? Something to do with Mr. Butcher? She didn't believe anyone on Timberoaks would talk, so how could he know she had killed the man? Accidentally. Still . . .

Holden had left very little of his gear. A couple of utensils and his canteen. But what did that prove? Those things could belong to anyone. She'd never noticed, not even the night she'd gone through his things, but maybe he'd scratched his name or initials into the canteen. Oh, lordy, she hoped not.

"Have a seat, gentlemen," Mattie said as Samantha entered the parlor. "Your coffee will be ready in a jiffy." She sailed through to the kitchen, clasping Lillibeth's arm to drag her along.

Samantha paused just inside the door and eyed the men warily. They removed their hats, then glanced around as if unsure how they had come to be there. Finally, Holden nodded at Hawkins, and the man took the settee while Holden settled into her father's chair. Each rested his hat on a knee. Neither said a word.

After some rattling from the kitchen, Mattie reappeared with cups of coffee on a tray. She walked first to Holden, then offered the remaining cup to Mr. Hawkins. Tray tucked under her arm, she motioned to Samantha.

"We'll leave the men to their discussion."

Her back straightened. *Not likely!* "You said there are no secrets on Timberoaks."

"That's true. But there are civilized ways to conduct business. And those proprieties will be observed."

"But—"

"Samantha!"

At that stern pronouncement, she complied, though her brow creased rebelliously.

As soon as they reached the kitchen, she glared at her aunt. "What are you—"

"I said we'd leave them to their discussion, Samantha." She grinned. "I didn't say we wouldn't listen."

Lillibeth choked and Samantha laughed simultaneously at the mischief dancing in Mattie's eyes.

"You are a devious woman, Mattie Crawford," Lillibeth said.

Mattie smiled. "Thank you." She placed the tray on the table, and crooked her finger for them to follow her back into the dining room. She motioned for quiet, then plastered herself against the wall next to the parlor door.

". . . and it looks like somebody murdered the old man."

"Why have you come to me with this?" Holden asked.

"The foreman told me you two got into it a while back. You shoot him in the hand and knee like Butcher claimed?"

"Hmm," Holden said.

"Is that a yes or a no?"

"Yes."

"Why? Seems to me you lamed a man for no good reason."

"Hmm." Holden remained maddeningly closemouthed.

"Who're ya?"

Samantha jerked back in surprise. Lillibeth clamped a hand over her mouth, golden eyes round in her piquant face.

"Give me strength," Mattie whispered.

"Hawkins, meet Miss Timberlake's brother, Guy," Holden said.

"Young fella," came Hawkins's sober voice.

"Who are ya?" Guy persisted.

"A Texas Ranger," Holden patiently supplied.

"Really?" Guy's voice rose an octave. "Whataya here for?"

Mattie'd had enough with that question. Boldly, she strode into the parlor and clamped a hand on Guy's shoulder. "Children should be seen and not heard, young man. Come with me."

"He's a Texas Ranger, Aunt Mattie. Ain't he funny lookin'?"

"Guy! You apologize right this minute."

"Why? He *is* funny lookin'."

"Guy!"

"Uh, ma'am, don't bother. I'm used to it."

"That is not the point," Mattie said heatedly. "There's no excuse for poor manners." She rounded on the child. "Guy, you apologize this instant or your backside won't be able to touch a chair for a week!"

"Oow!"

From the dining room, Samantha surmised that her aunt had pinched Guy's ear. She could remember that happening to her a time or two when she was about his age.

"OK! I'm sorry. But how come he's so white?"

"Guy—"

"Little man, do you know what albino is?"

"Sure. I saw a horse like that once't. Pa told me they got no pig . . . somethin'."

"Pigmentation," Holden said. "Sometimes people are born albino, too."

"Really? Well, I'll be! People, huh? Lots of 'em? How come we don't got none here?"

"Don't have any here," Mattie snapped. "Now, Mr. Nosey-drawers, let's get you to the kitchen for some vittles. Fill that mouth of yours with food instead of questions."

"OK. Bye, mister."

Samantha didn't want Guy to see her, so she inched back and wedged herself at the side of the hutch.

And sure enough, when Aunt Mattie ushered him ahead of her into the dining room, Guy blurted, "What ya doin', Miss Lillibeth?"

"Uh, just coming to see what all the ruckus was about."

"Did you see 'im? He's a Texas Ranger, and he's a albino," Guy said in a stage whisper.

"I know," Lillibeth retorted as the three passed into the kitchen.

Samantha breathed a sigh and crept back close to the doorway.

No sound came from the parlor until Holden said, "The boy is curious."

"And honest. Where were we? Oh, yeah. Why'd you shoot up Butcher so bad?"

"I had my reasons."

"So, I gotta wonder, did you go back, shoot him dead for good measure?"

"No."

Shoot? He fell on a rock! Samantha was stopped from barging into the conversation when Hawkins continued.

"Well, bashed him in the head, maybe?"

"That is how he was found?"

"Yeah."

Samantha heard the sheepishness in the ranger's voice. He'd tried to trip up Holden, and it hadn't worked.

"His rifle had been fired. You know anything about that?"

Silence greeted the question.

"Butcher'd gone missin' about three days when some of his hands stumbled on him—what was left of him."

Samantha shuddered and closed her eyes. She'd known wild animals would disturb the body. Even though she now understood why Holden had insisted they leave, she still regretted the desecration of a man's remains. Even vile Uriah Butcher deserved a decent burial.

"Where were you a week ago?"

"Hard to say," Holden evaded.

"Can't or won't say?"

Another silence.

"His boys said none of the gear they found belonged to Butcher. Don't suppose you'd know anything about that?"

Tell him, Holden! He sounds like a reasonable man.

But he didn't say a word.

"How long you been workin' on Timberoaks?"

"Since midsummer."

"I ain't accusing you of anything, Walker, but I'd appreciate you taking a ride with me. My colonel is breathin' down our necks about this. You sure are one tight-lipped feller, ain't you?" He laughed without humor. "You don't offer anything unless asked, do you?"

Again, silence.

"Well, what do you say?"

"Where is this colonel you speak of?"

"Main office in Lampassas."

"All right."

Samantha rubbed sweaty palms on her jeans. She couldn't let him ride off with this ranger. If he refused to answer questions, they'd pin a murder charge on him, for sure.

He'll get himself hanged.

She could not let that happen. Hands fisted at her sides, she marched into the parlor. "I killed Uriah Butcher."

Chapter Twenty-nine

Silence met her outburst.

The ranger's eyes narrowed. "You were there?"

"Yes—"

"No," Holden said.

She glared at him. "I hit Mr. Butcher to stop him from shooting you, Holden Walker."

"No—"

"Let the lady have her say, Walker."

"She need not—"

"Yes, I do. He's a reasonable man." Rounding on the lawman, she asked, "You are, aren't you?"

"Sometimes, yeah," Hawkins said.

"All right! Mr. Butcher planned to shoot Holden out of pure meanness. I sneaked up behind him and hit him on the head, but"—she swallowed—"he fell on a rock and . . . I didn't mean to kill him," she added quickly.

"Samantha—"

"Because Walker had maimed him?"

"That's what he said. And then his rifle went off. . . ."

"Yeah? And . . . ?"

"Uriah shot Holden anyway."

Hawkins gave Holden the once over. "He looks fit to me."

"It's the truth! Show him, Holden." When he sat unmoving, Samantha crossed the room and jabbed her finger at him. "Stubborn man!"

Holden batted her hand away. "You should not speak, woman."

"Well, she already has," Hawkins said. "You sporting a wound?"

"She's right. Show him, Holden," Lillibeth said from the dining room doorway.

Samantha swung around. It hurt like the dickens to admit it, but she was thankful for Lillibeth's interference. Maybe he would listen to . . . She looked directly at Holden but spoke to Hawkins. "Maybe the woman he loves can make him see reason."

"What's goin' on here?"

All eyes turned to Oscar as he stepped through the front door. He smiled when he spotted the ranger. "Well, ain't you a sight for sore eyes. What brings you to Timberoaks, Asa?"

"Oscar?" The ranger rose. "Oscar Dupree. Jesus. Wondered where you got to." He strode to the foreman and held out his hand. "Been a long time. Good to see you, old saw."

"More'n ten years." Oscar pumped the man's hand.

"You know each other?" Samantha asked in a squeaky voice.

"Sure do," Oscar said. "Rode together for a spell." He paused, his gaze roaming over everyone and halting on Lillibeth. A shy smile lit his eyes. He fell into that trance Samantha had seen more than once. Then he visibly shook himself and turned his attention to his friend. "So, what're ya doin' on Timberoaks?"

"Investigating Butcher's murder."

"Weren't no murder, Asa. Accident, pure and simple." He scowled. "Though the varmit deserved ta be shot or hanged a long time ago."

Relief, maybe premature, turned Samantha's knees to jelly and she sank into a chair. "That's what I've been trying to tell him, Oscar. I surely didn't mean to kill the man."

Oscar's eyes widened. "You told Asa ya killed Uriah? Why'd you do a fool thing like that, Samantha?"

"Exactly," Holden snapped.

"Because, because . . ." Holden's gaze held hers for a moment, but she ignored him. "He died! I hit him and he died, Oscar."

"Yeah, but only 'cause a rock got in the way."

Asa spoke up. "Miss Timberlake said Butcher shot Walker."

"Yep. Dug out the slug myself." He grinned at Holden. "If he weren't such a stubborn cuss, he'd a died."

Holden didn't respond to the taunt.

Perhaps, Samantha thought, because Oscar only spoke the truth. "So, what happens next?" she asked, concerned that Asa Hawkins might still cart Holden off to Lampassas.

"Where are your manners, young lady?" Mattie stood behind Lillibeth.

"My manners?" Samantha blinked in confusion.

"Didn't you ask the guests to sit down?"

"We've been a little . . . busy," Lillibeth said. "Mr. Dupree explained the situation surrounding Mr. Butcher's death, and everyone sort of . . . A bit of excitement, you might say."

As Guy was nowhere to be seen, Samantha guessed that Aunt Mattie had plied him with cookies and sent him out to play. With Uriah Butcher gone from this earth, her brother was no longer in danger. Thank God.

Everyone except Holden took a seat. He spoke to Hawkins. "If you are finished with me, I must leave."

No! How could she keep him from walking out of her life?

"Guess it's okay. I'll get the particulars from Oscar." He shrugged. "Butcher is buried, so there won't be no questions about his injuries. Where you off to in case we need to talk again?"

Holden hesitated and darted a glance at Samantha. "I do not know for sure. Waco, perhaps."

Oscar stood. "Hate to see ya go, Walker. We sure are shorthanded right now." Oscar's lips tipped in a half smile as he extended a farewell handshake. "If ya change your mind, you can work for me any day." He slid Samantha a questioning look. "Ain't that right?"

"Whatever you say, Oscar." Her spine stiffened. "But Mr. Walker has made it perfectly clear that he doesn't want to be here."

"Has he?" Lillibeth murmured.

Holden donned his hat, saluted Aunt Mattie and Lillibeth, then gave Samantha one last assessing look, lingering on her eyes. His were unreadable as he turned and left.

She would not cry!

Samantha crossed to the window and watched Holden stride purposefully toward the barn. His steps faltered when Guy rose from playing marbles next to the barn's entrance. Her brother brushed straggly hair out of his eyes as he looked up at the tall man. His uncle. Though Guy would never know that. Not now.

Suddenly, Guy lunged forward and wrapped his arms around Holden's legs. She couldn't hear what was said, but undoubtedly her brother had just learned that one of his favorite people was leaving.

After a moment's hesitation, Holden rested his hands on Guy's shoulders, then tipped back his head as if looking for guidance from above. He loved that boy. Samantha knew it as surely as she hitched in the next tear-clogged breath. He wouldn't have come back otherwise. Without a doubt, Holden found it difficult to leave him behind—again.

Holden pushed Guy to arm's length, then hunkered down on bent knee. Whatever he said to ease Guy's pain, Guy would have none of it. Breaking from Holden's grasp, he buried his face in the man's chest and wrapped sturdy arms around his neck. Even from this distance she felt Holden's heartbreak.

Unable to watch any longer, Samantha turned from the window. Without a word, she left the parlor and climbed the stairs. She eased the door shut as her gaze roamed over the familiar room.

For as long as she could remember, this room had been hers. A retreat when she was sad, confused.

Hurting.

And this hurt touched her soul.

She flung her coat toward the bed. It landed on the rug. Wrapping her arms around her waist, she rested her head against the door and closed burning eyes. Somehow she knew this gnawing ache would never go away.

Unaware of time, she stood there, unable to draw in air without searing pain in her chest, struggling to breathe past the tears in her throat.

Her brow creased when she recalled Holden's negligent good-bye salute to Lillibeth. If he loved the woman as Samantha had believed, surely he'd have taken her with him. Perhaps she'd jumped to the wrong conclusion.

Thoughts circled round and round as she absently rubbed her chest. More than once her father had admonished her that, once a decision was made, she should pursue it to the end. Only then could she know if it had been the right one.

Her brow creased. Should she confront Holden one more time? Could she persuade him she loved him and wanted him in her life? If not, what could he say to ease her pain? Would he even try?

Forbidding herself time to equivocate, Samantha ripped open the door and flew along the hall, then leaped down the stairs two at a time and burst onto the porch. She didn't close the door, never slowed her pace as she ran across the clearing and plunged into the trees where she'd last seen Holden's camp.

Her aunt's voice wafted faintly from behind. "Samantha!"

Torn between finding Holden at any cost and succumbing to lifelong respect for her aunt, she hesitated, then stopped. Mattie marched toward her.

"You can't stop me!" Samantha shouted.

"You're going to Mr. Walker?"

"Yes. I shouldn't have let him leave."

"I agree."

Samantha blinked in surprise. "I thought you didn't like Holden."

"I was wary of him at first." A gentle smile curved Mattie's lips. "He's a good man, Samantha. You'd be a fool to let him slip away."

Struck speechless by her aunt's change of heart, Samantha hugged Mattie fiercely until pushed away.

"Go, child."

She grinned, accepting "child" as the endearment it was intended to be. Spinning around, she raced on again and wondered if she'd stood feeling sorry for herself long enough for him to collect his gear and be gone? "Please, God, please, God," she gasped.

Dodging tree trunks, slapping naked branches out of her way, she stumbled over fallen limbs in her headlong dash to locate his camp. By the time she reached the stream, her lungs burned. Skidding to a halt in dead leaves, she leaned over, rested shaky hands on her knees, and sucked in labored breaths.

But only for a moment. Then she straightened and ran on.

It can't be far.

Holden heard her at the same moment she saw him. His gun magically appeared, the long barrel aimed directly at her. Eyes wide, he lowered the gun and jammed it into his holster.

"What do you here without your coat?"

She blinked. Her coat? Then she looked down and realized she'd forgotten it. But at this moment, it could have been fifty below and she wouldn't have felt the cold.

"I . . . I . . ." Putting her hand on her chest, she gulped a lungful of frigid air. It felt good.

She drank in the sight of him as he shed his coat and walked toward her. Before she realized his intent, he swung the coat over her shoulders, pulled it closed and held it with one hand. Delicious warmth, his warmth, engulfed her. His scent, wild, leathery, all Holden, filled her nostrils.

"Mmm. Thank you." She licked parched lips.

His gaze immediately dropped to her mouth. Something dangerous, compelling, inviting, flashed in his eyes. His hand fell away. He stiffened and stepped back.

"You should not be here."

"I could buy a horse if I'd earned a nickel every time you've said that."

He scowled. "But you should not be here."

"Yes, I should. I belong here on Timberoaks. And so do you!"

"No."

"Because you choose not to!"

Holden knelt on the blanket where he'd spread his belongings to organize and repack, hoping to buy a moment's time. Hoping to clear his head.

Did she speak truth?

He paused, one hand on the bow he had made for Guy. If he left, he would never give it to him. If he left, he would never see the boy again.

He heard Samantha approach, but still flinched when her hand settled on his shoulder. Against his will, his own came up to cover hers. He squeezed ever so gently as his head tipped forward.

"If it counts for anything, Holden, I love you."

Despair had not visited him for many years. Now it licked like fire at his soul. He hungered to hear those words again and again from this woman.

"I love how you talk to Guy. How you work with horses. The gentle care you've given Lillibeth. I even love your stubborn, hardheaded ways." She sighed. "A characteristic we share more than I like."

He shook his head. "You are a brave woman, Samantha. To run Timberoaks, you must be."

She dropped down next to him and chuckled. "You can call it brave; I call it stubborn."

His hands stilled. Settling more comfortably, he gazed across the stream, where steam rose from the narrow ribbon of water. It fogged his vision of the stark, winter-stripped trees.

Fogged his determination, too.

For what reason had he wandered rootless and footloose? Because that was what he had known as an Indian.

You no longer live in that world.

But it was the life he preferred.

Preferred?

Now he wondered. His gaze dropped to the bow and arrows. The time when he could have gifted them to Little Spring was past. He could not tell Guy of his heritage. The boy would be an outcast if others knew.

"Does your aunt know that Guy is part Indian?"

Samantha shook her head. "No. And I don't intend to tell her."

"It is well," he said aloud, though his heart ached within for what might have been.

He looked at Samantha. Could he commit to living on Timberoaks? His chest tightened. Should he admit his soul-deep love for her?

"Holden?" Her ebony eyes glittered with emotions that mirrored his own.

"I love you, Samantha."

Tears trickled from her eyes. Gently, he took her face between his hands, brushed the moisture from rosy, chapped cheeks. At that moment, the most compelling reasons for leaving stabbed his heart.

"Samantha, Guy now belongs to you and your aunt. When you learned I was Indian, when I explained I had left Little Spring, you recoiled from me. I must leave. I could not bear to one day see the love in your eyes again turn to fear or hatred."

"I have never feared you, Holden."

He dropped his hands and shook his head in denial.

"It's true." A smile trembled on her lips. "You've angered me, you bet. You left Guy on our doorstep. But you came back. You love him." She paused, raised her hand beseechingly. "Maybe I feared your gun a couple of times. But you could have easily killed Mr. Butcher and didn't." She clutched his shirtsleeve. "Holden, if I live to be a hundred, I could never hate you."

He searched her eyes and knew she spoke truth. He shivered, but not from the cold. "Samantha . . ." He yearned to touch her, to hold her. To never let her go.

She answered his prayer. Rising onto her knees, she placed her hands on his shoulders. "I love you, Holden. Please, love me back."

Her scent, her close warmth sent his senses soaring. He wanted her so badly that his breath stalled in his chest.

No longer able to deny himself or her, he crushed her lithe body against his, slanted his mouth over her sweet lips and drank her essence. When he deepened the kiss, a groan escaped. His or hers, he did not know and did not care.

Moments or maybe a lifetime later, Holden raised his head. Stretched on her back across his belongings, Samantha looked as dazed as he suspected he, himself, did.

"I am sorry." He started to pull back.

Both her arms circled his neck and held him tightly. "Don't you dare apologize. And don't leave, either! Understand? I want you."

"Not here. Not in the cold, on the ground."

"Why not?" she asked, mock-serious. "Where would you make love to me if we were in an Indian village?"

He blinked in surprise. Finally a sly grin turned up his lips. "Wherever privacy would allow."

Samantha turned her head awkwardly, looked right and left, then gazed up into his eyes. "Not a soul with a particle of sense is out here but us, Holden. Private enough for you?"

Of its own volition, his hand caressed her side and slid up her torso until he cupped her breast. Her nipple hardened against his palm, and she sucked in a breath. He nibbled at the corner of her lips as his fingers pleasured her through the material.

"You will freeze if I take off your clothes."

"You think so?"

He grinned. "Perhaps not."

In moments, Holden had disrobed her and himself. With infinite care, he explored the body he had longed to touch, to caress, to make his own from the moment he had first seen her on the porch so many months before.

Samantha's skin flushed from the heat building within. She explored Holden's taut shoulders, his muscled arms. "A beautiful man," she murmured.

"Not I," he argued.

He pulled back slightly and the fire in his eyes seared her clear to her core.

"I want you, Samantha. But if I take you, lie with you, then you are mine forevermore. Is that what you want?"

"As in married?"

He hesitated. "I do not need words from a preacher. If that is what you want, need, then I will repeat those words. But know this, Samantha. My love for you will live in my soul until I join the Spirits on the other side of eternity . . . and beyond."

Deeply moved by such a beautiful declaration, Samantha could do nothing but stare in wonder. Then she curled her fingers around his neck and urged him down to nibble on his lips.

"I can never ask for more, Holden. I return your love with all I have in my heart. I don't need anything but you. Make love to me, please. Make us one for eternity."

And he did, there on the cold ground, at Timberoaks.

At long last he had come full circle. Home. To the white man's world.

To love.

THE PIRATE HUNTER
JENNIFER ASHLEY

Widowed by an officer in the English navy, Diana Worthing is tired of self-important men. Then the legendary James Ardmore has the gall to abduct her, to demand information. A champion to some and a villain to others, the rogue sails the high seas, ruthlessly hunting down pirates. And he claims Diana's father was the key to justice.

When she refuses to tell him what she knows, James retaliates with passionate kisses and seductive caresses. The most potent weapons of all, though, are his honorable intentions, for they make Diana forget reason. They make her long to believe she's finally found a man she can trust, a man worth loving—a true hero who could rescue her marooned heart.

TEXAS STAR

ELAINE BARBIERI

Buck Star is a handsome cad with a love-'em-and-leave-'em attitude that broke more than one heart. But when he walks out on a beautiful New Orleans socialite, he sets into motion a chain of treachery and deceit that threatens to destroy the ranching empire he'd built and even the children he'd once hoped would inherit it. . . .

A mysterious message compels Caldwell Star to return to Lowell, Texas, after a nine-year absence. Back in Lowell, he meets a stubborn young widow who refuses his help, but needs it more than she can know. Her gentle touch and proud spirit give Cal strength to face the demons of the past, to reach out for a love that would heal his wounded soul.

WHITE SHADOWS
SUSAN EDWARDS

For years after his family was massacred, the half-breed Night Shadow harbored black dreams of vengeance—and the hope of someday finding his kidnapped younger sister. Now is the chance. His enemy shows himself and is to be wed. It should be a simple maneuver to steal the man's bride-to-be, to ride off with the beautiful Winona and reveal the monster she is supposed to marry.

But it is *not* simple. Winona is not convinced. Even the burgeoning desire Night Shadow sees in her eyes has not convinced the Sioux beauty of her betrothed's evil. Can love be born of revenge? There seems but one way to find out: Take Winona into the darkness and pray that, somehow, he and she can find their way to the light.

LEIGH GREENWOOD
The Independent Bride

Colorado Territory, 1868: It is about as rough and ready as the West can get, a place and time almost as dangerous as the men who left civilization behind, driven by a desire for land, gold . . . a new life.

Fort Lookout: It is a rugged outpost where soldiers, cattlemen and Indians live on the edge of open warfare, the last place any woman in her right mind would choose to settle.

Abby: She is everything a man should avoid—with a face of beauty and an expression of stubborn determination. Colonel Bryce McGregor knows there is no room for such a woman at his fort or in his heart. Yet as she receives proposal after proposal from his troops, Bryce realizes the only man he can allow her to marry is himself.
